THE VOYAGE OF

CONTEMPORARY

JAPANESE THEATRE

Senda Akihiko

Translated by J. Thomas Rimer

University of Hawai'i Press

Honolulu

Library of Congress Cataloging-in-Publication Data

Senda, Akihiko, 1940–

  [Gendai engeki no kōkai. English]

  The voyage of contemporary Japanese theatre / Senda Akihiko ;
translated by J. Thomas Rimer.

    p. cm.

  Includes bibliographical references and index.

  ISBN 0–8248–1722–2 (alk. paper)

    1. Theater—Japan—History—20th century.   2. Japanese drama—20th
Century—History and criticism.   I. Title.

PN2921.S4413   1996

792'.0954'0904—dc20   96–22961

                           CIP

Publication of this book was supported by the Saison Foundation.

University of Hawai'i Press books are printed on acid-free
paper and meet the guidelines for permanence and durability
of the Council on Library Resources

Book design by Paula Newcomb

THE VOYAGE OF

CONTEMPORARY

JAPANESE THEATRE

To Mae and Dick,
whose first encouragement made
this all possible

CONTENTS

THE VOYAGE OF

CONTEMPORARY

JAPANESE THEATRE

TRANSLATOR'S INTRODUCTION: FROM THE GROUND UP

I

The fact that postwar and contemporary Japanese theatre shows real creativity and accomplishment, and on an international scale, is by this point in time fairly well appreciated in Europe, the United States, and elsewhere. Yet, in and of itself, that bare piece of cultural information carries little freight. Barriers of custom, and of language in particular, continue to make it difficult for Western audiences to appreciate the excitement and significance of these last two decades of dramatic experimentation. There remains, therefore, the danger that synthesizing and summing up these developments without any requisite knowledge of the details involved risks diminishing the real level of accomplishment as well.

The present translation is meant to provide some of those necessary specifics, consisting, as it does, of some sixty reviews of productions staged for the most part in Tokyo between 1971 and 1988. The aggregate thus represents a view of theatrical activities in Japan, seen not from the heights but from the ground up. Better still, these details are never less than fascinating and compelling in and of themselves. It is from these details that the larger cultural and artistic patterns of change can be observed as they shift and grow, month by month, year by year, as new concerns, and talents as well, emerge, develop, mature.

The present volume represents an English-language adaptation of *Gendai engeki no kōkai*, here translated as *The Voyage of Contemporary Japanese Theatre*, first published in 1988 by Riburo Pōto in Tokyo. Its author, Senda Akihiko, is rightly regarded as the finest theatre critic in contemporary Japan. His articles, reviews, and interviews, many first published in the *Asahi Shimbun* (Asahi newspaper), of which he is a senior staff writer, have informed a generation on the importance of theatre as a means of expressing the concerns of contemporary Japanese culture.

Mr. Senda, born in Tokyo, studied at Tokyo University and joined the Asahi Newspaper Company in 1963. His various book-length studies span the wide range of his concerns and enthusiasms and include, in addition to the present study, *Open Theatre* (1976), *Theatrical Renaissance* (1983), *The World Inclines to Comedy* (1985), *Viva! Musicals!* (1994), and, most recently, *Japanese Contemporary Theatre* (1995).[1] As a critic, his erudition, sophistication, and sense of social concern have distinguished his work since the beginning of his career.

It has been my privilege to know Mr. Senda for some fifteen years, and the present translation can be said to represent in a very real sense a collaboration between the two of us. The original volume was roughly double the length of this English version, and the reviews translated here (slightly more than half of those found in the original) were chosen by Mr. Senda himself, his criterion for inclusion being some greater significance for the history of Japanese theatre during this period. In some cases, we have made small cuts within individual reviews of certain details too cumbersome, or of too little significance for readers outside Japan, to render into English. Most of these reviews were originally composed for newspapers and magazines, and, in that spirit, we have not included notes or other similar references but have rather attempted to work the requisite background information into the English text itself.

The fact that these reviews began as they did says something about the elevated and sophisticated nature of journalistic writings on contemporary culture (at least as practiced by Mr. Senda) in Japan today. Mr. Senda's style is often elegant, frequently abstract, and it consistently shows a canny and sympathetic understanding of theatre as it is practiced around the world. I hope that my translation can suggest something of the density and probity of his thought. In that regard, I have tried to remain close to the spirit, and so to the style, of the original. For Senda, as for many others, the theatre represents a privileged strategy for social, even spiritual criticism of contemporary Japanese civilization. In such a context, his comments must be read with care and discernment, for, in so many ways, this book represents a chronicle of the strains and tensions that Japanese society has undergone since the beginning of the 1960s, roughly a decade before the date of the first review included here.

In terms of theatrical history, too, it is important to note that Mr. Senda has chosen to include here a number of reviews of foreign plays and musicals, presented either by Japanese companies in translation or by visiting troupes from abroad. Given this heady mix of theatrical activity in Tokyo, it becomes easier for an English-speaking audience to understand something of the influences and counterinfluences that have helped make Japanese theatre what it is today. Then too, reading Mr. Senda's comments on the kind of fare familiar to American audiences, from Chekhov and Shakespeare to *Chorus Line* and *Sweeney Todd,* helps reveal the ways in which these Western works, classic and contemporary alike, entertain and inform within the context of other societies. Such glimpses are rare, and they are altogether fascinating.

By including such material, Mr. Senda reveals his conviction that the theatre can—indeed must—speak to a wider audience. From an American point of view, audiences seem more segmented in Japan than they are in our culture. Sophisticated audiences in larger U.S. urban areas may attend an avant-garde production one night, the opera the next. In Japan, however, audiences seem loyal, often intensely so, to the particular kind of theatre they enjoy and seldom seek to expand their consciousness by attending other forms. Those who patronize *nō* or *kabuki,* for example, seldom show an equal fascination for modern Japanese theatre *(shingeki)* or for the avant-garde. Mr. Senda watches it all and, with enthusiasm and skill, often manages to show the relations between these apparently disparate forms. This fact in itself, in my view, represents one of his most significant accomplishments.

If, as the expression has it, genius lies in the details, then what follows might be seen to represent an absorbing guide through what is to most of us a tantalizing and unfamiliar maze. As we go along, however, various signposts become more familiar, and the vitality and complexity of contemporary Japanese cultural life becomes all the more compelling.

II

For the reader coming on the phenomenon of contemporary Japanese theatre through the present translation, a bit of background may help explain the particular trajectory of Mr. Senda's concerns. Many of the plays reviewed here chronicle a powerful response by actors, writers, and theatre companies to the vicissitudes of contemporary Japanese culture. A number of the problems confronted by these plays, of course, are familiar to all contemporary audiences. The individual's alienation from a rampant consumer society, a search for transcendental values, and the ongoing pain of human relationships are subjects common, and current, to cultures around the world. There are, however, certain situations specific to Japanese political and cultural life that remain central to the artistic urges that underlie many of the works described by Mr. Senda.[2]

In this regard, any narrative of the period must commence with the struggles that began about 1960 in Tokyo and elsewhere in Japan against the renewal of the U.S.-Japan Security Treaty (Anpo). The issues behind these struggles were of course complex. Suffice it to say here that the conservatives, who were largely in sympathy with the U.S. attempt to repel Communism in Asia, were at odds with those of more progressive sympathies, who felt that the peaceful posture of the postwar Japanese constitution should be preserved, that the country should maintain no military and join no alliances. In the eyes of the progressives—a group composed mostly of young people, women, and those living in large urban areas[3]—the United States had through a strong military stance now actually come to betray its own best principles of peace and democracy, the same principles that had, in fact, been held up as models in Japan by the Americans during the Occupation years (1945–1952).

This radical split in the body politic grew throughout the decade. In 1965, the bombing of North Vietnam by American planes helped precipitate the formation of the Peace in Vietnam Committee (Beheiren), in which such prominent writers as Oda Makoto and Tsurumi Shunsuke were involved. By 1968, student strikes in Tokyo became more violent than those in Paris and New York, and the suicide of the celebrated writer Mishima Yukio (1925–1970) helped convince important sectors of the Japanese public that the political and social anguish voiced by the protesters and others was real. Relatively few may have applauded Mishima's conservative solutions, but many agreed with his analysis—that Japan had degenerated, socially and spiritually, into a malaise of empty commercialism in an age of vapid peace.

These issues brought fresh and unusual alliances between established intellectuals of the older generation and creative figures of the younger generation. Some of the playwrights whose presences loom large in this volume—among them Kara Jūrō, Betsuyaku Minoru, Shimizu Kunio, Suzuki Tadashi, and Ninagawa Yukio—were in their early twenties when they became embroiled, both politically and artistically, in the debates of this difficult period. These young people of the theatre were convinced that their work could change the consciousness of their audiences. Many of the intellectual elite of the older generation responded with enthusiasm to this striking countercultural effort.

For their attempt to change the mentality of their audiences, these young people could have found precedents within their own culture. The older modern theatre movement in Japan (usually referred to as *shingeki*, or "modern theatre," as opposed to the traditional theatre of *nō* or *kabuki*) also inclined toward the Marxist Left. Here, the models chosen by such powerful postwar figures as the director Senda Koreya (1904–1994) were Chekhov and in particular Brecht, whose own theories of "alienation" were created at least in part to generate new, thinking attitudes in his audiences. These young writers and directors, however, found the old ways of no use or interest in this time of political turmoil. The role models had shifted. The fascination with European drama was supplanted by a fascination with European film. Brecht and Ibsen were replaced by Arrabal, Samuel Beckett, Artaud, and Foucault.

By 1971, therefore, the trajectories of the members of the younger generation, whose later careers are chronicled by Mr. Senda in the present volume, were largely already determined. Studying Mr. Senda's reviews of their work in the theatre during the 1970s and after, it is clear that the stage was being set for a major shift. By the middle of the decade, their retreat from a direct confrontation with the politics of the present appears striking. Suzuki Tadashi and Ninagawa Yukio moved to the classics, albeit with very different motives; Shimizu and Kara began to look back, often with a note of regret, nostalgia, even an occasional sense of disdain, on the movements in which they participated in their youth. Newer and younger writers, notably Noda Hideki, Tsuka Kōhei, and Ōta Shōgo, moved into different realms of expression and expressivity altogether.

Perhaps one reason for this change was the devastating 1972 incident involving the Red Army Faction (Sekigunha), which disillusioned many intellectuals and turned them against overt social protest. The Red Army faction had emerged from the student struggles of 1968 as a kind of guerilla terrorist organization. Through the 1970s and even after, it carried out a series of bombings and robberies in Japan as well as international terrorist attacks. Although certain details of the faction's activities and membership remain unclear even today, its influence was severely curtailed when, in 1972, after the arrest of many of the faction's leaders after an intense siege of a lodge in the mountains near Karuizawa, a resort area north of Tokyo, it was revealed that a number of members had been tortured and killed by group leaders on the grounds of "ideological deviation."

Left-wing intellectuals and other student activists alike were appalled at these disclosures. The reception of Shimizu Kunio's play *When We Go Down That Heartless River,* performed in 1972, reveals that the tide had turned against the proponents of direct political intervention. Criticized for what many took to be his untoward sympathy for the Red Army Faction, Shimizu soon turned to the composition of dramas, which, although often powerful critiques of contemporary Japanese society, moved away from any suggestion of the promulgation of direct social action. The early 1970s were difficult years for all those of conscience involved in the politically engaged theatre, as Mr. Senda's own review of Shimizu's play makes painfully clear.

The reviews included here also chronicle the works of still another generation of young theatre professionals, who use fantasy, pop culture, even science fiction, to address their visions. Mr. Senda shows himself agreeably open to these new trends. Yet behind the enthusiastic response of audiences to these new departures can often be observed a lingering sense of pain. Like the generation of Americans who came of age during the U.S.-Vietnam conflict, the generation involved in the Japanese counterculture theatre of the 1960s remains marked forever. For them, some lessons are too painful ever to forget; indeed, to do so would for them constitute a real spiritual betrayal.

III

It remains for me to thank the Toshiba International Foundation, whose support provided me with some of the time necessary to undertake the translation of this work, and the Saison Foundation, for its assistance to the University of Hawai'i Press in publishing this English version. Both Mr. Senda and I are grateful that his seminal work can find a larger audience.

Finally, I should like to thank a number of people who have been of real assistance to me in the preparation of this translation. First of all, without the constant support and enthusiasm of the editorial staff at the University of Hawai'i Press, in particular that of Patricia Crosby and Cheri Dunn, this project could never have reached completion. Second, the text, so complex in the original, reads as well as it does in this English version through the consistent and highly skillful efforts of my copyeditor, Joseph H. Brown, who did indeed perform his own elegant miracles on my original version. I appreciate as well Paula Newcomb's elegant design.

The two anonymous readers of the manuscript chosen by the University of Hawai'i Press made trenchant and useful suggestions for the improvement of the first version of the manuscript. Ms. Sachie Noguchi, the Japanese bibliographer at the University of Pittsburgh's Hillman Library, was able to locate unusual and helpful background documents on the theatre of this period that were of great assistance to me in preparing this translation, and Mrs. Fumi Norcia, now retired from the Library of Congress, provided me with a good deal of useful background information as well. Hiroaki Sato gave me valuable assistance in locating some of the more obscure poetic and literary references found in Mr. Senda's text. Mrs. Mie

Kakigahara helped with the project at several crucial points. Most important of all, I would like to thank in particular my friend and colleague Professor Hiroshi Nara of the University of Pittsburgh, who guided me through some of the many difficult linguistic thickets found in the text.

J. THOMAS RIMER

Notes

1. Publication information for these books is as follows: *Hirakareta gekijō* (Open theatre) (Tokyo: Shōbunsha, 1976); *Gekiteki runessensu* (Theatrical renaissance) (Tokyo: Riburo Pōto, 1983); *Sekai wa kigeki ni keisha suru* (The world inclines to comedy) (Tokyo: Chūsekisha, 1985); *Biba! myūjikaru!* (Tokyo: Ashai Shimbunsha, 1994); and *The Japanese Contemporary Theatre* (Tokyo: Iwanami shinsho, 1995).

2. For reasons of space, this background can be sketched here only briefly. For the English-speaking reader seeking more detailed information about this period in general and about the theatre in particular, there are a number of studies that will be helpful. Tsurumi Shunsuke, one of the most outspoken Japanese writers of the period, offers fascinating insights in his *A Cultural History of Postwar Japan* (London and New York: KPI, 1987). Thomas R. H. Havens provides excellent background on the phenomenon of theatre in his study *Artist and Patron in Postwar Japan: Dance, Music, Theater, and the Visual Arts, 1955–1980* (Princeton, N.J.: Princeton University Press, 1982). J. Victor Koschmann has contributed a trenchant essay entitled "Intellectuals and Politics" to *Postwar Japan as History*, ed. Andrew Gordon (Berkeley and Los Angeles: University of California Press, 1993). I would like to call particular attention to "Alternative Japanese Drama: A Brief Overview," a brief but beautifully focused essay by the leading Japanese critic and scholar Takahashi Yasunari contained in *Alternative Japanese Drama*, ed. Robert T. Rolf and John K. Gillespie (Honolulu: University of Hawai'i Press, 1992). David Goodman's comments on the period in his *Japanese Drama and Culture in the 1960s: The Return of the Gods* (Armonk, N.Y.: Sharpe, 1988) are, as always, filled with provocative and significant insights.

3. See Koschmann, "Intellectuals and Politics," 406.

PROLOGUE

Is there a "New World?"—*The Voyage of Contemporary Japanese Theatre*

If one takes as a central metaphor that long voyage made by the Japanese theatre from the 1960s through the 1980s, in which new territories were sought out, would it be too romantic to suggest that such a voyage has constituted a striking adventure? There is a danger that my metaphor may sound that way. Indeed, I feel I can hear an echo of those lines toward the end of Brecht's *Drums in the Night,* "Stop that romantic gaping!"

Those young adventurers were sick of the boredom of the old theatrical world in which they lived, of its narrowness. Subjected to jibes about their "thoughtlessness," "ignorance," and "artistic clumsiness" and about the "nonsensical" nature of their vision, they have, one by one, boarded frail and poor boats of their own making (small theatres, small troupes) without any general plan for confronting the mighty deep. Would they find a place to land? Somehow, it seemed doubtful. And there were plenty of shipwrecks too. Still, despite everything, they did manage to cross over to a "new world"—through new dramatic structures, fresh acting skills, a changing sense of theatrical space, and new varieties of dramatic troupes. All these were developed by one small boatload of adventurers after another, as these new forms were discovered and then, given a justification for being, continued on. These voyagers came to constitute a new generation. So, if I succumb to the temptation of using the word *romantic,* it is because I do hold such an image of these theatrical adventurers.

As it turns out, there are several generations of such adventurers involved. If these voyages began with the "first generation" of small theatre troupes in the 1960s, there followed in succession a second, third, and fourth generation of those seeking a new theatre; content and consciousness alike would shift between them, like sections of a drawing that did not connect, as they worked to chart the still-unmapped "new world" of the theatre.

Nevertheless, there did exist a firm base from which to launch these voyages of discovery into this new theatrical territory. Indeed, in the activities of the theatre troupes in the 1960s, that very image of setting out on a voyage of theatrical discovery was given concrete dramatic expression.

The model was set by the man who led the "situational theatre movement," Kara Jūrō. For example, in his central early works *John Silver* (1965), *More of John Silver* (1968), and *A Beggar for Love* (1970), the image of a time consecrated to the great sea established there still resonates.

"Where is the sea? Not the sea we threw away, not Treasure Island; is there another Treasure Island?"

John Silver, a pirate of contemporary Japan modeled on the character in Stevenson's *Treasure Island*, escaping from the gentle path of everyday life, searches out "another" Treasure Island, seeks another new pirate adventure: such is the basic narrative image that lies behind this series of works by Kara.

This image of John Silver calls forth another tale of the vast oceans, Melville's *Moby Dick*. In Kara's novel *The Scroll of John Silver* (1969), his companion piece to the play *John Silver*, appear as well his guides, "the White Whale" and "Sister Makko."

In such plays by Kanasugi Tadao (the leader of the Nakamura troupe and another member of that "first generation") as *A Thief Who Lectures: The Story of Tami no I* (1972) and *An Uneasy Feeling after School Is Over* (1987), characters appear named "Ahab," "Starbuck," "Stabb," and so forth. They are men, roughened by their experiences with the white whale, who night after night chase after "Moby Dick," adventurers who make every strenuous effort to set sail for something that glitters in the distance, something "out of the ordinary."

In the play *Kangaroo* (1967) by Betsuyaku Minoru, the motif of "setting sail" surfaces again. In the prologue, the Singer in Disguise performs the following song, which, remarkably enough, appears to be a variation on the theme of John Silver.

Maybe, in the old days, I
Was a sea pirate, with an eye gouged out:
On a moonlit night setting sail,
Ringing the gong;
And maybe my boat,
Like a wolf,
For three days, three nights,
Chased its prey.

In Satoh Makoto's play *My Beatles,* performed by the Free Theatre in 1967, the images of a ship and a "sailing" to help mankind are clearly apparent.

"I've been waiting for the boat to arrive. . . . The Beatles will be on board. And I'll sail off with them. . . ."

There is even a case where these ideas of "departure" and "sailing" are reflected in the name of a theatre company itself. The example is that of the gifted troupe Riburesen (Freedom Boat Company), which staged two plays written and directed by Ōhashi Yasuhiko, *The Red Bird Has Fled* (1986) and *Godzilla* (1987). The meaning of the name of the troupe is as follows. *Ribure* is adapted from a Spanish word meaning "free." But, by writing the word in characters, a second meaning can be derived: *ri* means "separation," *bu* or *fu* can be construed as "wind" in the sails, *re* comes close to *rei,* or the human soul, and *sen* is a ship. Altogether, here is an image that resonates with a feeling of a grand voyage to the deep sea. Such a unique name for a theatre troupe suggests no brief voyage but one to some far shore.

But the playwrights who have used such terms as *sea, pirates,* and *Moby Dick,* men like Kara Jūrō, Betsuyaku Minoru, Kanasugi Tadao, and Satoh Makoto, have not tried to bring their dramas into being in any simple romantic way. On the contrary, the premise behind the "sea" they wish to conjure up is one filled with a basic sense of doubt: such statements as "Is there still a sea?" and "Whatever may be, John Silver, there's no sea for you . . ." (*John Silver*) suggest the sense of fright and of loss that is conveyed. Even though they talk of "another Treasure Island," that "other sea" across which they must row in order to get there may well have disappeared. There is a Samuel Beckett–like impotence that seems to undercut every impulse from the beginning.

Betsuyaku Minoru, Kara Jūrō and the others of this "first generation" took as a point of departure the stimulus received from Beckett's *Waiting for Godot* (first produced in Paris in 1953 and in Japan by the Literary Theatre troupe in 1960), it seems to me. Thus, while the characters in the plays of Kara and Betsuyaku talk of "departures" or call out, "Well, shall we start off?" "Yes, let's move out," their leave-takings seemed immersed in the *Godot*-like paradoxes of Vladimir and Estragon, who never manage to go anywhere.

Thus, the "pirate" song in Betsuyaku's *Kangaroo* is, in the end, filled with despair.

Maybe I
Grew old
Maybe my boat
Has already sunk. . . .

The young girl in Satoh's play who waits for her saviors to come and save her is in a similar position, for, when those saviors appear, they turn out to be no more than four self-styled "Beatles" who work as gangster freight handlers, and what they bring her are four "plain wood coffins."

"That's right. The Beatles have all died, you know."

It is the same with Kanasugi Tadao's weary middle-aged man, who every night repeats and repeats again "White Whale. . . ." Other than setting out on a regressive trip to the nostalgic "kingdom," under the aegis of "the past," he can go nowhere. Why? Because it has been solemnly pronounced that, "indeed, Moby Dick has already died."

In such a situation, when the "sea" has already disappeared, such impotent departures, so filled with peculiar paradox, in which "another Treasure Island" is sought with such passion, appear to be a common feature of the plays of all these writers. Yet Kara, Betsuyaku, Suzuki Tadashi, Satoh, Terayama Shūji, Ōta Shōgo, Shimizu Kunio, Ninagawa Yukio, and the others did manage to make their own theatrical voyages with their small companies during this "first generation," despite the fact that in their plays these voyages, which represent "something lost even before begun" (Shimizu), in the end "cannot be accomplished." When one considers the aggressive spirit with which they set about creating these small theatre companies, the contrast of their purposeful activities with this expressed sense of "loss" and "impotence" seems surprising indeed.

In all this, one can surely read something of the atmosphere of frustration felt by the younger generation after the struggles over the U.S.-Japan Security Treaty in the 1960s. But, in terms of something more basic still, it is worth recalling the words of Suzuki Tadashi expressed at the time of the founding of the Waseda Little Theatre (now SCOT):

> True enough, the riots over the treaty were a factor, and situations were shifting; yet, in one sense, we believed that nothing had changed. We thought to put on plays because of the sad lot of humankind.

Thus it was that, on the basis of this fully "life-size" human misery as well as the notion that "structures and systems were to some extent unchangeable," thereby constituting "the only thing that can be counted on," Suzuki and Betsuyaku created the Waseda Little Theatre. They believed that, when making a play, only those feelings that "neither affirm nor praise the future" should be represented. Or, to put it another way, this pitiful "sense of loss" or "impotence" was now taken to be the normal condition of man; these writers took the point of view that, through the energy of great passion, the essential human drama might make sport of this misery. Thus, this sense of "loss," which in everyday terms represents a minus, might very well, in the fabricated world of the theatre, become some kind of trump card, a real theatrical plus.

It was this sense of "pitifulness" that was taken up in the 1970s by such "second generation" writers as Tsuka Kōhei, who with his glittering comedies of the pitiable buried ordinary life in an excess of theatrical art and brought forth the order of "artistic man."

Nevertheless, the kind of difficult voyage envisioned by Kara Jūrō, a voyage to his "treasure island," his "new world," sought "an unprecedented world," a world that he was to posit. For Kara, this "unprecedented" factor represented, not an even number capable of taking its ordered place between two odd numbers, but still another "odd number" that, in his vision, might actually exist.

"What if, between the odd numbers 1 and 3, there is found, not the even number 2, but yet another odd number, one yet to be discovered? This is what I would identify as this 'unprecedented factor,' " he wrote.

Despite the playwright's theatrical mystification and fanciful rhetoric, Kara did indeed conceive of this "flight from the world of reality to this world of the unprecedented." And what he imagined was not merely a choice between odd and even numbers or an escape from some ordinary conception of the "old world" to a "new world." Rather, he sought an entirely unprecedented world, a permeable space between two realities, "still another new universe."

If I were to explicate the situation of the theatre in Japan in the 1960s and 1970s, I would suggest that its future lay neither in the established theatre nor in the "tent theatre" that opposed it but rather in "still another new theatre." At the time, Kara Jūrō himself wrote of the "trap of structure" into which "the happenings of the 1960s" or "the protest tent theatres" were prone to fall. Kara, the standard-bearer who himself had championed the "tent theatre," by no means wished simply to pose the tent theatre as an alternative to the more traditional forms of modern drama. It is well to remember that what he had sought from the first was a glimpse of this "unprecedented world," "another new universe."

> If you start with a childish culture, that idiocy of inevitability that demands uniformity—for every right, there must be a left—then everything will finish in some sort of fluctuating movement, but fixed in a closed order. If this were not so, then the underground would be on as solid earth as the ground.

At the same time, Kara's observations possess a larger meaning that surpasses any mere description of the theatrical situation. They suggest that such actions, supported by some kind of dynamic that is capable of opposing ordinary reality with this "unprecedented world," may well be able to bring about a complete change in the way in which we live our lives, hinting at a world that must require a "new flight."

There is visible a similar consciousness of a "new world" in the work of the playwright Kōkami Shōji of the Third Stage, which was part of the so-called fourth generation of theatrical activities that began in the 1960s. For example, in the introduction that he prepared for his play *Taking along a Sunset like the Morning*, which was published in 1983, he wrote the following.

> In order to surpass the traditional methods of storytelling, which were brought to their highest peak four hundred years ago, all sorts of experiments have been tried, one after another. Still, "telling a story"—that "illness smeared with meaning"—apparently continues to spread itself in all its ease. By now, though, we are disgusted with the shock of any explanation that shows some flawless karmic connections. We must search around for some new type of drama. Like travelers going here and there, we seem to be setting out on a journey. As for me, I have decided to take my first steps, however obscurely, toward that labyrinth.

Kōkami Shōji has written plays that, again and again, not only seek to identify some new form of drama but also, in terms of our own contemporary sense of life, attempt to find a means to "make a hole in the wall" behind which we have been sealed; he hopes to create plays that can show us how to "escape" from the world in which we are imprisoned.

Still, as Kara Jūrō said in the first place, "John Silver, there's no sea for you . . ." (*John Silver*). A closer view of that same situation can be found in a work like Kōkami's *Angels Who Close the Pupils of Their Eyes*, published in 1988. "We are closed in by walls we cannot see; and there's no way out." Although the periods in which they wrote differ and the quality of their talents is not at the same level, the work of both playwrights nevertheless reveals similar concerns. Both believe that we can indeed begin to ask why we should try to escape from a situation from which we "cannot break out," one in which we are limited by the dynamics of a spirit that aims for an "outside" away from the territory in which we find ourselves trapped. Their variations on this single theme constitute a matter of the greatest interest.

By the same token, it should be noted that many of Kōkami's plays differ from those of Kara, which face in the direction of a nostalgic past; those of the younger writer serve as sectors of experimentation for the future.

In Kōkami's *Angels*, which chronicles the history of a "street" created by those few survivors of an atomic catastrophe in which "the world has finally ended," this area, "surrounded by a soft wall that no one can see," becomes the setting for the drama. This ominous "wall," which appears to be "in a form somewhere between solid and fluid," is described in the following, suggestive manner.

> This wall spreads out far, so very far. You can't really get out beyond it, but you can go for a long, long way.

The image of this almost infinitely wide wall gives the sensation of vastness, of a soft, constructed society in and of itself. Within it, one may do whatever one wants; one can follow one's desires "for a long, long way." Yet there is no way to "get outside" the confines of this "wall."

Thus, although one may "set sail" on a sea, traveling on and on as the days and months pile up, one finds oneself still within the confines of a vast bay, still confined within a system that forbids any egress into the open sea beyond. The scene of this mysterious "inner sea" spreads widely, but it is surrounded by this "soft wall that cannot be seen," one to which even those adventurers of old, Captain Ahab and John Silver, never managed to row.

In this instance, those mariners who seek to escape are not those adventurers seeking the roughness of the open sea. Instead, they must be those with clear heads who seek a plan of escape from the "inner sea."

What is of particular interest in Kōkami's play is that a plan is developed to break through the "wall," not by individuals, but as part of a group enterprise, one that has "subjugated all the media." A process is instigated in which the whole population is marshalled and, through a television relay, a media event is created in which an "adventure" is staged in order to "get to the other side." I know of nothing else that speaks with such force to the degeneration of the concept of "adventure" in our generation, for, despite the fact that the stage is set "in the future," the situation enacted is obviously a clear description of contemporary Japan. This drama of Kōkami, with its adventures moving from the open sea to the "inner sea," the "outside" becoming the "inside," and the "adventurers" no longer individuals but participants in a group enterprise, allows to float up before us a reality that, despite its casual appearance, is deeply frightening.

In his stage works, Kawamura Takeshi (who manages the theatre company the Third Erotica) places before us on the stage in all its raw power a world that reveals the degeneration of the idea of a "voyage," one that has lost its contact with the outside world and has retreated to the "inside."

In his 1984 play *Japan Wars*, Kawamura creates a group of male and female androids who have been trained for battle and who are now on a voyage over a "black sea" in a submarine called "The Whale." (It is easy to note how the motifs of "ocean" and "voyage" alternate.) These androids lead an existence in which their consciousness of past memories sustains their identity, so that even the sense of "love" itself has been scientifically imprinted in them.

In watching the drama unfold, what strikes the viewer most is the spirit of revolt born in the androids as they attempt to revolt against the structures within which they have been programmed to function. The androids gather their forces together in order to destroy the computer that commands the activities of the submarine and emits its own "brain power." At one point, their revolt seems successful. Just at that moment, however, it becomes clear that, astonishingly enough, although the androids do truly wish to rise up, that act itself is merely the result of a carefully programmed sense of "revolt" already implanted in them, a revolt that in and of itself constitutes a "final lesson" with which they must comply.

> Once the soldiers of our country have tasted the sweet wine of "rebellion" in the course of their training, they will rush forward to the front lines. This idea of revolt, don't you know, is just one more element in our programming. Every few years they have shown us a wonderfully exciting rebellion. Come now, don't you agree?

This kind of suggestive stage dialogue, in which our own phantom concepts of revolt are exposed, relativized, is rare indeed. What if, for example, our own participation as audience in a desire, an ardor for a successful outcome for this "revolt," represents nothing more than a program already imprinted in us? What if that participation results only in a strengthening of the very system against which the revolt is to be staged? What if, indeed, as in Arthur C. Clarke's novel *Childhood's End,* the very concepts of "revolt" and "revolution" amount to no more than the imprint of some vast program within us?

In Kawamura's play, the dreams we have within ourselves of "change" are shaken, prodded. Yet these androids, who themselves possess a consciousness of the fact that they bear this imprint within themselves, are nevertheless determined to undertake a final effort against the system in order to occupy a submarine to be used in "our war." It might be said that, compared to the power of the ruling classes as portrayed here, the final image of these androids undertaking their own "departure" might seem a bit too heroic. In any case, however, there is strongly expressed here the truth of the vision that there exists within all of us a strong human desire, a will to escape from the kind of overpowering standardization to which our actions, thoughts, and expressions are constantly and stealthily subjected.

When we hear the words *adventure* and *voyage,* we naturally associate them with the concept of the "far away." Kawamura, on the other hand—

quoting Ninja no Kagemaru, the hero from the comics, "We've come from far away. Then we'll go far away again"—possesses within himself no concept of any such distance.

> What does it mean to say that something is "far away"? If you transpose this for easy understanding to "a place that doesn't exist, anywhere," then *is* there any such place at all? Far away, close by, isn't it like some element following the laws of perspective in a landscape painting? Just as it seems that, through the intervention of these laws of perspective, words like *far* and *near* can be absorbed quite easily, that dream of "going far away" is already crumbling.

So writes Kawamura in 1984, in the afterword to the text of his play.

Yet, as far as this playwright is concerned, the fact that what is "far away" can vanish is intimately linked to the destruction of the "self" and the collapse of the idea of the "story" or "tale" itself. None of these changes came about in isolation; they all occurred together. It is rare to find such a concise rendering of this world that Kawamura has confronted so directly.

> Indeed, myth has collapsed. And to a satisfying degree. After its destruction, its disappearance, we have begun to spin our own tales. Thus, the illusion of "the distant," under the patronage of myth, just like the myth of our own selfhood, can no longer be depended on.

These remarks in turn bring to mind a play from the 1960s by Fukuda Yoshiyuki, *Going Far, Far Away*, first produced in 1961. The play, which took as its subject the Algerian War, derives its title from a poem by Yoshimoto Takaaki. It created quite a stir: in fact, a group of new-Left students used the title of the play for a magazine they created. Toward the end of the play, there is a striking speech from Jean, the protagonist. He has left the French Communist party and deserted the occupying army as well in order to join the Algerian struggle for independence. His lines seem to speak for the feelings of those young students who, following the battles over the U.S.-Japan Security Treaty, sought some "far distance."

> . . . Well then, if you've started out, then you can't give up. [*Pause.*] So we'll go off into the distance, as far as we can. That's right. Just as far as we can.

This expression of determination is certainly heroic; nevertheless, in that statement about going off "just as far as we can" I feel there lies a suggestion as well of some modest sense of hesitation. At this point, the very urge to depart in and of itself suggests the existence of a territory that can be obtained; there is no doubt but that, with the proper willpower, it can be reached. The curtain can come down, with the excitement that "going as far as we can" serves as some sort of communal password. This was a strong and healthy age indeed.

Now, some twenty years later, when Kawamura Takeshi speaks of a "distance," he can go no further than to suggest that, no matter how far you travel, you can do no more than traverse "the laws of perspective in a landscape painting." The very illusion of "distance" itself has collapsed. The world has shrunk, become homogenized. And it has become expressionless. Even in terms of geography, we live in a period when the camera in a man-made satellite can photograph the entire globe in units of a few centimeters; there no longer exists any "distant" place as yet unknown. The relentless logic of capitalism has unified us all; even our extreme ideas about seeking out that "distance" have by now been cataloged, then placed in an orderly display in some showroom of ideas.

In the metaphors of Kōkami Shōji, we are completely wrapped in that "soft wall" that "extends itself endlessly." We have lost our "exterior," and our "interior" voyage cannot be urged on for any romantic reasons because, however far we may go, we will never achieve the far distance of the open sea. Rather, there exists a sense in which our voyages end by "going backward."

Although there came to be a fantastic increase in theatrical activity during this period, it is suggestive that so many of the dramatic efforts that sprang to life might be defined as metatheatre, that is, a theatre that deals with theatre, a theatre that stresses the fact of its own fabricated nature. It would be no exaggeration to say that, in going to see productions performed by these young troupes, I found that well over half were of this type. Dramas that inserted into their own world the framework of some already famous theatrical work. Plays that centered on characters who were, in terms of their own personalities, nested like some sort of intricate set of boxes, those sorts of human beings who in their everyday lives show an excess of performing sensibilities. Dramas in which are layered with minute precision the characters in the play as well as those of the actors who perform them. Metatheatre has shown its myriad possibilities in a bewildering variety of colors.

Among the plays that exhibit these qualities, the following must surely be mentioned: Kisaragi Koharu's *Romeo and a Dining Room Table with Freesia* (1979), Kōkami's *Taking along a Sunset like the Morning* (1981), Ichidō Rei's *A Tale of Imposing Appearance* (1984), Kawamura Takeshi's *The Shinjuku Version of the Tale of Eight Dogs, Vol. 1, The Dog's Birth* (1985), Ikuta Yorozu's *Children of Night* (1986), Noda Hideki's adaption of Hagio Moto's *The Demi-God* (1986), Kitamura Sō's *Duck Soup* (1987),

Takahashi Isao's *Goodbye to Walter Mitty* (1987), and Ōhashi Yasuhiko's *Godzilla* (1987).

It goes without saying, of course, that the presence within the theatre of methods peculiar to metatheatre does not represent any particular new development. In the case of Japanese theatre, metatheatrical techniques have been in place since the coming of *nō* and *kabuki,* and metatheatre has played an important role in Western theatre from Shakespeare through Brecht and Genet.

In any case, the vast increase in metatheatre is not the result of any single factor found in modern reality; it surely developed from an attempt to grasp a many-sided, multilayered collage of circumstances. In characterizing his own dramatic methods, Kawamura Takeshi has written as follows:

> When one wishes to grab hold of "the present," drama represents a form of storytelling that is not merely flat, nor are its characters. As a hunter, when I wish to show my prey, which is "the present," I have already shown the conditions of that "bottomless swamp." It is multilayered, not flat at all. To show the realities of "the present," which is by no means level itself, we cannot make use of any "flat" dramaturgy in our storytelling.

I myself as a critic have taken cognizance of the necessary qualities inherent to metatheatre as a form of drama, and I have found much pleasure in observing the excitement of its development. I have sensed a new kind of energy in these sorts of experiments, which can show all the surprises and new techniques one might find in some delicate, exquisite computer software, beginning with the manipulation of time and its transformations. In this kind of conception, the multilayered construction of such plays, complex as a maze, becomes central; such experiments are in the process of moving away from that kind of drama that might attempt to explain to us the nature of this "bottomless swamp" toward some other kind of vision altogether.

It really does seem to me that this phenomenon is closely linked to the fact that we have lost our sense of the "exterior" and are now moving closer to a totally "interior" world. Indeed, the age in which many in the theatre attempted to do battle with those elements in the drama that normally belong outside it—the nation, society, urban existence, even the fact of the audience itself—is ending. The idea of some influence for change on the "exterior" has dimmed. All energies now seem concentrated on the drama of that "inner" world.

The playwright Terayama Shūji once said that, like the traces of some sort of reviewing stand in the sky, an experimental drama studio must "serve as some mystical form of intervention in order to 'overturn society.'"

One would now be hard put to find such robust words in any discussion of the contemporary stage. In their place, with the exception of the striking glitter with which time and memory can be manipulated in this dramatic universe of the "interior," where plays of considerable complexity and delicacy can be created, there is little that can be considered exceptional, on any international scale, in the dramas of this kind now being created by the small companies in Japan today.

Is it really true, then, that much of the contemporary theatre has lost any sense of "the exterior," has compromised with reality, and so has finally shut itself in? I am not convinced that such is always the case. It is certainly true that the larger-than-life scale of the type of plays presented in the 1960s has been altered and that the most common type of drama presented now remains on a humble plane, conceived without bombast or exaggeration. Yet do these new plays not in fact represent just the kind of attempt described above? And does not the fact that they can picture on the stage this "soft wall that cannot be seen" of the kind so repeatedly adumbrated in the works of Kōkami Shōji as the one that "we must manage to cross" represent in and of itself an attempt at a protest, a wish to find at least an airhole leading out of this "interior world"? Surely the posture of a writer like Kawamura Takeshi—who, in the midst of a system that would encompass every aspect of society, attempts to set up a "body to question that system" (using many scenes and a variety of theatrical apparitions) as a means to try to find a way to "swim onward"—reveals the acceptance of a strategy to break out of this "interior world."

In the 1986 play *The Never-ending Tomorrow of the Eternal Optimist*, Takahashi Isao has created a kind of comic vision in which his prisoners are punished in a perpetual attempt to flee from a lenient prison, one in which the arts and culture are in fact encouraged. I believe this play can be understood as a work that shares similar intentions. This prison in which severe judgment is rendered against anyone who attempts an escape into the "outward world" surely represents an allegory for the tolerant oppression of contemporary society.

In June 1988, I remember well that it seemed as though on stage after stage there appeared fascinating visions, directly created, of those who would move from the bureaucratic realities of our contemporary world to the "open sea." I found myself strangely moved. In a Tokyo private theatre and elsewhere, the first performances took place of *Cosmos Columbus*, written by Tamaki Michiko, with direction, sets, and costumes by Kushida Kazuyoshi. Although there were incoherent aspects to the production, the play kindled a great deal of excitement, particularly in a period when all too clearly we have lost our will to "escape."

In the play, we are shown both the glory and the tragedy of the life of Columbus, who would discover the "new world." His life is placed alongside that of one Kusano Hiroshi, a "salaryman" who, while living his ordinary life as a mid-level administrator in the kind of corporate society that Japan represents, nevertheless dreams secretly of setting out on his own "voyage." With the appearance of a surprising youth who can travel at will and who is not concerned with time, the two narratives become mixed, despite their different time lines, in a most surprising way. So it is that Kusano can cross time and space and, with this youth, who styles himself as "the son of Columbus," board the explorer's ship in order to set out on a voyage over the great sea to the "Indies."

The device of creating the character of such a youth as this, appearing as he does in contemporary Japan, is a striking one. One day, Kusano finds himself trapped in the revolving door of a tall building; however many times the door turns, despite his desire to get out, he is always thrust back into the "interior" again. Just as in Luis Buñuel's film *Exterminating Angel*, the world painted here is altogether of the interior; the exterior has disappeared. In that sense, this scene creates a certain outlandish, vivid reality. At this point, the youth appears and pushes the door, and the two together manage to make their escape "outside," into the real world.

The audience has the sensation that the stage is superbly filled with the sense of a "great voyage." Indeed, there is here a sense that this setting out on a voyage, so full of adventure, to that vast "exterior" can set up waves capable of touching our own private oceans. Even the set seems redolent with a sense of festivity. In particular, a scene that takes place at the bottom of the sea in which various sea monsters exchange anecdotes seems to me a most delightful moment.

However, when Kusano awakes from his "dream of the great voyage," he finds himself again closed in by the world of industrial Japan. Then, one day, when the elevator door opens, the youth appears again, attempting to tempt Kusano to another "departure." He points to a gondola with windows on the roof of the building and says to Kusano, "I'm going to get into this gondola and sail off to the Indies."

But the gondola that the youth has boarded falls to the right side of the building; Kusano, in a state of terrible agitation, goes down to the street, but the youth is nowhere to be found. Then, as Kusano looks up blankly, a kind of wilderness seems to spread out endlessly beyond the building.

In this period in our culture, when we have lost sight of any "voyages" out onto the "great sea," our actions are limited, in the perplexed words of Kusano, to an interior trip since, "domesticated as we are, there is nothing to do other than seek out the 'Indies' we can locate within ourselves."

By the same token, the youth who has urged Kusano on has chosen a very different path; he is making his voyage toward what Kara Jūrō called "an unprecedented world." But has Kusano, as expected, even actually seen that gondola?

The contemporary theatre reveals a bewildering variety of subject matter. Yet, if one listens with great care, passing beyond time, situation, and the cultural moment, one can pick up the sound of a continual motif of "setting out" for "the world beyond," which flows on ceaselessly, setting up a kind of ground bass. If that is so, then the sound of the bell that calls us to the performance can serve as an invitation to a voyage itself. In this theatre we call a boat, boarded by the staff, actors, and the audience as well, we set out each night on the seas toward a "mysterious island" with an engine powered by the imagination. The voyage of the contemporary theatre toward that "new world," which surely must exist, is still somehow under way.

Scene I: 1971–1973
The First Period

I suppose that, in personal terms, this "first scene" can be said to have commenced when I began to write articles on the theatre on a regular basis. Otherwise, there is, indeed, no special significance, theatrically speaking, to the year 1971 in and of itself. The work of the early experimental theatre companies in Tokyo came to a peak in the mid-1960s, culminating in those Red Tent productions presented by Kara Jūrō's Situation Theatre in 1967. At that time, I was no more than a fascinated spectator.

The activities of that "first generation" of those small companies reached a peak during 1969 and 1970. Created as they were in the context of a struggle against the Japanese national authorities by the radical student movement and the anti–Vietnam War protest organizations, these performing companies gave rise to theatrical manifestations that were both boldly experimental and filled with a sense of adventure. The early productions of Suzuki Tadashi, Satoh Makoto's Black Tent, and Ninagawa Yukio's productions, all of which involved in one way or another contemporary problems, gave a fresh sense of shock to all of us.

From 1971 to 1973, however, subtle changes began to occur. The incident of the Japanese Red Army purges of their own members brought profound reverberations in the minds of a public that could find a sense of pity and gloom only in a play such as Shimizu Kunio's *When We Go Down That Heartless River.* In 1971, established troupes dissolved, and new companies began to form. As a result, the whole map of postwar theatre as we had come to know it began to shift. And a "second generation" of small groups began to emerge. Such names as the Theatre Troupe and Space Performance began to become familiar to us.

Such was the nature of those years.

1. A DRIFTING COMMUNE

Diary of a Voyage to the West

Written and directed by Higashi Yutaka

THE TOKYO KID BROTHERS

1972

On a cold day early in April 1972, I went to see the new Kid Brothers production, *Diary of a Voyage to the West*. I must say that, in terms of my own actual emotional responses, I found their work truly striking. There were certain sections of the play that I found genuinely moving. Yet what was "moving" for me cannot be simply described in terms of this one production itself. As I watched the performance on the stage, memories of these "Kid Brothers" flashed in and out of my mind; now, after a lapse of time, I was able to "rediscover" this troupe and to take cognizance yet again of the special kind of persuasive power they can assert.

And at that moment I remembered too phrases that Higashi Yutaka had written on the first page of his recent book *A Drifting Diary of a Cherry,* to serve as a kind of epigram. I read this some months ago, but I remember that his words were something like the following:

> The petals of the cherry flutter to the ground, but the fruit remains. And, just like the cherries on a tree, these fruit may be tiny, but I would like to build through them a gentle sense of togetherness.

In the middle of April, the Tokyo Kid Brothers plan to embark on their third overseas tour, with a troupe of some 150. They will visit various countries in Europe, and then, after returning home, they plan to begin construction, and with their own hands, of their "Cherry Commune" on a large plot of land in Tottori Prefecture.

My own personal experience of the "Kid Brothers" can be divided into three periods. The first was the summer of 1969, when I first "discovered" the group for myself. At that point, the troupe was virtually unknown, as the Kid Brothers had not yet been picked up by the journalists and the mass media. Thinking back, this first "encounter" was truly a very happy one. The troupe was performing in a kind of coffee house theatre in Shibuya that could seat sixty at most (the place was called Hair, a name so

The 1972 production of *Diary of a Voyage to the West* by the Tokyo Kid Brothers, directed by Higashi Yutaka. (Photo by Katō Karoku.)

typical for the time!). I went there for two nights in succession, and the company provided me with quite an unusual set of impressions.

That presentation, called *Tokyo Kids*, was actually a kind of homemade musical presented by these down-and-out young performers. These youngsters, separated from any purpose or joy while living in the city of Tokyo, seemed to shrug their shoulders together in sympathy as they sang of their dreams that could in no way be fulfilled. In terms of the pressures of everyday life, they could do nothing; on the stage, they provided an unanticipated sense of freshness precisely because this theatrical fantasy represented what their ordinary lives could never mean for them.

But then came a second period, one of disillusionment and despair. The group came back from a tour of America in January 1971, flushed with the success of their performances there. They now presented their production *The Golden Bat Comes Home*, a presentation planned, like the window of some souvenir shop, for the pleasure of a foreign audience. I found the results very disappointing indeed. The whole production seemed designed simply to show off their successful return, and I found myself sufficiently disgruntled that I wrote badly of them in a magazine article, to the effect that their *The Golden Bat Comes Home* should have been renamed *A Bat for a Foreign Audience*. It seemed to me at that time that they had forgotten the basic principle of their philosophy, that "solidarity" of which they always spoke.

Now, however, they have moved into a third period, and I must admit that my point of view has again changed completely. As before, I still harbor some doubts as to their shallowness of principle and about the way in which they try to please their audiences in too easy a fashion. On the other hand, it has become clear to me that their intention to take seriously the concept of a commune has real value. This change in my thinking, I believe, has come about since I myself have been reading extensively on communes as they exist outside Japan and, in addition, because, in the process of collecting the material for a writing assignment, I had the experience of visiting what has been termed a "typical Japanese commune," the "Mountain Riverbank Society," located in a small village in Mie Prefecture.

In general, it can be said that, until now, the left wing in Japan has failed to take up the concept of the commune. In their view, a "commune" was rather to be regarded as a faction, a progressive organization whose purpose was to advance revolution throughout the entire society. Communes were seen as functional groups that fulfilled a need existing at a certain stage of a larger process; any idea that a commune could be created in and of itself to bring about a sense of "happiness," and that it might exist for its own purposes, would have been denied as nonsense. This is because any movement to gather together a small group of like-minded sympathizers in order to construct an idealistic society "in miniature" would have been seen as flying in the face of a movement established on the principle of serving the cause of a total revolution designed to free all the people at one time. Indeed, this first principle of social revolution actually resulted in the putting off of any individual "personal revolution" far into the future, as a kind of second consideration. And it might be noted as well that those very left-wing intellectuals who cried out for the abolition of personal property often held strong "personal" views of their own. It was no accident that they often reserved a position of privilege and retained the right of private ownership for themselves. These are the kinds of elements to be noted when observing the process by which the revolution took on a Stalinist character.

Those inspired by the communal ideal itself proceed from a very different set of assumptions; they believe in a personal "revolution" and the eradication of public property. For them, the idea of becoming "fighting revolutionaries" belongs to a separate dimension of the problem. These believers are sensitive to human realities: affection, gentleness, weakness, even stupidity; in this, they possess a genuine self-awareness. Their idea that an ideal society might be constructed by linking together one commune after another is, of course, surely overly fanciful. Still, it is true that each of us has only one life to lead; in that context, such an attempt to build a small and

ideal society is certainly not without value. Indeed, I must admit that I did
find a surprising sense of ease and peace when I observed communal life as
it was pursued at the Mountain Riverbank Society. And this despite the fact
that the standard of living commune members enjoyed was very, very low
indeed.

As I came to adopt this new point of view, I began to see the attitudes
of the Tokyo Kid Brothers in a new light. Let me quote again something
that Higashi Yutaka wrote in the book I cited above:

> I dislike dreams that belong only to one individual. I would like for us all to
> dream together. In the dark period in which we live, it is difficult to escape
> from the self and arrive at the point where all can exist together; still, "we"
> really do wish to try to carry on; and in this is the meaning of the fact that we
> are "floating."
>
> At the end of our "floating" will come a shift from the isolated individual
> to the individual who belongs in a group; perhaps indeed we will be able to
> give birth to a truly "communal body."

It is easy enough to diminish the significance of the Tokyo Kid Brothers
if one judges them merely in terms of their artistic skills. However, if one is
to achieve a more just evaluation of their work and a surer understanding of
the context within which that work is created, their communal thinking is
then surely the place to begin.

2. THE RED TENT IN GOOD HEALTH

A Tale of Two Cities

Written and directed by Kara Jūrō

THE SITUATION THEATRE

1972

There is nothing as joyful for me as an encounter with a fine piece of theatre, and it is in this spirit that I am writing these few remarks. Since I have

The Situation Theatre's 1972 production of Kara Jūrō's *A Tale of Two Cities*. *From left to right:* in the rear, Kara Jūrō, Fuwa Minsaku, and two minor players; in the foreground, Ōkubo Taka and Ri Reisen. (Photo courtesy of *Asahi Shimbun*.)

begun reviewing theatrical productions, I must have written about some fifty plays, but in truth I have seldom felt such a seething excitement as I did when watching this current production of *A Tale of Two Cities*. The play is a masterpiece that shows off at its richest one aspect of Kara's powerful romanticism. What is more, the production itself reveals that Kara's company is now in a happy state of artistic health.

For some time, Kara has made public his desire to present one of his productions at the famous Shinobazu Pond in Tokyo's Ueno Park. I believe that it was his intention to stage his important 1971 production *The Vampire Princess* in that location.

Kara's vision: those fleeing the fires of the 1923 Tokyo earthquake rush off in a confused fashion to the woods of Ueno, where the roar of the lions at the zoo suddenly changes to the roar of the sea. Across from those same woods, new, dark straits now open, linking Japan directly to the mainland. Is this splendid scene not a perfect expression of Kara's romantic temperament? At last, managing to evade the tiresome regulations of the Tokyo government, Kara was able to set up his tent on the site he had longed to use for such a long time.

Entering the concert shell erected over one end of the pond, I sat down on one of the benches provided inside the tent, which was flapping about in the evening breeze. The front of the tent itself had been opened up, and the whitecaps that could be seen on the pond seemed quite close to the stage, which itself undulated from the movement of the water. On both sides lay the broad expanse of the wide pond, which in the dying light was beginning to turn the color of steel. Indeed, this stage itself served as the most important "player" in the production, creating a device by which the roar of the straits between Korea and Japan could echo in the dark corners of our all too human hearts. A startling moment opened the performance: the characters who first appear are stowaways newly arrived from Korea, the ghosts of those "original Japanese" who now seek their proper family register books. These figures (played by Kara, Ōkubo Taka, and the others) actually swim through the dark and chilly waters of the pond, then appear dripping wet on the stage.

From that moment onward, all of us became quickly and easily caught up in the magic of Kara's stagecraft. We followed his tale through its labyrinthine ways, sometimes descending into the darkest valleys, often rising high with our most optimistic dreams. So it was that we could experience again the terror and exaltation the Situation Theatre can bring into being. The high-pitched roar of sound, the abrupt transformation of the characters from one persona to another—these sudden flashes could in an instant turn on its head what had seemed a set of meanings that held up an artificial world.

The art of Kara does not depend on any panorama of static images springing from the imagination of a poet; nor is his work the product of an analytic intelligence, skillfully weaving together the contents of a box of magic tricks. Rather, his is a dynamism that must rush forth toward some dark and final destruction, a romantic world filled with both the hot-blooded and the gentle.

There are a number of gripping scenes. Take, for example, the moment when, in answer to the cries of the young girl Riran (played by Ri Reisen), there suddenly appears above the black straits a mysterious red merry-go-round. Or the moment when Riran, resuscitated when she takes a hundred-yen coin, thrown in charity into a spittoon, has her hideous dream linking Tokyo and Seoul. Or the moment when the bandage that has been covering the face of the girl named Mitsuko (played by Taguchi Ikuko) is suddenly transformed into a glittering white flower fluttering above that same merry-go-round. We watch these moments as children, in self-abandonment, our hearts pounding, as we exalt in these experiences.

Having said this, *A Tale of Two Cities* is not, as far as I am concerned, to be compared to such a vast and synthetic work as *The Vampire Princess*. As the title of that earlier work of Kara's suggests, he achieves there a level of fear and terror that, in comparison, gives the impression that the present work is one truly conceived on a smaller scale and possessing a certain sweetness.

In a recent review of the play, the critic Saeki Ryūko wrote that *A Tale of Two Cities* is "viciously left wing," but I certainly do not believe that his view is correct. In terms of its content, the play is neither to the Left nor to the Right; *A Tale of Two Cities* shows none of the fanatic gleam that Kara revealed to us in *The Vampire Princess*.

Why is this the case? It should be noted that, as originally conceived, *A Tale of Two Cities* was written for a staging planned to take place in Seoul, where students and the general population, under the most difficult conditions, were continuing to resist the pressures of the Korean government. Indeed, the play was presented on 23 March in the suburbs of Seoul, on the campus of Sogang University, with the support of the radical poet Kim Ji-ha and others. Aware of his reputation for a kind of fanatic passion, Kara held himself back so that his play would not be condemned as "left wing," as might be expected in Korea. Such self-control limited the scale of the play and so permitted the creation of this small and exquisite personal universe.

All the cast worked valiantly. Ri Reisen in particular revealed an increasingly pleasing level of skill. It was impossible to take your eyes off her. And she, Ōkubo Taka, and Nezu Jimpachi gave performances that exist at the cutting edge.

3. A LOGIC SURPASSING ANY
DECLARATION OF DETERMINATION

When We Go Down That Heartless River

Written by Shimizu Kunio

Directed by Ninagawa Yukio

THE CHERRY COMPANY

1972

Among the plays I have seen in 1972, there is one that truly seized my attention and yet has left me tormented and uneasy ever since. It is Shimizu Kunio's *When We Go Down That Heartless River.*

When I first read the script, I remember feeling that, unusually for this author, there seemed something incomplete in its conception; later, when I saw the production in rehearsal, I experienced, on the contrary, a deep sense of sympathy. And I was much moved as well when I attended the opening night of the production. Yet, in the days that followed, after I became weary through thinking over the various and complex issues concerned, I wrote a number of articles about the play in various newspapers and magazines in which I expressed the fact that, while in general the production certainly did elicit a deeply felt response from me, I nevertheless sensed a need to add certain criticisms concerning Shimizu's play.

Yet at the same time I must certainly admit that this is a work that, in the ordinary sense of the word, is difficult to *criticize.* This is not a drama in which the text itself can easily capture the realities of what has gone on beyond the confines of the theatre. The level of fear caused by the actual situation, which can be evoked only in the play, is one that has come to pursue us in our own daily lives. Therefore, should I add any critical comments to my description of the play, I would be stating my own views concerning those dark and difficult circumstances in which the political Left now finds itself in the aftermath of that infamous 1972 incident in which the Red Army Faction, the radical extremist group that first developed in the 1960s, cruelly executed a number of its own members in a purge-like action. It goes without saying that the situation has become a very tangled one. I know a number of active members of the Left who, when they attended the production, found themselves deeply moved. Yet, when it came time for them to describe in precisely what fashion they had been stirred, they could only remain silent. Their thoughts were heavy indeed; any words of explanation would simply have sounded frivolous, unworthy.

In the last scene of the play, the older brother (played by Ishibashi Renji)—who binds to his own body the bloodied corpse of his younger brother (played by Kanie Keizō), whom he has stabbed to death—literally merges with his victim as he decides to descend that "heartless river" forever.

> OLDER BROTHER: . . . Anyway, let's go as far as the riverbank. I've got you tied right to me now, and you won't be able to slip away. And if we can get safely to the bank, we can send off a boat. And even if it is a frail boat, frail as an October butterfly, we can at least begin to row. . . .

The older brother now "disappears, with the body of his brother, down the evening path," while onto his head, the stage directions continue, "pure

The climactic scene of the 1972 production by the Cherry Company of Shimizu Kunio's *When We Go Down That Heartless River.* Here the father (Honda Tatsuhiko) is on his knees before the older brother (Ishibashi Renji), who carries his younger brother the poet (Kanie Keizō) bound on his back.

white snow begins to fall." This is the same winter snow that presumably fell on the heads of the cruel young Red Army members on their march in the mountains near the resort town of Karuizawa as they carried along the frozen bodies of their slaughtered comrades.

True enough, I did feel an emotional response to the peculiar beauty that the scene provided; but at the same time I found myself forced to resist those feelings. "Even if it is a frail boat, frail as an October butterfly, we can at least begin to row. . . ." There is no question that there is a certain moving quality in a determined declaration of this sort. Yet, frankly, all this seems completely wrong to me. In the aftermath of the Red Army murders, public sentiment has not reached the point at which a beautiful, lyrical declaration of this sort would be found acceptable. In order to grasp the cruel horror of the incident, some kind of stern and cruel "logic," one that would twist out our very vitals, would first have to be found acceptable. And, for that situation to come about, we must first express certain fundamental suspicions concerning that phrase "we can at least begin to row." We know all too well the future of that "October butterfly."

Whatever meaning is ultimately found in the incident, its perpetrators cannot claim to have put forth a viable declaration on the emotional level. They had no more right to do this than did those comrades who carried out the cruel executions in the Soviet Union during the 1930s. Both incidents take their place in a growing international history of the kind of purges that occur in the aftermath of Stalinism.

In order to contain these Stalinist attitudes, it is necessary, first of all, to develop a strong logic capable of sharply criticizing attempts to justify such actions with theories of "self-criticism" or "aiding and abetting the enemy." Indeed, this Red Army incident in Japan reveals all too clearly that the members of the Left in our country, born itself from an anti-Stalinist impetus, now find themselves cornered, for want of any close study of the nature and history of purges in the Soviet Union. And because it is clear that the sort of attitudes conducive to Stalinist logic and action still lie concealed within their thinking, the cruelty found in the present situation seems therefore all the greater.

Such are the arguments that have occupied my thoughts. Yet I suddenly asked myself, what kind of person am I, after all? I am at best no more than an onlooker. I have certainly never experienced the sensation of strapping the cold body of a comrade to my back. And, when I speak of the need for some "strong logic" to replace any "declarations of determination," it is true that I am by no means prepared to explain just how the development of such a "logic" might come about. So it is, then, that, in pointing out any possible flaws in Shimizu's work, I can only admit my own poverty of imagination in terms of understanding how to move beyond what he himself has accomplished. In other words, on what basis do I make these "criticisms" of Shimizu's work?

In the end, when it comes to those "criticisms" of the play that I have written, I now realize that I have been able to provide no more than an outside, "objective" level of comment. My own powers of imagination have been frozen, crushed, by the horrors of the situation itself.

Eventually, in the January 1973 issue of the magazine *Teatoro* (Theatre), Shimizu himself published a strongly worded article expressing his opinion of the criticisms of this play and stating as well his views on the critics. In this article, he pointed out, with some anger, the real lack of constructive criticism in today's theatre world. He describes this situation, in terms of his own "lyrical expressivity," as a failed criticism in which "the ego and the drama cross swords, until blood flows from both." Why, he asks, do the critics not realize that they are at best "looking in from the sidelines?" Since they cannot see or experience every aspect of a drama, why, when discussing a play that they cannot totally possess and that they cannot allow simply to pass by, do they insist on revealing their own egos, and with such apparently transparent sincerity?

I myself believe that the kind of writing on the theatre with which Shimizu finds fault must be clearly and simply done away with. Many kinds of words have been spilled over plays that have been written in the memory of some actual blood that has been shed. Some of those words have been complimentary as well. I believe that Shimizu has expressed himself in the way he has because of his anger over the fact that our perceptions of this bloodshed are too indistinct, our hidden subjectivities too powerful. As for myself, I have no intention of changing either my observations or my criticisms of his play. However, honestly speaking, as far as such "theatrical criticism" goes, I must admit that of course I have never shed even one drop of blood. I flee from any exposure of my own limitations or any cruelty that I myself might experience. And, therefore, I avoid the expression of any views that would intrude on my "theatrical criticism." And so, perhaps, I must acknowledge, I make my apologies far too late.

Still, I believe that what I am aiming at is to carry out my own investigation, using the kind of "logic" I have called for, of a means to "cross over," but in another direction, that "heartless river" Shimizu has shown us.

4. THOSE SLIGHT STIRRINGS OF THE MAN IN THE WIND

A Tale of the Smallpox

Written, directed, and performed by

Hijikata Tatsumi

1972

One of J. G. Ballard's science fiction novels is entitled *The Wind from Nowhere*. The protagonist in this tale is not a human being but the wind itself. This fierce wind begins blowing with a strength and velocity beyond the human imagination. Every building, every city or locus of human habitation, is destroyed in what becomes Ballard's legend concerning the end of the world, a theme that governs his novel *The Drowned World* as well. When I saw Hijikata Tatsumi's *A Tale of the Smallpox*, the first part of a projected larger work and his first production in some four years, Ballard's powerful images came rushing back into my head.

In Hijikata's vision, there is also an uncompromising wind that serves as master to a great darkness. This is the fierce wind that blows from the fro-

A scene from the 1972 Hijikata dance performance *A Tale of the Smallpox*. Hijikata is the figure in the upper center of the photograph. (Photo by Onozuka Makoto.)

zen fields and mountains of the Tohoku region of northern Japan, and it is the sound of this wind that, along with the distant echo of horses' hoofs, sings out the tight rhythms that give tension to the entire performance.

In these two works, however, the wind functions in a very different fashion. Ballard's "wind" works against humankind; it stands as a physical force capable of blowing over walls made even of concrete and provides the kind of violence that brings with it the possibilities of physical subjugation. Hijikata's "wind," on the other hand, is one that locates itself within the human condition. For him, humanity *is* the wind, and the wind is within humanity; the wind therefore not only blows on us from outside but wells up as well from within, making our human flesh cry out as though it were a pair of bellows.

And what a strange beauty this "flesh" of Hijikata's possesses! I was able to see his famous 1969 presentation *The Revolt of the Flesh;* after that I saw his work only in films or on the flat performing space used by his performing group, the Human Theatre. And I must confess that I began to weary a bit of the somewhat boisterous "Hijikata legend." This year as well, with the exception of Kasai Akira's January recital, I found myself disappointed in the contents of a number of the *butoh* performances I had seen, which confirmed my continuing suspicions concerning the value of these experiments.

Now, faced with this vision of Hijikata's "flesh," I found myself susceptible to a truly fresh stimulus. For the first half of the production, the pure and exquisite melodies of the Canteloube *Songs of the Auvergne* poured out into the auditorium; in the midst of the atmosphere this romantic music created, Hijikata, in all his nakedness, like a beggar crouching to warm himself in the sun, seemed to become a squirming insect, only shifting his body slightly from time to time. And what poverty in this "flesh"! His ribs seemed to float to the surface of his chest, his legs only sinews, poles thrust forward; he appeared to be facing his own death as he dragged along his own weakened body, or so I thought, watching him in a state of vague apprehension myself. He really did manage to reveal to us "the eyes of the dying." Yet within those eyes shone the glitter of a rapture approaching intoxication.

In this there is nothing perverse, for these eyes look on his own body with the greatest intensity as he watches happily, and virtually without movement, the destruction of his own flesh, while the seasons move and the unstoppable wind permeates all things. For Hijikata, there is no specific gesture in his dance that seems necessary. Faintly, faintly, he moves himself ever so slightly, and through this means, surprisingly, his "story of the body" is richly spun out. The novelist Dan Kazuo has captured this quality precisely when he writes of this performance that Hijikata "has buried his flesh and spirit in the wind itself in the midst of a void that surpasses the very concept of dance itself."

Then, too, it seems to me that I here encountered still another way of using the "body." Take, for example, the actress Shiraishi Kayoko, perhaps the greatest performer in Suzuki Tadashi's troupe. When we observe her "body," one posits another kind of physique, the kind trained in a gymnasium and modeled on the Western concept of "bodybuilding." In her case, therefore, it would seem that physical and emotional gestures can reach a climax together in a total fusion and that boundaries between the two cannot be drawn. Considered in this way, perhaps Hijikata's sense of the "body" does not differ so widely from hers. Yet, in his case, body and spirit alike find their stability and their fusion through the fetters placed on them by the physical features of the very earth to which he is bound. So it is that, if Shiraishi's "body" gives us a sense of the vitality of life, Hijikata's gives us a sense of the body as inanimate object. The gestures that create the image of this trajectory, this transformation, already half completed in the present performance, suggest that this "flesh" resembles some shrub that has had its roots thrust deep into the ground.

A week or so before this performance, I requested an interview with Mr. Hijikata, and I went to call on him in the Meguro section of Tokyo. He was sitting upright on the boards of the rehearsal floor, his shock of hair uncombed. This "wind man" kept talking as he peered into the eyes of all those to whom he spoke; for me, he had a rare attraction of the kind I have seldom felt in all the interviews I have conducted. On the whole, the things he told me were similar to those he has often spoken of and written before, yet the refrain so typical of this remarkable person was no less interesting for all that.

"In Tohoku, the northern part of Japan, you can dress yourself in the wind and stand in the door. When the spirit of the wind comes into the room, you have the dance right there." As he said this, into his mouth came the melancholy range of sound of the wind blowing, from high to low.

I left him about two hours later, much stirred by what he had told me. When I got home, I decided to listen to the tape of our interview. I turned on the recorder, and the tape spun along just as it should, yet no sound issued from the speakers. I was surprised and somewhat flustered. The sound of Hijikata's voice, which should have captured his vibrant, intense conversation, had suddenly vanished as if blown away by the very wind itself.

5. A GHASTLY MASTERPIECE WITH CRUEL INTENTIONS

The Great Doctor Yabuhara

Written by Inoue Hisashi

Directed by Kimura Kōichi

THE MAY TROUPE

1973

This current staging of Inoue's new play is extremely striking. It ranks with Kara Jūrō's *The Bengal Tiger* as the most effective theatre piece of 1973. And it surely represents Kimura's greatest success as a director in many years.

As I watched the progress through the play, so closed in with spiritual darkness, of the blind protagonist, the musician Sugi no Shi (who later takes the name Yabuhara), pushing his cane along until he reaches the final bloody denouement, yet another blind man came to mind, one who tapped his cane in a similar fashion as he moved himself along toward a similarly ghastly end. Both these blind men resembled each other, in their birth, their upbringing, their rise in the world, even in their last moments.

What I found myself calling to mind was Uno Nobuo's *The Phosphorescent Blind Doctor*, first written in 1960, then revised a decade later. Despite the fact that both plays offer similar blind men as their protagonists, one can sense at once the great differences between these two works; indeed, Inoue presents the more extreme of the two versions of the story.

Among the sources for both Inoue's *The Great Doctor Yabuhara* and Uno's *The Phosphorescent Blind Doctor* are a written Tokugawa account and Kawatake Mokuami's *The Great Doctor Yabuhara*, based on the same account and written for the celebrated *kabuki* actor Onoe Kikugorō V. As a result, the two contemporary plays resemble each other in many ways.

In both plays, the protagonist's father is a poor fishmonger who kills a masseur and whose son, the protagonist, is later born blind (to show the workings of fate). (Interestingly, Uno cut this material when he revised the play.) Both protagonists show a certain guile and a desire to get ahead in the world. Both kill an ill traveler with an acupuncture needle in order to steal his purse, and both hire henchmen to murder their teacher in order to steal the officially inherited title of blind musician. And, in the end, it is the coming to light of an insignificant crime that brings both men to execution.

Despite the use of similar materials, however, the two plays seem altogether dissimilar. The characters of the two writers are in the end so different that their dramas strike out on very different paths.

Quickly said, Uno Nobuo's play inhabits a logical, rational universe. No doubts are expressed about the ordinary nature of reality. His protagonist, Tomi no Shi, is a heretic within this commonsense environment. Although he shows a spectacular talent for truly evil behavior and his life follows a grotesque trajectory, his evil stands alone. The world itself remains as always regular and orderly. Tomi no Shi is, himself, a kind of hero who leaves behind him the vision of an exhilarating, somehow glamorous wickedness that stands in opposition to the orderly boredom of everyday life. Thus, when he is arrested, the world at large returns to a state of quiet and balance. Given the logic of this vision, when Uno revised his script, he was able to leave out the notion of the protagonist's fated birth, so that the hero becomes merely a modern sort of wicked man.

In the dark and decadent world that he has captured in *The Great Doctor Yabuhara*, Inoue, on the other hand, reveals a blood-soaked universe, a veritable hell. His blind protagonist Sugi no Shi (played by Takahashi Chōei) is not a single, warped figure but a living representative of the evil and grotesquerie that pervades all of society. As opposed to Tomi no Shi,

The May Troupe's 1973 production of *The Great Doctor Yabuhara* by Inoue Hisashi. The protagonist *(left)*, Sugi no Shi (Takahashi Chōei), clutches his mistress O-Ichi (Taichi Kiwako). (Photo courtesy of the Seibu Theatre [now the Parco Theatre].)

who represents the embodiment of calculated wickedness, Sugi no Shi remains merely his cruel self. In this hellish, illogical universe, the boundaries between good and evil, value and loss, begin to blur, becoming almost indistinguishable. At no time is a sense of tragedy evoked; rather, the world is something to be laughed at. Only a sense of cruel comedy remains.

This clear alignment between comedy and this hellish world comes to life with particular strength during the ghastly comic scene in which Sugi no Shi himself is killed. These qualities center in the person of O-Ichi (played by Taichi Kiwako), the paramour with whom he has become increasingly entangled. However ghastly this moment remains for Sugi no Shi himself, the fate that attaches itself to O-Ichi, doomed as she is to receive sexual advances from such an ugly presence, is far more dreadful.

In this play, then, is Inoue suddenly changing his character as an author? This brilliant writer of beguiling comedy, who has brought such genuine laughter to the theatre, this gentle wordsmith, this friendly agitator who wrote in one of his popular plays "Take up your arms, tomorrow will be beautiful!"—has he suddenly been transformed into a pessimist?

No, I don't believe so. Inoue Hisashi has remained consistently himself. He is one of the comparatively few writers who has not sought to provide any thorough personal confession in his work. Why? Perhaps because of his propensity for clowning, Inoue's work can take many directions, and as a result, the ideas embodied in his work so far represent only one aspect of his total vision. Inoue is the kind of writer who will ensure that at least some of those very characters who sang "Take up your arms, tomorrow will be beautiful!" will find that, when that "beautiful tomorrow" does arrive, they may harbor certain doubts after all.

In that regard, it can be said that Inoue, himself a Roman Catholic, stands diametrically opposed to Yashiro Seiichi, another Catholic writer whose work consists of a confessional profession of faith (although this is sometimes concealed in a style representing a disguise of evil). Inoue's interior spirit reveals a vast and desolate space where dark fires burn, regardless of the sense of God's salvation that may be hidden there.

And so, for these very reasons, Inoue dons verbal armor, using a glittering style of puns, plays on words, and verbal games. Rich and fecund in their details, the plays Inoue has continued to write show this mannerist spirit.

In any case, in the present *The Great Doctor Yabuhara*, Inoue has finally provided us with at least a fleeting glimpse of his darker intentions and of the spectacles that pass within him.

Scene II: 1974–1979
Tsuka Kōhei and After

The year 1974 turned out to be symbolic. The experiments of the 1960s were now supplanted, and a whole variety of new and unexpected changes came about.

The most brilliant manifestation of these tendencies can be seen in the activities of Tsuka Kōhei. His 1973 play *The Atami Murder Case* won the coveted Kishida Kunio drama prize. His company, the Tsuka Studio, presented one brilliant work after another, among them *Revolution for Beginners: Legend of the Flying Dragon* and *The Story of a Stripper*. The productions staged by his young troupe, performing in the Shinjuku section of Tokyo, created a virtual "Tsuka boom." For him, the glamour of the performer was to remain the center of his vision of the theatrical experience. With his considerable skills he developed this tendency, which could already be seen in the productions by the experimental troupes active in the 1960s. His sometimes bitter comedies, filled with exaggerated theatricality, spurred on in turn the development of sparkling comic drama, but these were dramas that, unlike their ardent predecessors, revealed a shrewd and observant glimpse of a period "vacant of ideology."

In 1974, after an earlier period as a director of an often radical theatre, Ninagawa Yukio began directing a series of productions for Tōhō that began with *Romeo and Juliet*. On that occasion, he left his radical group, the Cherry Company.

By that same year, because of the oil shock, the Japanese economy experienced its first year of negative economic growth, and long-held assumptions about the Japanese economy were called into question. In this climate, entertainment began to reach a new stage of commercialization, and young audiences in particular were much influenced by new publications advertising contemporary culture.

This new period saw unique work by such companies as Space Performance and the Troupe of the Slanting Light. Yamazaki Tetsu began his celebrated series of productions entitled *Field Notes for Crimes*. And a new, third generation of troupes began their activities, among them Noda Hideki's company the Dream Wanderers and Watanabe Eriko's Three Circle Company.

It was during this period as well that those "first generation" theatre companies that began in the 1960s reached maturity and fruition. Kara Jūrō's Situation Theatre, with its famous Red Tent, had a real success with *The Kara Version: Matasaburō of the Wind*. Suzuki Tadashi's company began its famous festival performances at Toga, deep in the mountains of central Japan, and Terayama Shūji's experimental productions, with their unsettling social implications, included such street theatre pieces as *Knock*. It was at this time that such important figures as Ōta Shōgo, Satoh Makoto, and Saitō Ren did their best work and attracted a genuinely popular following.

6. THE INTOXICATION OF A "MYTH" THAT SOARS

The Kara Version: Matasaburō of the Wind

Written and directed by Kara Jūrō

THE SITUATION THEATRE

1974

I have seen this new production of Kara's Situation Theatre twice, first on an island in Tokyo Bay, then at Shinobazu Pond at Ueno Park in the northeastern part of the city. On both occasions I enjoyed myself immensely. Kara's three-act play, which takes more than three hours to perform (and is by far the longest of his plays to date) captures the undivided attention of his spectators from the opening scene through the final climax; I would say that the present script and the skill of Kara's direction make *Matasaburō* a virtually "well-made play." By the same token, the richness of imagination that Kara reveals here as he spins out his tale is truly astonishing.

Certainly, in all Kara's recent works, he has revealed to us an imagination so rich as to be outlandish, couched in a virtual torrent of exalted language. Given the productions we have seen in Kara's Red Tent, it is easy to fall into the illusion that his works apparently inhabit a dimension altogether different from our contemporary culture, one in which, according to George Steiner, the universe of words has shrunk, a world in which, as Martin Esslin has pointed out concerning drama after the coming of the theatre of the absurd, the value of the words themselves has been diminished, if not eradicated altogether. Such is the vision we encounter in the work of a Samuel Beckett or a Betsuyaku Minoru, who conquers with abstinence, a loss of speech, or conversely the kind of chatter that possesses a signal equal to that of silence itself, as in the work of a playwright such as Shimizu Kunio.

At this point, however, I do not mean to compare Kara's use of words with the strategies employed by such other dramatists. Rather, I would like to point out that, in *Matasaburō of the Wind*, Kara has again created what is for him a prototypical tale as he struggles to find what might be called a new popular "myth."

As those who have seen or read Kara's work already know, he has long

The 1974 production by Kara Jūrō's Situation Theatre of his *The Kara Version: Matasaburō of the Wind*. Nezu Jimpachi as Oribe *(left)* and Ri Reisen as his sweetheart Erica. (Photo courtesy of the *Asahi Shimbun*.)

been the creator of such stories. He always picks up images and fragments of the same variety, ones that closely resemble each other, then exchanges and rearranges them; and, while piling them one on the other, he creates a myth-like structure that appears in some whirlpool, screwlike shape. Each of the individual plays staged by his Situation Theatre company represent one twist or turn, and, as these stages or moments are tied together, we can envision a sort of swirling nebula through which we can see the larger significance of Kara's work.

We can find the early myths of Kara in the tale of the comings and goings of the vulgar one-legged John Silver, who has stepped out of Stevenson's *Treasure Island*. To borrow the observations of the theatre critic Tsuno Kaitarō, this is the tale of a romantic search undertaken by the pirate John Silver, who has "fled the sea" but who now takes up again the life of a wanderer.

After these early tales of Silver, however, Kara went through a period during which he composed his "Manchuria plays," again in an apparent search for something new. Since the time when he first produced the play that best represents this series, his masterpiece *The Vampire Princess* (1971), it seems clear that he has been following this new line of thought, as can be seen in such productions as *A Tale of Two Cities, Iron Mask, The Bengal Tiger,* and *Fang of the Sea.* In terms of the images employed, these are works that place violent images of the Korean Straits on the stage. These plays deal with problems of Koreans living in Japan or with the history of imperialist Japan and its incursions into Southeast Asia juxtaposed with the transformation of the Japanese nation into a great postwar democratic and economic power. Such are his raw materials. But these complex matters are not presented in terms of some postwar humanistic outlook. For Kara, rather, this period of history represents a time in which the very souls of his citizens are mired in a swamp in which love and hate are mixed.

At the risk of misinterpreting his work, I would conjecture that, from *The Virgin's Mask* of 1969 down to *The Virgin's City, A Beggar for Love,* and *The Vampire Princess,* this series of "Manchuria Plays" has been conceived of as a means to confront directly the situation of our society in the postwar period. If some of his spectators may have considered that, early in his career, he was entangled in some sort of "right-wing fanaticism," the plays of the past few years are works that, if anything, adopt a "left-wing" stance in terms of their critique of modern Japanese culture.

However, to be deceived by the raw materials Kara employs, or by the convenience of making certain ideological distinctions, is to overlook a real advance that has been made in Kara's own evolving dramaturgy. First, one must acknowledge the fact that all his recent works have been centered on the relationship between his heroines (played by his wife, the Korean actress Ri Reisen) and their younger lovers, the "romantic leads" (performed by Nezu Jimpachi). Thus, rather than continuing to utilize the rough sorts of male characters that inhabit the myth of John Silver, Kara here is spinning out the myth of a new Orpheus and Euridice, using his two stars to suggest the pain of living in a cruel and wounded world.

The purest image of these two mythical lovers and their cruel environment is crystallized in *Matasaburō of the Wind.* In this play, it seems to me, Kara has put aside his critiques of contemporary life and his use of mere exterior elements in order to concentrate on creating the image of a true Orpheus and Euridice living in contemporary Japan. As a result, he has moved a long way away from creating simple melodramas about the dreams of the poor for a higher realm occupied by a genuine sense of the mythical.

By the same token, it must be said that this Orpheus and Euridice configuration merely brushes past the original myth as it goes on toward its own destination. Here, Orpheus is a young man named Oribe, who has managed to escape from a hospital for the mentally ill in Miyazawa. Euridice is transformed into Erica, a bar hostess in the town of Utsunomiya, near Tokyo. They are not true lovers in any ordinary sense. Their frail connection is made possible only through the agency of a limitless sense of a soaring freedom and love gained through a youthful reading of *Matasaburō of the Wind*. In order to return to his youth, Oribe has begun to dote on Matasaburō. Erica entrusts an image of Matasaburō to her lover, an officer of the Self-Defense Forces named Takada, who has escaped with his vehicle to the bay of Kashima and cut off all communication with the world. Now the two leave this world and, through the aid of the four-man "deep detective company," trudge through the labyrinth of Oribe's bloody ear, which has been cut off, in order to reach the Kingdom of the Dead, where they again meet Matasaburō, that is, Takada himself.

From this starting point, Kara once again creates a tale that can stand as an archetype; yet it is clear that this kind of popular "myth" that he has established is far different from the kind of work he created in his earlier days.

Above and beyond all other considerations, Kara's final scene, in which the two scarred "lovers" are now metamorphosed into Matasaburō and fly off into the dark night sky outside the Red Tent, their phantom airplane rising until it disappears from view, remains one of intoxicating beauty.

7. THE APPEARANCE OF A NEW TALENT

The Legend of a Flying Dragon:

And Then a Crow

Written and directed by Tsuka Kōhei

TSUKA STUDIO

1974

Among the new playwrights who have appeared since such now established figures as Betsuyaku Minoru, Kara Jūrō, and Satoh Makoto, none can rival the talents shown by the uniquely gifted Tsuka Kōhei.

The first point that makes his work unique is that, unlike those who have merely pushed forward the kind of vision first proposed by Betsuyaku and the others, Tsuka engenders feelings in his own work that are altogether different. He represents no "conscious" epigone of Kara or Satoh as represented in their work of the 1970s. His vision does not resemble theirs. In a theatrical world now seemingly filled with those still writing under the influence of these powerful mentors, Tsuka's appearance, and his development, suggests that, at last, new horizons are appearing.

Of course, it can be observed that, in the delicacy in the construction of Tsuka's dialogue, his work certainly reveals the influence of Betsuyaku's early plays; nor is it hard to imagine that he certainly must see his own work in the context of his senior colleague. Still, each describes a totally different world. Take, for example, Betsuyaku's masterpiece *Elephant* (written in 1962) and Tsuka's *Revolution for Beginners: Legend of the Flying Dragon,* or, as it is retitled in the present version, *The Legend of the Flying Dragon: And Then a Crow.* Both works may arise from the same source, but the results show that the two plays are put together very differently and to different ends.

What then represents the characteristics of this special universe of

A climactic scene in Tsuka's play between Kamada (performed by Hirata Mitsuru) and the Girl (played by Inoue Kanako). This photograph derives from a 1979 revival by the Tsuka Studio of the original version of Tsuka's 1974 *The Legend of a Flying Dragon: And Then a Crow,* first produced in 1973, entitled *Revolution for Beginners: Legend of the Flying Dragon.*

Tsuka Kōhei's? From what I can observe, it is a "world of relationships" that he depicts, one he has developed to a remarkable level of perfection.

In Tsuka's artistic vision, it is not as though he, or anyone else, is attempting to put forth some serious philosophic argument, set out some brave declaration of purpose, or make a profound personal confession. None of the activities he portrays are meant to show any such high significance of meaning. He is concerned rather with how, in the midst of human relationships and in any given situation, effective gestures and expressions can manifest themselves and what the responses are that those gestures and expressions can engender.

Through his theatrical vision Tsuka attempts to create a world based on just such a concept of absolute relativity, one that is missing any sense of absolute values and standards. In this environment, everything moves with a sense of life, but one that remains vague and undecided, one controlled by the nuance of relationships. Everything passes through this net of relationships; conversely, the skillful use of these connections allows Tsuka's characters to live out their lives in terms of empty "performances" that serve to manifest their own heated and unfulfilled thoughts, their dreams that cannot be achieved. The goal is to bring into vivid being a theatre in which life itself is represented by the idea of "performance." Such, I believe, are the main themes that underlie Tsuka's plays.

So it is that, as in much contemporary drama, Tsuka has moved away from themes that can be expressed only in verbal terms; indeed, Tsuka's dramatic presence begins with a delicate sense of the very collapse of such themes. To put it another way, for him, human existence is itself a performance. Tsuka explained his views in a 1974 interview with the playwright Miyamoto Ken:

> You see, I write plays about the part of life that leaves us feeling flat. I don't really emphasize anything special, and because I feel the situation objectively, not subjectively, most of the relationships I depict with others are decided in that light. . . .

In the case of the present production—which he both wrote and directed for his company, the Tsuka Studio—what "leaves us feeling flat" is the "struggle between the classes in Japan," a struggle aimed at the "victory of a world revolution." An earlier version of this play was presented by another theatre group at Waseda University in the spring of 1973. The present version has been extensively revised and as a result considerably enriched. The result is a fully realized work of art of the sort that is rarely encountered these days.

While the "interest" of the production lies in the hearty laughter that it provokes, in the hearts of the many spectators who jam the theatre there arise a set of complex and deep emotions as well as an occasional sense of being jabbed by a sharp needle in uncomfortable places. This play casts a sharp, shrewd, and unforgiving eye on the last days of the bankrupt "revolutionary faction" from the 1960s, observing the survivors as they trudge along, living out their lives, with an awareness, and often a cruel one, of their own sterile situations. This view can give rise to a certain humor. Indeed, Tsuka paints the situation in an accomplished satirical fashion.

There are only three characters in the play. The first is Kumada (played by Hirata Mitsuru), the former leader of the "revolutionary faction," who is now middle aged and often in ill health. He lives in the memory, emotionally speaking, of his days of glory in the midst of the struggle. The second is a girl (played by Iwama Takako), the bride of his son, who had collected stones to sell for throwing at the government tanks during the demonstrations.

The third is Onodera (played by Miura Yōichi), the leader of the fourth squadron in the government's tank brigade, Kumada's archenemy, who mercilessly and relentlessly hunted him down. Onodera now has left his government position and, while serving as a counselor to ex-convicts, manages to eke out a living arranging tables in a center that provides school lunches for children.

It turns out that Kumada, with happy memories of battles bravely fought, takes up his dream to return to the front lines, while that "devil Onodera," who looks back on those fierce days when he fought the students as though his life depended on it, now plans to live out his own empty life by opposing him, on the pretext that Kumada still "plays his role" of "class hatred." And so it is that these two middle-aged men, who in truth have little to fight over, find value in their lives by indulging in a painful game: the "23 January Panda Observation Memorial Battle," a tussle in front of the main gate of Ueno Park in Tokyo. It is a situation that gives rise to considerable dark laughter. At the same time, it is the aptness of Tsuka's bitter humor that makes the play sufficiently fascinating. Some of us who watch Tsuka's production must take cognizance of the fact that, indeed, an important postwar period has ended.

In terms of the theatrical finish of the production, it can be said that the three performers are not in fact all that highly skilled. Still, they do have a sense of the kind of "reality" demanded by a work of Tsuka's. These performers, who first appeared in Tsuka's 1973 production at the Literary Theatre's Atelier, have certainly gained in theatrical technique, and this current offering is quite a bit more interesting than that first production. All in all, a real discovery.

8. MINUS DYNAMICS,
ALL SCOOPED OUT

Chairs and a Legend

Written by Betsuyaku Minoru

Directed by Sueki Toshifumi

THE HANDS COMPANY

1974

The present production of Betsuyaku's play *Chairs and a Legend* reveals a maturity of vision that is rarely seen these days. In fact, the play shows great spirit.

I must confess that I maintain a powerful admiration for Betsuyaku's early plays, such as his 1962 *Elephant* or *The Little Match Girl* of 1966, and, indeed, these early works have maintained their high reputation. Within his texts woven from everyday language, Betsuyaku manages to impart astonishing tension and cohesive power. Since the author's vision

The 1974 production of Betsuyaku Minoru's *Chairs and a Legend* by the Hands Company. *From left to right:* Woman 2 (Hara Sen), Man 2 (Tagi Hitoshi), and Man 1 (Naitō Taketoshi).

exists in a purposefully sharp competition with everyday reality, his text can soar up through of a kind of poetic centripetal force unrelated to the usual sorts of outpourings judged to be of the usual lyrical or sentimental sort.

However, ever since Betsuyaku established himself as a commercial playwright, it seems to me that his work has lost some of that sharp edge revealed in those earlier works in which he posited such a competition with everyday reality. Now he depends merely on the creation of an individual style. Yet, since he does not surrender himself to romantic lyricism or establish a firm philosophical basis as a thinker himself, Betsuyaku goes on polishing his style, developing his texts simply to express feelings through the use of images that now seem static. His works risk becoming merely obvious in terms of the metaphysical images employed. His style has become increasingly smooth, and his technical skills as a dramatist have become ever more prodigious. Still, I cannot push away the thought that somehow his works have grown weak; they have lost that tension that I tried to describe above.

Chairs and a Legend, however, is altogether different. Here, Betsuyaku has escaped from a drama driven by style. Rather, he has adopted as a central strategy a new method that might be termed "the logic of a slip of the tongue." In doing so, he has succeeded in creating a new species of drama. It would seem that, after a long period of groping, he has managed to bring a new dimension to his work. The style in which this play has been composed is, by its very logic, quite powerful.

This is a work that has revealed through the great efforts of its author those dark and cruel "negative dynamics" that essentially permeate any collective society.

The set is nothing more than a guardrail surrounding an empty space in which have been placed some five or so miscellaneous chairs and a desk. In this space appear four men and three women; they proclaim this space a "liberated zone." In the words of Man 1 (played by Naitō Taketoshi), this space is defined as that within which "a hidden experiment is taking place. . . . This is not a space that is created in order to spring back from some pressure brought from the outside, but one that comes together through a mutual under-standing developed from within. . . ." The group is thus a sort of voluntary commune.

However, it soon becomes clear that this commune is certainly not sustained and supported by any extensive "mutual understanding." The characters in this play listen to the words of a well-intentioned newcomer to this "liberated area," Middle-aged Man 1, and then, following the stubborn logic of his "slip of the tongue," bind him hand and foot; without any real discussion, they simply set him up as a "traitor" to the group.

Along with a "traitor," a "sacrificial victim" is needed as well. In the same way, Young Man 4, who has recently joined this "liberated zone" and does not yet know the rules very well, is chosen, first of all, to have his eyes gouged out with a knitting needle by Woman 2 during a collective lynching party. Then he is stabbed to death with a knife placed in the hands of Man 1, the "traitor."

No longer motivated by the "positive dynamics" of ideology or shared commitment, the group has passed its apex and, in its decline, knows only a "negative dynamics" of censure and punishment. There is a need to create both traitors and victims.

This kind of conception is not new with Betsuyaku. Such activities were actually undertaken by the nineteenth-century Russian revolutionary Nechaev, later portrayed with such effectiveness by Dostoyevsky in his long novel *The Possessed,* which deals with just such a small revolutionary faction. And Abe Kōbō's 1971 play *Involuntary Homicide* showed the same process of decay. All these examples reveal all too clearly the workings of such "negative dynamics." In Japan today, such an absolutist logic has surely overtaken the Red Army Faction (witness the recent lynchings). Even our national system of justice itself, in terms of its own exploitation of these "negative dynamics," now seems reduced to seeking out and punishing victims merely in order to keep functioning that large legal machine that has been created.

There is in addition another important meaning hinted at in Betsuyaku's *Chairs and a Legend,* no less than a new interpretation of the story of Christ and the disciples who surrounded him. In an essay written in connection with this production, Betsuyaku says, "I find it difficult to believe the tradition that first Christ appeared and then gathered about him his twelve disciples. I believe, rather, that there first existed a group of thirteen, held together by some sort of unshifting, yet peculiar relationship; then, at the end of their ceaseless wandering, in the context of the Jewish faith giving rise to Christian belief, the idea of this special 'relationship' was somehow perfected." Whatever else may be said, Betsuyaku has certainly found an unusual way to interpret the New Testament.

There are, unfortunately, many disappointing things about the direction and about the production itself. Perhaps most important, the performers do not exhibit the kind of heightened emotional style that would allow them to move suddenly from the realm of everyday perceptions through a kind of peculiar exaltation to the depths of madness, necessary to suggest the blood and horror of a play dedicated to themes of massacres and purges.

It seems a shame, therefore, that the complex perceptions that underlie that clarity and the "everyday quality" of Betsuyaku's drama have not been expressed in the production itself.

9. THE CROUCH AS A CRITIQUE OF THE MODERN

The Trojan Women

Written by Euripides

Adapted and directed by Suzuki Tadashi

AN IWANAMI HALL PRODUCTION

1974

At this certain point in the day, when the bicycle races finish in the suburbs of Tokyo, one sees large groups of men, crumpled racing sheets in hand, on the platforms of suburban railway stations, squatting down, heads drooping, waiting for their trains. Even in the crowded trains, surrounded by dowdy, middle-aged men in jumpers and *tabi,* the traditional workingmen's white socks, they will continue to squat. And you can also see young men in well-cut coats who disdain the posture of the straphanger and instead block the aisles as they squat together.

It is rare to see this kind of communal squatting posture among the ordinary commuters who crowd the stations and the trains. Those traveling to work either sit quietly on the interior seats or, pushing away their fatigue, gather their courage and stand, to be jerked about as they hang on the leather straps hung from the ceiling. Still, it should be observed that many of us, should we enter into that state of absentmindedness that follows from the physical fatigue that develops when we learn that we have merely thrown our money to the winds, might well find ourselves thoughtlessly, naturally, forgetting our "modern" conceptions of "good posture" and slipping into that same crouching position.

Concerning the "squat," the essayist Tada Michitarō has made some interesting observations:

> It would appear that [in Japan] the position of squatting is regarded as something extremely ill bred. No position appears so uncouth in public, and it is acceptable only in private when going to the toilet. This position has been suppressed through the advances of modern culture.

Tada writes as well that

> "squatting" somehow suggests a sense of "low class." . . . Indeed, this position, which suggests neither standing nor sitting, hints at a certain attitude of insubordination toward one's superiors. *(Gestures and Japanese Culture)*

It is also of great interest that, in a program note accompanying this production, the critic Noguchi Michizō wrote that, in order to investigate "the essence of human behavior," he examined the most ancient forms of Chinese writing and their pictorial symbols. He was surprised to find, as he writes, that "there are almost no examples of characters based on the human figure standing erect, with both feet together," while, on the other hand, there are so very many drawn from figures that are "squatting, crouching, or bending."

Thus, it would appear that this "low-class" gesture of crouching or squatting, apparently so far from our modern consciousness, represents a basic bodily stance not only for the Japanese but for all Asians, including the Chinese. Furthermore, it seems a most natural one.

From that point of view, consider the touching scene toward the end of the great Ozu film *Tokyo Story* where two of the characters, dressed in mourning clothes, exchange a few words while squatting down on the embankment; for us, as Japanese, this scene is highly poetic and leaves a strong impression.

I have gone on at such length about the squatting position because Suzuki Tadashi's production of *The Trojan Women* at Iwanami Hall makes uncompromising use of this "vulgar" posture. Indeed, it is the very basis of his conception of the play.

In truth, this "crouching" constitutes the chief glory of Suzuki's conception as employed in *The Trojan Women*. At the beginning, the members of the chorus, draped in rags, enter one by one, sliding their feet and crouching as they walk. This basic posture is never abandoned. And, when Queen Hecuba, played by Shiraishi Kayoko, enters amid the chorus, she too crouches, except on occasions when she is half standing or sitting. When Cassandra (performed by Ichihara Etsuko) performs with the chorus the "dance of sadness," she creates this powerful moment in a low crouch as well.

In the spring of 1974, the National Theatre of Greece visited Japan, and we were introduced to productions of *Oedipus the King* and other classic plays; but it must be said that, in comparison to their chorus, which moved about in a vivid fashion, standing upright as they danced and sang, Suzuki's chorus exhibited a strikingly unusual expression of both fleshly substance and sensibility.

It seems to me that Suzuki's experiment has taken the stuff of Greek tragedy (which constitutes, after all, the source of all Western drama) and "reread" it altogether in terms of the Japanese national sensibility and body movements, creating in the process what is essentially a new form. Further, such a production constitutes a strong critique of the kinds of productions of Western drama presented until now in Japan, productions that privilege

The 1974 Iwanami Hall production of Suzuki Tadashi's version of *The Trojan Women* of Euripides. Shiraishi Kayoko *(left)*, with Kanze Hisao *(center)* and Ichihara Etsuko *(right)*.

traditional, European interpretations of the texts, thereby denying any role to authentic Japanese (indeed Asian) sensibilities. The very appearance of this "squatting" posture constitutes one vivid model of such a critique. Suzuki is deliberately setting out to question at the most basic level our methods of ingesting "modern culture," a process that privileges the conceptual and denies a unique Japanese physicality and sensibility. In this context, it seems to me that there is a real significance in the fact that this production is being presented at the Iwanami Hall in Tokyo, originally built to stage productions that appeal to the "Iwanami person of culture."* Now, Suzuki has brought his sense of resistance, of disturbance, to that very spot that so strongly symbolizes this older approach to Western culture.

At the same time, I should mention that, in his version of the Greek original, Suzuki has created a special dramatic structure quite unlike those employed in any of the translations or adaptations that we have seen to date. While he has retained the basic framework of *The Trojan Women*, he has added a new element: an old man (played by Kanze Hisao), struck down and burned out of house and home at the end of the Pacific War, spinning out his own "vision of Troy." By this device, the tragedy of Troy is personalized, extended into the historical moment, indeed the very physical sensations, of those who experienced the grim realities of the immediate postwar period in Japan. Suzuki thereby creates a double layering effect, at once strange and unsettling. So it is, then, that we are able both to witness this tragedy of ancient Greece and to have the rare experience of a drama set in contemporary Japan.

In terms of the production, the three main performers, Kanze Hisao, Ichihara Etsuko, and Shiraishi Kayoko, do not shy away from the effort required to bring verisimilitude to their roles. They can make us tremble. Supporting them is the chorus, which shows a stern agility of movement that deserves the highest praise.

---

*An amusing reference to Iwanami Shigeo (1881–1946) and his famous Iwanami Publishing House, which did so much during the interwar years and indeed still continues to make available Japanese translations of the great works of Western culture in popular editions.

10. AN OBSTINACY WELL WORTH MENTIONING

Tosa Genji

Written, directed, and performed by

Sakamoto Nagatoshi

THE ACTOR'S THEATRE

1975

Among those actors who have undertaken their training in the context of the orthodox modern theatre, Sakamoto Nagatoshi, I find, has continued to draw my special admiration. Part of the reason for this is that he has gained from this experience a truly successful acting technique, one that matches his unique personality. At the same time, however, while he began with this realistic school of acting in his work with previous troupes, he has since attempted a number of experimental and avant-garde productions with the company Transformation and has recently been performing in privately produced productions, even in a "romantic porno." In sum, he has been active in many areas, and these various efforts have brought his talents to a real fruition.

On this occasion, he has prepared a special solo production, *The Best of Sakamoto Nagatoshi,* which has been given a limited run at the Actor's Theatre in Tokyo's Roppongi district. The concept behind this evening is to fulfill a desire on his part to present the best efforts of his varied career.

The program is divided into two parts. The first seems more of a mere curtain-raiser. Here, Sakamoto borrows a number of tricks from the kind of popular theatre championed by a producer like Fukuda Yoshiyuki, yet his attempts to please are in the end mostly irritating, since performance and text alike are pretty thin stuff.

The second part, however, *Tosa Genji,* is quite another matter. Here, we enter into the real world of this vastly gifted actor. By any standards, even his own, this sketch represents one of the most remarkable achievements of recent times.

Surprisingly enough, this was the fourth time I have seen Sakamoto in *Tosa Genji.* And each time I have seen this solo production, which lasts less than an hour, my sense of attachment to and admiration for his work has continued to deepen.

The first time I saw this monologue was in February 1967, at a so-

Sakamoto Nagatoshi in his 1975 *Tosa Genji*. (Photo by Mizumura Takashi.)

called nude theatre, the Modern Art, in the Shinjuku section of Tokyo. At
that time, the so-called little theatre movement had suddenly begun to
thrive, and Shinjuku in particular had become the mecca for these movements, among them Kara Jūrō's Red Tent, the Scorpion Theatre, and the
Art Theatre Shinjuku. Thanks in part to this kind of atmosphere, even the
managers of the little strip joints of the time decided to mix in some avant-
garde material with their main numbers, so that there were a number of
"avant-garde entr'actes" being presented, among them this early version of
Tosa Genji. Although I visited the little theatre where Sakamoto was playing a number of times, the other skits and acts have completely faded from
my mind. My first impressions of his work, however, remain extremely vivid
and fresh. This was the first presentation that Sakamoto had made of this
material, and I was grateful to have chanced on his work.

I next saw a version of *Tosa Genji* two years later, in 1969, when it was
produced by the company to which he belonged, Transformation, in
Tokyo's Yoyogi district. I saw it again five years later, in 1974, in a ninety-
ninth commemorative presentation in a theatre in the Aoyama area. What I
learned was that Sakamoto had spent several years polishing and perfecting
his art in venues I never would have known of: coffee shops, snack bars, the
homes of friends, the dining halls of factories, lofts above movie houses,
wedding ceremonies, even firemen's meetings. Now, finally, has come my

fourth time to see *Tosa Genji,* on the occasion of its hundredth performance as part of *The Best of Sakamoto Nagatoshi.*

This *Tosa Genji* is by no means an avant-garde play. Rather, it is a skillful adaption in monologue form by Sakamoto of the recollections and memories of the actual Tosa himself as recorded by the anthropologist Miyamoto Tsuneichi, who met this unusual character holed up in his little nest
under a bridge in Kochi Prefecture (traditionally referred to as the Tosa
area). From the point of view of the subject matter of Sakamoto's sketch,
his is a naive tale that might well be classified as a kind of contemporary
folklore.

Be that as it may, when the actor appears from the depths of the stage
disguised as a beggar, in the flickering candlelight and with the harsh sound
of the old-fashioned Japanese lute, the *biwa,* there is something awesome
about him as he takes away a straw mat that had concealed his face and,
blinking his blind eyes, begins to tell his own tale of long ago. This story of
his own experience seems to touch us directly, as though a hand has reached
out directly to us.

True, the story that he tells is naive enough. But this man, who grew up
in extreme poverty and ate horse fodder as a child, who spent his life
"mixed up with women," and who, as wages for his sins, spent the latter half
of his life as a blind beggar, makes a powerful impression on us when he
says of the women who were attracted to him that "I never ever cheated
one of them." He tells of the life he has led with a grave composure. The
title of this sketch is particularly appropriate, for the meaning of *Tosa Genji*
comes from the popular idea of the "Shining Genji" who lived in Tosa,
going all the way back to popular versions of the lives of characters adapted
from the eleventh-century novel *The Tale of Genji,* by Lady Murasaki. One
must praise the unforgettable beauty of the simple eroticism with which
this piece is infused.

As it has developed through its various incarnations, however, *Tosa
Genji* has not always been performed with such extraordinary skill. During
the course of its hundred performances, many different effects were tried
and abandoned, many different devised used and revisions made.

As far as my own taste in the matter is concerned, the first production
that I saw in 1967 and the present version are by far the most successful. In
that very first version, Sakamoto wore a brighter sort of costume, and he
moved very little, sitting upright on his platform like some traditional Japanese doll. As he pushed along the story, some species of weird beauty radi-
ated from his energy and passionate emotion.

Then came Sakamoto's period of "theatrical realism," during which,
when performing this sketch, he tried to dress and speak as much like a real
beggar as possible. The results were surprisingly flat and boring. He has

finally, however, returned to his original, powerful conception, and with a symmetry and balance to his formidable technique that have given rise to this present, astonishing performance, surely a highlight of his career.

Given the present state of contemporary theatre in Japan, where things are used up, then thrown away in a state of virtual amnesia, I would insist that a very special value accrues to the obstinacy of an actor who can constantly strive to perfect his art through a hundred performances. A performer who can sustain his work to this extent is a strong one indeed.

As a final cautionary note, however, I can't help adding the thought that, if merely repeated again and again, this very dedication can also risk transforming itself into a kind of passive, conservative inertia.

11. A DRAMA OF A NEW AND FANCIFUL GEOGRAPHY

Knock

Planned and arranged by Terayama Shūji

THE PEANUT GALLERY

1975

Let me state the truth right from the beginning. There is no way that I can write what might pass as a straightforward "review" of this street drama called *Knock*. In the first place, no one spectator could possibly verify all the "events" planned as part of this production, which took place over thirty hours, from 3:00 P.M. on 19 April until 9:00 P.M. the next evening. These "happenings" were spread across twenty-seven locations in Tokyo's Suginami Ward. From the moment that we, as spectators, began to stroll through the streets ourselves in search of some "theatrical event," we too became part of the actors' stratagems. We surpassed our usual role as spectators, transformed as we were into minor players, and in precisely the fundamental, theatrical sense envisioned for this production.

To put it another way, our own power of imagination and our curiosity had to be put to use in order to discover what constituted these "theatrical events" brought into being on the streets. We worked alongside Terayama's performers, in roles of varying importance, and this personalized experience brought us to a new awareness of the connections we ourselves had made during those thirty hours with the streets on which we continually walk and with what we can find there.

My own personal "drama" began at a corner occupied by a small real-estate agency diagonally across from one of the exits of the East Terminal of the Shinjuku railway station, one of the busiest areas of Tokyo, where a strange man, draped completely in black and with a bandage over one eye, exchanged my "entrance ticket" for an illustrated map. The map, centering around the Asagaya station, located in a residential section of the city, provided a layout for the whole of Suginami Ward, listing the times at which various "events" were scheduled to happen and indicating the appropriate locations. I was therefore supposed to select from among those "events" some that seemed of particular interest to me and so make up my own "theatrical course," that is, my own "plot."

However, most of the events listed on the map were extremely puzzling. It was virtually impossible to know exactly what might be taking place. For example, what could be the meaning of "The Disappearance of the Drosselmeyer Clock Shop"? What sorts of happenings could be described as "Empty Houses That, Depending on the Hour, Change Places Thirty Times" or "Strollers in the Air"?

I started off walking around the Suginami area with my mysterious map, and it was at that point that I suddenly realized that this street, so familiar to me, had now suddenly been transformed in some subtle way. It was true, of course, that, at least on the surface of things, the crowd was simply walking along nonchalantly in the usual fashion. But now I began to think of decoding what I saw; anything might be a hidden signal that something had become a "theatrical space."

For example, I noticed a small watch-repair shop on a side street. There was something peculiar about this store. In front of it were lined up altogether a whole mass of old-fashioned clocks with no hands, clock faces, and wall clocks. Some of them were upside down. In the grimy shop window I noticed a mound of unidentified rubbish that resembled bits and pieces of broken toys. Inside the shop, there was no one in sight. Had this shop always been here? Or had this place been created especially for this piece of street theatre? When I spoke to people in the vicinity, I learned that this shop had always looked this way. Yet, so far as I was concerned, armed with these strange phrases from my map about "The Disappearance of the Drosselmeyer Clock Shop," it did seem to me that I had somehow solved one of the puzzles posed by this mysterious "theatre."

Terayama Shūji's 1975 street drama *Knock*. The performer Kotake Nobutaka is using this strange device to walk through a park at night. (Photo by Senda Akihiko.)

Perhaps, I thought, Terayama's actors actually performed none of these "events" themselves but were content merely to write up myriad peculiar statements and then hand them out in map form. Thus, the efforts to seek out the various events that were made by those spectators whose sense of expectancy and powers of imagination carried them on their walks would presumably constitute the "drama" that each person experienced.

And those who created this "theatre" certainly did work out their conceptions cleverly. For example, when I went to investigate one "incident" in the area, which was listed as "Billiards at Number 42," with the alternative title "Address for the Collection of Plans for Frenzied Suicide," I found a whole group of other spectators. We walked around the area, asking questions of those in the neighboring shops and houses, no doubt causing all sorts of confusion and consternation. The problem was that, at Number 42, no incident of any kind occurred. Rather, the title involved a pun using the word *shi*, which means both "four" and "death" in Japanese. This fact occurred to us only after we had walked around the area for some twenty minutes.

Actual events, too, took place at all sorts of different locales. Two friends and I tried to verify a number of them. We did nothing but walk around continuously on the nineteenth from a bit after 3:00 in the afternoon to sometime after midnight. At one point we followed two performers who were rushing along at top speed while indulging in a fierce husband-and-wife quarrel. In the end, we and all the other spectators followed the couple late into the night, having become involved in this "marathon drama." Looking back on this experience, it was doubtless an interesting one. Yet, in the eyes of those poor souls who lived in the neighborhood, what on earth was the meaning of this line of people hurrying past, led by a man and woman in the midst of a fierce quarrel? (Needless to say, the policeman in his stand on the corner became alarmed and bicycled after the couple in order to question them, and a patrol car was dispatched as well.)

Then I saw a group of four men and women emerge from a manhole; one of them appeared to be a mummy, swathed in bandages. Appearing in the middle of the park at dusk, they seemed to me to be participating in some sort of elegant formal dinner. Then, late in the evening, I saw on a sports field some kind of contraption that supported a "car" on which a man in a black cloak "walked," seemingly in midair.

On the next day, Sunday the twentieth, I found myself soaking in a tub at a public bath called the "Peony Pool," where I witnessed the birth of the "drama" called "The Incident of the Men in the Peony Pool." What made this particular adventure so cumbersome was the fact that the bath was full of patrons, all of them naked. Who were the actors? Who were the spectators? It was impossible to tell. People like me, who had rushed in and filled the bath to capacity in order to see what this "play" might be, found our-selves looking at our unclothed neighbors without trepidation and demand-ing to know, "Aren't you an actor?" We waited for what seemed an endless time until the three actors among us began speaking their lines, one after the other.

In the end, however, I must confess that, on the basis of my own expe-rience (to which I must of course limit myself), I did not find these "events" to be particularly "theatrical." What seemed theatrical to me were, instead, the puzzle-filled maps, which turned the familiar streets into ciphers. Even now, I remember the sense of freshness that my observations had as I looked on heretofore familiar sights with new eyes. In those moments, this "theatricality" seemed to allow the city to transform itself into something peculiar and strange.

This "street theatre," therefore, did give me a new means of looking at the urban environment. This "street drama" *Knock* was indeed a drama that gave rise to a new and fanciful geography.

12. HARVEST: AFTER A YEAR AND A HALF

The Comic World of Shōwa

Written and directed by Satoh Makoto

68/71

1975

After a year and a half, the 68/71 Troupe has broken its silence and is begin-ning a national tour using as a performing space Satoh's famous Black Tent. As his opening presentation for the tour, Satoh set up that tent on a piece of reclaimed land in the Kōtō area of Tokyo and presented his *The Comic World of Shōwa*, which includes three of his earlier works.

These excellent productions, it should be said, tower over anything seen recently on Tokyo stages; they are absolutely superb. Perhaps the most important thing to note is the fact that Satoh's actors have now moved beyond his original dedication to "put the play first," heretofore so important, and so have begun to bring into being a kind of communal power in performance. When I have written previously of the 68/71 Troupe, I have concentrated almost exclusively on Satoh's plays themselves or on the effective elements in his direction. This fact may be taken to suggest that there has been on my part a certain dissatisfaction with the lack of energy and a certain brittleness shown by his performers.

This time, things are different. On the whole, it is hard to come to any quick judgment as to whether this break of a year and a half has been good or bad for the company itself. Then too, some of his main performers are not involved in the present productions. In any event, a new power and level of skill have been revealed in the company as it is now constituted.

Of the three plays that make up *The Comic World of Shōwa*, the first two are revisions of earlier works. The first, *Abe Sada's Dog*, is based on the 1973 play *The Comedy of Abe Sada;* the second, *Cinema and Spies*, is a reworking of the 1972 *February and Cinema*. The third, *Shanghai in Spring: Killing Blanqui*, is, strictly speaking, the only totally new work being presented.

The revisions of the two earlier works are a distinct success. Basically speaking, Satoh is the kind of playwright who, while repeatedly utilizing one theme, nevertheless so successfully fills out his plays with a series of variations on that theme that his one basic vision can support a series of dramatic works. I have previously referred to Satoh's works as "plays for the study of secret codes," but it can also be said that one of the essential characteristics of his dramas lies in his technique of rewriting and reworking his material in such a way that, as he opens one door into the maze that he has created, he throws down a key that can help in turn explain the ciphers he has previously provided. Thus, in his revisions, the mazes begin to open, and his meanings become clear. On this occasion, Satoh's means of expression takes on a glittering grandeur, and his plays take on a wide appeal.

The first two plays in this series are constructed in this way. The third, however, involves Satoh's synthesis, from the vantage point of 1975, of an incident in the history of Shōwa in which both ordinary people and the revolutionary minded lost the common ground that had existed between them, with cruel results. Satoh's vision is not an emotional or a romantic one. It constitutes rather a cool and clear-eyed critique of our current situation. Indeed, it is this cruelly "comic" point of view that informs Satoh's entire vision of the period. Watching his plays, our normal, everyday habits and perceptions are set aside, allowing us to perceive a new type of con-

Satoh Makoto's *The Comic World of Shōwa,* presented in 1975 by the 68/71 Troupe. The photograph is from the first of the three plays, *Abe Sada's Dog.* The actor Mizoguchi Junsuke holds an umbrella over his partner, the actress Arai Jun.

temporary history play, one in which the many layers of "those realities of the truth itself" are set directly before us.

For example, in *Abe Sada's Dog*, nostalgic melodies, handled in somewhat the same fashion as in Bertolt Brecht's *The Threepenny Opera*, allow the effective contrast of the passions of Abe (who represents the quintessence of the popular man) and the revolutionary spirit of those right-wing officers who rose up and, on 26 February 1936, assassinated the prime minister in the name of a government to be controlled directly by the emperor, a government "purged of politics." Satoh starkly defines this entire period as one in which "revolution did not exist since the Shōwa emperor himself remained untouched" (indeed, at the end of the play, he peacefully continues his long, God-given life).

In *Cinema and Spies*, Satoh has created a scene in which the heroine of a melodramatic film calls out in romantic fervor, "Soon the sun will rise! Tomorrow will be the day of revolution!" This incident is given a richer texture because it is made to take place on the very day that the greater war in East Asia breaks out, thereby depicting a process all too painful to witness. In this production, these two plays are presented as popular spectacles, in an atmosphere redolent of aerial stunts and fireworks.

With the third play, however, *Shanghai in Spring: Killing Blanqui*, our impressions of Satoh's theatre are changed in an instant. Here remain no elements of popular spectacle or appeal. Text and staging alike are curt, concise, even strict, unyielding. I was surprised at such excessive control, since the play represents the final synthesis of Satoh's ideas. His direction stripped the various scenes portrayed of any warmth or emotion, even to the extent that a certain feeling of boredom ensues. Yet this play is doubtless no different from other works by this author. It too will at some point be revised and so reveal the meanings of heretofore secret codes to the audience.

Nevertheless, it should be noted that, even though the text is sometimes difficult, the play is something more than a mere puzzle. Set in Shanghai, in a manner that suggests the atmosphere of the infamous Shanghai Incident of 1931, in which Japanese troops invaded the city despite an already-declared nonaggression pact with China, the play portrays the resuscitation of the nefarious revolutionary "Foreigner" who, at age seventy-six, has been in jail for thirty-six years and five months. Constructing complications between this "eternal revolutionary" and a former Japanese anarchist who, after multiple recantations, is now a terrorist spy for the Japanese right wing, this play represents another experiment in juxtaposing past and present as a means toward getting at Satoh's concept of "revolution" in Shōwa Japan.

So it is, therefore, that, after killing the young girl who has taken into herself the spirit of the "revolutionary foreigner," Sankaku can whisper the following speech, the words of which seem so heavily laden for a contemporary audience.

> So it is that, at this instant, countless numbers of us, who stand on top of countless bridges, with the killing of countless corpses we must face, have now lost our way. We have been mistaken. Countless numbers of us have been mistaken. . . . But, among us, there are a few who will discover the correct solution. That's not impossible. . . . Are we in Shanghai?

The play ends with this final question. It is never answered. But we who watch the play do know the answer.

> Yes. Yes, this is Shanghai. And, of course, at the same time this is the Japan of our own days.

Yet is this "actually" the "right interpretation"? At the least, it should be said that, at least at this moment, we can give no other answer.

13. A FIRST TRIP TO A DISTANT VILLAGE

A Night's Feast

Arranged and directed by Suzuki Tadashi

THE WASEDA LITTLE THEATRE

1976

Usually when we think of watching a performance, we are limited by habit to our usual position inside the confines of a theatre. The same mentality ensues even if the playing area happens to be outdoors. Yet, in fact, our dramatic encounter begins the moment we come in contact with the performance space itself. Such was my reaction on seeing Suzuki's troupe

perform in their newly opened theatre in this remote village in the mountains of Toyama Prefecture, where they staged this memorial production.

The sense of distance between Tokyo and this empty mountain site lost
in the depths of the countryside seems very great indeed. As this memorial
production was to be presented on only one occasion, 28 August, it was
necessary to plan a trip that in the end took me virtually four days. Used as
I was to getting to any production in the city easily, I felt spiritually replen-
ished by my trip into the deep country. The experience was a rare one,
almost dream-like, one in which ordinary reality had somehow taken on an
element of the fantastic.

In the course of making the trip, I remembered my visit to the Greek
theatre of Epidaurus. To get to this huge theatre today requires a drive of
several hours from Athens, then further travel on foot—hence a night spent
in the country. In ancient times, the entire journey took place on foot, and
people had to devote several days to the venture. Why put this outdoor theatre in a place so difficult to get to? I wondered at the time. Now, I suddenly realized that I had come to understand at least part of the reason:
removed from our ordinary life and concerns, one is far more open to an
unusual theatrical experience.

Those of us attending the play got off the train at a local stop and
boarded a local bus for Toga (the bus runs only three times a day). As the
bus wound over its rugged course, it was hard to believe that anyone could
live on these steep mountain slopes. Eventually we arrived at the village of
Toga with its thatched farmhouses and their sharply pitched roofs. Suzuki
had built his theatre inside one of them. It was the afternoon of 26 August.
Inside this multistoried farmhouse, Suzuki had left the beams and dark,
lustrous pillars and created a stage with a side-elevated walkway. Thin matting was spread on the floor on three sides for the spectators. The total
effect created was both relaxed and gracious.

The actual rehearsals began that evening. Suzuki's usual training methods, in which his performers exercise their lower bodies to the rhythm of
Japanese popular songs, filled these actors with a sense of physicality and
bodily tension; these methods virtually constitute, more than merely a "theory of the Japanese," but instead a "theory of Japanese physicality."

Even though the performance took place in August, the mountain air
was clear and chilly, and, just as Suzuki had planned, the extremely austere
rehearsals were redolent of some quasi-religious discipline. The various
performers slept, men and women separately, in two of the tall farmhouses
that lay clustered so close together. They cooked two of their spartan meals
by themselves but went to eat the third together in the local village welfare
kitchen center.

On the twenty-eighth, the day of the performances, a cold drizzle

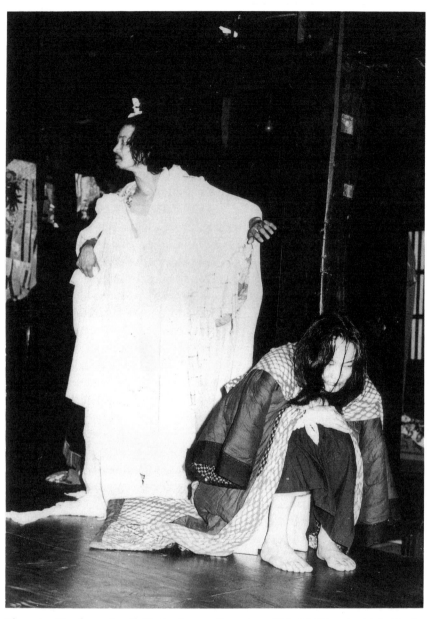

The actor Toyokawa Jun *(left)* stands over the actress Shiraishi Kayoko *(right)* in the 1976 production of Suzuki Tadashi's *A Night's Feast*. (Photo courtesy of the Editorial Department of the journal *Bijutsu techō*.)

began to fall in the morning. At one in the afternoon, a free performance was given for the villagers living in the area. Roughly four hundred people packed themselves into the theatre.

At six in the evening, some six hundred visitors from all over the country pushed inside to see this opening festival production. Following a lion dance performed by local folk artists, the nō actor Kanze Hisao and his two famous brothers presented their production of the medieval nō play *Tsunemasa*.

Because the walkway was located on the spectator's right instead of on the left, as in traditional nō theatre, a number of the movements performed by Kanze Hisao had to be executed in reverse, as it were, which presented him with what must have seemed unreasonable demands. Yet, in the end, these very difficulties called forth a sense of dramatic tension not ordinarily witnessed in nō. This performance of *Tsunemasa* seemed to give forth a sharp atmosphere of unusual beauty.

The third part of the play, which Suzuki entitled *A Night's Feast*, was assembled from various works that he has previously created and directed. Scenes from such diverse productions as Chekhov's *Three Sisters, The Bacchae, The Trojan Women*, Oka Kiyoshi's *The Heart of the Japanese*, and Beckett's *Waiting for Godot* were altered and juxtaposed in a collage-like fashion, which gave this packed audience a remarkably nuanced and layered sense of what it actually meant to be Japanese. His cast, among them Shiraishi Kayoko, gave appropriately powerful, tension-filled performances.

This production included no "leads" or any major plot to be revealed as the drama progressed. Rather, it was we, as spectators, who were being urged through the power of our own imaginations to create our own drama. In this sense, Suzuki's production created for us an intellectual experience and, at the same time, at least from the point of view of those grounded only in traditional Japanese theatre, a dramatic conception based to some extent on Western modes of dramatic expression. The final images, which grew from the sparse words exchanged in *Waiting for Godot*, abruptly juxtaposed with music from Carl Orff's *Carmina Burana* played at ear-splitting volume, suggested as well a certain fanaticism that lurked within.

14. A QUESTION TO THE MAN WHO BLEW THE FLUTE

The Rats of Hamelin

Written by Kara Jūrō

Directed by Satoh Makoto

THE SEVENTH WARD TROUPE

1976

As its opening production, the new Seventh Ward Troupe, founded by six prominent avant-garde theatre personalities, presented a new play by Kara, *The Rats of Hamelin,* directed by Satoh Makoto. More than a new troupe seems to have been created, however; a number of problems have surfaced as well.

The first of these involves doubts as to just what kinds of new theatrical experiences these artists might create since most of them have split off from such established companies as the Modern Peoples' Theatre or the Cherry Company, where, under the direction of Ninagawa Yukio, politically avant-garde and radical plays by such authors as Shimizu Kunio had been presented from the late 1960s through the early 1970s. Without such artists, what could they now accomplish?

The second problem concerns the nature of the radical drama of social criticism Kara could have written on this occasion, given the fact that he himself has remained so critical of the work of these other companies.

This opening production was staged in a western section of Tokyo, in an abandoned movie theatre, the Fujikan. There was a good deal of tension in the atmosphere when the curtain went up. I must confess that I too had certain misgivings at that moment, for, despite the fact that the troupe spoke of its "new beginnings," the group was depending far too much on outside talent. In one sense, I suppose, this is what those in charge of the troupe were referring to when they spoke of their "new beginning." However, the use of Kara, who has his own troupe, the Situation Theatre, as well as of Satoh, who has the 68/71 company, and the addition of the Waseda Little Theatre's Suzuki Ryōzen and the Situation Theatre's Kobayashi Kaoru to the Seventh Ward's small number of players made it difficult to tell precisely what this new spirit and style might be. Would we be asked to accept the artistic deficiencies of the troupe, deficiencies presumably validated by their brave and energetic struggle to break new ground? Thus my concern.

Kara Jūrō's 1976 *The Rats of Hamelin*, presented by the Seventh Ward Troupe. Midori Mako as Kyōko *(left)* and Ishibashi Renji as Manzō *(right)*.

I am sorry to report that my fears were not entirely unjustified.

True enough, the staging had been more than tolerably well managed. The brilliance of Satoh Makoto's direction, in which he set out to "show" us what Kara wanted us to understand, brought energetic, dancing images to the stage. The beautifully wrought performances of Ishibashi Renji and Kobayashi Kaoru were unforgettable. Despite these successes, however, the divergent personalities involved in the production seem to have been unable to come together and conceive a unified social critique; the occasion never seemed to rise above a medley of "spots" starring celebrated entertainers. Satoh is a master of directing technique, yet he was unable to overcome the mixed message of both friendship and ill-will, of administering both poison and antidote, that Kara seemed to be sending to his former associates in the Cherry Company. Suzuki's performance in particular seemed determinedly out of harmony with those of the other actors; the austerity that makes his work elsewhere—with, for example, Suzuki Tadashi and the Waseda Little Theatre—so memorable came across here rather as clumsy.

This play was based on Kara's 1974 short novel *The Full Moon inside the Full Moon.* By making use of a device that figured in the novel, he has constructed *The Rats of Hamelin* as a kind of defiant explosion.

In the play, the idea of "rats" holds a double meaning. The authorities are hunting "radical left-wingers," and the ensuing chase is staged to suggest a kind of "roller skate war." These revolutionaries have now been caught in their trap. Central to this aspect of the story is Kyōko (played by Midori Mako), now a hostess in a cheap cabaret; she has been expelled from her neighborhood association because her former lover was a student who constructed terrorist bombs.

Now a man has been killed by a bomb constructed by her lover, who subsequently committed suicide in prison. The murdered man, an innocent victim who had no connection whatsoever with any of these political affairs, had two sons. The first of them is named Setsuzō (performed by Suzuki Ryōzen), who works in a cleaning store and is in love with Kyōko. His brother (played by Kobayashi) is the chief of the neighborhood youth association.

This setup supplies the second meaning of the idea of the "rats," one that is established through the cruel words of the students themselves, who are quite willing to sacrifice to their cold logic all those who follow them. These ordinary people, who lead such miserable lives, constitute the "rats" who are abandoned by the "revolution."

Kara is obviously invoking the legend of the Pied Piper of Hamelin, who led the rats of the city to the river, where they drowned. Here, as well, the "rats" are made to dance at the command of their masters, and in the end they, too, in effect drown. They symbolize all those nameless followers of the left-wing revolutionaries who were simply pawns in a larger game and who were ultimately abandoned. Because such companies as the Modern Peoples' Theatre and the Cherry Company, using such performers as Ishibashi Renji and Midori Mako, continue to side with the radical young and heroically perform their pathetic revolutionary dramas, Kara seems to question subtly whether those who play the pipes of the revolution are not forgetting the mass of people under them who say nothing, whether revolutionary words spoken on the stage actually constitute a revolution.

The tenor of Kara's questions, and of his larger message, becomes altogether clear when, near the end of the play, Kyōko and the wounded Setsuzō and Manzō (also performed by Ishibashi Renji), walking shoulder to shoulder, look at the river as they cross from the stage into the auditorium itself, with the words, "Sometime, just in this way, there will be two men who will be wounded, just like this. . . ." In a 1972 production by the Cherry Company of the Shimizu Kunio drama *When We Go Down That Heartless River*, Ishibashi himself played a scene in which he went out into the audience, looking in the darkness for the river he sought. So it is that, in the present play, Kara consciously adds to this memory an additional layer, one that also serves as a critique of that earlier work.

In the end, I do not believe that Kara's play provides any definite answer to the kind of inflammatory questions that he raises in the course of the play. Indeed, it seems to me that, for better or worse, to find answers to these questions is too heavy a charge to give to those who have shouldered the burdens of our time. Such responses cannot be quickly and clearly formulated. Rather, at least in theatrical terms, they must emerge gradually, concretely, and from the experiences gained during the course of productions carried out by a genuinely independent theatrical movement.

15. THE *NŌ* STAGE, NEWLY ACTIVATED

The Legend of Komachi

Written and directed by Ōta Shōgo

THE TRANSFORMATION THEATRE

1977

Ōta Shōgo's *The Legend of Komachi,* produced by the Transformation Theatre in 1977. Satō Kazuyo plays the old woman, once a great beauty. (Photo by Sugizaki Taku.)

For a critic of the contemporary theatre like myself, there is no pleasure greater than being present on those occasions when the theatrical frameworks employed in the past are ruptured, transcended. It may well be that we exist as journalists precisely in order to encounter, and report on, just such moments.

Yet such a task—waiting for new talent to appear, then responding to it and explaining it when it does—requires perseverance and patience, for there is usually little to report. Such fresh and attractive talents and performing groups do not appear with any great frequency, and finding truly new talent requires witnessing a bewildering number of small groups in performance. And, even when one meets with a happy surprise, one cannot always get one's views into print in time to attract an audience to what is often a short run.

In this context, it should be said that there are often periods, as in the 1960s, when a striking number of new, talented groups emerge. But circumstances are very different now toward the end of the 1970s. In recent years, with the exception of Tsuka Kōhei, there has been very little in the way of genuine new talent to appear.

Ōta Shōgo's company, the Transformation Theatre, proved the rare exception with its production in January of *The Legend of Komachi,* performed on a *nō* stage in Tokyo. This was superb theatre. On this occasion I was able to experience the kind of thrill that only a live performance on stage can produce. Without doubt this production represents the richest of the treasures harvested from this season's offerings.

It should be noted that Ōta's Transformation Theatre is not really a new group. The troupe first appeared in 1968, under the direction of Hodoshima Takeo, and now possesses virtually a decade of performance experience. Yet until now their performances have been rather subdued, and the group has not attracted wide attention.

When I first saw their work, in March 1970, Ōta had become a mainstay of the company. He wrote and directed *Nine Scenes about Buses,* and I retain the memory of his clever dialogue, somewhat in the style of Betsuyaku. I later saw the troupe perform in a small theatre in the Akasaka district of Tokyo. Each year, their experience and expertise has steadily increased. But of course, when it comes to creativity in the contemporary theatre, personal character and sincerity in and of themselves may count more as a minus than as a plus. In that context, as director of a 1970 production for modern actors of Tsuruya Namboku's classic *kabuki* play *The Scarlet Princess of Edo,* Ōta produced much more striking results than he had previously when directing his own plays.

Now, however, with this current production of *The Legend of Komachi,* Ōta's troupe has in one leap created a totally new theatrical experience. The results suggest a man who has been climbing through the tortuous paths that wind, hidden away, through the steep mountains; then, suddenly, when he reaches the top, he unexpectedly commands a vast view over myriad peaks. In Ōta's case, the crest he has reached is startlingly high.

There are, it seems to me, two reasons for the success of the current production. First, rather than using the kind of performance space typical of such small groups, the company has for the first time chosen to use the stage of a real *nō* theatre. There have been many theories about the theatrical efficacy of the *nō* performing space, yet there have been few cases in which it has been successfully employed by an experimental theatre troupe. It has often been remarked that the *nō* theatre space is a sacred one; by invoking an ordinary, mundane space for *The Legend of Komachi,* a stimulating rivalry between these two conceptions is created.

Second, the dialogue is pared down to a minimum, so that two-thirds of the play, which runs for two and a half hours, proceeds without dialogue of any kind; Ōta has organized his presentation as a kind of daring, silent drama. Those of us who have somehow forgotten the richness that silence can have can now experience it anew. Most remarkable of all, this play, which comes close to pantomime, is performed with such skill by Ōta's players that the audiences can follow along without any sense of boredom or fatigue right until the very end.

As the play opens, the stage area is already lit. From the bridge leading to the *nō* stage, an old woman (played by Satō Kazuyo), slowly enters. She has long, unkempt hair, and her clothes, apparently made of tattered mosquito netting, trail behind her. She does not walk with the usual sliding motions typical of the *nō;* rather, she employs a peculiar way of walking, in which the toes of both feet are crunched up together as she shuffles along. She moves as though in some slow-motion film; it takes her fully five minutes to traverse the fifteen-odd feet of the bridge to the stage.

Once the old woman arrives on the stage proper, she continues to move with these peculiar slow steps. Eventually, she arrives in the middle of the playing space. We in the audience, pulled in by this slow method of movement, which surpasses any category of realism, seem to enter into an unreal, a dream world. She stands there with the vaguest of impressions on her face. We begin to hear the subtlest movements of the wind in the upper sky; then softly, surprisingly, with a kind of gently thudding sound, in the now dim light, we begin to hear music, a mild and yielding piccolo piece by Vivaldi, as from the bridge a group of peculiar-looking performers enters with various household goods on their backs: a shabby old dresser, a tea chest, a Japanese-style low dining table, torn sliding wall panels. It is just as though they were bearing some sort of magic objects through this space. They move forward, floating through the gloom, and then construct around the old woman, still standing there, the dilapidated room of an apartment. The room they create is constructed with minute realism and in its everyday vulgarity seems to constitute an invasion of the sacred *nō* space.

The old woman, as before, carries on with her slow movements (which, incidentally, continue in this fashion until the end of the play). She washes her face at the basin, heats water on the electric hotplate (yes, she actually boils water on a *nō* stage!), and cooks a package of instant noodles for her breakfast.

From this point on, while making and eating her breakfast noodles—an action that in real life would take only minutes—this sad old woman lives through her dreams and fantasies and so becomes involved in several episodes with those who live in the apartment building and nearby. That is to say, just a few minutes of real time are extended to two hours in her dreams, just as though the folds and pleats of her consciousness, her fantasies, could be probed with a microscope. In this state of gentle relaxation, we become aware of the unexpected richness of life and of all the pain, beauty, and cruel humor that lie within the depths of this reticent hag, now so badly dressed and altogether forlorn.

The peculiar stateliness pervading every aspect of this play owes nothing to the style of *nō* itself but flows rather from the skillful use of a device that, thanks to a rupture in the speed of everyday life, can pull forth a delicate sense of the things that can be located at the bottom of human consciousness, feelings that can be grasped only at a very slow speed. Therefore, the choice of a *nō* stage seems altogether appropriate.

While the old woman waits for her noodles to cook, a man (played by Masuda Saiki) appears before her, dressed in a uniform of the Japanese imperial army. If the old woman is meant to represent the legendary Heian beauty Komachi, then the man must correspond to the Fukakusa General, who, in the celebrated *nō* play, visited Komachi every night in the hope of attaining her favors. From the old woman's decrepit phonograph comes the mournful sound of Edith Piaf singing "La Vie en Rose" and "Dark Sunday," symbolizing the days of a youth long passed. Yet is this "Fukakusa General" really a memory, or is he merely an emblem of her desire? We cannot be sure.

Suddenly, the old woman's daydream is broken as her landlord (played by Segawa Tetsuya) appears. The landlord cannot but hope that this old lady, shut up within herself, half ill, without family, friends, or money, and who therefore cannot pay her rent, will die as soon as possible. For that reason he calls on her every day, talking on and on, but the old woman never opens her mouth. Indeed, as Satō Kazuyo plays the role, she never utters a word. According to the landlord, the old woman has spoken only three times in seventeen years. What did she say on those occasions? That particular fascinating mystery remains unsolved at the end of the play.

The means of emotional expression that Satō has chosen for this role are quite unusual. The expression she adopts (is it the rapture of imbecility or a misplaced joy that crosses her face?) has mixed within it, hidden away, the pain of carnal desire, so that we as spectators seem to find before us the real presence of an old person who, despite the misery of her condition, has found a kind of radiance in the solidity of her own existence. This is no tearful tale of an old person doomed to misery and destruction. One important factor that gives the play its humorous effect, and to such an astonishing degree, is the way in which Satō manifests her misery in such a positive fashion.

The next incident of the morning involves an amusing encounter with a neighboring family of strolling players, traditional Japanese *chindon*, who function something like "sandwich men" as they go about the streets to advertise some local establishments or products. After this incident, by means of mental associations, the old woman imagines that she is to have an assignation with the young man of the family. Yet this dream as well is shattered as the landlord breaks in, bringing with him a doctor and a nurse. He tells her she is on the verge of death, and there follows a peculiar exchange of questions and answers concerning the actual state of health of this woman, who apparently will never die. Suddenly, as the sound of a folk dance,

"Oklahoma Mixer," played for some athletic meet, wafts in through the open window, the doctor and his aides line up and, following the music, dance out in a single line. As yet another daydream of the old woman, this device provides a theatrically striking moment.

Then, suddenly, the wind begins to blow, and the performers enter again, dismantling the apartment that had been built up around her and carrying the parts off, back up the bridge and out of sight. She has still another vision of an erotic dance with the young man next door, yet that too suddenly vanishes, and she is once more left alone on the stage. She crouches down, and the play ends.

It is true that Ōta's presentation has a number of undigested bits and that certain roles need some adjusting. Nevertheless, I have no hesitation in stating that a group that can produce a work as stimulating as this one has reached a real peak in its performance history. Such, for example, was the case in Suzuki Tadashi's Waseda Little Theatre production of *On the Dramatic Passions II* or of Tsuka Kōhei's *The Atami Murder Case*. Not only did these works seem to express one particular sense of the moment. But the vision comprehended by these works goes further, deeper than the writers may have imagined, representing a peak in their power of creative conception. From now on, Ōta and his Transformation Theatre may well decide to play out variations on the great theme that they have created here, but I do not believe that the original can ever be improved.

In sum, Ōta should be praised for the fact that, for the contemporary Japanese theatre, he has opened up new territory. This production does not depend on dialogue or on any form of dance, nor is it a kind of "collage play." The methods that form the basis of his dramatic conception—for example, using a Japanese sensibility and Japanese physical movements to create a sharp yet wonderfully humorous critique of life in present-day Japan —are unique and highly creative. In particular, his use of the traditional *nō* stage space, which is usually shunned by contemporary performers but which Ōta here suggests can suit very well the work of an experimental company, is marvelously suggestive.

16. MAKING THE CONNECTION: KILLING THE BEGGAR

Thirty Days Hath September

Written by Betsuyaku Minoru

Directed by Fujiwara Shimpei

THE ATELIER OF THE LITERARY

THEATRE

1977

"Not everyone can be classified as treacherous. And all victims cannot be dismissed as pitiful. Often, people are merely indifferent." So Betsuyaku Minoru wrote at the beginning of his early success, *Elephant* (1962). Now, on seeing this production of his new play, *Thirty Days Hath September,* I was powerfully impressed by the fact that, beneath what appears to be his nonchalant way of regarding the world, there lies a fiercely dramatic urge, one that is altogether unforgettable.

I have not consistently found myself responding so strongly to Betsuyaku's work. More often that not, for me, his plays begin by seeming merely nonchalant, only to end in the same fashion.

However, along with his *Bubbling and Boiling,* produced by this same troupe a year ago, this new work, which is closely linked to that earlier endeavor, also allows us to glimpse a shocking violence under the veil of nonchalance. Here is revealed to us a side of Betsuyaku that we have never clearly seen before. At the risk of misinterpreting, it seems to me that both these plays can stand as signposts pointing toward a blurred vision that he posits concerning "God" and "salvation." In other words, these two plays seem to reflect a powerful religious sensibility. As for their effectiveness in the theater, I would judge them as roughly equally successful. In the present instance, the performance of Yoshino Yukiko is particularly adept at suggesting the flow of some dark vortex bubbling below the surface. And the performances of both Kadono Takuzō and Kobayashi Katsuya are effectively buoyant.

The meaning of the title *Thirty Days Hath September* is not precisely clear. However, the idea may be that, as the odd months of the year (January, March, May, etc.) are regarded as "positive," the even months (February, April, June, etc.) are regarded as "negative." In that context, the title may seem to suggest that this drama represents a sort of "alias" for a life in

Betsuyaku Minoru's 1977 *Thirty Days Hath September,* presented by the Atelier of the Literary Theatre. Kadono Takuzō as Man 1 *(left)* and Yoshino Yukiko as Wife 2 *(right).*

the realm of the "negative." In other words, we are shown the image of contemporary life perforce compressed into a minus.

As might be expected in such a vision, the stage arrangements are extremely simple. The printed stage directions indicate simply, "At stage left, an electric light pole. Under it a bench." (Indeed, Fujiwara, the director, has even done away with the bench.) They continue, "There is nothing more. It is evening. The wind is blowing."

The cast is limited to five people, two couples and a beggar. The two couples very much resemble each other. The two husbands are timid, weak spirited; because they were so often delinquent at work, they have lost their jobs; in fact, the very houses they lived in have now been taken away from them. While both have dreams of becoming inventors, they can only tramp the roads and highways as vagabonds. Their wives, who go from one disappointment and difficulty to another, bear their situations with humility.

The invention they have come up with, their "device to catch a beggar," reveals both bizarre humor and a terrible cruelty. To construct this device, a rope is first thrown over the top of the electric pole. A heavy stone is then hung from one end, and directly underneath is placed a pillow and some bedding. Easy as it may be to see through this artless device, the beggar (Tamura Katsuhiko) brought along by Wife 2 (Yoshino Yukiko) humbly lays himself down. Wife 2 cuts the rope with a thrust, dropping the stone on him, which crushes his face and kills him.

It is not clear why the group actually created this sort of machine. However, it appears that Man 2 (Kobayashi Katsuya) first thought of the idea, which was then actually carried out by Woman 1 (Kurano Akiko). She indicates that she wants to put everything in the world "in a state of total disorder." And it seems that Woman 2 decided to use the device on the old beggar because she had allowed her baby to die of malnutrition. In her view, only the beggar knew that the baby she was carrying on her back was already dead.

If such is the case, just what kind of man is the beggar himself? This man, realizing the situation in which Woman 2 finds herself, and knowing of the existence of the machine, lies down in order to be killed. Who can he be? He is surely Christ himself, the Christ who allows himself to be killed, a sacrificial lamb who, knowing all, takes the sins of the world on himself. Facing the dark rage created by the oppression they feel, the two couples choose this beggar to serve as the one to bear their misery and the meanness of their lives. In killing him, they move from the role of victim to that of aggressor as they carry through this ghastly ceremony of blood, one that apparently serves to represent a desire on their part to connect with some new circuit, a fresh existence in which they will be freed from the poverty of their present lives.

Such questions bring to mind the sister work to this play, *Bubbling and Boiling*. In this case, there are also two couples on stage, couples who appear to be close cousins to the characters in *Thirty Days Hath September*. These four are also unlucky; they are frightened and attempt to carry on their lives in stealth, as though in a quiet corner removed from the world. At the final curtain, a beggar also appears on stage in somewhat similar circumstances. In this case, Man 1, an older figure, and Woman 1 speak in a tone of unanticipated violence.

> MAN 1: (*Whispering, as an incantation.*) I call on you, God. We . . . we have lived. Yet we do not want anyone, anyone to know of it. . . . God, we have been unhappy. We have borne with our troubles. But we want to tell no one of this. God, please allow the snow to fall. . . .

As he says this, an unexpected event occurs. As the stage directions indicate, "From the midst of the darkness, *precisely as though expressly selected for this purpose*, one white snowflake begins to flutter down."

There was thus some sort of short circuit when their "God" was called on. This play of Betsuyaku's reveals an unusual direction in his work, one filled with a passion and a fury that is scarcely smoothed over. Here, it seems, we can catch a reflection of some higher power that, while gravely aware of the misery of human life, can still, in response, merely send along a snowflake that has been "expressly selected."

The God here depicted is not merely the one to whom prayers are offered and confessions made. If one had to choose between definitions for such a figure, Betsuyaku's God is closer to the kind of fictional deus ex machina who sends help in the course of a drama. In any case, the God of this scene does not resemble the God described in the work of Japan's Christian novelists and playwrights, one who might suggest unsought religious faith. Instead, it seems to me that Betsuyaku opens up before us a real territory in which a sharp religious yearning is central. While we may watch this drama quite aware of the fact that, for all we know, there may indeed be no God, through Betsuyaku's art we can witness nevertheless the power of one person's whispers, in a thirst for a God who cannot be found. For contemporary audiences, perhaps the sternest kind of religious drama that can be written might well involve the very fact that, sadly, we are completely cut off from any God.

These characters are reminiscent of the kind of figure suggested by Man B in Betsuyaku's first play, *A and B and a Girl* (1961). They resemble as well the man in *Elephant*. There are also connections to be found with Older Brother, the "habitual offender" who inhabits his 1967 *Landscape with Red Bird*. All these "negative" characters, with their sham and casual behavior, are now seen to face in what I have come to realize is a new direction.

17. A HUMBLE SELF-EXAMINATION

The Dressing Room

Written by Shimizu Kunio

Directed by Akihama Satoshi

THE TREE IN WINTER TROUPE

1977

While put together in a modest fashion, this production of Shimizu's new play *The Dressing Room: That Which Flows Away Ultimately Becomes Nostalgia* is one full of theatrical excitement. In this play, which takes only a little more than an hour to perform, it is clear that the author shows no overblown ambition, no unnecessary eloquence. In that sense, the style of the play resembles the suggestiveness of the title; Shimizu shows here a tendency toward a moderated silence. But this whisper, in which what is spoken differentiates between simple nostalgia and the force of silent thought, becomes an extremely striking one.

It would appear that Shimizu has finally said good-bye to his loquacious period. As far as *The Dressing Room* goes, the images and dialogue that Shimizu permits himself as a means to reveal his thoughts do not find an immediate target. Rather, he uses an indirect method, and an extremely effective one, that of collage.

When one speaks of a "drama of collage," one thinks immediately of the astonishing success in developing such a technique achieved by Suzuki Tadashi; indeed, it cannot be said that, in the present play, Shimizu has escaped altogether from echoing these methods. In one sense, both playwrights make use of a similar technique in which dialogue or phrases already known to the audience are released into an altogether different dramatic environment and a new sense of meaning is thereby plumbed.

The 1977 production by the Winter Tree Troupe of Shimizu Kunio's *The Dressing Room. From the left:* the Actress (Matsumoto Noriko) and two of the ghosts who surround her (Abe Tamae and Nakano Reiko).

By the same token, it can be said that Suzuki himself is obstinately attached to the use of collage. For him, the technique has become the most useful tool with which to carve out a theatrical experience in contemporary terms. He once wrote that "the theatre is constructed on the basis of the disparities, the slippages between word and word, body and body, body and word." Indeed, Suzuki's art consists of allowing the drama to float up from a theatrical situation in which dialogue is taken from other sources and reused—in both a verbal and a physical sense—to create a multilayered performance text.

Until this present play, however, Shimizu, blessed with his natural talents as a storyteller, has not himself drunk from this particular spring. It is true, of course, that, in *The Dressing Room,* portions of Lady Macbeth's speeches and sections of Chekhov's *The Seagull* are used, but their function here is quotation, not collage. However, toward the end of the play, when the last scene of Chekhov's *Three Sisters* is performed by the three characters in Shimizu's play, Shimizu does create here an exciting and a true collage. Although new verbal and physical readings are not given to the scene, the slippage between Chekhov's dialogue and the scene Shimizu himself presents provides the kind of theatrical situation in which a new sense of meaning and understanding can emerge.

The characters in the play are an actress (played by Matsumoto Noriko) and the ghosts of three nameless actresses who never in their lives achieved fame in their profession (performed by Abe Tamae, Nakano Reiko, and Shinno Kayoko). These three might be considered as warriors fallen on the battlefield of the theatre; now, having remained tenaciously faithful to this same theatre, they haunt the dressing room, waiting to play those parts that in fact they will never be called on to undertake.

When, however, the ghosts of these three women decide to enact their own imitation of Chekhov's *The Three Sisters,* which they never had the opportunity to play during their real lives, their assumption of the roles of Olga, Masha, and Irina strangely transforms the all too familiar Chekhov original.

> ACTRESS B: . . . Oh, listen to that music! They are leaving us . . . we are left alone to begin our life over again. We must live. . . . We must live. . . .

Such is the appearance of these three women, who doubtless seem to represent "soldiers reflected in the mirror" who, on the theatrical "field of battle," have fallen by the wayside or who have been forced to desert. Shimizu is surely showing us here, in lyrical fashion, a strikingly fresh image of those radicals who were killed in Japan's political battles in the 1960s. These dead, here whispering Chekhov's words, see through those still living. And those words, so familiar from their original context, now take on a fresh meaning that becomes virtually tragic.

> ACTRESS A: Time will pass, and we shall be gone forever; we'll be forgotten, our faces will be forgotten, our voices, and how many there were of us. . . . Oh, my dear sisters, our life is not over yet. We shall live! The music is so gay, so joyous, it seems as if just a little more and we shall know why we live, why we suffer. . . . If only we knew, if only we knew. . . .

Then too, at the same time we also see here the person of Shimizu himself, who assumes the aspect of the dead as here presented. Having himself given up the battle halfway through and yet still feeling a desire to "get up and go," which he can never abandon, he feels his own existence to be one close to those dead he has portrayed. "Those people will get up and go. Only I will be left behind. . . ."

Yet, in actuality, who among us can at this point actually "get up and go"? We know all too well that we cannot. So it is, therefore, that this drama represents a humble self-examination.

Akihama's direction reveals his great skill. Reading the play in its published form, it should be pointed out, shows even more clearly the power of Shimizu's conception.

18. A SCENE OF RIPENING

The Bacchae

Written by Euripides

Adapted by Suzuki Tadashi, translated by

Matsudaira Chiaki, and directed by

Suzuki Tadashi

AN IWANAMI HALL PRODUCTION

1978

In April 1972, Richard Schechner's Performance Group presented in Tokyo a program of "situational theatre" under the auspices of the American Cultural Center. Seeing that performance, I was reminded of the documentary film made of his famous production *Dionysus in 69.* This adaption of the Euripides *Bacchae* went so far as to involve the audience itself and remained one of the most famous theatrical productions of its time; nevertheless, as I watched one scene after another in the filmed version, I found it clumsy and naive, and I remember my disappointment in discovering what I described as a "rough and decidedly *un*-erotic parade of naked flesh." In that production I sensed a real lack of harmony. My description, written in 1969, was as follows.

> Brawny men and women performers moved around, naked, in a lively fashion. They leaped, they ran, they even rushed up into the seating area, they screeched, they hugged female members of the audience as they tried to tempt them into joining the group, they sang, they danced. On the surface of things, they provided a fulsome banquet of Dionysian flesh in a contemporary mode. Yet . . . there was something too crude and unsophisticated about all this. These naked bodies rushing about before one's very eyes seemed more like thick logs; in the end, it was hard to call this "nudity" in any artistic sense of the word. From the scenes presented, the effect was more like some healthy athletic display; what was missing altogether was any sense of a deep human depth from which a true sense of "eros" might arise.

Whatever else might be said, Schechner's attempt to realize a Dionysian space in his production was somehow an optimistic one, one representing an effort that reflected in and of itself the "revolutionary intentions" of the ideology of the 1960s.

Yet how could such a space be realized in actuality? Narumi Shirō, who saw the first performances in New York, wrote as follows.

> When King Pentheus, restrained in shackles, was murdered, the people carried Dionysus on their shoulders as he shouted, "I announce my candidacy for president!" opened the large garage door, then went right out into the street. As this was the end of the performance, the audience, applauding all the while, followed them out. This surely represents the ultimate social magnification of a theatrical experience.

All in all, it must have seemed a satisfying idea at the time.

Now, however, six years have gone by. In Suzuki Tadashi's present production of the Euripides *Bacchae,* his work is at every turn opposed to Schechner's version. Naïveté is replaced with cruel convolution. Rather than a show of the firm, gymnastic flesh seen in the earlier production, there was an intensity, both emotional and physical, concealed beneath a calmer surface; instead of a Dionysian praise of revelry, the cynical line of vision employed here aims rather at a portrayal of those humans who find themselves forced to seek out such a dark vision. There is no more audience participation, no more rushing out into the street. On the contrary, Suzuki's version from the beginning, classical crimson curtain included, is, rarely for him, a handsomely restrained and mature production.

Yet, as I reflect on the matter, it is actually surprising that this production does in fact give an impression of restraint. Most of the productions in which Suzuki has been involved until now have provided a sort of bouillabaisse of various elements and ingredients, in which the slippages between these disparate elements are scrupulously employed in order to assemble his dramatic framework. Therefore, these encounters, these slippages, even should they be ingeniously humorous, divided as they are between feelings and pleasure, manage to give off a certain creaking sound; there is something contrived in their conception, a sense that makes us uneasy, for these productions can show a sort of critical ill will that forces too complete a level of generalization.

In the case of this performance, however, Kanze Hisao brings to his performance the base of his great abilities as a _nō_ actor. Along with his beautifully rhythmic performance of King Pentheus comes that of Shiraishi Kayoko as Queen Agave; and they in turn are supported by the skillful efforts of other members of the Waseda Little Theatre, among them Sugiura Chizuko and Tsutamori Kōsuke. At first, I thought that Suzuki was using the wild music of Perez Prado in the production, but it turned out to be the music of Mori Masako and the Nippon Ondo— "Everyone's looking for the road to tomorrow, shaba shaba shaba . . ."— and, to an operetta melody from _Diabolo,_ Mori Shin'ichi howls out the finale in a husky voice.

Yet, on this occasion, such diverse ingredients did not produce any sense of disharmony; rather, they contributed to the performance of a theatrical structure here scrupulously woven together. In Suzuki's adaption of the Euripides original, there is nothing that reaches toward mere excess or any sense of the grotesque. Rather, he has tried to marshall the various elements at his command in order to achieve a kind of controlled theatrical form. In this effort, he has largely succeeded. From the beginning, Suzuki has shown us his well-ordered sensibilities, but on this occasion they have truly begun to function in a fundamental way. In that sense, in terms of the kind of forms he wishes to create, this production serves as an interim report, if not indeed a final balance sheet.

I was deeply stimulated by the fascination of his ripened vision. This

The 1978 Iwanami Hall production of Suzuki Tadashi's adaption of *The Bacchae* of
Euripides. Kanze Hisao and Shiraishi Kayoko.

was indeed one occasion on which I could truly say that my excitement was
deep. A sense of theatrical mastery was evident, particularly in the scenes
in which Pentheus, played by Shiraishi, and Dionysus, played by Kanze
Hisao, faced off against each other on opposite sides of the stage. The
scene in which they question each other was masterfully realized. Seething

emotions seemed to boil up from unseen depths as the two faced each other, Shiraishi squatting down to bring her center of gravity closer to the earth, Kanze Hisao filled with a deep joy, with a look stretching to the heavens. Altogether a remarkable encounter. Then too, Shiraishi revealed her always superb technique, which can permit her to move quickly back and forth from the melancholy to the comic. As for Kanze Hisao's performance, among his roles undertaken outside the nō theatre, this was surely his most dazzling accomplishment. Their surging speeches found a beautiful harmony in the force exerted by those of the blind man, played by Tsutamori Kōsuke.

Suzuki has constructed this play from two overlapping conceptions. One is taken, of course, directly from Euripides. The other, his own, concerns those men and women who are driven to seek a vision. These men and women in turn are divided into two groups. One turns away from everyday reality, becoming "vagrants" who rush to seek the revelry of the Dionysian space. In Suzuki's view, however, these vagrants also possess a spiritual and an intellectual dimension. By this I believe that he means to suggest a double image in which he portrays Japanese intellectuals altogether fascinated with Western ideologies. Indeed, in one scene he shows us a group of men infatuated with their dreams of Bacchus as they wrap themselves in the red curtain, all of whom wear the kind of eyeglasses preferred in Japanese intellectual circles.

Beyond this, however, when the space of revelry is finally achieved, the sharpest impression is that made by the disillusioned old man and woman (played by Tsutamori and Shiraishi), who have lost their roots and their children as well. They have perforce made this frenetic way of life their own, yet what remains to them from their commitment seems now only an inevitable sense of cruelty and betrayal. Here, Shiraishi seems to personify these feelings in her portrayal of Agave. It is surely in this scene that Suzuki's biting sense of protest against all such frenzied movements comes across most clearly.

If I were to add one note of caution concerning this vivid piece of theatre, it would be to note a certain thinness in Suzuki's controlled and intellectual vision. What we see is overwhelmingly colorful, yet it is not the deeper kind of emotion that could be pulled up from the depths of the hidden world of the play. This is despite the fact that Suzuki probably meant this production to be the fullest and most complete statement of his art.

The run of this production was cut short because of the illness of Kanze Hisao, who was hospitalized for cancer. He was soon to die at the age of fifty-three. With the exception of some nō performances, this was the last theatrical production in which this great actor appeared.

19. A CRITIQUE OF MIYAZAWA KENJI AS A *TABLEAU VIVANT*

Directions to Servants

Written by Terayama Shūji

Directed by Terayama Shūji and J. A. Caesar

THE PEANUT GALLERY

1978

I always enjoy looking at Terayama's photographs or at still shots made from his theatrical productions. Several collections of these have been published, and I never tire of leafing through their pages. In fact, I have hanging in my own study a signed photograph of Terayama's, presumably an original, which I bought some years ago at a one-man exhibition of his photographs held at the Aoyama Gallery in Tokyo. In the photograph, tinted in such a way as to give it an antique cast, there is an easy chair, surrounded by a stuffed owl and an eagle; on top of the chair is sprawled a woman's body; behind her, in the darkness, the background flickers and burns. The image suggests some movement through a labyrinth, and the effect is like that of an old postcard from the end of the last century.

Like all Terayama's photographs, this one is a *tableau vivant*. He catches his figures in deliberate and exaggerated poses, seemingly struck for eternity; the effect produced is that of wax figures lined up on display. He has created an artificial world in which the natural, the casual, the unguarded, the bashful, and the timid are altogether rebuffed. Those figures posed in his pictures quiver with the joy they find in turning themselves into beautiful objects precisely at the moment Terayama captures them. Most of us who examine these photographs are satisfied to delve no deeper into their meaning than this. Yet, however decadent these photographs may appear at first glance, Terayama's art finds healthier foundations, from which he creates images of those who are *seeking* to desire. His art itself is not decadent; rather, his works show the systematization of desire felt by those who search out decadence.

Every time I see a production of Terayama's, I am drawn to remember my impressions of these *tableaux vivants.* Indeed, rather than being constructed from a sequence of shifting dynamics, his plays usually instill in the memory of his spectators certain powerful images of fixed poses. Little else seems to matter; consistency of story line seems unimportant, as any narra-

A 1982 photograph of *Directions to Servants* taken in Paris at the Palais de Chaillot during the European tour of Terayama Shūji and his company.

tive elements seem created only in order to prepare for these scenes. One has an image of Terayama himself whispering softly to us that he has made his play in order to reveal just these special moments.

On a cold January evening in 1978—a night so cold that it gave me the impression of being trapped in a vast refrigerator—when I went to see the production of Terayama's *Directions to Servants*, I found that such techniques were apparent again. Yet, in order to create a series of striking images, Terayama, it seemed to me, had been forced to create a play that ran for over two hours.

Take, for example, the opening sequence. The audience entered a large and empty hall, the Tokyo International Trade Center, where Terayama staged this experimental work. The space was enormous. In the midst of this vast, black darkness lay what appeared to be a small, abandoned island. This was the stage, surrounded by seats for the audience. As J. A. Caesar's music rose to intoxicating heights, huge shutter-like contraptions opened in front of the audience and some twenty-odd figures, as peculiar as alien beings from another dimension, suddenly faced the crowd, stirring up an intense visual excitement as they came forward.

Or examine the final scene, in which a kind of flashy festival that the "servants" concocted flashed past while they reveled in disorder. They danced wildly, they shrieked, they disguised themselves, they provoked, they adopted lewd poses. Suddenly they were surrounded by an eerie mantle of smoke, and a dim blood-like glow of light announced the end of the play. Such a device calls to mind the moment close to the end of the Andrezej Wajda film *Ashes and Diamonds* in which can be seen the dim figures of those ruined aristocrats dancing in the gloomy dawn. Indeed, the chance to witness this final striking scene in Terayama's production does seem reward enough for having sat through over two hours of verbosity in an icy railroad car.

It should be pointed out as well that this play represents a unique critique, a send-up of the work of the much-loved modern Japanese poet Miyazawa Kenji.

Opperu, Jobani, Kūbō, Gōshu, Kanpanerura—these names, given to the servants who inhabit Terayama's mythical mansion, are taken from some of Miyazawa Kenji's most beloved characters. These servants have no master. In that sense, they live in the kind of free and untrammeled commonwealth imagined by the poet; their world constitutes a twisted reminiscence of the kind of clean and pure human society imagined by the poet some seventy-odd years before. Terayama's is thus a drama describing the ruin of what might have been.

It is clear that these servants have wearied of any imagined equality. They decide to construct a fantasy of social structure based on their feelings of an erotic pleasure and style of life. In such circumstances, one leader from among them must be duly chosen. This constructed society is based on the equality of hedonism, in which all can become masters as they sink into the pleasures of masochism.

However, class lines are not firmly drawn in this society. In their pursuit of pleasure, all are free to move from one role to another. These servants cannot, however, bear the absence of a master. And, in these images of men and women seeking sufficiency in pleasure, Terayama gives us a spectacle in which we hear his own boisterous laughter.

20. THE CONFLAGRATION OF AN EXPLODING LEMON

Lemon

Written by Takeuchi Jū'ichirō

Directed by Wada Shirō

THE TROUPE OF THE SLANTING LIGHT

1978

This was the first time I have seen the work of this troupe. In fact, I was not sure who had put this group together. So it was, then, that I sat in a dreary little theatre in a building in Tokyo's Shimokitazawa district (the first floor housed a *pachinko* parlor, the second a sauna), waiting with no great expectations for the performance to start.

However, soon after the play began, I found myself astonished at the vigor shown by the troupe. The script, the direction, the staging, all revealed considerable power. One sensed real talent. And, despite the fact that the play was purposefully constructed in a somewhat bizarre fashion, the larger lines of the story were never submerged. The results were amusing, yet serious, lighthearted, yet severe. There was a strong sense that the theme that had been chosen was no mere borrowed dress.

When the play was finished, the reaction of the audience was profound. We all applauded with great sincerity for the kind of vigor revealed in the performances, an energy all too rare in a young troupe of this kind.

The play concerns the fortunes of a young salaryman of thirty-two named Shin'ichi (played by Nishimura Katsumi), who, having abandoned his efforts to "battle the repressive powers of the government" during the demonstrations of the 1960s, now works as a "contented deposit teller in a credit union," "gallantly engineering the reactionary lives of city dwellers." Into his garden one morning comes the detective Takashi (played by Koide Shūji), a friend of his youth who served with him on the battle lines. This kind of plot line would certainly suggest to many the ideas taken up in Tsuka Kōhei's *Legend of a Flying Dragon*. As the events of the drama unfold, that superficial impression remains, for there are also echoes of Tsuka's style of writing in Takeuchi's clever dialogue. Both authors employ youthful laughter in order to make light of the lives of those who have turned away from earlier, radical positions.

Nevertheless, *Lemon* reveals a universe unique unto itself. Indeed, if

The 1978 production by the Troupe of Slanting Light of *Lemon* by Takeuchi Jū'ichirō. Yamaguchi Ei as Yoshirō *(at the right)* and Koide Shūji as the Detective *(to his immediate left)*.

there is a resemblance between the two dramas, it lies in the fact that both reveal how widespread this pattern is in contemporary life, the valiant struggle against government repression in youth abandoned and the despised working world embraced in a life of fractured days.

By the same token, the two playwrights take different attitudes toward these "turncoats." True, both find it humorous that, while having abandoned left-wing politics, they still remember their days of glory. But Tsuka Kōhei's eyes are wide open, and his point of view is chilly, his critiques filled with malice, as he distances himself from these men and women.

Takeuchi, on the other hand, while ridiculing these people as well, by turning the cold smile of an often cruel satire on them, does not distance himself from them. They seem somehow to be a part of his own experience. His play is thus more than a critique, more than an explanation written in desperation. Rather, it is a long and earnest look at the current situation. In it there is no attempt to flee reality or to turn reality into some narcissistic tragedy. Rather, it is a vision of reality that is pliable and modest, one that remains comic to the end.

Perhaps a few lines spoken toward the end of the play by Yoshirō (played by Yamaguchi Ei), one of the characters who wishes somehow to go on fighting, will give some idea of the author's point of view.

Today, I heard something wonderful. Light, when there is nothing for it to be reflected from, cannot shine. . . . So then, even if a starry sky looks black from somewhere else, it's really filled with light, all on its own. . . . I guess I'm just promoting my own interests here, though, when I say that the darkness is really filled with light. . . .

But the playwright does not divide things so simply into "darkness" and "light." His use of stage rhetoric is canny indeed. In fact, the play's special interest lies on the way in which Takeuchi overrides the usual theatrical conventions. Particularly striking is the casually bizarre arrangement in which Shin'ichi lives in his apartment with both his wife (played by Yajima Hitomi) and his mistress (played by Jō Sanae). Takeuchi sketches these peculiar relationships with skill and daring.

The title of the play—taken from the famous short story "Lemon" by the highly esteemed Kajii Motojirō (1901–1932)—provides us, therefore, with a double image. Kajii's "lemon explosion," a crystalline vision conjured up in a dream-like narrative, is indeed actualized when, toward the end of the play, a wall of old newspapers suddenly topples down, revealing a real street scene in Shimokitazawa, and the beauty of the lemon in bright conflagration in that space leaves an indelible impression.

The actors in this production are by no means uniformly brilliant, but they do reveal a collective energy and power more than sufficient to put across the comic flavor of the script.

When the play was over, I learned that most of the performers, with the exception of Takeuchi himself, had been connected to the Cherry Company, the troupe managed by Shimizu Kunio and his associates, which made their present success more understandable. Most of them have been playing smaller parts in that company.

Still, it has been four years since Shimizu's company disbanded. Now these performers have sought out their own means of expression and their own themes, conducting this search right in front of us. In that sense, *Lemon* provided a moving spectacle.

21. THE WHIRLINGS OF A WORLD
AT BIRTH

A Tale of the Original Japanese

Written and directed by Okabe Kōdai

SPACE PERFORMANCE

1978

Among the younger playwrights who have appeared in recent times, Okabe Kōdai here shows his quite remarkable abilities as a genuine man of the theatre. What I mean by *genuine* is that he possesses his own strong sensibilities and shows an ability to write in a style beholden to no other. Through the organization of his own theatrical skills, he has been able to establish a troupe capable of giving a real sense of direction to his performers.

A comparison of those figures who have appeared in the world of the theatre in the 1970s to those who came from the world of the small theatre companies in the 1960s reveals certain weaknesses that are all too apparent. The newcomers have been accused of showing a lack of genuine theatrical vigor, a frequently stated opinion that, more often than not, is on the mark. Yet, when I saw on the stage this play written and directed by Okabe (first performed in 1975), the refreshing performance made such comparisons superfluous. True enough, there are rough spots in the production. But at the same time there is a genuine responsiveness in the players, a real core to the work. His prodigious energy concentrated in creating his troupe's work, Okabe reveals his talents in the kind of reckless animation that he and his troupe can manifest (an animation that surely grows from the privileges they assume because of their lack of maturity).

The instant the curtain goes up, the audience is inundated by a flood of dialogue in the Kyushu dialect, which is spoken on the southernmost island of Japan (at first I could understand less than half of what was being said). The actors seemed divinely inspired, Okabe's direction utilizing the energy packed into the lines and his actors' dynamic physical performances to create a droll humor. Both in the use of local dialect and in the humorous yet charged effect, I was reminded of the work of Akihama Satoshi (who hails from northern Japan) with the Group of Thirty.

It is easy, however, to point out the differences between the work of these two playwrights. Akihama's dialect serves to surround and shape its speakers: the heaviness, the whispers, the twistings. His characters are by nature taciturn and show no skill in speaking. Spurred on by their loneliness or their fear, they express themselves only fitfully.

The 1978 production by Space Performance of Okabe Kōdai's *A Tale of the Original Japanese*. "Firecracker Tetsu" (Akō Zenkei) is leaping *(center)*.

Okabe's work, on the other hand, might be interpreted as a refracted drama concerned with social issues. Behind his vision lies the kind of firm design inherited from more orthodox models of modern drama. Okabe himself, born in 1945, left Kyushu when he was eleven. His dialogue, which resembles the undulations of a lovely sea, reveals the talents of a lively chatterbox and shows no dark undertones. The characters he creates are by nature great talkers. They know nothing of silence or unfinished sentences; their words wash over the audience like waves on the beach, and they never tire of chattering away. On the basis of this play, at least, Okabe possesses a profound belief in the kind of frank energy that derives from the dramatic combustion with which the lives of his characters are filled. So it is that this kind of drama, positive and openhearted (so rare in Japan)—while drawing to some extent on the perverted aesthetic of the "dramas of oppression" all to familiar to our generation—may be seeking something that does not actually exist.

At the beginning of the script, the following verse makes clear indeed the openhearted nature of the play.

The wind rushes in the star-filled sky
In the rushing wind the clouds swirl about
In the rushing wind the rough sea glitters
In the rushing wind the dust storm swirls

The play is set in Kyushu in a place called Matsuura. Two groups of young men face off. One is a group of miners working in the coalfields; as one mine after another closes down, Matsuura has become a virtual ghost town. The other is a group of fishermen; for generation after generation, such men have made their living there from the sea. One of the fishermen has "smooched up" to the daughter of one of the coal miners. The play reaches its climax one evening when, overflowing with excess energy, the two groups face off and fight after fight erupts along the beach.

The play takes its model from the musical *West Side Story*, yet the connections between the two seldom came to mind as I watched the performance. *A Tale of the Original Japanese* creates its own unique environment. It is set in the present, but the world one watches seems one of primal forces, undifferentiated energies swirling about, feelings that suggest one meaning contained in the title. The players overflow with energy. I cannot say that they are highly skilled or particularly polished, and all too often they seem content simply to hurl their words at the audience. Still, witnessing the dervish-like theatrical skill that emerged from this integrated force gives enormous pleasure, a pleasure all the more remarkable for the fact that these actors, so different in sensibility and disposition from most professional performers, could have been brought to work together as a true ensemble. As a director, Okabe certainly shows charismatic qualities.

Within this ensemble, there were a number of remarkable individual performances. Koseki Yasuhiro, who played Policeman Yasuzō, worrying over his various complexes, showed delightful qualities with his absent-minded humor. Firecracker Tetsu (played by Akō Zenkei), who created a chaotic atmosphere every time he hurled his firecrackers around the stage in the most nonchalant of manners, and Hyōdō Ippei (played by Torimaru Mitsuhiro), who cheered himself up by launching into the fight with his examination book in his hand, revealed a winning individuality in their performances. As a whole, the coal miners seemed better delineated on stage, the fishermen a bit more colorless.

Still, what are we to make of such a buoyant atmosphere, one that seems so transparent? What confuses us, I think, is that for too long we have become accustomed to plays dealing only with the kind of dark energies that arise from a sense of refraction and oppression.

22. LAUGHING OKINAWA

Anthropology Museum

Written by Chinen Seishin

Directed by Kōki Ryōshū

THE CREATION TROUPE

1978

This August, this Okinawa theatre group presented its first Tokyo performances (four in all) in its seventeen years of activity.

If that were all there were to it, this fact would not amount to any big news in and of itself. Recently, quite a number of regional theatre troupes have been performing in Tokyo, and a number of them, particularly from the Kyoto-Osaka region, have been particularly worthy of note. But I believe these present performances to be of a truly special significance.

In the first place, this is the first time to my knowledge that an Okinawan theatre troupe performing modern theatre has appeared, not just in Tokyo, but anywhere in mainland Japan.

Chinen Seishin's 1978 *Anthropology Museum*, performed by the Creation Troupe. Kitajima Sumiko plays the Woman, Sakihama Shigeru the Man.

Second, the play that they are presenting, *Anthropology Museum*, directed by Kōki Ryōshū, is the first original play by an Okinawan author that the troupe has staged. That the play exposes the feelings of discrimination that lurk in the hearts of Okinawans has allowed the company successfully to mount a rich and multilayered drama, one that rises above the more accusatory style that has heretofore been so familiar.

The play represents a reflection of the artistic subjectivity of those involved in the modern theatre in Okinawa, and the level of confidence that the troupe possesses is attested to by the very fact of these Tokyo performances. Although the play is short and involves only three performers, the problems that it undertakes to explicate are surprisingly profound and wide ranging. The Tokyo audiences, which, including standees, must have numbered some two thousand during this short run, can scarcely have overlooked these remarkable facts.

Anthropology Museum was first staged in Okinawa by the company and directed by the author himself in the summer of 1976. The production attracted a great deal of attention, and, as a result, the text was published in a magazine dedicated to new Okinawan literature in the same year. The play was later reprinted in serial fashion in the Tokyo theatre journal *Teatoro*. It was then performed on the stage in Tokyo by the Rekuramu Company, a young group of actors directed by Akaishi Takeo, in October 1977, and this beautifully controlled production received excellent notices. As a result, the author was awarded the prestigious Kishida Kunio drama prize for that year.

The author, Chinen Seishin, was born in Okinawa in 1941. He came to Tokyo to further his studies but abandoned them before finishing. He entered an experimental troupe, the Youth Theatre Arts Troupe, run by Fukuda Yoshiyuki, Okamura Haruhiko, and Yonekura Masakane. Among his fellow students were Kara Jūrō and Satoh Makoto. In 1963, he returned to Okinawa, where he took a job with the local Okinawan Broadcasting Company. At the same time, he joined the Creation Troupe. *Anthropology Museum* was, in fact, his first play.

The play concerns what the history books refer to as the Osaka Anthropological Museum incident, which took place in 1903 at the Fifth Osaka Industrial Fair. In what was described as an "academic anthropological museum," two streetcorner prostitutes were displayed as typical Okinawans, along with "Ainu from Hokkaido" and "Koreans." The guide, whip in hand, treated them as animals, referring to them disparagingly as "these creatures." As a result of vigorous protests from the Okinawans, this "display" was closed within a month. Nevertheless, the incident left deep scars.

The play updates the incident, setting it in the contemporary period. In a kind of tent show dubbed "Anthropology Museum," the Circus Trainer (performed by Uchima Yasuo), whip in hand, laughing in polite collusion with the audience, talks of the fact that "on the basis of the concept of the universality of humanity... no discrimination of any kind will be permitted." As "models" of Okinawans, a Man and a Woman (played by Sakihama Shigeru and Kitajima Sumiko, respectively) are placed on display. The Man, who has a criminal record, is a coward who gets by through bluffing; the Woman is a prostitute. Their words and actions identify them as humorous characters. While they mix the Okinawa dialect with standard Japanese, the Circus Trainer speaks an all-too-smooth standard language. His sadism is apparent, as he heaps disdain on these people he despises, and he is violent as well. He forces the Man to call out "Long live the emperor!" but the Man can pronounce the phrase only as, "Bong live the emperar!" The Circus Trainer then hangs a sign around the Man's neck, identifying him as a "dialect criminal."

The Circus Trainer consistently plays the role of the oppressor from the mainland of Japan; the Man and Woman become the oppressed of Okinawa. According to the logic of this "sideshow," they are to play out one incident after another in the complex history of the prejudices and difficulties suffered through by the Okinawans since the Meiji Restoration of 1868. The various scenes of that history—the military squadrons Okinawans were forced to join during the war, prostitution during the Vietnam era, and other degrading episodes—all are blended into the bizarre games played by these three characters as they condense time and space.

In one of the wartime scenes, however, there is a sudden reversal. The Circus Trainer suddenly stops using standard speech; he stutters; then he too begins speaking the Okinawan dialect fluently. The very character who embodies the mainland's hatred of everything Okinawan is, it turns out, Okinawan himself and has been unable to succeed in Japan because of that fact. I must admit that, because the next scene—in which all three discuss the issue of self-determination—was spoken entirely in dialect, I had difficulty following it; nevertheless, it was clear that, through this rupture, a scene of unusual tension and beauty had been created.

In the end, the play takes a surprising turn. In a sudden accident, the Circus Trainer falls down, and the Man immediately takes up his role; it is now he who carries the whip, and he adopts with great glee the words of the Trainer: "Today, it is our pleasure to welcome you to our Anthropology Museum!"

Now the circle of prejudice has closed. The wheel has turned all too smoothly.

What strikes me as remarkable about *Anthropology Museum* is the fact that it sets out to identify and attack the prejudices and the desire for control hidden in the Okinawans, even though they are themselves the victims of similar oppression from Japan proper. Nothing here resembles the other sorts of plays that take the point of view of the oppressed to make emotional accusations. On this occasion, the Okinawans look at themselves objectively and in a mercilessly clear light. For that reason, there is a severity in their laughter. The three Okinawans presented have been fleshed out in a striking manner; they have indeed been "humanized."

To put the matter in another way, the history of Okinawa, which has always been explained as a "tragedy," has now been turned, at least in the terms posed by *Anthropology Museum,* into a grotesque comedy. The laughter has a bitter ring to it for all that; these are jokes that are not to be undertaken lightly. Nor is the humor polished and refined. Still, the author seems to suggest, if the Okinawans cannot turn their tragedy into a comedy of disinterested self-scrutiny, they will never achieve any true sense of autonomy. Seen in this way, this comedy represents a serious effort on the part of the author.

As for me, I wished to experience this play as though it were borne along on the rhythm of a popular song, for it seems that, in such a rhythm, the strong satiric sense of the current protest movements in Okinawa might find its proper expression.

The significance of this work is not limited merely to an increased consciousness of the history of Japanese prejudice against Okinawa. There floats up here in a curious upside-down fashion, both among those who are oppressed as well as among those who oppose the system, a sense of self-inflicted prejudice and discrimination that seems in the end unrelated to the sense of injustice created by the system itself. In that sense, we all find that we inhabit an *Anthropology Museum.*

My impression was that this current production, directed by Kōki Ryōshū, moves along at a relaxed and reliable tempo. Mounted as it was by young actors from Tokyo, the Rekuramu Company's production of the play last year moved much more quickly, had a harder, more powerful edge to it and showed a greater sense of focus. The present production takes the opposite approach. It is performed without frills and moves calmly and with dignity.

At first I found myself a bit confused by the slower rhythm. I thought that this relatively listless pace might be difficult to tolerate. However, as the play progressed, I realized that I had judged too hastily. There was a real basis for this slow tempo. The company's sense of pace was unrelated to that kind of restless movement to which we have become so accustomed in Tokyo; rather, the director was here making use of the kind of unhurried serenity that can be found in the traditional Okinawan performing arts. The group is uninvolved in the whirl of Tokyo rhythms. They show here their will to create and reveal a rhythm authentic to their own sensibilities.

In one sense, it might indeed be said that a real contemporary Okinawan theatre begins with this *Anthropology Museum.* And, as for us, we have at last moved within range of their criticisms.

23. A RIPENING OF MELODY

Shanghai 'Vance King

Written by Saitō Ren

Directed by Kushida Kazuyoshi,

music by Koshibe Nobuyoshi

THE FREE THEATRE

1979

No recent production has brought me as much pleasure, or made such a deep impression on me, as this truly delightful production of Saitō Ren's *Shanghai 'Vance King.*

Actually speaking, this kind of work is rarely written for the stage these days. The audience follows the fate of Saitō's fascinating characters as though poring through the pages of some adventure novel. Will they manage to live out their destinies? Or will their dead bodies end up floating in the Yangtze River? With trembling hearts we follow them in their joys, their pains. We worry over the fate of each one of them, over their loves, over the inevitable coming of the war. This is truly a melodrama for all seasons. Should I be talking about theme? construction? dramatic technique? None of these things we critics tend to chatter on about should apply here. Given the circumstances, even to ask such questions would seem to me ungentlemanly.

It seems to me that we have long forgotten just how much pleasure there is in watching a story like this unfold. There have been few opportunities for us to worry about the ups and downs of stage characters as they move toward their respective fates. This is surely because, in most productions of what we term *contemporary theatre,* the real interest for the audience lies not so much in the activities of the protagonists as in the very construction of the play itself. So it is that we find ourselves talking about structure, technique, and device, and we have come to worry very little about the lives of the characters on the stage.

In this case, however, the author has used very skillful techniques to create this remarkable melodrama, which never pales, never bores. Saitō Ren has managed all these tricks with extraordinary ability. And behind this seemingly nonchalant yet scrupulously prepared production lie ten years of experience, beginning with his masterpiece *Red Eyes* in 1967, then *Trust D.E.* in 1969. Without undue boasting or undue modesty, he has been able, with the present ripeness of his talents, to bring a polished melodrama like

The 1979 Free Theatre Production of Saitō Ren's *Shanghai 'Vance King.* Yoshida Hideko as "Madonna." (Photo by Ide Jōji.)

Shanghai 'Vance King into being, and the results can be described as altogether chic.

The scene is Shanghai during the period stretching from 1925 to the coming of the war in 1937. As Japan approaches a wartime footing, it becomes more and more difficult to perform jazz altogether, so two jazz men —Bakumatsu (played by Sasano Takashi) and Hatano (played by Manako Keiji)—have escaped, as it were, to Shanghai. These two plus their wives, the Chinese woman Lily (played by Tanabe Satsuki) and Masaoka Madoka (played by Yoshida Hideko), sometimes known as "Madonna," constitute the chief characters.

Despite the fact that controls in Japan proper are tightening, these characters believe that the good life in Shanghai will continue forever: jazz, women, wine, gambling and, when the money runs out, loans with no worry. Yet, when the war does arrive, they realize that they will have to pay everything back, and at a painful price indeed.

Intertwined with these central figures are a number of other colorful characters: the boss of Shanghai, Larry (played by Tsuruta Shinobu), who whispers all sorts of weird tidings; Shirai (played by Arifuku Masahi), a very correct Japanese military officer; Hirota (played by Ōmori Hiroshi), a former left-wing agitator who has now become a rightist; and the old man Fan (played by the director himself, Kushida Kazuyoshi), a brilliantly intellectual Chinese servant.

Each of these varied roles is played with style and humor, and the atmosphere created in the theatre is gratifyingly bright and busy. Kushida's direction is scrupulous and appropriately nostalgic, with a sense of elegant playfulness of which his audiences never tire.

Among the performers, Sasano Takashi in the role of Bakumatsu is particularly effective. His face is so typically Japanese, and he shows both a shallow and a fidgety side to his character as he rushes about in the course of his hectic life. Yoshida Hideko's Madonna is also well sketched. Under her brightness is revealed a languor and sadness, and her cool performance makes a deep impression on her audiences. Lilly as played by Tanabe Satsuki shows an appropriate listlessness as well, and Tsuruta Shinobu's Larry is completely successful in his comic exaggeration.

What I most want to take note of here, however, is the real delight to be found in the music. Not only is the score charming, but most of the male members of the cast are musicians and so perform the musical numbers themselves. Even though they are not highly accomplished professionals, the effect is astonishing. These days, given the increasing cost of live musicians, it has become increasingly common for musicals to use prerecorded soundtracks. In the face of what these actors have achieved, however, this logic is not persuasive.

Seeing this production reminds me of another ten years ago, when in his production of *Trust D.E.* Saitō Ren also had his performers pick up their instruments, filling the theatre space with the same vivid energy. From that time on, Saitō became known as a playwright of unusual ability. Yet his very prolificacy has often resulted in a lack of focus and inferior craftsmanship. With *Shanghai 'Vance King*, however, he has managed to bring his fecund imagination under control. The first volume of his collected dramatic works, *Red Eyes*, has also just been published. The direction that the work of this prodigious talent will now take remains to be seen.

24. YOHEI WHO LIVES ON

Double Suicide, after Chikamatsu

Written by Akimoto Matsuyo

Directed by Ninagawa Yukio

A TŌHŌ PRODUCTION

1979

This present production of Akimoto's play, directed by Ninagawa, is a beautifully mature piece of stage artistry.

I know little about the stagings of Akimoto's earliest plays, but it does seem to me that, since 1967, when her work *Kaison the Priest of Hitachi* was first produced, the stagings of her plays have not lived up to the potential inherent in the texts themselves. There can be no denying the ardor and single-mindedness of the troupes that have performed her work. Great energy has been forthcoming in every case, and I have vivid memories of a number of brilliant actors and performances. Still, the creative energy manifested on stage has, surprisingly, never matched the creativity that Akimoto has invested in her work. To put it differently, the originality and extravagance that truly successful productions of her plays demand has not yet been forthcoming.

It seems that, in the end, Akimoto's plays have been composed with such strictness that there is little room to introduce an individual interpretation or any sense of playfulness when mounting productions of them.

In that sense, the encounter between Akimoto and Ninagawa has been extremely fortunate and fruitful, for Ninagawa has confronted the text of her *Double Suicide, after Chikamatsu* both on its own terms and on his own terms as director. As it turns out, I read the play in published form before seeing the stage production, and I must confess that I received a more powerful sense of shock, and of exaltation, from the production than from my own reading. This experience has thus been an exceptional one for me, particularly as I think back over previous productions of her plays. It is true, however, that Ninagawa has a reputation not only for taking firm control of a production but also for making of his productions "events," at least in terms of noisy excess. I therefore waited apprehensively for the play to begin.

Yes, this *Double Suicide, after Chikamatsu* indeed, an event, in the good sense, one that is beautifully realized. While watching the stage, the audience felt a deep sense of satisfaction and no sense of uneasiness what-

Ninagawa Yukio's 1979 production for Tōhō of Akimoto Matsuyo's *Double Suicide, after Chikamatsu*. Kanno Naoyuki *(left)* as Yohei and Ichihara Etsuko as O-Kame *(to his right)*.

soever. From the stage was conveyed no arbitrary sense of shock or defiance.

In a word, the production was so skillfully managed that the audience was lost in admiration. The keen and clever sharpness of Ninagawa's vision spun itself unceasingly before us, helped considerably by the dark, murky atmosphere created by the brilliant lighting of Yoshii Sumio and the evocative stage settings of Asakura Setsu, which kept the tension the director wished to create smoldering. Therefore, rather than adopting a stance that might introduce a sense of a disparity between her vision and his own, Ninagawa's realization of the play worked to build a strong sense of aesthetic consciousness in the sensibilities of the audience.

As the drama unfolded, a song (with words by the playwright herself and music by Inomata Koshō), sung by the popular singer Mori Shin'ichi, proved astonishingly effective. In its freshness, this music brought precisely the right kind of rhythm and emotion to this drama, which is in itself so typically Japanese in conception. There was nothing intrusive about its use; indeed, as intended, the song served as a wave that helped wash together all the emotions being expressed.

By the same token, Ninagawa remains himself. What he has given us previously we now see again. As before, we have presented to us violently romantic emotions, the exaltation of eroticism and death in the manner of Georges Bataille, details of stagecraft polished in the most fastidious fashion, the sort of structure appropriate to a popular extravaganza that enraptures the eyes.

The keenness of Ninagawa's vision is ever sharper. For example, in act 3 there is a moment in the large public room of the Echigoya brothel (a moment of no particular significance in the larger drama) that I find unforgettable. The space is so large that it seems cold, the depths of the room dim and remote. The space itself is roofless, revealing a number of two-story buildings that surround it. The whole is sunk in murky darkness. On the left side of the stage, a group of women who work in the brothel are trimming the lamps, crouching quietly. On the right side, an old woman, perhaps a servant, bends low as she quietly, soundlessly cuts across the stage space. In the darkness, one sprig of early flowering cherry, which she has stuck in her hair, stands out, strikingly crimson. Now, suddenly, it seems that, here and there near the tops of the roofs of the surrounding houses, dim in their own alleys, other cherries eerily open as well. Flowering alone in the darkness, the clusters of blossoms seem to symbolize passion and death: in this seemingly nonchalant fashion, we are given an momentary glimpse of Ninagawa's vision, to be frozen in our minds forever.

Yet, along with the familiar themes and sensibilities that Ninagawa has always shown, one now senses a change as well. In this production, he has shown his control in a more relaxed fashion. His productions always take risks, but, on this occasion, he has been less obvious in exploiting them at the expense of the rhythm of the production as a whole. The energy that sometimes breaks forth from the stage is here confined within it, and that single-minded sense of excess so characteristic of his previous productions has been modulated into a clear-headed intensity, here transmuted into an aesthetic refinement not always apparent before.

One reason for this polish, I am sure, is his contact with Akimoto Matsuyo's original script. In particular, there is one character in the drama who has a great influence over this modulated intensity. This is the character of the umbrella shop owner Yohei, played by Kanno Naoyuki. I found Yohei to be a most striking and memorable stage portrait and Kanno's buoyant, cruelly humorous portrayal to be of the highest caliber. For me, Yohei is the central character among all those whom Ninagawa has brought to life.

Akimoto has extracted from among the fifteen-odd plays of the great Tokugawa dramatist Chikamatsu Monzaemon (1653–1724) dealing with love suicide the characters of Umegawa and Chūbei from *The Courier from Hell* and, from its sequel, the characters of O-Kame and Yohei, and she has constructed her drama by blending and transforming these two originally separate strands. Perhaps, therefore, it is a bit peculiar of me to choose Yohei from among all the characters who inhabit this complex world.

However, from the very moment Yohei first steps before our eyes, mixing with the throng of men seeking to purchase a woman for the night in the brothels of Osaka's Shinmachi district, we cannot help but take note of this forlorn figure, who, unlike his partner, has remained alive after a failed attempt at a love suicide, one who has given up as well on an attempt to hang himself in remorse. Ninagawa has realized in a strikingly realistic fashion the final stage direction calling for "a vast crowd in a phantom brothel district": Yohei walks through this penultimate scene, sad and alone, repeating the opening moments of the play. Yohei therefore becomes pivotal, linking the beginnings of the tragedy with its end. The whole production thus becomes, in one sense, a device to reveal the nature of the phantom drama in which he himself has become implicated. The possibility thus arises that Yohei, this wretched man, has created in his wild fancy a kind of straightforward tragedy such as that of Chūbei and Umegawa, one in which he cannot participate himself.

The love suicide of Umegawa and Chūbei, on the other hand, is created within the world of pure tragedy. The pair rush headlong into their universe of passion and eroticism, and their smiles of rapture float up with them; they never waver or hesitate but plunge directly into their deaths. They are committed; they are gallant. There is nothing that separates their love and their lives; they are ignited together. In that sense, their love, which knows no doubt, is doubtless a healthy one. Yet, since they never examine the world outside themselves, their purity seems somehow sealed, a perfection within themselves; it is as though the pair inhabits a tiny globe reserved only for themselves. They seem to represent human beings who are almost too pure; there is something cold about them, and they lack human interest. The same may be said of their realizations on the stage. While Taichi Kiwako, who plays Umegawa, and Hira Mikijirō, who plays Chūbei, are capable of performing with the requisite passion, they can reveal only the perfection, and the hardness, of pure crystal.

On the other hand, Yohei and his wife, O-Kame, may seem at first to have been conceived as comic characters; yet, in revealing their human weakness and foolishness, they manage with their bitter laughter to break open the play, moving away from the atmosphere of tragedy established by the two lovers. The paths of the two couples zigzag back and forth in a striking fashion; yet, since Yohei and O-Kame live in a fashion so different from the lovers, they create a somehow refreshing comic atmosphere that stands in contrast to the all-consuming passion found in the conduct of Chūbei and Umegawa.

The performances of Ichihara Etsuko as O-Kame and Kanno Naoyuki as Yohei are vividly conceived. Still, it may have been easier for them to deal with characters who reveal so obviously both human weakness and tragedy.

Yohei shows a remarkable passivity. Everything slips away from him. No concerns seem to pile up before him—not his work, not his love, not even his dissipations. He is gentle, quick-witted, generous with his friends. Always clearheaded, he has a sense of the limitations of his own interior world; he is never intoxicated with fantasies. And, because he has a firm sense of his own smallness, he shows true respect for others and tries insofar as he can to match his conduct to their desires. Even when he and O-Kame decide to commit suicide together, he shows an objective understanding of her consuming passion to participate in a suicide pact that will confirm and crystallize their love, remove their uneasiness. So it is that the scene of their love suicide at the Shijimi River, which reveals the differences in their characters (although she dies, Yohei throws the short sword with which he intended to commit suicide into the river and remains alive) and in which things are settled in such an unsightly way, is the most affecting moment in the work. It is from their love, rather than the passion of Umegawa and Chūbei, that a light shines, a light that can illuminate our contemporary lives.

The most important aspect of Yohei's actions, however, lies in the fact that, having behaved badly, he has created an existence for himself that is altogether at odds with the kind of exquisite beauty in death sought by Umegawa and Chūbei. Yohei sees himself as a bad person who has impudently chosen to continue on with his life, however vile he may thus appear. Such is the path that he has overtly chosen for himself.

In the last scene of Chikamatsu's original, Yohei, still alive after the earlier suicide attempt, follows his love by bravely killing himself with a razor, but Akimoto's character dares to go on living. Having failed to hang himself, Yohei whispers the following lines in the middle of the falling snow:

> O-Kame. . . . I am . . . really . . . a terrible person. I just can't manage to kill myself. Please take mercy on me. . . . I'm sorry to ask this, but . . . let me go on living out my life.

His words are meant to show his weakness, but they are shrewdly conceived. If he were actually prepared to die, there would have been plenty of opportunities for him to do so. He is really saying that he does not intend to die by his own hand. So it is that he nonchalantly announces that he intends to go on "living out my life."

To put the matter another way, Yohei has chosen here the path not of tragedy but of comedy. He himself is small, weak, foolish, even comic;

there is not one speck of grandeur in his whole existence. Still, he does not mean to interfere with anyone else's life. Indeed, he is aware that he is a comic figure, one who seeks only to prolong his own existence. Precisely because he knows his own failings, he is humble in the face of the enormity of a world that, in its ultimate absurdity, cannot be understood by even the wisest of men. In the end, it is not he who has consciously chosen a comic role for himself. Rather, in his fantasy, his bitterness, his weakness, he has passed through the dark tunnel within himself in order to grasp the world as a comedy.

25. A PLAY GOES ON "OUTSIDE THE WALLS"

Lemmings

Written by Terayama Shūji

Directed by Terayama Shūji and J. A. Caesar

THE PEANUT GALLERY

1979

Watching Terayama Shūji's new play *Lemmings—Going along to the Edge of the World,* I felt as though I were experiencing two works at once.

Then, after the performance, I realized that what *Lemmings* called to mind was something I had just finished reading, the distinguished novelist Sono Ayako's lengthy new work *The Empty Room*—despite the fact that Sono takes a position as a writer that seems diametrically opposed to Terayama's.

In her novel, Sono, a Catholic herself, presents a cruel snapshot of a religious order that, because of the "rationalization" of church rules at the Second Vatican Council of 1967, has lost its vision of God and so has become increasingly secularized. Sono particularly emphasizes those moments that signal the beginning of the loss of faith. Born in the wake of the democratizing tendencies of the 1960s, the nuns, who until now had spent their lives working together in one large room, begin to demand privacy. Their wishes are granted, and each receives her own room with a lock on the door. When one of them wishes to be alone, she simply hangs a "Do Not Disturb" sign on the door, just as in a hotel.

On the face of things, it would seem that, within the convent walls, the environment is such as to permit a true inner experience of God. Ironically, however, the nuns have lost sight of the divine altogether. The nunnery has, in effect, become nothing more than a women's dormitory. It is God who is missing from "the empty room."

Terayama's current play makes a similar, albeit secular, statement. For Terayama, the all-consuming search for individuality that pervades contemporary life throws up symbolic walls around each one of us (what Sono conceptualized as rooms). If only we could find a way to tear down those walls, to move beyond a sense of the self in isolation, we would discover, not a divine being who orders nature, but a random universe, a reality that is wider and more complexly layered than the one we have known. Here, it seems to me, the two artists transcend their differences and strike surprisingly similar notes.

In Terayama's play, very much as in his previous success, *Directions to Servants*, he has used the large floor space available to him at the City Gymnasium.

As always, Terayama's visual devices are striking; and, with the provocative music of J. A. Caesar incessantly jangling our every nerve, we are shown the tiny room of Wan (played by Wakamatsu Takeshi), an apprentice cook in a Chinese restaurant, who lives in a dormitory in a poor section of Tokyo.

Suddenly, the walls of his room melt away.

As they vanish, Wan's life takes a turn for the theatrical. We see the next room, where the Girl in the Wheelchair (played by Ran Yōko) and her Elder Brother live. And that is not all. These walls, which constitute our sense of the realities of everyday life, in turn disappear, and, in a universe rather like that created by science fiction, unexpected sorts of people invade Wan's space and involve him in their own affairs.

The beautiful girl who calls herself Movie Star (played by Niidaka Keiko) seems the central figure in a group of film technicians at work, who pass through in shadowlike fashion; Wan himself becomes part of the film and, when shot by the Movie Star, dies a sweet death. Now the dormitory is suddenly transformed into the ward of a mental hospital; each person there thinks that the others are mad, and they become involved in a dissipated so-called entertainment remedy. Four jailbirds, who have been in prison for twenty years, now open the door painted on the side of the prison wall. The very moment it seems they can step safely out, a remarkable and illogical

The 1979 production by the Peanut Gallery of *Lemmings* by Terayama Shūji. The Beautiful Girl (Niidaka Keiko) stands above the ensemble in the center.

episode occurs: they are shot and killed with a hunting gun by a dwarf, who has suddenly appeared after an expedition to Africa. This bizarre moment is one of the most effective scenes in the play.

More took place, however, than that which transpired on the stage in front of the audience. The second time that I went to see *Lemmings*, the performance was sold out, and I could find no place to sit, so I clambered up onto a platform that had been set up behind the performance area and watched the play with ten or so other brave souls. That vantage point gave me a panoramic view of the entire theatre space, and I could see that there were all sorts of dramatic moments taking place that were not visible from the regular seats, all happening at the same time.

The dwarf from the African expedition had indeed "broken out of the walls" and was running about soundlessly as he repeated again and again his "breaking away." A number of men and women clothed in black loitered about looking like pieces of sculpture. A huge white balloon floated above the floor, moving ever so slightly.

In other words, in Terayama's conception, the very fact that the audience traditionally focuses its attention on the main stage constitutes itself a kind of wall. The genius behind this production lies in the fact that it allows for many "dramas" to take place outside the walls of individual consciousness. It is this variation on the theme of walls that makes it possible for

Lemmings to approach the level of success achieved by *Directions to Servants*. That same Terayama who shouted, "Put down our books and out into the streets!" is obviously alive and well.

26. OBSTACLES TO ABANDONMENT

Two Women

Written by Kara Jūrō

Staged by the directing unit of the Seventh Ward

Troupe

THE SEVENTH WARD TROUPE

1979

On those occasions when Kara Jūrō writes for a company other than his own Situation Theatre, he alters his customary style, often creating works constructed in quite unexpected ways.

Among his many plays, for example, certain works reveal a classic clarity of structure, such as *The Virgin's Mask,* which he wrote in 1969 for the Waseda Little Theatre Company. Such plays do not manifest the expansive, baroque constructions of those he writes for the Situation Theatre. The control and sense of dramatic tension that he shows in writing for other companies seem closely related to a sense of conformity to autonomous dramatic forms.

The Seventh Ward Troupe, which centers on the work of two accomplished performers, Ishibashi Renji and Midori Mako, who mounted their first production in 1976, has now broken a three-year silence to present Kara's new play *Two Women*. This work must be counted as among his most accomplished. While the direction is billed as a collaboration, Ishibashi has obviously taken the lead, and, although there are occasional defects here and there in the production, the presentation is always vigorous, and, in the end, the performance made a powerful effect.

Remarkably enough for Kara, his new play is an updating of certain

The Seventh Ward's 1979 staging of *Two Women* by Kara Jūrō. Kōichi (Ishibashi Renji) is set on by Rokujō (Midori Mako). (Photo courtesy of the Editorial Department of the journal *Bijutsu techō.*)

sections of the classic eleventh-century novel *The Tale of Genji* by Murasaki Shikibu. In 1975, Kara was asked by NHK, the national radio network, to contribute a script for an episode of a series entitled "My 'Tale of Genji' "; the result was the radio drama *Rival Courtiers in Love.* In 1978, he transformed this material into a one-act play, *The Sixth Room,* which has now been expanded and revised again as *Two Women.* This newest version is by far the most theatrically effective of all.

The material for the play is taken from the *Aoi* [Hollyhocks] section of *The Tale of Genji,* in which the Princess Rokujō, burning with jealousy over the fact that she has lost Genji's affection, becomes a living ghost who causes grief to Genji's wife, Aoi, eventually pursuing her to her death. Kara sets the play in the present. Genji becomes Kōichi, a doctor dealing in mental illness. Aoi is now his fiancée, and Rokujō is a former patient, already abandoned by him, who continues to yearn for his affection. Thus, a triangular relationship is reborn. The roles of both women—Aoi, who eventually becomes pregnant, and Rokujō, the "woman of fate" for whom Kōichi feels a powerful attraction—are played by the same actress (aided by a series of rapid costume changes), with thrilling results.

In addition, Kara further refracts the relationship between Rokujō and Kōichi. At one point, Rokujo had joined a "military group." There she meets a man and is deserted by him; it is his image that she later projects onto her doctor, Kōichi. Kōichi, in turn, is seized by a passion for Rokujō, who closely resembles his wife, Aoi. During the period of his relationship with Rokujō, Kōichi comes to realize just how much of his own life he has thrown away—in the sense that, as a physician and therefore a member of the elite, he has taken no part in the political and social struggles he has lived through. The connection between these two begins as a kind of hallucination, and their meeting has about it a sense of inevitable ruin.

In fact, however, as it is conceived here, this love triangle far transcends a simple affair between one man and one woman. What emerges from Kara's version of the tale is the question of how to determine, in human terms, what, if any, meaning might exist for that which has been purposefully abandoned. The theatre companies in which these two performers have been successively involved, from the 1960s through the mid-1970s, have worked to take a stand on serious social issues; now that this era of activism is over and done with, the play subtly queries the nature of those continuing obstacles that those who now participate in the Seventh Ward Troupe evidently feel they now confront. These issues make up material for a rich theatrical experience.

The small stage used by the company has been covered with coarse sand, which serves a variety of purposes, beginning with the scene in which Rokujō, now a patient in a mental hospital by the sea on the Itō peninsula, confesses her feeling of closeness to the ants that burrow there in the sand. The play then moves inside the hospital, then to a road circling Mount Fuji, then to a room in an apartment building. All these scenes are performed in the sand. When the characters stretch themselves out on the floor of the apartment as though on straw matting, they are covered with grit; when they chase each other around on the stage, a sandstorm erupts, engulfing the first few rows of seats.

At first glance, this use of sand may seem to represent nothing more than a typical trick used by a small theatre company fond of "grime," but, in this case, the sand performs a powerful theatrical function. Its meaning becomes blindingly clear at the final curtain, when Kōichi, who in the grip of his powerful emotions seeks to follow his wife in death, attempts to strangle Rokujō on the beach.

As they struggle, he manages to push her down into the sand. At this point, Midori Mako's Rokujō shows a mysterious blush of color in her face. Twining her legs about the man's body, she suddenly pulls herself up on top of him as though she were riding a horse. She whispers to him, "So now, let's go home . . . slowly go home. . . ." Showing herself to be the mistress of the hideous ants who burrow in the sand, Rokujō now drags Kōichi into a hole; both seem to become insects as they disappear together into the earth.

Since Kara's 1974 *Matasaburō of the Wind*, he has created no final spectacle as striking as this. However, so far as *Two Women* is concerned, the earth goddess descends to reveal her frightening power directly. This sort of magical force in turn gives new life to the lesser energy that has been abandoned. Dynamic, destructive, this beauty sends chills down the spine.

Midori Mako plays both female roles with overwhelming effectiveness. Her artistic powers have in no way declined; in her present performance, it is as though she has residing within herself both a young girl and an old woman. She possesses the theatrical skill to manifest a natural simplicity and an unparalleled ability to suggest a pretense at understanding. The male actors in the play perform with vigor, but the play would be more effective still had they allowed for the appearance of more alluring and individual personalities. The direction is careful and detailed, yet filled with power. The figure of the young man from the parking lot (played by Ōkubo Makoto), who appears as a giant in the shadows, was particularly well managed.

27. IN THE MIDST OF
A WEAKENED ART

The Lady of the Camellias

Written by Alexandre Dumas Fils

Directed by Takemura Rui, translated by

Watanabe Moriaki

A NISSEI THEATRE PRODUCTION

1978

As it turns out, I have just finished reading a new Japanese translation of the famous *Letters to d'Alembert* by Jean-Jacques Rousseau (1712–1778), the French philosopher born in Geneva. I found them to be of the greatest interest. Among the many classic and modern texts on such subjects, there exists no similar example of such a clear diatribe against and critique of the art of the theatre. This curious disharmony between the author's love and hate for the stage surely derives (although Rousseau would surely deny it) from the nature of his own character. What comes across in print, of course, is the image of a Rousseau who interrogates the theatre, then denounces it. Yet, by the same token, there is conveyed as well a certain forlorn quality when he takes up his sword to attack the "evils" of the theatre, for what permeates his writing is a vision, and a correct one at that, of the theatrical arts of France, the country he has left behind. Thus, even though I feel that much that he says is riddled with error, I found myself at the same time filled with admiration, even as I chuckled.

In the book, Rousseau judges the theatre, first and last, from the perspective of one who would maintain the conventionalities of civic life. He takes the position of one who supports the quiet daily life of those who work patiently at their respective labors and who live within a unified culture. From that point of view, the theatre, with its dizzying sense of difference, upsets the balance involved in such a round of daily life. The thrust of his critique is to judge between the "good" of custom and the "beauty" of art; and, in that context, it is not surprising that the theatre appears to be dangerous. From its beginnings, the theatre by its very nature has undercut the flow of daily existence, pulling us toward energies that are indeed divorced from such simple patterns. Rousseau's harshest judgment is therefore reserved for the very attraction that defines the theatre.

Rousseau's critique is class based: he does not categorically condemn all theatrical activity everywhere. He makes the point strongly that, in a small city such as Geneva (or so he judged the size of the city to be in 1758, when he wrote these letters), daily life is conducted simply and modestly. For the citizens of Geneva, therefore, the theatre constitutes a positive harm. Yet, in a large metropolis such as Paris, where the life of its citizens is so often idle and degenerate, the art of the theatre constitutes an essential distraction. This is because, for the two hours' duration of a play on the stage, the spectators are effectively hindered from participating in something "still worse": "If the citizens are degenerate, the theatre becomes a perfect distraction; if the citizens are virtuous, it is a bad thing."

As it turned out, I was reading this tract at precisely the time I saw the famous female impersonator from the world of *kabuki*, Bandō Tamasaburō, perform the leading role in the celebrated Dumas play *The Lady of the Camellias*. This juxtaposition was a curious one for me. If I took up Rousseau's idea that beauty can be criticized from the everyday ethical point of view, there could scarcely be a more perfect example to seize on, and to censure, than the performance of Tamasaburō, who had no other idea than to create "beauty." Interestingly enough, with Rousseau's critique fresh in my mind, I was able to appreciate such beauty all the more.

Even though I know Verdi's opera *La Traviata,* which is based on the Dumas play, I had never before seen *The Lady of the Camellias* staged. There is, of course, no question but that the drama itself takes up a fascinating subject, which depicts so well the manners of its time. Still, I had never imagined that, as a play in and of itself, it constituted any sort of masterpiece. The character of its heroine, Marguerite—who, while an inhabitant of the demimonde, is able to abandon even her life itself because of her love for the young Armand—never seemed to me adequately realized in the dialogue, and the tale of the heroine's descent had always seemed insufficiently dynamic.

Of course, a proper production, which would take into account the world in which the play moves, could create the necessary theatrical magic to draw the audience in. In this instance, however, it did not seem to me that the results were uniformly successful.

Takemura's direction appeared, here and there, to show certain real successes. The first and second acts were performed at too low a level of emotional intensity, and there was very little of beauty to be seen in the movements of the performers. In the third and fourth acts, however, thanks at least in part to the costumes and the lighting, the play began suddenly to come vividly to life. In the scene in act 3 at the country villa, a greenhouse was placed center stage, and through the glass and the open door one could see out into the green fields beyond, with truly fresh and attractive results. At the opening of the act, the atmosphere is clear and full of happiness. Then, during the time when Armand's father (played by Yamagata Isao) visits and asks Marguerite to give up his son, followed in turn by the moment in which Armand is angered at what he takes to be Marguerite's duplicity, the sunlight fades, to be replaced by a patter of raindrops. This convergence is tense and beautiful.

In the scene in act 4 in Olympe's salon, the dark wine-red color of the room, echoed in the gowns of the women, gives off a strange sense of beauty, like the flow of congealed blood. This device too is effective. The sense of dissipation and passion, even destruction, that fills the atmosphere of the salon converges with the anxiety conjured up by the color red to create an overwhelming sense of tension.

Indeed, it can be said that, in this production at least, the talents of the director confine themselves to what amounts to a series of still life stage pictures; there is little attempt to ferret out or expand on the internal dynamics of the work. Measured against the totality of any truly successful theatre experience, the direction here rises to the occasion only fitfully.

The same can be said of the performers, who reveal their talents only

Bandō Tamasaburō as Marguerite in the 1978 Nissei Theatre production of *The Lady of the Camellias* by Alexandre Dumas Fils. (Photo courtesy of Shōchiku.)

in fits and starts. Those who take up the minor roles have been drawn from among those actors who usually perform smaller roles in regular modern theatre companies; their performances betray no powerful fires; all they can do is provide a competent and reliable framework for the principals. Tachikawa Mitsuki as Armand is solid; he makes no errors and is appropriately youthful. Yet he lacks precisely the kind of magnetism surely required for the role. Kiki Kirin, who plays Prudence, gives a debased performance, worthy only of a soap opera, and it is no wonder that many in the audience were forced to laugh at her portrayal. In short, none of the supporting players gave a performance that was truly inspired, as the material requires.

But, of course, the whole production was created, after all, so that Tamasaburō's Marguerite could wring our hearts. And I must admit that Tamasaburō did create one of those dazzlingly glamorous stages presences for which he is renowned. Yet his portrayal never moved beyond the glitter, never focused in on any underlying, half-hidden sense of beauty. Compared to the standards of truly brilliant performance, Tamasaburō's performance was variable at best.

Tamasaburō certainly called on all of his many and various skills as a performer. As his Marguerite unfolded before us, he seemed to be presenting us with a series of variations on his vision of the crumbling heroine. Thus her beauty would be revealed in a series of poses, head thrown back, or a sense of her failing health conveyed by the way he moved his hands or moved an object.

Unluckily, whatever the situation—whether being visited by misfortune, or being reproached, or falling sensuously onto the chaise longue, or even dying in Armand's arms—Tamasaburō's Marguerite seemed continually to be sinking, albeit with a beautiful, floating languor, as though her very life force were being consumed from within. Her swoons were not those that come at the end of one's strength, when the various energies of mind and body vie with each other, collide with each other. What we are shown is rather a simple slipping away, a gasping for breath, an instant of feeble beauty, like a butterfly caught on a pin, a congealed specimen of beauty. It might well be said that we are given here various idealized visions of enfeebled beauty from among which to choose. The gestures, even the various passions revealed, seem to mimic some perfect model as they are calmly set out, one after the other, for inspection. Even the device of the white petals of the camellia pinned to her breast fluttering down in such profusion is duplicated again and again, as a variation on the aesthetics of enfeebled beauty. Now it was time for *me* to gasp for breath.

The special beauty of Tamasaburō's performance comes from the skill of artifice, devolved, in my mind, from an aesthetics of quotation. It is the opposite of that kind of simple beauty that flows naturally from the soul of a living person; it is a beauty, rather, that creates pleasure from the art of calculation. In that regard, Tamasaburō's performance is quite different from one that is built from within. Here the performance constructs itself from an exaggeratedly grandiose repertoire of quotation.

What I witnessed therefore was Tamasaburō himself and, within him, an elegance constructed from a sense of the frailty of true beauty. Nevertheless, even on the basis of such a conception constructed from bits and pieces instead of from a unified concept of the whole character, there is no denying that the results are striking and possess their own keen and vivid charm.

Perhaps it is his concentration on momentary details rather than on the role as a whole that prevents Tamasaburō from manifesting in his portrayal of Marguerite some broader theatrical reach or powerful attachment. He certainly manages to show the various layers of emotion that exist in the role, but, faced with this heroine's simple devotion, he has largely forfeited the chance to convince us of its fascinating power. When Tamasaburō plays evil women, such as those in the *kabuki* plays of Tsuruya Namboku, or the princess in the celebrated 1917 ghostly melodrama *The Castle Tower* by Izumi Kyōka, or Shakespeare's Lady Macbeth, he fills such parts with vibrant life, yet in any more modestly feminine role such as Desdemona in Shakespeare's *Othello* his artistry seems weakened. In the case of Marguerite, who is, after all, a nineteenth-century high-class courtesan, there is no question that she is a naïf. Yet it has been denied this actor the power to portray the simplicity of her willingness to die for love—the central point on which the drama turns and precisely what fascinates us so about Marguerite. Nothing more is left Tamasaburō than the creation of isolated moments of beauty.

It is certainly not my intention to criticize this production on the basis of the beauty of the particulars that it shows. Yet, if I may side for a moment with Rousseau, this production of *The Lady of the Camellias* can reveal to us at best only a generic model.

I do not accept Rousseau's critical theories about the theatre. It seems to me absurd to apply everyday moral judgments to the theatre, which of course draws its essential energy from the unusual. Rousseau was speaking out against what he saw as the evils of the theatre of France in his day. Still, his very conception betrays his attraction to the form—theatre (for him, the French theatre) gives its victories not to the glittering brave ones of this world but to the worst human beings of us all. Nevertheless, Rousseau's critique, paradoxically, can give us material with which to reflect on the state of contemporary Japanese theatre.

Not only does the theatre derive its sustenance from the unusual, but it has the ability to penetrate beyond a rational sense of the good in order to seek out the very territory of evil. The theatre reveals that it can dig below the apparently healthy surface of everyday life and reveal the strange passions that exist there, seemingly unrelated to the normalities of ordinary existence. The illumination gained, therefore, from an eerie and peculiar passion or illness, created through the perilous art of human performance, can allow the theatre to make important discoveries about the human condition that can truly reach us, the spectators.

Yet, among all the plays being performed these days in theatres large and small, how many can show the requisite strength, even in their "evil" manifestations? How many can truly celebrate the glamorous victories of the "evil ones," so as to give us a fresh look at human nature and the human condition? On the contrary, as spectators we seem to have far too much contact with those sorts of ambiguous plays that, rather than giving rise to the creative powers and energies necessary to combat Rousseau's critique, seem rather to incline toward his dictum, "When we see a play, it does not draw close to us but moves further away."

To put the matter in another way, as we perfect and polish a sense of detail and refinement, we seemingly succeed merely in weakening our ability to pose crucial questions concerning the human condition. The more we crave and pursue some sort of elegant brilliance, the less we seem to find the spirit to raise the questions that for our own sakes we must ask.

We find ourselves now in an environment where, insofar as we seek the beauty of detail and the refinement of a moment, we can discover no relation between the parts, which in turn might help our comprehension of the whole. Indeed, we already make up a part of that environment. "The rapture and unease generated by the beauty of individual moments"—as I watched the beautifully wilting art of Tamasaburō's performance, such were the thoughts that came to me.

Scene III: 1980–1987
The Period of Metatheatre

Significant changes came to the Japanese contemporary theatre in 1980. National and local government became more tolerant of these theatrical activities, and, hoping to improve its image, big business began subsidizing individual artists and companies. A number of large and well-equipped theatres were opened with the help of such subsidies, and the number of small companies operating in Tokyo grew to an astonishing degree. More and more productions were also underwritten by the private sector.

In this milieu, such hitherto small companies as Noda's Dream Wanderers, Kōkami Shōji's Third Stage, and others began to attract large audiences. The plays written for these companies could no longer be considered as minor "experiments," and they were now composed for more diverse audiences.

In the midst of this explosion, the small groups whose work is described in the reviews that follow surely deserve special mention. Their productions ranged from those close in spirit to the commercial modern theatre to the experiments of such groups as the Freedom Boat Company and Pappa TARAHUMARA.

The 1980s also brought forth a profusion of dramas that might be considered metatheatre, nesting boxes of plays within plays. In one sense, these dramas might be considered strategies to construct multifaceted and precise critiques of contemporary culture; yet many of these metadramas, which set out to create universes of their own, were in and of themselves reflections of the floating and unsettled nature of the times.

Beginning with Suzuki's Toga festival in 1982, and continuing with the first Tokyo International Theatre Festival in 1988, similar special productions and performances began to spring up all over the country. In addition, such directors as Suzuki and Ninagawa began to send their companies and productions overseas, usually garnering successful reviews. At the same time, more and more troupes from abroad, particularly those presenting foreign musicals, toured Japan. The rise in the value of the yen on international markets made it easier—indeed, almost a matter of course—to "import" foreign directors to prepare Japanese-language productions mounted by commercial troupes, both in Tokyo and elsewhere.

In the midst of all this excitement and activity, however, one quiet change also came about: the older generation of drama companies began to disappear. Terayama Shūji's company, the Peanut Gallery, was dissolved on his death in 1983. Kara Jūrō's company ceased performing in 1988, after he divorced his wife, the Korean-born actress Ri Reisen. Ōta Shōgo dissolved his company during the same season. For that "first generation," a corner of their bright sky was to become dull and empty.

28. MACBETH IN A FOREST OF CHERRY TREES

NINAGAWA Macbeth

Written by William Shakespeare

Directed by Ninagawa Yukio,

translated by Odashima Yūshi

A NISSEI THEATRE PRODUCTION

1980

Shakespeare with a Buddhist altar and a forest of cherry trees in full bloom: once the idea of this curious mixture was born, Ninagawa's production was already half realized.

We sat, listening as music from the Sanctus of the Fauré *Requiem* floated by in all its exquisite softness. The stage of the Nissei Theatre was filled with that enormous, black Buddhist altar, its doors opening in a gentle and easy fashion, while, behind the scrim, the cherry trees glittered in full bloom as the wind began to stir the blossoms. In terms of these profoundly sensual impressions at least, Shakespeare's own vision was truly reborn within our own culture.

Such efflorescence, however, by no means conveyed a sense of fullness or health—for, as the novelist Sakaguchi Ango wrote, in the midst of a forest of flowers, men can go mad.

What was the anxiety that seemed to cut into us, happy under that line of nodding, blossoming trees? What was the shadow of a chill that spread into the audience, rendering hollow all this beauty? Of course, we have the term *flower chill,* a sensation created when the flowers bloom early and the weather is still chilly; but such was not the case here. The forest has fallen silent, absolutely still; suddenly, "a wind roars through it, despite the fact there is no movement." So Ango has described the awakening to this uncanny sensation.

This stage picture speaks to a basic sense of beauty in Japanese culture, an image that always shows a double meaning: extravagance and unease, life and death, triumph and corruption, eternity and the moment, flourishing and silence, the sublime and the coarse. The composite qualities of all

126

these rhythms were rendered with great theatricality on the stage, so that the theatrical space created in this Ninagawa production could indeed be explicitly labeled "Macbeth in a Forest of Flowers."

Two images: the domineering black of the huge Buddhist altar and the layering of the blowing blossoms. The erotic fusion of death and life was astonishingly effective, creating a strong impression on the audience's sensibilities. Yet our reactions were by no means merely in response to some ideological vision. While the sensibility that moved us was aesthetic, the flavor of the production arose rather from the what one critic has called "the viscera of our spirit." In other words, this was no *Macbeth* that came to us as a visitation, a drama from outside our culture. We took in this story of Macbeth and his consort as something from within us, a kind of internal memory emerging from that huge altar decorating the stage.

Ninagawa's direction followed a consistent strategy from the start, separating with clarity the important moments from the incidental. There was a particularly good example of this in the final scene, just at the death of Macbeth (played by Hira Mikijirō). As he fought, now one lone figure against a host of enemies, a shockingly large, red moon floated into view. Then, at the moment Macduff (played by Yokouchi Tadashi) struck Macbeth down with his sword, the moon abruptly turned pale. In that gathering

Hira Mikijirō as Macbeth in the 1980 Nissei Theatre production of *NINAGAWA Macbeth.*

darkness, Macbeth, lying flat on the ground, was visible in a single ray of light that pierced the gathering darkness, as he slowly pulled in his arms and legs as though he were a fetus, seemingly content to die. Macbeth seemed to be retreating to the sky as to a womb; the universality of human life, and death, was powerfully conveyed as a sensation common to all of us who witnessed it.

Kurihara Komaki was an exceptional Lady Macbeth. Heretofore, she has not always recognized her theatrical potential in performance, but on this occasion she showed a remarkable luster. Not that she played Lady Macbeth as an elegant aristocrat. On the contrary, this Lady Macbeth's upbringing was rough; she is churlish, and she seems all too anxious to seize power from her husband. Hers is a fascinating presentation of a despicable personality. "You are unmanly," she says, as though slapping her husband's cheeks. Surely this is the first time in the performance history of this play that Lady Macbeth has been presented in quite this striking a fashion.

During that final scene, in which Macbeth is surrounded in battle, was heard the continuous sounds of pistols firing. The sound was surely much like that made by the kind of tear gas weapons used these days by mobile police troops. From the 1960s into the 1970s, when Ninagawa himself was producing a series of radical dramas with two small troupes, he must have heard those very sounds time and again on the Tokyo streets. (Later, according to what Ninagawa himself told me, what we heard was the sound of the kind of tear gas guns used against the students who barricaded themselves inside Tokyo University in 1969.) At this point in time, as these sounds piled up one on top of another, it did not seem to me that their meaning remained quite so profound. Still, as those muffled sounds reached our ears, Ninagawa's own opposition to the repressive politics of those years, his dreams of resistance, lying somewhere at the bottom of his heart, seemed somehow still apparent, however dimly we might now perceive them.

29. A DUCK WITH TWO DIFFERENT WINGS

The Seagull

Written by Anton Chekhov

Directed by Michael Bogdanov,

translated by Kurahashi Ken

A TŌHŌ PRODUCTION

Directed by Andrei Serban,

translated by Suwa Tadashi

THE FOUR SEASONS THEATRICAL COMPANY

1980

Are these truly two productions of the same work? I found myself vaguely mumbling after seeing these two productions, for they were as different as they could possibly be.

The journalists dubbed this the "War of the Gulls" since the productions were staged simultaneously in two different theatres in Tokyo. The Geijitsuza brought in Michael Bogdanov, from the National Theatre of Great Britain, to direct, the Nissei Theatre the Rumanian-born Andrei Serban, now so active in Europe and the United States.

It is certainly true that this is a period in which our views of Chekhov are changing. It was thus no surprise that I had high expectations for these two versions of the play.

Yet what was the result? If it were a question of the presentation of a fresh and stimulating point of view, I would unhesitatingly give the prize to Serban. His production, so full of humor, was conceived altogether in accord with Chekhov's explicit dictum that *The Seagull* is "a comedy in four acts." Filled to overflowing with bold ideas, the production revealed a keen sense of beauty. The actors in the Four Seasons Company, who perhaps lacked the scale and grandeur of personality necessary to sustain such an interpretation, mitigated to some extent the power of the directors' vision; still, there was no doubt but that the result was one of blinding originality. In contrast to Serban's, Bogdanov's realistic production presented a dark stage picture; his version was scrupulously reliable but lacked freshness, sparkle.

Serban's direction took two major approaches. The first involved Chekhov's specific conception of the play as a comedy; indeed, the director's intention seemed in places to be to turn the play into out-and-out farce. The direction therefore emphasized the exaggeration inherent in the text and the cartoon-like aspects of the play, making the gestures and actions of the characters conspicuously comic—a daring experiment, one that anticipates the criticism that one needn't "go all that far." Take, for example, the way in which Mita Kazuyo played the role of Masha. Serban sought a character whose inner excess of enthusiasm and flexibility turns into comic excess, and Mita's clowning revealed this vividly.

Had the other performers portrayed their characters in a similarly comic fashion, the result would have been a delightful ensemble. They did not, however. Their performances—especially that of Arkadina (played by Fujino Setsuko)—were awkward and overly one-dimensional. Any sense of softer emotions or spirituality—of the human oppression and suffering—so often privileged in productions of Chekhov was thus ruthlessly expunged, creating an acerbic comedy, one where the humor is all on the surface and the characters, essentially hollow inside, are free to float, glittering, before our eyes.

Along with this basic "comicalization" of the play, Serban also emphasizes the discrepancies between the various levels that exist in every phase of human activity. What is most theatrical in Chekhov's art (what is most comic, one might add, since it amounts to the same thing) is his sense of how human beings never manage to find a way to connect with one another, of how disjunctures inevitably appear between their words, their bodies, and their hearts. Serban is able to take these slippages and spread them brilliantly before us, enlarging comically the sense of the play.

One clever example that caught my attention was the way in which the painful gap in the love of the writer Trigorin (played by Kusaka Takeshi) and Nina (played by Kuno Akiko) was revealed. Chekhov's own stage directions indicate that Trigorin is always writing memos in a notebook, collecting material for his novel. In Serban's version, however, this note taking becomes "memo fever." Trigorin never lays aside his notebook, even for an instant; everything he sees must be recorded. And, as a result, he appears more than eccentric.

As far as Trigorin is concerned, reality exists only if it has already been recorded in his notebook. Therefore, in the scene in act 2 in which he again encounters Nina, he must consult his notebook in order to remember her appearance from the week before: "Ah, can I remember? . . . Yes, you were wearing a stark white dress." (Needless to say, there is no such stage direction in the original.) Then again, when the curtain comes down on this act, despite the fact that the moment is intended to represent a love scene

Andrei Serban's 1980 production of Chekhov's *The Seagull* for the Four Seasons Theatrical Company. Ichimura Masachika as Konstantin *(to the left)* and Kuno Akiko as Nina *(to his right)*.

between Trigorin and Nina, Trigorin must stop to take note of her appearance: "Those beautiful eyes, that gentle, beautiful smile. . . ." (not in the original either). In the end, Trigorin's passion for Nina represents no more than an experience to be recorded in his notebook. And, while Nina appears to love this middle-aged writer—or, more precisely, this apparition of a writer, at least as far as he himself is concerned—passionately, she represents to him no more than the "topic of a short story." Or, more precisely, Nina exists because Trigorin has his short story.

Serban's direction emphasizes these perverted situations, and their humorous aspects certainly invite the audience's laughter. Yet that laughter is poignant. Chekhov's literary genius allows us to connect with the characters as human beings. There can be few in the audience who, in laughing at the absurdities on stage, can honestly feel that none of the satire applies to them. All too often theatre people allow the play and the world of the theatre to become their primary reality, the real world receding to little more than background and therefore becoming that much harder to grasp. Because Serban understands this reversal so well, he can force us to laugh at Trigorin with his memos as an extension of ourselves. He penetrates into our very being.

The second device of which Serban makes use is the lake. At the beginning of act 1, Chekhov writes explicitly that "the lake cannot be seen." But this audacious experiment goes far beyond anything suggested by Chekhov's stage directions. Not only has Serban created part of the lake on the stage—he uses real water and sand, and the light reflected from the tiny waves invests the set with a sense of magic—but he has also given the lake a role to play in the drama. Just as Doctor Dorn (played by Mizushima Hiroshi) says at the end of the first act, this fascinating, "seductive lake" dominates the drama.

As the play progresses, it is clear that the lake in no way functions merely as a background. It manipulates the characters; it represents the reflection of something deep, gigantic, that rules over all of them in a frightening fashion. When characters move close to the lake, they open their hearts, and love blossoms; when they move away from it, Trigorin's capricious affection begins to wither, for example, and Nina's career as an actress encounters ever more obstacles. Thus, when in the final act Nina returns to her old home, it seems more than anything else the lake, that fountainhead, that powerful life force, that has pulled her back. The bloody ghost of Konstantin (played by Ichimura Masachika), who has managed to commit suicide with his pistol, walks soundlessly at the back of the stage, then sinks to the bottom of the lake, certainly a moment without authorial sanction. A scene like this, created certainly for shock value, seems also meant to show that Konstantin's soul has returned to the lake, and, in the flow of this production, it has a persuasive power. The lake itself might be considered to correspond to the forest on the outskirts of Athens in Shakespeare's *A Midsummer Night's Dream.* The powerful and bewitching "charm" of this lake has been created on stage in what might be described as the most "fashionable" possible terms, an impression strengthened by the effective costumes created by Kanamori Kaoru.

In a pamphlet prepared for a 1978 production of *The Cherry Orchard* by Tokyo's Four Seasons Theatrical Company, Serban emphasized that "there are two sets of words involved in the theatre": "the words which manifest themselves in the dialogue itself" and "the true words, which are hidden beneath that dialogue." For him, the second set of words is the more important. In his direction, Serban mixes both layers, creating a visual representation of the "hidden words." Since that production of *The Cherry Orchard,* Serban's application of this kind of excessive directorial technique to the plays of Chekhov has been considered a blow to the deeply rooted deification of Chekhov so common until now. Perhaps. But I find this excess altogether fascinating. I believe that, if we are to find a renewed vitality and freshness in these texts, we must move beyond the narrow confines of "correct" interpretation. We must search as widely and deeply as possible if we are to attain the rich and complex world that Chekhov has created.

Of particular interest to me was the staging of the lines spoken by Nina in act 1 (and repeated by her in act 4) in the play-within-a-play written by Konstantin:

> Men and lions, partridges and eagles, spiders, geese, and antlered stags, the unforthcoming fish that dwelt beneath the waters, starfish and creatures invisible to the naked eye; in short—all life, all life, all life, its dismal round concluded, has guttered out.

The scene takes place on a temporary outdoor stage, and Nina's delivery is foolish and flat, a perfect comic imitation of the way in which Arkadina herself speaks throughout the play. The effect is simply amusing. By the time the lines are repeated in the fourth act, however, Nina and Konstantin have abandoned their "radiant, sunny" lives, and for the first time the true meaning of the speech becomes apparent. The passage, which describes the "uncanny," the "cold," and the "declining," represents the very state of their souls. The lines are delivered very slowly and disjointedly. The direction, accentuating as it does a sense of rupture, sheds a sharp comic light on the way in which we proceed through our own ordinary lives.

If we compare Serban's direction and its new discoveries to Bogdanov's "reliable" interpretation, the latter leaves us feeling incomplete. Cer-

Michael Bogdanov's 1980 production for Tōhō of Chekhov's *The Seagull*. Kurihara Komaki *(seated)* is Nina; Kondō Masaomi is Konstantin.

tainly Bogdanov fails to show us, unlike Serban, the hidden aspects of Chekhov's text.

This is not to say that Bogdanov does not make use of fresh devices nowhere to be found in Chekhov's original stage directions. In the area surrounding the space used by the actors, steel frames stand close together. As the play progresses, this eerie forest of steel poles grows thicker, quickly shrinking the space in which humanity, as represented by the characters in the play, can live. The play was written during a period of rapid industrialization and violent social change. To suggest these ruptures, the stage has been dressed in a peculiar green, which is literally invaded as the drama progresses.

This concept is indeed a bold one. During the blackouts that cover the changes of scenery, the horrible noise of construction work rings out, and the stagehands, wearing construction helmets, move mechanically as they go about their work, surely a remarkable and stimulating spectacle in a Chekhov play.

The difficulty is making a connection between the invading forest of metal and the concerns of the characters themselves. According to the explanation provided by the director, Konstantin does not commit suicide of his own volition; his death is the inevitable result of the violent destruction of the natural world wrought by the industrialization of Russia. Such an interpretation is scarcely justified by the plot of the play itself. Even in terms of Serban's "hidden" text, this interpretation seems forced.

The performances of the actors in this production appear a bit slack. The most interesting is that of Kurihara Komaki as Nina. In the fourth act, her acting, a veritable outpouring of cruelty, is far more effective than that of her counterpart in Serban's production, and, within the limits imposed by the director's vision of the play, such an interpretation shows that Bogdanov has a fresher sense of the role's meaning than does Serban.

Until these productions, the interpretation usually given to Nina's situation in the last act is that, despite bad luck and poverty, she has at last found her footing as an actress, and the role is played in this fashion. Kurihara's Nina, however, shows us a woman without talent caught in the cruelest of situations; she delivers the famous line "I am an actress" in a fashion that reveals a terrible disjunction, one in which only the words themselves are beautiful.

This interpretation of Nina, in which the end of the play shows a closing in of some unbearable, cruel darkness, seems to me so much more suitable than a final curtain presented in a light or comic fashion. After all, Chekhov was a courageous writer of comedies, a man who pointed in this particular play called a "comedy" to a cruel darkness that is indeed difficult for us to bear.

30. A DIFFUSED REFLECTION

Travel of Twenty-seven Thousand Light Years

Written and directed by Noda Hideki

THE DREAM WANDERERS

1980

Among the various notable young writers working in the theatre today, there are few as facile and amusing as Noda Hideki, the head of the Dream Wanderers, a playwright possessing a talent whose reflections penetrate everywhere. Noda spins out dialogue that is chatty, filled with the energy of his quick wit. His conceptions often involve the play of rhyming words, and he tumbles things about again and again in order to create a sense of surprise. His dramas, in which all sorts of situations pile up together, give his audiences the sense that he skips three, if not four sections at a time, leaving them with an amusing impression of a brilliant and virtually limitless

The 1980 production by the Dream Wanderers of Noda Hideki's *Travel of Twenty-seven Thousand Light Years.* Noda himself *(at the left)* with two other members of his company, Saegusa Kiwami *(center)* and Sadoi Kenta *(right).*

scattering. The greatest pleasure to be gained from these plays involves the arbitrary magnifications and deviations that he creates as he jokes with the surface of things, seemingly endlessly.

Nevertheless, when one of his plays moves toward its conclusion, certain motifs that have heretofore been scattered in various layers suddenly come together; indeed, many of his productions end on a surprisingly serious, lyric note. The audience is thus left with a sense of surprise, realizing that the true talent of this playwright has been to create before us a realistic reflection of a complex world out of seemingly arbitrary parts.

Noda is more than just a playwright. He is the head of his troupe (founded in April 1976), he is a director, and he remains the chief performer in this crazy group of talented actors. In this sense, he is blessed with a total theatrical talent, calling to mind an older figure such as Kara Jūrō.

Noda was born in 1955. I first saw him on stage in October 1976 in the second production mounted by a new student troupe at Tokyo University, the Dream Wanderers. In order to seek out and encourage new talent, Tsuka Kōhei had sponsored a competition for young, unknown troupes at Van 99 Hall in Aoyama in Tokyo. Of the seventeen groups who entered, two —one of them the Dream Wanderers—were chosen to give special presentations of their work at Tsuka's theatre. The play that the Dream Wanderers performed, *Run Merusu: Do You Like the Burning Underwear?* (written by Noda and directed by Takahagi Hiroshi), was full of movement and speed. I was amazed by the unmistakable talents shown by the troupe and, in particular, by the feelings conveyed by the clever use of all those words that spouted forth. In the midst of such frenzy, Noda himself, who appeared on the stage as a comic *onnagata*, a *kabuki*-style female impersonator, directed a production that seemed a kind of miracle in and of itself.

Since that time, Noda's company has staged two productions a season; and, with performances of Noda's plays, in which his spectators seldom know what to expect, his audiences have expanded. In particular, in the fall of 1979, with the troupe's production of *Boy Hunt*, staged by the director Shinozaki Mitsumasa, who had been especially invited for the purpose, a real turning point was achieved.

Then came the production of *Travel of Twenty-seven Thousand Light Years*, written and directed by Noda himself. The work was a thoroughly revised version of a play staged three years before and similarly titled; the new production revealed yet another delightful sample of Noda's great skills.

The plot line is constructed in a way that undercuts ordinary dramatic conventions. Rather than beginning at the beginning and moving from there directly to the end, it instead follows myriad, seemingly unrelated paths, scattering its meaning here and there as it moves along, its true beginning known only after the audience has struggled along to the end. In fact, the story turns out to be serious, even pathetic. And, because the serious elements that it contains anchor the narrative, the author has felt free to skip about as lightly as he pleases.

The play concerns a shocking case of cannibalism and is based on *A Eucharist in the Andes,* an account of the experiences of the passengers of a plane forced to land in the Andes. While on the surface the play jokes about "eating people," underneath it is concerned with the way in which humans, on a basic level, really do devour each other. Such at least is the basic contrivance, one fully typical of Noda.

The story concerns forty-odd young people stranded in the Andes. Two young men among them, "the Nameless One" (played by Noda) and "the Warrior" (played by Enjōji Aya), strike out west, seeking help. But, before they go, the group takes an oath—committed to paper and signed in blood, an oath so strong it requires them to eat their own fingers—that, if help does not arrive, they will eat the Nameless One's younger sister. Help does not arrive in the time agreed on, and the girl dies, but the two young men who sought help are rescued. The play tells the story of these two young men. By its end, the Nameless One carries the emotional burden, not only of his sister's death, but of the Warrior's as well.

In comparison to the brilliance of the mad scramble that has preceded, the final scene seems saturated in a kind of classical lyricism. The author seems to conceive of it as crystallizing a moment crucial to an understanding of the psychology of young people. My only complaint is that, no matter how lyric or pathetic this final moment may be, the tale that the play tells is in the end not particularly profound, at least as far as what it reveals about basic human nature.

The performers are all quite youthful; most are highly skilled and give great pleasure. Noda's own frenzy is as striking as ever, and both Saegusa Kiwami and Enjōji Aya exude a fascinating charm. In sum, the kind of theatrical speed and energy that this troupe can summon up is rare indeed.

31. DECIPHERING MIYAZAWA KENJI
WITH CRITICISM AND SYMPATHY

The Theatre Train of Iihatōbo

Written by Inoue Hisashi

Directed by Kimura Kōichi

THE MAY TROUPE

1980

In the spring of 1980, I had the opportunity to make a trip to Indonesia with Inoue Hisashi. This was just after he had finished the first half of his play *The Theatre Train of Iihatōbo.*

This was the first time we had ever traveled together. After visiting Jakarta, Jogjakarta, and Solo on the main island, we flew to Bali, where we saw dance plays presented over a series of several days, listened to gamelan music, and visited famous ruins and well-known temples. It was an exalting, extremely happy time. Both of us had visited Indonesia before, but this time we felt somehow possessed, and our fascination with the culture of Southeast Asia grew to a fever pitch.

What surprised me most during the trip was Inoue's passion for note taking. In the airport, in the hotel, even while concentrating on the dances and the music or touring the ruins, he took notes diligently and tirelessly. Everything was fixed and set down in his notebook; all that he saw, everything he heard, every perception of the world around him, became part of his written record.

Inoue was particularly good at illustrating his notes; for example, he carefully sketched the splendid ruins at Borobodur and Pramabanan, and he even went so far as to copy the label on a bottle of Indonesian-made beer. He seemed to me driven by a stubborn streak, one that forced him to record on paper, even to excess, every aspect of reality with which he came in contact. Inoue is blessed with extravagant powers of imagination, but he is the type of writer who is always aware of the fact that his imagination risks losing sight of the real world. Thus, he proceeds with care as he writes. He is not one who is happy to dance just as he pleases, high above the ground.

Given his disposition and posture as an artist, Inoue's new play, *The Theatre Train of Iihatōbo*, directed by Kimura Kōichi, made a strikingly fresh impression. Until now, Inoue's works have been biographies of histor-

Inoue Hisashi's *The Theatre Train of Iihatōbo,* produced by the May Troupe in 1980. Satō Kei as Miyazawa Kenji's father *(on the left)* and Yazaki Shigeru as the young poet himself *(on the right).*

ical figures. This play is no exception, in the sense that it is based on the life of the poet Miyazawa Kenji (1896–1933). Miyazawa himself studied agriculture with the hope of helping the poor farmers in northern Japan, where he was born. Inoue has rendered certain periods in Miyazawa's life with great fidelity and in painstaking detail. Nevertheless, his use of a number of striking devices and techniques places the play firmly in the kind of theatrical world that he himself as a playwright inhabits. The production made a profound, an unforgettable impression on me, for it captures the unique glow of those works of Miyazawa's that I myself so love to read. Along with Inoue's *Kobayashi Issa* of 1979, which dealt with the life of that celebrated eighteenth-century haiku poet, this is one of this popular playwright's most impressive achievements.

During his short life, Miyazawa Kenji (played by Yazaki Shigeru) made the trip from northern Japan to Tokyo nine times and even lived there briefly. Inoue creates a superbly lively and comic treatment this short and intense period in Kenji's life by focusing on the poet's fourth visit to Tokyo—the one that proved to be such a turning point in his life—and particularly on the atmosphere inside the car on the night train to Tokyo. This is the first of three theatrical devices that makes the play so successful.

The second device is that, while the night train, which occupies such an important place in the staging of the drama, represents a telescoped version of the poet's life, it also serves as an improvisational theatre for the souls of those poor farmers of northern Japan who have abandoned this world and are moving on to the next. In this way, an image of Miyazawa Kenji is created by those farmers who "play" the poet who, despite his deep interest in country people and in their artistic possibilities, never did become a farmer himself. The portrait thus created of Miyazawa Kenji is both affectionate and critical. Many who write about him fall into the trap of adopting an extreme view, one of either uncritical praise or unnecessary severity. Inoue has constructed his play, however, in a wonderfully clever way, avoiding such extremes through the evolution of an alert, synthetic spirit that contains both elements. In doing so he has created an accurate portrait of the poet, one that shows us his virtues and his weaknesses simultaneously.

The third device is the way in which the farmers on the night train lead the audience into the mental world of the poet Miyazawa Kenji, since they serve as characters in his well-known children's story *Night Train to the Milky Way*. The "Tall Conductor Who Wears a Red Hat" (played by Matsukuma Nobuyoshi), who functions with such energy throughout the whole play, serves as the "Conductor to the Stars." The last scene of the play, in which the dead bodies of the farmers are borne up on the rapid night train, against a background of the Milky Way in the night sky, led on with such gentleness by the conductor, is one of the most beautiful moments in the whole drama.

Inoue himself, so much bound to this earth, surely wanted to convey the message that, however much their thoughts and desires might remain unfulfilled, Miyazawa Kenji put his faith in them. The theme is repeated again and again, as Inoue pours out one pregnant phrase after another: "In Japan, we have no more need for farming villages now"; "Farmers, face away from the cities . . ."; "The cities can be of no help to you now . . ."; "Farmers, work for self-support and self-sufficiency . . ."; "Soldiers, prostitutes, and rice, this is what the villages have largely had to offer. Now it's time to stop all that. . . ."

This play continues in the same vein as Inoue's 1979 *Kobayashi Issa*, in which he also takes a critical view of city life. As far as I am concerned, born as I was in a city and having lived only in an urban environment, his conclusions appear so weighty and significant that I find it impossible to comment on them.

32. THE BACHELORS WHO
CONTINUE ON

That Raven, Even

Written and directed by Takeuchi Jū'ichirō

THE MYSTICAL ZERO TROUPE

1980

Takeuchi Jū'ichirō is a playwright who does not perform his tricks in any ordinary, run-of-the-mill fashion. The troupe with which he formerly worked disbanded last year; this fall, his new group, the Mystical Zero Troupe, made its debut with the kind of thrilling and puzzle-ridden production that is rare indeed. To say that much, however, is not to suggest that to watch *That Raven, Even* may cause undue confusion. From the beginning of his career, each of Takeuchi's stage works has happily romped its way past audiences in a highly entertaining, if curious and unorthodox, fashion. Yet, while we laugh along with him, there always comes an instant when, in the midst of his gleeful comedy, we are struck by the sense that a vivid, deeper, often painful subject lies hidden beneath his facile devices.

This opening production of Takeuchi's new company (reportedly named for a tarot card motif) is filled with such devices and tricks. The events on stage are playful and the conception amusing. Yet, while *That Raven, Even* does maintain a light and bantering tone, we do catch the sense of a surprising undercurrent just before the final curtain falls.

The present production takes its basic tricks, beginning with the title, from the work of the celebrated Dada artist Marcel Duchamp (1887–1968), and it does so in a delightfully comic way. The play shows a real chic. The whole text is studded with quotations from the artistic world of the famous French painter. Indeed, the play as a whole seems to embody Duchamp's dictum that people "think too much" when looking at his art. It is in such a context, then, that we must begin to observe the play.

At first glance, the plot seems unexceptional. Three men spend all their time carrying a huge sheet of glass (invisible, of course, to the audience), which seems enormously heavy, and they grouse at each other as they move it from one location to another. That is all that happens. The men are supposedly delivering the glass to someone named "Yamada," but they cannot find his house. Seemingly doomed never to find it, they pass the time in a fashion reminiscent of Beckett's *Waiting for Godot*, stumbling around, complaining about the weight of the glass, arguing with each other, ever in a bad mood.

The 1980 staging by the Mystical Zero Troupe of Takeuchi Jū'ichirō's *That Raven, Even.* Kiba Katsumi, Moriwaka Ryūichi, and Koide Shūji carry that invisible piece of glass. (Photo by Matsunaga Yō.)

The "big glass" that they continuously talk about is in fact a reference to perhaps Duchamp's most famous creation, the large work *The Bride Stripped Bare by Her Bachelors, Even,* which he created over a span of years from 1915 to 1923. The Japanese title of the play involves word games, and the word *even* is tacked onto the title as well, in homage to Duchamp. The "three movers" represent bachelors 1, 2, and 3 of the nine in Duchamp's picture, and they are costumed to resemble them. The fact that there are three movers derives from Duchamp's indication that "the number three is employed as the refrain that continues."

In the center of the stage is a building marked "the Sanjō House." That house has a kitchen door, which is locked. It soon becomes clear that this is what the three men have been referring to as the "Yamada house." It is occupied by a former child singer, now a porn star named Sanjō Harumi. This woman, who corresponds to the "bride" in the Duchamp painting, is featured in a soft-porn series entitled "The Bride Collection." She never appears on stage.

The three men yearn for her (or, at least, their fantasy of her). They keep trying to get into her house, which is surrounded by a fence. Here is evidently suggested an allegory of sexual intercourse, a device that apparently has its origins in a famous "memo" of Duchamp's concerning the painting, in which he indicates that, because of a "refrigerator," the "bachelors" are "separated" from the "bride," who "hotly," not chastely, denies their "intemperate request."

The "Sanjō house" also has a "violent aspect." There are two hoses outside the house, which are leaking; when the men leave, the hoses stop dripping. This scene is also evidently meant to evoke Duchamp's 1945 window display "Lazy Hardware." In the second half of the play, there is a scene in which the men peek into the porn star's house through a hole. And, of course, the sight they see of the reclining nude woman is directly borrowed from this famous painting. And so on, and so on. The more one knows of the hidden meanings in Duchamp's work, the more significant the various moments in the play itself become.

However, there is no denying that *That Raven, Even* contains a number of devices that can be manifested only in the theatre. For example, there is that clear pane of glass, which, thanks to the skill of the "three bachelors," eventually becomes quite real for the audience. True enough, they are carrying nothing more than air, but they take themselves so seriously in every detail that, through the intensity of our own will to believe, their performance makes the glass seem heavier and heavier and so brittle that it might break at the slightest shock. We become convinced that this thrilling piece of glass is absolutely real. Thus the theatrical imagination turns the lie of the glass into the truth.

On the other hand, the second part of the play brings a sudden reversal. Bachelor 2 (played by Koide Shūji) and Bachelor 3 (played by Morikawa Ryūichi) take the glass off stage. Soon Bachelor 1 (played by Kiba Katsumi) staggers on stage carrying the glass, which, as we all know by now, is much too heavy to be carried by one person. In that instant, we suddenly realize that, however heavy the pane of glass may seem to them, it has no more existence than the men themselves do: all are part of the same illusion.

And so it is that the huge glass reverts from being the "truth" to being a "lie."

In the end, our understanding is reversed yet again. A small stone is carelessly thrown, a horrendous noise is heard, and the glass breaks into countless glittering fragments. The next instant, showing no sign of being at all upset by the sudden turn of events, the three men "go off to find another huge glass somewhere else." Bachelor 3 apparently doubts the reality of the glass. Bachelor 1 answers him in a speech that reveals the serious intent that lies beneath the play's humorous surface:

BACHELOR 1: Yeah. . . . I don't really know whether it's there or not . . . but I got used to carrying it, you know. It was the feel of it. . . .

The glass has once again become real. The three men resume their "heavy" burden and carry it through the kitchen door of the house, just where it was intended to go in the first place.

Nothing that the dramatist writes or the performers do—other than pretending to carry the glass—is directly intended to further the illusion. Yet, because of the emotion evoked by the play's simple devices, the huge sheet of glass changes before our very eyes from lie to truth back to lie, a transformation made beautifully manifest on the stage. Through the power of the imagination, nothingness gives birth to reality, surely the most transcendent movement that any drama can create.

The three men, of course, know that this "great glass" is only an illusion. Nevertheless, this fantasy has taken concrete form in their spirits. As Takeuchi writes at the beginning of the published version of his play, "This is not merely a joke. Things that we cannot see can be very heavy indeed."

True and direct exchange between human beings cannot be accomplished so simply. Perhaps, it is suggested here, we can only share among ourselves what amounts to a common illusion, a brittle, heavy "pane of glass" that has actual substance. Therefore, however vexing or amusing we may find this image, our laughter contains within it both a critical spirit and a real sympathy.

However, it should be said as well that much of the appeal of the play lies in the coming and going of the bachelors, in the sharpness of the response we feel to their loneliness, their closeness, their melancholy, in their will to carry on. Although the bachelors know all too well that their work, which is "very heavy indeed," represents an illusion that is itself as frail as glass, it is nevertheless work that they must perform. This "huge glass" that they must treat with such care must somehow be delivered to this "bride," in whom they believe as well. So it is that they show an ability to play on this "refrain that continues." And while that refrain makes full use of the playful devices of Duchamp, it nevertheless attempts to show how man himself can deal with the times in which he lives, thus leaving a fresh and lively impression. This is true for someone even as foolish as me, even.

The energy and wit of the three actors is impressive, and it should be said that the skill of their genial performances remains memorable.

33. DREAMS THAT ARE RUFFIANS

A Tale of Mannen-town in Shitaya

Written by Kara Jūrō

Directed by Ninagawa Yukio

A SEIBU THEATRE PRODUCTION

1981

When I approach a particular play that purports to shock and stimulate, I apply one criterion: there must at some point exist a moment that opens up some door within me, one that can call forth thoughts and feelings of which I had previously been unaware. Then, suddenly, lights begin to burn in some interior territory of which I have only the dimmest of recollections, of which I had no prior consciousness. It is not enough for me to live within the world of the play. At some point, the action on the stage must bear some relation to my own sense of self, of life. Such an experience allows me to go beyond what the director, playwright, and actors can create. It allows me to become a co-collaborator, adding my own vision to theirs. Together, then, we create a new, composite work of art.

Kara Jūrō's new play is directed by Ninagawa Yukio. This effort is their first joint production in seven years. For me personally, the play offered just the sort of experience I described above. Kara's strong script and Ninagawa's alluring staging, so rigorously coordinated, had a truly powerful effect on me. I felt doors opening within me and lights moving, illuminating one dark spot after another. I do, however, not mean to suggest that this production is without flaws. There are portions of the play that are overly verbose, spots that need to be cut, and sections that appear self-indulgent. Yet, even taking these irregularities into account, there is no denying the power of the play as a whole, opening as it does our receptivities to the full. The play brings to mind a statement of Jung's about archetypes, when he writes in his *Modern Man in Search of a Soul* that man "has the sense that he may have grown wings," that he "has a sense that he has the strength to capture eagles."

Such is the case in the first act, when Bunchan, the "Youth" (played by Tsunekawa Hiroyuki), suddenly begins to talk of the huge lizards that Darwin saw on his trip to the Galapagos Islands. The introduction of the subject may seem arbitrary, yet it is by no means unrelated to the play as a whole. This is because, in a work by a playwright like Kara, who speaks in "archetypes," Jungian fables, "we are not individuals; we are a species."

Memory in this play works on a level beneath any sense of individuality and reaches down to "vestiges of a self-generating genealogy." Therefore, by moving parts of the story back "several tens of years" ago in a section of town that has since even been renamed, Kara has created in this Tokyo "Mannen-town in Shitaya" a place where, to borrow Jung's words again, "ancient words echo through ordinary speech." Through his art, Kara is able to define this place as "a domain in which what was once destroyed and has perished is given new life."

Still, what is to be made of the ebullient mania on stage, a recreation of this uproarious "town" in 1948, when "the homosexuals who have come to live there are boisterous, with the tango blaring from their phonographs, dancing around like flies." In front of that "superrealist" set designed by Asakura Setsu, in which real green water ripples in a gourd-shaped pond in front of a two-story tenement house, fully seventy-nine actors, in their midst a group of men dressed in women's clothes, seem to embrace with their whole beings the reverberations of the tango and the outrageously sensual rhythms of the boogie-woogie, so redolent of the unprecedented vitality of those early postwar years just after Japan's defeat in 1945. This music, providing as it does a nostalgic framework, gives the play a rich sense of thickness, of substance. Such a nostalgia is capable of making us virtually swoon away in rapture. Yet, rather than simply using this musical frame in order to push toward the creation of a brittle memory play, Kara has instead provided an overflowing sense of villainous energy, one that agitates us with its vibrant sense of deviant life. I very much liked the phrase that Kara employed in the first act of his 1967 play *Hoffmann of Shitamachi,* in which he spoke of "the dream of a vagrant." In this new play, we are now shown multiple "vagrant dreams, of a vagrant," in which preposterous reveries and recollections, "shaken awake by the town at night and best forgotten," nevertheless now come gushing forth.

Seeing this production, I am reminded of the American writer Albert Finney, whose work also concerns the power of nostalgia. Finney too explores the past; his particular imaginative wanderings lead him to the America of the 1880s and 1890s. Finney's nostalgia, however, contains nothing of Kara's wild energy. Nevertheless, for both writers, the past is not just a lifeless series of events that follow meaninglessly one after the other and are immediately forgotten; rather, the past takes on a life of its own and is capable of coming back to haunt us when we least expect it. If one's emotions are attuned, therefore, to beloved times and places past, the turn of any corner and the sight of a street, perhaps, or a row of houses could very well call forth a strong sense of nostalgia. In this regard, Kara and Finney share the same convictions concerning the power of time to evoke these feelings.

In Kara's play, it is certainly no time machine that transports us back to the past; rather, he uses the astonishing device of a syringe that "removes the air" from the human body. In this scheme of things, young people become adults by having their bodies filled with air, like balloons, a process that leaves behind a "blister of feeling." The process can also be reversed. When, for example, the syringe enters the arm of the "Man" (played by Kara Jūrō himself), "that long air of time" is sucked out, the Man falls asleep inside, and the "Youth" that he was so many decades before returns, saying, "I think that I can get by without sleeping anymore." Thus Kara has found a clear way to set up his sense of that rough "youthful feeling" which is at the center of his concern.

Another device that I found quite effective was the fact that both the "Youth" and the "Young Man" Yōichi (played by Watanabe Ken) were born "owners of a sixth finger." Both retain "a scar in the space between the thumb and the first finger, where something had been cut off in ancient times." This "sixth finger" is crucial to Kara's conception. It is at first explained as a useless growth that has simply been removed. Yet like the past, which is also invisible, this finger has an existence of its own: "It appears in my dreams and makes my heart jump strangely."

In one sense of the word, this "sixth finger" represents deviance, a way of life that is out of the ordinary. We require only the five fingers that we

The 1981 Seibu Theatre production of Kara Jūrō's *A Tale of Mannen-town in Shitaya*. Ohyō (Ri Reisen) addresses the crowd.

normally have; a sixth is useless and can be removed without harm as extraneous. But these "sixth fingers" persist in spirit; in fact, they grow bigger than the other five. This "sixth finger" binds together the "Youth" (Bunchan) and the "Young Man" (Yōichi) and also ties them to Ohyō (Ri Reisen), who is the very incarnation of the "sixth finger." In the third act, Ohyō uses a syringe to grow herself a sixth finger and faces off against Oichi (Shiojima Akihiko) and the group of homosexuals who hold the power in Mannen-town. As she says, this finger "must do something, but I don't know what it is."

The homosexuals of Mannen-town live a life of excess, of deviance, the kind of lifestyle that rejects the democracy sought in the immediate postwar period—hence their ostracization as the tribe of "six-fingered ones." So it is that Ohyō, Bunchan, and Yōichi only appear to oppose Oichi and the other male prostitutes; their opposition is more like a "festival of blood," a family feud. The real opposition comes from the "five-fingered tribe," in the person of the police inspector who single-handedly takes on all the "six-fingered ones." In fact, the real quarrel seems to me to be that between a sense of time in which everything is gently forgotten and buried and that stubborn sense of time maintained by the playwright, who insists on keeping alive a time when life was lived with vigor, excess, and confusion. At the end of the 1960s, Kara wrote, "At present, I have more respect for obstinacy than for amnesia." On that point, at least, his attitude has changed little since then.

The second act is particularly strong. The noisy carnival of the opening scene represents a superbly dynamic accomplishment by the director, involving as it does the amusing quarrel between Ohyō and the male prostitutes. After their happy chorus, there follows an abrupt shift of emotion when, caught up in the brilliant sweep of this energy, Ohyō's pitiful past is revealed. Then too, there is the scene in which Ohyō, poisoned by the drugs she has taken, thinks to play Julien Sorel locked behind iron bars in his prison sickroom, where "I can chase cockroaches." As she barely touches the bed, then crawls around on the floor, we are given a moment of blinding brightness, of striking and cruel humor.

The last scene is adeptly executed as well. The "Youth," who has fallen time after time into the middle of the pond, as he becomes the middle-aged "Man," now goes into the water to exchange places again; his final words are, "Good-bye, you town . . . where the frames still stand for drying clothes . . . ," words so laden with nostalgia that the image sticks with us long afterward.

Even then, the play takes an unexpected last turn. "No, I don't think that I will go back there . . . ," says the Youth, who in the end refuses to slip back into the sleep of his past. He thrusts down into the water again the

"Man," who represents another aspect of himself. In the place of the "Man," who disappears into the water, the drowned "Yōichi" appears, as a sign of the present moment, carrying on his shoulders Ohyō, soaking wet; holding out his hand, he says, in a cheerful voice, "Let's go, Bunchan!"

Here, the past still lives, in every sense. And, more than that, the past of those "six fingers" can push aside the present with its "five" at that instant when life is first truly experienced. In this, Kara's agitation is truly beautiful to behold. The play is not a requiem for lost dreams; rather, it seems a stout hymn of praise.

34. TWO BLANCHES

A Streetcar Named Desire

Written by Tennessee Williams

Directed by Sharon Ott

THE MILWAUKEE REPERTORY THEATRE

1981—Jealousy

Written by Shimizu Kunio

Directed by Fujiwara Shimpei

THE ATELIER OF THE LITERARY

THEATRE

1981

Just what kind of creatures are we human beings, anyway? The various schools of art and philosophy are so numerous because of the many ways in which people have tried to approach this eternal question. Just as the lives that people live are complex, the answers to the question must be complex as well. An answer that seems to have pinned down the basic nature of humanity may be correct in its own way, but at best it can be only a partial answer.

Keeping such limitations in mind, one useful answer might be that "a human being is a creature that spends its existence playacting." Indeed, it would behoove us to think more carefully about our deep-seated urge to perform in our own personal "theatres." Such actions on our part are by no means limited to the sort that might appear on a real stage, set off from everyday reality. We act on the "stage" of our ordinary lives as well. In his *The Presentation of Self in Everyday Life,* Erving Goffman postulates that such roots exist for all human activity; he finds in all cases a connection to the "theatrical." In his view, we are all actors who play our own roles, whether consciously or unconsciously, a situation that perforce gives rise to countless ambiguities.

I have recently seen two plays that take as their basic premise the notion of life as theatre and human beings as players. Tennessee Williams' play reveals a special luminosity that I found particularly satisfying.

The first play, *A Streetcar Named Desire,* was the first production of the Milwaukee Repertory Theatre (MRT) to be seen on their tour of Japan. Sharon Ott directed. The MRT's is the second in a series of tours by non-profit regional theatre groups from the United States; the first was by the American Conservatory Theatre (ACT) of San Francisco in 1967. These productions offer sober and reliable performances, far removed from Broadway glitter; this is a different kind of American theatre, one that flourishes outside New York City.

In recent years, Japanese audiences have acquired a greater apprecia-tion of the high standards of such regional groups; I myself once had occa-sion to see a production at the Arena Stage, the well-known theatre in the round in Washington, D.C., and I was much impressed. While the ACT's choice of repertory caused certain problems and the impression it left was too sober, even pallid, the MRT's production was highly successful, despite a similar propensity for sobriety and orthodoxy.

The scenery (created by Laura Maurer) used by the MRT tended toward the realistic and showed a certain severity: there was little decora-tion, and the colors employed were restrained. When Peggy Cowles first entered, in her nonchalant fashion, I was surprised to see so healthy a Blanche, even at the very start. The actress was quite tall and by no means thin. The darker, eccentric side of her character was not apparent; rather, she carried about her an atmosphere of artless good cheer. She used very little makeup. Compared with the description of her provided by Williams in the stage directions ("she has the kind of beauty that cannot be exposed to the light"; "somehow, she makes one think of a butterfly"), this Blanche seemed too simple, too healthy. Perhaps I reacted this way because of the many occasions on which I had seen the part portrayed by the Literary Theatre's Sugimura Haruko as a self-conscious eccentric. Compared to her

Peggy Cowles as Blanche and Tom Berenger as Stanley in the 1981 Japan touring production of Tennessee Williams' *A Streetcar Named Desire*.

Blanche, Peggy Cowles' seemed almost a normal woman, little inclined to any sudden peculiarity.

Yet, as the play progressed, these various images of Blanche in my mind began to join together, and my sense of uneasiness began to disappear. Peggy Cowles gave a performance punctuated by occasional humor and showed us a Blanche who only appeared healthy but who was all the time crumbling inside, a conception of the character quite different from one that sees her development as the growth of some basic abnormality. Jenni Brenn gave a riveting performance as Blanche's younger sister, Stella, revealing the character's bitter edge. Had she performed the role of Blanche, she might well have given us a heroine much sharper and more pitiful.

Nevertheless, my strongest impression was of a Blanche who from beginning to end "playacted" the part of a human being, doing so in high relief. Take, for example, the way in which she articulated her lines. As opposed to the ordinary speech employed by the other characters in the play, she always spoke in a mannered style, as though she were, verbally speaking, using artful makeup. Those lines that, in the author's words, "bear magic" cannot, of course, be properly rendered in Japanese translation, and previous Tokyo productions of *Streetcar* have therefore, it seems to me, not made such distinctions clear. What is now strikingly clear from Sharon Ott's MRT production is that the play is in some sense a battle of words. And the language that the character uses makes it clear that Blanche strikes a defiant attitude toward those who, beginning with Stanley (played by Tom Berenger), merely use everyday language. Peggy Cowles exaggerates the differences, making her language and speech as broad as possible. As a result, her Blanche seemed the heroine of some classic play, lost and wandering in the vulgarities of everyday reality. The effect is cruel, yet comic. Watching this production, I gained a strong impression that, in so many ways, *Streetcar* is a drama closely aligned to Chekhov's *The Cherry Orchard*.

If I were to define the nature of Blanche's "theatrical existence," I would say that it lies in the aesthetics of magic. In scene 9, Blanche faces Mitch (played by Henry Strozier) and says, "I hate the truth. . . . I prefer magic." She then continues, "I never tell the truth exactly as it is. I state what the truth *ought* to be." Here, she seems to have running through her the strength of a Don Quixote. In the musical version of Don Quixote written by Dale Wassermann, *Man of La Mancha*, Don Quixote has a powerful line, "Facts are the enemy of truth." Blanche's words seem to echo the same insight. Blanche here opposes with all her might the "truth" that must be with her own "performance," a dramaturgy based on her own whimsical spirit, crushing ordinary reality before her like some rolling bulldozer. This image of Blanche in jest, amusing and pitiful at the same time, gives a sense of a painful courage and the energy that accompanies it.

It cannot be said that the MRT production is altogether highly polished or that the direction and the acting open any astonishing new vistas. Yet a production like this one, which puts Blanche's "acting out a life" in such high relief, can bring to life the true beauty of the theatrical world of Tennessee Williams.

The second production I would like to describe is that by the Atelier group of the Literary Theatre of the new Shimizu Kunio play *1981—Jealousy,* directed by Fujiwara Shimpei.

In a word, this is a production in which all the elements of text, direction, and acting have been scrupulously blended. There is nothing flashy, or sensational, to be seen. A high level of energy underlies this careful production, and watching the play gave me an enormous amount of pleasure.

Since the beginning, Shimizu has been well known as a playwright who too conveys a sense of the theatricality of existence in his dramas. Even his one-act plays provide successful vehicles for this vision. And, particularly in this new work, Shimizu seems to echo the world of *Streetcar.* Matsushita Sachiko gives a striking performance as the Elder Daughter, conveying her as at once a humorous and a bedraggled version of Blanche. It was that aspect of the production that I found particularly fascinating.

Shimizu Kunio's *1981—Jealousy,* produced by the Atelier of the Literary Theatre. *From the left:* the Elder Daughter (Matsushita Sachiko), the Husband (Kadono Takuzō), and the Middle-Aged Man (Kanno Naoyuki).

There is not one word in Shimizu's text to suggest any direct connection between his work and Williams'. That connection is one that I have made myself. Still, if one compares the way in which the two plays are constructed, certain parallels suggest themselves.

Look, for example, at the disposition of the characters in the play. First, there is the Elder Daughter (Matsushita Sachiko), who lives alone in her dead parents' house, surviving on a surfeit of illusions. Then there is the Younger Daughter (Ninomiya Sayoko), the reliable type, and her Husband (Kadono Takuzō). Finally, there is the Middle-Aged Man (Kanno Naoyuki), who lives nearby and who shows a great deal of kindness and goodwill toward the Elder Daughter. *Streetcar* is structured around the same constellation of characters: the older, unmarried Blanche; Blanche's younger sister, Stella; Stella's husband, Stanley; and the bachelor, Mitch. The plots of the two plays even follow similar lines: just as a psychiatrist and a nurse come to take Blanche away, a doctor (Shimomura Akihiro) and his nurse (Saitō Shirō) want to put the Elder Daughter in the hospital.

From the beginning of his career, Shimizu Kunio has shown a strong interest in the plays of Tennessee Williams, on whose work he even wrote his graduation thesis. Therefore I cannot help but think that Ms. Matsushita, who until now has performed the role of the younger sister, Stella, in the Literary Theatre productions of *Streetcar,* has now graduated to the role of the elder sister and that Shimizu has created for her his own version of a Blanche. Indeed, there is in the character of the Elder Daughter not only something of Blanche but clearly something also of the delicate Laura of *The Glass Menagerie.*

As in other of Shimizu's plays, the characters in *Jealousy* go on "playing" their lives. The Middle-Aged Man, an eccentric tailor, carries on as though living a lonely monologue. This character, who is passionately fond of films, behaves like Captain Ahab as performed by Gregory Peck in *Moby Dick;* he is James Dean in *East of Eden.* The Younger Daughter's Husband, a university lecturer who is mad about the movies, lives his life the same way; both use the same devices in order to "perform." There is a delightful scene in which the two circle around each other, brandishing pistols, imitating an American western (the script itself does not contain these directions, as it turns out), which sets in high relief the amusing way in which their "playacting" helps their sense of having a good time together.

More important is the continuing, peculiar "peep show" in which the Bachelor and the Elder Daughter surreptitiously engage, despite the fact that their houses are separated by a wall. Of course, in reality, no actual "peeping" can occur. Yet the Elder Daughter harbors the grand delusion that the Bachelor has been observing her steadily for some forty-six hours; he in turn knows this, and the fact excites him all the more. As the Younger

Daughter puts it, "Actually, don't you think that they really hate each other? . . . Well, let's suppose it's a modern miracle. Let's suppose there are forty men and women who live as congenial spirits, each holding their breaths to listen behind the walls. . . ."

Both the Elder Daughter and the Bachelor are nursing the extravagant power of the imagination that lies within them, and, even though they have no contact with one another, the fiction that they maintain allows them to exercise that power and to continue living in the euphoria thus created. The two never show their faces to each other. They know all too well that they can achieve these theatrical feelings only as long as they maintain the agreed-on limitations. Both the Elder Daughter and the Bachelor are superbly theatrical figures. And the Younger Daughter's Husband has something in common with them as well.

But the Younger Daughter does not. All she can manage is to feel jealous of her older sister; all she can do is scheme to have her locked away in a hospital. In the second part of the play, it becomes clear that the Younger Daughter, seemingly so reliable, is actually far more neurotic and ill than her sister could ever be. In this "playacting"—which becomes a kind of daring employment for the Elder Daughter, a staving off of the barrenness of her everyday existence, something the Younger Daughter cannot understand—is revealed the painful irony sought by Shimizu.

No matter what else might be said about the production, Matsushita Sachiko gives a superb performance. Until now, as I have mentioned, she always assumed the role of Stella in *Streetcar;* now that she has graduated to the "Blanche" role, she carries it off in a truly striking fashion. Her skill at suggesting particularly fine delineations of character has always set her apart from other performers of her generation. To this particular role, which requires an interpretation that will in some way transcend the clumsiness and formality inherent in it, she imparts the grace of an opening flower. No other actress could play the part as she does, bringing to it both a reserved elegance and a glittering sense of the comic. It is clear that her success with this role rivals her long success with Stella; in fact, this role suits her even better. Here, her art seems perfection itself. When she first appears on the stage like some young girl, a shabby doll in her hand and a backpack slung over her shoulder, she creates a truly charming impression, giving us a clear picture of a "disheveled Blanche" or, better yet, a "disheveled Laura." A brilliant and satisfying image indeed.

35. THE MAGIC OF ASSORTED MIRRORS

Run, Merusu—a Girl's Lips Are Dynamite!
Written by Noda Hideki
Directed by Noda Hideki and Takahagi Hiroshi

THE DREAM WANDERERS

1981

When I see a play by Noda Hideki, I often have the sensation that I am watching a kind of beautifully constructed magic show, filled with miracles that make me roll my eyes. A scene will go innocently along, then suddenly vanish, some seemingly unrelated situation taking its place. Then, before you know it, this new scene will have been transformed into something else altogether different and preposterous. Like a magic box that shows one blinding image after another, one vision after another, Noda's technique is to present us with a series of apparently unrelated images, thereby creating momentum. Yet, at a certain point, the implicit connection is revealed. The result is a brilliant, composite whole, worked out in minute detail, often filled with bizarre ideas. Indeed, Noda is the great magician of this kind of intellectual theatre.

His current work, now playing at the Molière Theatre in Shinjuku, which he has codirected with his colleague Takahagi Hiroshi, is called *Run, Merusu—a Girl's Lips Are Dynamite!* and shows off all the effects that represent the specialty of this master trickster. Everything is brilliantly connected, using one trick after another as scene after scene rushes by with dizzying speed. The talent and wit of the playwright are clear, and we can see his intelligence, as it were, working at such breakneck speed that it sometimes seems hard for the spectators to catch their breath. It is the intelligence behind it, in fact, that allows the play to move beyond the merely clever. On the surface the play seems an elegant joke. Yet the way in which the various sections are juxtaposed allows us the occasional glimpse of something more significant below the surface. I have often chosen the image of a rubic cube to explain the fascination of Noda's stage works. The present play creates that kind of impression all the more vividly.

Run, Merusu! was first staged in 1976, in a small Tokyo theatre located in Aoyama, the Van 99 Hall, a performing space that has since disappeared. That spring it was Noda's troupe's second production and the first time that

The 1981 production by the Dream Wanderers of Noda Hideki's *Run Merusu—a Girl's Lips Are Dynamite!* Surume (Danda Yasunori) shows his passion for the lovely Fuyō (Takeshita Akiko).

the young company had performed away from Tokyo University, where the group was founded. The play was then titled *Run, Merusu: Do You Like the Burning Underwear?* and Takahagi Hiroshi directed the production. The fascination of the crazy antics being performed was apparent at once to audiences, and Noda's performance (he was then only twenty-one) disguised as a girl was truly comic (it remains so in the current production).

If my memory serves me correctly, however, the contents of the play have been considerably altered for this second production. The original play was less complicated and contained fewer tricks. As always, Noda's cleverness is evident from the outset, but that he has fully matured over the last five years is fully evident here. When we hear the title *Hashire, Merusu!* everyone in Japan, of course, thinks of the famous story by Dazai Osamu, *Run, Merosu!* [Run, Melos!], one of the short classics of modern Japanese literature that every schoolchild reads. But why is Noda's orthography not M*e*rosu, but M*e*rusu? The change is indicative of one of the most clever, perhaps the greatest of all the tricks played in the course of the play. Yes, it must be Me*rusu*, not Me*rosu*. But why?

In Noda's play, the image of the heroic youth Merusu is turned upside and reappears as Surume, a poor fellow whose life seems little more than a wallowing in poverty and degradation. When the syllables of the name are reversed, *Merusu* becomes *Surume*. Or, to put it another way, the comely Merusu becomes the slovenly Surume, his mirror image. This theatrical trick reminds me of another clever device used in Inoue Hisashi's 1973 *A Strange Bible.* In that play, everything takes place in a world inhabited by dogs, but only in the final scene did the point become apparent: *dog* spelled backward is *God.* The vulgar, canine world is turned upside down, becoming the realm of the saints, all light and glory.

Noda has used the oppositions created by the concept of the two sides of the mirror to structure the play. The contrast between *Surume* and *Merusu* is, on the surface at least, nothing more than a play on words, but underneath the puns and the playful use of language is a serious message, as in Inoue's *Strange Bible.*

Run, Merusu! unfolds through the device of a mirror stand used by the young girl Fuyō (played by Takeshita Akiko). There are two sides to this mirror (metaphorically, it is as though there are two banks to the river) between which the play switches with bewildering speed. Most of the actors play two parts, one on each "side" of the mirror. It is not ever made clear, however, which side of the mirror, which bank of the river, represents a true image of life and which merely a ghost image. There is a difference in the play between what is "heavy" and what is "light", yet both are real and at the same time fictional, unreliable. It is this structure, in which the two halves of a polarized world interact with each other, that reveals Noda's view of life.

Let me attempt to sum up what these two polarized "shores" or "banks" signify. In the first place, between them lie the straits of Naruto. On "this side" of the bank is the city of Naruto, in Tokushima Prefecture; here lives the young man Surume (played by Danda Yasunori), who was born in the town of Kurume; he is the wretched thief who steals women's underwear and lives in a messy room. Surume has developed a passion for the young girl Fuyō and has stolen her underwear; he hopes to make contact with her, but this impertinent young woman provokes his feelings and teases him from beginning to end, continually repulsing him. There are others in their circle: the Big Landowner (Sakakibara Totsu), the Big Wife (played by Noda himself), her son Hyakutarō (Tayama Ryōsei), and the Accounts Administrator (Haruta Osamu). There is something slightly old-fashioned about this group. In the world of "this shore," most of the characters wear old-fashioned Japanese-style clothing, and the weight of their poverty-stricken lives is evident; Surume and Fuyō pass their days waiting for the arrival of something "they can't give up on." Within the world of the play, their lives suggest a history of oppression.

On the other side of the straits lies the "other shore." Here is a world of bantering, a modern fiction, all surface, a world seemingly "without oppression." Here our poor underwear-stealing "Surume of Kurume" is transformed into the singing star "Meruku no Merusu" (played by Matsuzawa Kazuyuki). Here, the girl who teased Surume becomes Reiko (performed by Torii Emiko). The group that surrounds these two consists of, first, the "seven detectives," who seem right out of some television drama. Then there is the writer and critic Kirishima Yōko (played as well by Noda), who lives in the world of toys and fairy tales, and the three girls. In other words, this "other shore" is, in the words of Reiko, "a world of crystal, where we can decide anything we want." At the same time, this is an empty world, "a blank hole," a "hollow cavity." All standards of value have collapsed completely, and this "blank hole" represents a place where anarchy reigns.

The Naruto Straits are suddenly reflected on both sides of the mirror, so that both characters (Surume and Merusu) can somehow understand that the other is "someone I've not yet met." For Surume, with his burdensome existence, to observe the heedless youth Merusu through the mirror is like witnessing a dream. On the other hand, caught up in the emptiness of contemporary life, in which "nothing settles in" and "everything just seems to float away," Merusu must recognize in turn his "other half."

Both young men make use of the mirror that separates these two worlds as they rush madly about, at full speed. There is a thrill for the audience in the very dizziness with which the play skips from one incident to another, as when, for example, the "Einstein Youth" (smarter still than Newton with his apple and the laws of physics) suddenly comes bursting forth.

Merusu himself managed to penetrate the mirror and to cross over to Surume's side, thus encountering his "other half." The results are as exciting as any science fiction encounter with the "unknown" of an interior universe.

Then too, there is the superbly fresh device by which Merusu reaches the other side; soaking in a hot bath, his toy boat becomes a "green celluloid warship." As he summons up the distant memory of "the aroma of a Japanese bath," the sound of the theme song from *An Escape to Glory* sounds, and a fleet of "some hundred great warships" appears; Merusu, the highest-ranking admiral, boards his warship and majestically sails forth across "the great whirlpools of Naruto."

Another remarkable scene in the play shows both worlds at the same time: a cube of sugar is burned, and in that "shadow of an instant" they appear together. Through yet another play on words, the burning of the sugar is linked with Surume's burning of his hometown of Naruto in the final scene. Ultimately, the poor boy is arrested as a criminal for having stabbed Chiyo, the girl he loved so much. Suddenly, at this point, we as an audience understand that what we have witnessed has perhaps been played out within the interior universe of this lonely youth with criminal inclinations, a tale with a significance quite different from what we originally expected.

What we have here is a play that, for all its clever devices, its plays on words, of a flutter from one level of sport and teasing to another, can reveal another side, the painful interior world of a youth destroyed by his dark side, despite his bright dreams of an alter ego. Suddenly, one remembers that the play begins with the sharp cries of young, "parentless" Surume, "Dad! Oh, Dad!" Then it becomes clear that, unable to bear the emptiness of his solitary existence, Surume creates that "other world" of Merusu's in order to realize his dreams. His inner life "extends over the Naruto Straits." "I go back and forth, one way and the other," he repeats, and he exhausts himself in the effort.

Noda's play paints a surprisingly earnest portrait of the pilgrimage of this remarkable youth, so filled with a sense of his own "emptiness." Under the luxuriant and witty exterior that is the text runs a vein of profound seriousness. For some spectators, the play may seem little more than entertainment, worth seeing for its verbal wit and amusing byplay; but, for those who seek a more profound level of understanding, there is the puzzle of attempting to decipher this hidden, serious core, which provides a very different kind of pleasure. In this regard, Noda has become the consummate, impertinent master of that reflecting mirror he so brilliantly uses in the play.

In all its aspects—direction, script, acting—this current production of *Run, Merusu!* is the most perfectly realized of any of Noda's productions that I have seen. In a production three months ago at the Kinokuniya Hall of the play *Boy Hunt*, complete harmony was not achieved, but, in this present production at the Molière, the actors were filled with a sense of vitality and seemed to identify with their characters closely. The atmosphere of a small theatre suits Noda's troupe perfectly.

Noda himself plays two roles, the "Big Wife" and the writer Kirishima, and, as usual, his comic abilities shine brilliantly. Women's roles seem to suit him very well. The performances of Danda Yasunori as Surume and Takeshita Akiko as Fuyō are also fresh and quite well done.

36. SIGNPOSTS ALONG THE WAY

A Legend of Fish: A Teacher Kills His Student at

Rikkyō University

Written and directed by Yamazaki Tetsu

TRANSPOSITION 21

1981

This play seems like an attack. The power and emotional impact of this production goes far beyond such issues as its "success," its sense of "completeness," or how well it is performed. Frankly speaking, the experience made me feel as though some dark and heavy object had been thrown right in my face. "I give up!" I whispered in my inner being when the play finished, for, just as the title of this play suggests, Yamazaki's production represents an invasion, a violation.

A Legend of Fish is without doubt the most successful drama, and the most polished production, ever prepared by Yamazaki and his group. In terms of the quality of work being done in the Japanese theatre today, this production stands out; indeed, it is so good that I wonder whether Yamazaki can ever surpass what he has accomplished here. *A Legend of Fish* is a landmark for his troupe in the way that certain productions have been for other companies: Suzuki Tadashi's *On the Dramatic Passions II*, Kara Jūrō's *The Vampire Princess*, Ōta Shōgo's *Legend of Komachi,* and Tsuka Kōhei's *Atami Murder Case,* for example. The question inevitably arises as to whether the artistic levels established by any of these productions can be exceeded.

Yamazaki's company, Transposition 21, was formed in 1980 when the members of an earlier group, disbanded in 1979, joined with the chief actors of a company called the Theatre Troupe. The original version of *Fish* was presented as their opening production, but unfortunately I didn't get an opportunity to see it. The present staging is a revival. Yamazaki, born in 1946, has sometimes been regarded as a minor figure in the second generation of the small theatre movement that began in the 1970s, but *Fish* reveals a new burst of creative energy, generating a sense of great excitement in its audiences.

As is clear from the subtitle of the play, the drama is based on an infamous incident that took place in 1973, when an instructor at Rikkyō University strangled a woman student with whom he had been having an affair, in the process involving four other people, all of whom joined him in a joint love suicide on the beach at Izu. As the story is retold here, it has been subjected to a number of bizarre twists and turns. As in his earlier *Field Notes for Crimes* or his 1981 *The Family Adrift—the Jesus Ark Incident,* Yamazaki distorts the original material in order to bring out unusual elements, all with the clarity of a candid photograph.

As the play opens, we meet a patient in a mental hospital, a woman (performed by Shikimachi Chako) jealous of her husband's affairs, finally driven mad by them, and ultimately hospitalized. Her escort, a university instructor who works under her husband, is played by Fujii Bin. The play is set in motion when the pair meets another patient (played by Kuriyama Michi), a young girl who is purportedly the lover of the woman's husband. At this point, the focus of the play tightens in a frightening, sharp focus on the "incident" of the murder itself.

That the trajectory that events take, from the collapse of the family to the love suicide, is so compelling owes much to the author's use of elements of Shimao Toshio's novel *Thorns of Death.* The hysterical wife who cannot stop berating her husband because he has taken a lover, the husband who cannot stop apologizing—the picture created is one of sheer hell. We see with shocking clarity the horror of the lives of all those involved in the incident, and at the same time we see the grotesque humor inherent in such a painful situation.

Among the cast, Shikimachi Chako gives a dazzling performance as the

The 1981 production by Transposition 21 of Yamazaki Tetsu's *A Legend of Fish.* *From the left:* the University Instructor (Fujii Bin), the Wife (Shikimachi Chako), and the Old Man (Tane Rakuko).

wife. From the moment the curtain went up, when she appeared so sweetly in her red wool dress ("Is it all right? This is what it means to be cheerful, you know . . ."), to the instant her mask-like face was broken by a startling smile, I found it impossible to take my eyes off her. She performed the extremes of her role—the gentleness of everyday life as well as the heights of frenzied passion—with commendable self-possession. The issue is not simply one of a passionate performance. Her technique is rich and resourceful enough to undercut with violence her character's essential femininity and, at the same time, to create a sense of comic lightness. Watching her perform, I was reminded of the multiple intensities of some of Shiraishi Kayoko's early performances with Suzuki Tadashi's company.

There was much that was fascinating as well in Kuriyama Michi's performance as the twisted young girl in the wheelchair. And there was a surprising amount of freshness shown in the work of Tane Rakuko, who played the old man who tried to turn himself into a famous boxer of yore, Piston Horiguchi.

In the end, I really felt that I had experienced a series of remarkable theatrical moments, in which the performers, so full of charm and strength, took up the text with commendable vigor and skill. After all, the text itself represents only one aspect of the total theatrical experience; it is the performer's job to bring to the fore the rhythm of the words on the page. In that regard, it is quite clear that Yamazaki's troupe truly embodies the accomplishments of the small theatre movement of the 1960s. If truth be told, it is some of the other companies that have undergone a "transposition." Transposition 21 has continued right on from its audacious starting point; so, from this point of view, the paradox proceeds.

The young man admitted as a patient (Kinouchi Yorihito) keeps repeating his symbolic fantasy of "two fish" swimming leisurely "at the bottom of the Euphrates" (his attempt to escape from an unpleasant reality), a clever rhetorical device to be sure. At the end of the play, he picks up the crazed wife and, seemingly with her consent, drowns both himself and her in a reservoir that is all too real. The final image is thus one of the "two fish" going home. They leave behind them a powerful sense of shock.

37. A SNACK BAR IN
THE WOODS OF ATHENS

A Midsummer Night's Dream

Written by William Shakespeare

Directed by Deguchi Norio,

translated by Odashima Yūshi

THE SHAKESPEARE THEATRE

1981

It really seems as though lately *A Midsummer Night's Dream* is turning up every season. Certainly there have been quite a few stagings this summer. Besides the Shakespeare Theatre's anniversary production, there has been a musical version at the Actor's Theatre, another staging at the Jean-Jean Theatre in Shibuya, and yet another production is expected in August.

Apparently, *A Midsummer Night's Dream* is a frequent summer offering in Europe and the United States as well. According to the drama scholar Takahashi Yasunari, the play is presented outside in Regent's Park in London virtually every summer. Some time ago, when I made a trip to Europe during the summer months, I had an occasion to see an open-air production of the play in Stockholm. At that point, virtually every theatre was closed for the summer, and only this outdoor production was running. What I saw was perhaps in and of itself nothing special, but a temporary stage had been set up in the courtyard of an old residence, and there was a special charm in seeing the play performed in the white light of a Scandinavian summer night.

Deguchi's current staging of *A Midsummer Night's Dream* has its own special power. Over the course of six years, from 1975 until the spring of 1981, his group has presented all thirty-seven of Shakespeare's dramas. Their productions were confident and successful, combining a high level of energy and a touching, shadowy charm.

Calling themselves "Japan Shakespeare," the group was largely composed of young performers, who adopted a casual look, wearing street clothes and using no makeup. These simple productions, without props or sets, were typical of the group's efforts. With the project now complete, this "memorial festival," which opens with *A Midsummer Night's Dream,* is being given a more elaborate staging. For these productions, the group makes use of costumes and settings prepared by Abe Machi, which add to the festival's overall sense of style.

The set represents a great forest of trees, some of which support a tent in sober gray, from which two large pieces of dark gray cloth are hung to form a canopy. This tent is placed in the middle of the woods near Athens. The colors employed in the set are all dark, mostly blacks and grays. This kind of harmony and restraint provides a very practiced and polished look.

The disposition of the play has been strikingly reconceived. In the director's vision, the "play" of A *Midsummer Night's Dream* is "performed" by the guests and employees of a contemporary Japanese late-night snack bar. When this production was first presented in October 1979, this device seemed extremely fresh; now, seeing this version again, it is even more effective.

As the curtain rises, the snack bar has not yet opened, and the scene is dark. The employees arrive for work. It is a quiet moment of the day. Preparations for the opening are made in virtual silence. In the midst of this, one of the young waiters (played by Ishizuka Unshō) is absorbed in a book. Several employees get ready for customers, who soon begin to arrive. At this point, the young boy imaginatively invests his fellow employees with the personae of the characters in the play he is reading. In his imagination, the plot of A *Midsummer Night's Dream* begins to unfold in the snack bar. The shop owner and his wife (Matsui Junrō and Takamura Mayumi) become the king and queen of the fairies, Oberon and Titania. The waitresses become her fairy attendants, and the boy himself turns into the comical, jesting Puck.

What is of particular interest in this conception is the fact that the business of the play and the business of the snack bar proceed contemporaneously: while the play is performed at the front of the stage, behind it in the snack bar the owners and the waitresses continue on with their work, time passing for them just as it would in the real world. For example, the waitresses boisterously thank their "customers" whenever "actors" in the "play" leave the stage. This connection between the two staging areas serves to emphasize the illusory nature of theatrical reality, and it is maintained as the performance moves vigorously along.

This device provides a splendid framework within which to develop a sense of what the play is really about. Juxtaposing the action of the play against the "action" in the snack bar—which represents life at its most ordinary, indeed its most vulgar—adds even more layers of meaning to what is already an extravagant dream, one that encompasses all the basic human desires, including the baser instincts. The boy's own fantasies, spawned from the loneliness of his wretched existence, provide the pretext for the play. In this context, the boy as Puck is no jovial, carefree sprite. Even his

The 1981 production of *A Midsummer Night's Dream* by the Shakespeare Theatre. Kawakami Yasunori plays Bottom.

eerie makeup suggests his darker side, a disdain for the world of the ordinary. And the grays and blacks of the set reflect the shadowy world that he inhabits. Seen this way, *A Midsummer Night's Dream* surpasses ordinary fantasy, shining in its own hard light.

In this production, the roles of the menials are played with enormous skill. Their easygoing energy and the skillfulness of their humor are outstanding; watching them is like being billowed up by a soft, warm breeze. Proud of their ability to perform comedy, this troupe has long specialized in assembling as many tough and stalwart male actors as possible. Kawakami Yasunori was particularly successful as Bottom; I have rarely seen this role performed with such seemingly endless energy. In their recent production of *Henry VI, Part 3*, the actors portrayed their characters as multifaceted individuals and gave strong, lively performances. When the actresses in the troupe reach a similar level of maturity, an even deeper and more resonant production of *A Midsummer Night's Dream* will be possible.

Because the dialogue in this production is delivered so clearly and quickly, the audience has a sense of being struck relentlessly by the text, as though we represented Shakespeare's target ourselves. This effect is another specialty of this troupe's. The entanglements of the four lovers are most amusingly displayed, yet their suffering is evident. And, even though all their problems are resolved and the play ends on a happy note, no sense of final resolution is conveyed. We are left instead with the impression that, on still another night, in yet another dream, they might forsake their proper partners and pursue illusion once again.

As the players wake from their dream at the approach of dawn and Titania, Oberon, and Puck speak of "the earth," "the globe," and "the moon," a sharp image of a universe beyond the wretched and selfish dealings of mankind appears. That such a clear, and cruel, image is invoked attests to the skill of the director, Deguchi Norio.

38. LAUGHTER IN A GOTHIC MUSICAL

Sweeney Todd: The Demon Barber of Fleet Street

Music by Stephen Sondheim,

book by Hugh Wheeler

Directed by Suzuki Tadashi,

translated by Kurahashi Ken and Kai Marie

A TŌHŌ PRODUCTION

1981

A new and exciting kind of musical has appeared on the stage that changes the very nature of the form and, indeed, breaks new ground. When *Sweeney Todd* opened on Broadway, it was referred to as a "musical thriller," but it shows certain connections to the gothic novel, most popular in the eighteenth and nineteenth centuries, and so it seems to me that we might equally well consider it a "gothic musical." This work blends terror, black humor, and a sharp critical spirit; in that sense it stands as a masterpiece, and Suzuki's direction is dynamic and intense. It might also be said that the producers have shown a spirit of adventure in planning for a run of two months at the large Imperial Theatre, a long time for a production of this sort.

The original New York production opened in March 1979 at the Uris Theatre. It won eight Tony awards that year, including best musical, best book, and best score, a remarkable accomplishment that was much talked about. *Sweeney Todd* is the newest product of the partnership of Harold Prince and Stephen Sondheim, a pairing that has already produced such works as *Company, Follies, A Little Night Music,* and *Pacific Overtures.* Yet, although the critics lavished praise on the production and it continued winning prize after prize, the show never had the long Broadway run it surely deserved. For New York audiences, *Sweeney Todd* may well have been too "advanced," created more for the enjoyment of theatre professionals than for the entertainment of the average audience. Doubtless the show struck a sour note with many, so far removed as it was from the familiar conventions of romance, comedy, and a healthy humanism that have been the mainstays of the musical.

That *Sweeney Todd* is not a typical Broadway musical should not, however, bother Japanese audiences, given the different theatre traditions with which they are familiar. For example, the show is very close in spirit to the works of the great *kabuki* playwright Tsuruya Namboku (1755–1829), sharing the characteristics that define his work—the sense of the beauty and cruelty that reside in terror, a taste for the grotesque, black humor, and the correspondence between the glittering attraction of evil people and the evils of society they represent. Central to the plot of *Sweeney Todd* are dead bodies: victims' throats are cut, and the corpses are sent down a chute to the kitchen below, where the remains are made into meat pies. This startling conception has its own intrinsic interest, yet to a Japanese audience it also seems to be a cunning variation on the kinds of murders dreamed up by Namboku.

Should Japanese audiences resist Sondheim's work (and there was evidence of such a reaction in the Tokyo audiences), it would only be evidence of how far we have distanced ourselves from our own traditions. It would also be evidence of a refusal to recognize an inherent darkness in our nature as well as of a weakening of our spirit of inquiry.

The ingenious machinery for this production has been designed by Takada Ichirō. The curtain opens onto a residential street in nineteenth-century London, the houses leaning in eerily one on the other, the street receding into the depths of the stage space. On both sides of the upper part of the stage can be seen the interior of a dilapidated factory, with huge pillars soaring upward. There are cogs installed everywhere. Such, by implication, is the hidden structure of a society that resembles in its workings the vast mechanisms of a factory itself. The image created very effectively suggests the enormous changes wrought in England by industrialization. Indeed, the musical begins with the raucous sound of the factory siren. As the story progresses, an iron bridge moves people smoothly up and down; even the barber chairs used in the shop are moved by a crane. All these

Tōhō's 1981 production of Stephen Sondheim's *Sweeney Todd*. Ōtori Ran plays Mrs. Lovett, Matsumoto Kōshirō the Barber.

devices contribute to this picture of society as a vast factory. Because of this complex installation, the stage of the Imperial Theatre does not, for once, seem overly large, and a tense theatrical space has been created. Yoshii Sumio's lighting is also effective.

The protagonist of the piece is the barber Sweeney Todd (played by Matsumoto Kōshirō), whose very soul is bent on revenge. Fifteen years before, through the machinations of an evil Judge (played by Nakamura Takao) and his henchman, the Beadle (Yamaya Hatsuo), his wife had been seduced, his daughter, Johanna (played by Sawada Ayako), stolen from him, and he himself, innocent of any crime, deported. Now, he has returned from abroad and is back in London. He and the pie maker, Mrs. Lovett (Ōtori Ran), rent the second floor of a shop, where he again opens a barbershop. There he begins his bloody revenge taking.

In the end, Sweeney avenges himself on the Judge and his underling; but, more important to the plot, he kills not only them but many of the customers who come into his shop, one by one. Mrs. Lovett transforms their dead flesh into meat pies, which she sells successfully in her own shop. Thus, the pair figure not only as avengers serving a just cause but also as miscreants who sink deeper and deeper into evil. Here, the usual banal formula, "The sacrificed equals the good, the avengers the bad," is not applied. If the society that has banished the innocent Sweeney and robbed him of his daughter can be compared to a cruelly efficient and emotionless factory, then why should the man who fights it show only gentleness and goodness? In such a world, even the bird seller (Kijima Shinichi) nonchalantly puts out the eyes of his "merchandise" so that they will sing the better.

TODD: Those crunching noises pervading the air?
MRS. LOVETT: Yes, Mr. Todd, Yes, all around—
TODD: It's man devouring man, my dear,
    And who are we to deny it in here?
MRS. LOVETT: Then who are we to deny it in here?

This is a universe that "eats men up." The cruel, black humor of people being murdered and their flesh cooked in pies nicely suggests the realities of a society in which men are indeed "consumed," and the cruelty serves as a cynical method of proving the point. In that regard, *Sweeney Todd* comes close to the powerful atmosphere of the Brecht/Weill *Threepenny Opera.*

Until now Suzuki Tadashi has worked exclusively with the avant-garde theatre, and this is the first time he has had a large space in which to reveal his finely honed skills. His direction here is precise, tense, and exciting. And this production shows him to be a director skilled at mounting more orthodox and large-scale productions.

As conceived by Suzuki, Sweeney is a man of the people. He is indeed their creation—the hero who, in their name and without hope and against all odds, will single-handedly take on the soulless, mechanized evil that society represents. At the beginning of act 1, we see a group of silent, robed figures who suggest the shades of the dead; from their midst, the figure of Sweeney floats up. In that instant, Suzuki's plan of attack, as it were, becomes clear, for those robes are a glittering white, the color of shrouds and of the repose of souls—and salvation as well. In the final scene, as Sweeney steps onto the steel platform behind a row of figures who line the stage, brandishing his razor, he himself glitters white, the very image of the lonely warrior who has earned an honorable death in battle.

The methods by which Suzuki has placed his production in the context of the oppressed people are extremely effective, and, in that sense, *Sweeney Todd* represents a natural extension of the Japanese director's own vision of the work. In the scene in the mental hospital in act 2, which is much altered from Hugh Wheeler's original script, we suddenly catch a glimpse of Suzuki's work with his own Waseda Little Theatre.

Among the performers, Matsumoto Kōshirō and Ōtori Ran are brilliant. Sondheim's music, relying as it does on dissonance and chromatic intervals, is difficult and suggests the score for a contemporary opera, yet both these performers have mastered the score. The woman beggar, played by Ichihara Etsuko, is also quite well done. Some of the minor parts, however, have been given to performers who, while familiar with the techniques of more usual musicals, have difficulty singing together as a chorus; they are unsure of Sondheim's complex pitches and so lower the tension of the drama.

This exciting production shows us for the first time that change can indeed come, even to the conservative world of musical theatre.

39. THE POWER OF THE OLDER SISTER, THE POWER OF THE MIRROR

Night Shadows—a Gentle Ghost Story

Written and directed by Watanabe Eriko

THE THREE CIRCLE COMPANY

1981

This was the first production by this troupe that I have seen. I had been hearing for some time that, of the various young companies now active, this one was particularly worthy of note. So it was with a certain degree of expectation that I set out to see this performance. When I saw the crowded theatre, filled beyond capacity, I thought of my crushed legs and feet and wondered whether I would have to cry out in pain. Yet, as this remarkable production started, I realized that my expectations would be far surpassed. And, while my poor feet were indeed put through agony, I no longer felt compelled to protest. Any discomfort was more than made up for by the fascination of this stimulating production.

The Three Circle Company was founded in 1979, and *Night Shadows* is its seventh production. The talents of Watanabe Eriko as writer, director, and even performer show considerable promise for the future. True enough, I have only the evidence of this one production on which to base my judgment, but it nevertheless seems clear to me that the kind of theatrical sense shown here is altogether exceptional: a strikingly extravagant conception, allied with a genuine sense of the realities of actual life, an altogether individual writing style, and the ability to mirror the complexities of human life on the stage.

Born in 1955, Watanabe Eriko is now only twenty-six, and her youth offers great promise for the future. There are a number of bright young playwrights at work now, and her name must be added to their number. And it should be noted as well that there are quite a number of skilled actors who can show off their own skills as they perform with the troupe.

As *Night Shadows* begins, we see the interior of what appears to be a two-story house, a rising staircase disappearing in the gloom. The opening scene is a *tableau vivant*. In the center is an artist, sporting a goatee, who is looking up at his canvas as he twirls his paintbrush. To his right is a nude model, who hides her breast with a cloth. Various people surround the pair. In the silence, it strikes me that I have seen this "picture" before. . . .

Of course! It is the famous painting *The Studio* by the celebrated nineteenth-century French artist Gustave Courbet! He painted it for the 1855 Universal Exposition in Paris, but, because of its "radical" contents, the picture was refused. It is thus a painting "with a history." The picture has a long subtitle: "A True Allegory Summarizing a Period of Seven Years in My Life as an Artist." Why are the actors striking this now familiar pose, and what does it have to do with the beginning of Watanabe's play?

Watanabe Eriko's *Night Shadows*, produced by the Three Circle Company in 1981. Amamiya (Shintani Kazuhiro) shows his interest in the girl student Chigusa (Motai Masako).

As this scene fades, we move to another area of the stage, where a young student, a girl named Chigusa (played by Motai Masako), dressed in a sailor suit, is sitting on her bed. Unable to sleep, she repeats some ordinary English constructions as though they were some kind of mantra. Now the relatives who constitute her "family" come on stage. We are now in the main room of the shoe store the family operates. They are in the process of holding a typical 1950s Buddhist memorial service. Now we encounter a young man named Awao (played by Sasaki Mitsuru), Chigusa's younger brother, who is extremely shy. The play proper can be said to begin with an image of the closeness between the older sister and her impressionable, clumsy younger brother, who is both apprehensive and fearful.

Soon, however, the play takes a totally unforeseen direction. A hole is rent as it were in the prevailing reality, and unanticipated, bewildering invasions now take place, as the stage turns into a glittering surprise package. Yet real life, the life of ordinary, common people, with all its colors and smells, still remains visible beneath the images soaring overhead.

As this process continues, it becomes possible to speculate as to why the play began with the *tableau vivant*, which essentially serves to epitomize the action of the entire play, thereby providing a key to what follows. Here is how I would interpret the opening.

Courbet's famous picture puts the artist in the center and places different groups of people on either side. On the right are the artists and intellectuals, who are carefully studying the work in progress. Among them are the poet Baudelaire and the philosopher Proudhon, critics, patrons of the arts, women models, their lovers—in short, all those for whom art is life.

On the other side, however, is a group that represents the nameless, faceless masses, those who labor for their daily bread—a hunter, a woman who works at funerals, a priest, a seller of old clothes, a laborer, a grass cutter. These figures scarcely notice the artist at work but rather huddle together, oblivious to their surroundings. This striking disparity represents for Courbet the nature of reality. As he said of this painting, "It represents seven years of my life." The artists face the picture directly. Yet Courbet, for his part, looks toward the ordinary people who inhabit the left side of his picture.

So it is that the structure of the play resembles that of the painting. Virtually all the characters are drawn from the working classes. Assembled for the service are the family who runs the shoe store; a tailor's family; a teacher who drinks too much (played by Mizuno Kimiharu); his old student Dasai Osamu (played by Tōdō Takaya), an aspiring but so far completely unsuccessful novelist; and one Utako (Watanabe Eriko herself), the teacher's middle-aged ex-wife who now lives with Osamu. Altogether, this is an affecting and somehow comic crew.

Once the action is set in motion, however, the original deployment of characters changes dramatically, as in Watanabe's remarkable vision the worlds of the intellectuals, the working people, even the artist himself, increasingly overlap and merge, creating in effect a theatrical double image.

The impetus for these transformations is a work of art, not the landscape that Courbet depicts himself as painting, but the portrait of Chigusa, the high school student nervously biting her lip, that figures in the *tableau vivant*. And the imagination of the one who looks at her with such adoration (whose identity will be clear by the end of the play) uses the power inherent in her portrait to transport ordinary people into an extravagant imaginary world.

A superb device affords entrée into this world of fantasy. Chigusa, who cannot sleep, is in the room she uses to study when she receives an unexpected visit from Amamiya (played by Shintani Kazuhiro), a young man much taken by her. Her younger brother, Awao, back from the Buddhist funeral ceremonies, joins them. Amamiya begins to chant a spell—"Derederoten, derodoradon. . . ." Meant as a joke, the charm soon shows its true power.

Suddenly, the walls of this ordinary girl's room open out, and, like some strange night wind, a black knight on a black horse, a white knight on a white horse, and a red knight on a red horse come riding in, crisscrossing the room before they disappear.

"Don't waste a second! Time is fleeting! Riders of a thousand, ten thousand skies, come!"

Suddenly, the barrier between the real world and the fantasy world dissolves, and we join Chigusa and Amamiya as they rush to follow the horses into the unknown universe beyond. The experience is almost like waking inside a carnival.

This fantasy world is not the fairy tale that we would expect of a young girl's imagination. We find ourselves instead in the cheerful salon of the painter Maneet, the failed novelist Osamu (never to become the celebrated Dazai Osamu!) transformed. The owner of the shoe store (played by Sugano Hisao) becomes "the white rabbit of the shoe store," Imipuramin, and the owner of the tailor shop (played by Egami Shingo) "the black rabbit of the tailor shop," Hidorajin. The old man who repairs shoes (played by Azuma Ginnosuke) becomes Maneet's steward. Despite the transformations, however, all these fantasy figures bear some resemblance to their models in the real world. For example, Maneet, aware of his own inferiority, resembles the real Osamu, whose passion for Yayoi, the beautiful wife of the shoe store owner, had raised eyebrows. And when the painting by Maneet is refused by the Salon, Chigusa and Amamiya take on the names "Baudelaire" and "Georges Sand." From these guises, it is clear that the Courbet painting is being parodied.

It is interesting as well that, in the "reverse sorcery" of Amamiya, a multiple image of young Awao now appears. She is his aunt, Awahi. The role is played by Mitsunaga Yoshie, the actress who also plays the role Yayoi. She is a lovely woman whom the boy secretly adores most among all his relatives. As she changes into her new self, she drags him off into this new world like some Peter Pan.

As these fantasies continue, the play becomes increasingly lively and complicated, drawing us through several plot turns. Then, just before the end of the play, a most unexpected scene occurs—Chigusa's funeral. She has willingly outstripped the world of fantasy; her portrait with a black ribbon is now installed in a place of honor, and various friends, dressed in black, are mourning her death.

At this moment, I suddenly came to realize that from the beginning the whole play has been about memories of Chigusa; indeed, it is a kind of requiem for her. The one who remembers her with the most affection is her younger brother, Awao. "I'm even lonelier than my older sister, and I'm going to breathe life back into her," mutters Awao. Is he not the architect of this extravagant fantasy drama?

It seemed to me that this was certainly the case. Yet the play reveals several important disjunctions as well. As Amimiya borrows those words spoken by Awao concerning his older sister, Awao himself now disappears. For at some point Amimiya has assumed the identity of Awao; he now speaks as though Chigusa were *his* older sister.

Then, in the penultimate moment of the play, the play shows us still another "disjunction." The old shoemaker's helper, who until this point in the play has only performed a minor role, whispers the phrase "Oh, my older sister . . ." from the depths of the darkness into which the stage has been plunged. At that instant we are shown still another *tableau vivant*. We see Awao chasing after Awahi. And we see Chigusa, pursued by Amamiya.

In that momentary flash, we understand. This is a play about the profound dreams of three generations of men who seek an image of the eternal "older sister." The boy Awao, the young man Amimiya, and the old man all reach after this image, so crucial to them; they live out their lives as they call out "Oh, my older sister! . . ." From childhood through youth, this beautiful "power of the older sister" guards these males from the rigors of the outside world, seeks to encourage them, manages even to scolds them, all in order to allow them to stand on their own feet. This universal symbol of the older sister haunts these men throughout their lives, acts like a tender spirit that has secretly settled in their very hearts. The author has captured this vision with great affection and, making use of her abilities to create complex dramatic structures, fleshes them out with real inspiration.

There is a well-known essay written in 1940 by the anthropologist Yanagida Kunio entitled "The Power of the Younger Sister," in which he points out the force that, traditionally, the younger sister held over her older brothers. Yanagida discussed the influence gained from the fact that, from the beginning, such women were considered to possess shamanistic powers. At the same time, in a review of Yanagida's essay, the writer Hayashi Tatsuo noted that, while he agreed with Yanagida's premises, he felt that there was a case to be made as well for the power of the older sister, citing examples ranging from the Greek tragedies in which Elektra and Antigone appear, to the heroine of Mori Ōgai's touching *Sanshō the Bailiff*, a classic of modern Japanese literature. Inspired by this review, another well-known writer, Shibusawa Tatsuhiko, wrote an extremely provocative essay entitled "The Power of the Older Sister." He saw both "the power of the older sister" and "the power of the younger sister" as stemming from the same fundamental mythical structures, locating early examples in Greek myths and later ones in those of India, China, and Japan. He points out that, in these cases, the "power of the older sister" is ubiquitous. He pointed out that the same characteristics were shared by such diverse figures as the Greek goddess Demeter, the Great Earth Mother, Kannon, the character Princess Terute in *Oguri Hangan*, and the figure of Shintoku Maru in medieval performance legends. In Shibusawa's view, all these women occupy a place "somewhere between mother and lover." For men, then, they serve as eternal images of the feminine.

What strikes us with such force, living as we do in the world of everyday reality, are the various sorts of violent forces that stand in opposition to that basic "power of the older sister," created as it is on a structure of love. To put it another way, there is the "power of the mirror," which can divide us up into countless, multiple images. This "power of the older sister," which from the beginning attempts to guard and protect a sense of congenial closeness, is thus opposed to that "power of the mirror," so full of evil intent, which seeks to break and scatter. Attempt as we may, we cannot escape from the complications of these dynamics (although, of course, in order consciously to seek a sense of union again, the mirror may be necessary for us as well). In that sense, Watanabe Eriko's drama plunges right to the deepest level of our lives.

True enough, the atelier scene as created here falls a bit flat, but this is only a slight fault. I expect much from Watanabe's fresh talent, overflowing as it is with such creativity and wit.

40. DINING AND A SENSE OF FREEDOM

Bubbling and Boiling

Written by Betsuyaku Minoru

Directed by Fujiwara Shimpei

THE ATELIER OF THE LITERARY

THEATRE

1982

Betsuyaku Minoru is the kind of playwright who makes every attempt to avoid references in his plays to many of the vital physical functions of his characters. In the world that he creates, there are no references to sex; his plays are somehow temperate, dry. They show a certain still, hard brilliance.

On the other hand, it is remarkable how many scenes there are in his plays in which his characters are eating or drinking. There is, for example, the unforgettable scene in his 1962 *Elephant* where the "patient" and the "wife" eat their rice balls wrapped in seaweed. Similar scenes come to mind in certain of his other plays, such as *The Little Match Girl, Landscape with Red Bird, The Move,* and several others. Indeed, this "crude custom" of "chewing," as he defines it in *The Revolt of the Soyosoyo Tribe,* is often shown; and, in that sense, Betsuyaku reveals a physiological side after all.

Betsuyaku's play *Boiling and Bubbling* has been restaged after six years, in a production directed by Fujiwara Shimpei by the Literary Theatre. Here too, I realized afresh, there is a surprisingly effective scene of "eating." Indeed, from the point of view of food and the means by which it is consumed, Betsuyaku's plays reveal quite an unusual, and a larger, concern that is in itself extremely striking.

In the present play, this "eating" occurs in the third scene. The bridegroom, Man 1 (played by Kadono Takuzō), is dressed in formal Japanese clothing, his wife, Woman 1 (beautifully played by Yoshino Yukiko), in a white bride's kimono. Both sit upright in a somewhat gloomy fashion next to a telephone pole as they begin to consume their lonely bridal dinner, served on two lacquer trays.

Noticing that something unusual is floating in his soup, the man tells his wife, "There must be some sort of mistake, don't you think?" half apologizing. Then, aware that he is ashamed of his stinginess, he attempts to

Betsuyaku Minoru's *Bubbling and Boiling,* produced by the Atelier of the Literary Theatre in 1982. Man 1 (Kadono Takuzō) and his bride (Yoshino Yukiko).

show his generosity by passing over his pickles to his wife. "Even if it's over here, or over there, we should be able to eat freely what we want together, . . ." he proposes. Such is Betsuyaku's discourse on commonality and freedom, posited in terms appropriate to the dining table.

Unfortunately, going along with his logic, the bride suddenly puts out her hand to take one of the small sardines on his tray. The Man is vaguely confused. "That . . . is that what you want? . . . My? . . . Well, I don't mean *mine,* but it *is* over here. . . ." Thus, he reveals all too clearly that he cannot escape his former logic, in which there is "mine" and "yours."

Within his brain are planted quite clearly the concepts of "commonality" and "freedom," but his desire and the functionings of his own body cause him quickly to undercut any merely intellectual understanding. Flustered, he continues, "No, no . . . it's all right, really." "Really, it's nothing. . . . Do as you like naturally. . . . Feel free to do as you like," he says by way of apology. His wife, somewhat intimidated, says, "You mean, once out of three times? . . ." The atmosphere becomes increasingly awkward as any sense of freedom disappears. In the end, the Wife hangs her head down and whispers, "I . . . I don't know why . . . but . . . it's really very hard to eat. . . ."

We laugh while the couple fidgets. Yet, at the same time, it is clear that we are being shown—so sharply as to be almost unbearable—the basic issues of freedom and commonality between human beings. Betsuyaku adds no critical comment but simply and quietly creates this suggestive moment. And that is, of course, quite enough. We are struck by the force of a moment that, although presented in a seemingly nonchalant fashion, strikes us with great force. And we are forced, therefore, to question our own deepest assumptions. We can talk coolly about "freedom," just as we can talk about "food," yet understand nothing of what we say. Betsuyaku's image of humanity points out all too clearly the absurdity of the human condition.

The contemporary theatre has moments when it can convey more than any novel. This moment is surely one of them.

41. A WORLD IN WHICH THE COMPOSITION IS NOW COMPLETE

Song of Praise and Thanksgiving

Written by Kitamura Sō

Directed by Ōsugi Yū

KATŌ KEN'ICHI STUDIO

1982

There are certain plays that, when simply read, do not reveal their scope, or their depth, texts that can be grasped only in performance. There is no better example of such a play than Kitamura Sō's *Song of Praise and Thanksgiving*, which, in these terms, strikes me as a remarkable discovery.

Kitamura Sō, who was born in 1952, first published this one-act play in 1979, when it attracted more than a usual amount of attention. Now, in 1982, two productions of the play are running concurrently in Tokyo, one at the Free Theatre company, directed by Kushida Kazuyoshi, and the production under review here. To say the least, this is a most unusual dramatic contest.

I have seen both of these productions, and it seems clear to me that Katō's company's is far superior. Compared to its sophistication and clarity, the Free Theatre's stagnant staging is a far cry from their earlier work, such as the superb *Shanghai 'Vance King*.

The 1982 Katō Ken'ichi Studio staging of *Song of Praise and Thanksgiving* by Kita-mura Sō. *From the left:* Hoshi Mitsuru as Christ, Katō Ken'ichi as the Man, and Miwa Yumiko as the Woman.

In a Japan virtually destroyed by a worldwide nuclear holocaust, two theatre performers, a man and a woman (Katō himself and Miwa Yumiko), who have somehow been spared, are pulling along their bicycle-driven cart. Suddenly, they encounter in front of them a weak and sickly "beggar" (played by Hoshi Mitsuru), who turns out to be Christ. For a certain time the three travel together, eventually parting to go on their separate jour-neys. Such is the drama we witness. The two performers, who resemble high-class stand-up comedians, mix their heavy Kyoto/Osaka dialect with the pure, elegant standard Japanese of the Christ figure. Although the play takes up a very serious subject, the treatment is as light and carefree as a comedy, which makes its reception more pleasant. To cite an extreme example, the miracle of the loaves and fishes is treated here as a "crowd attracter" of a street charlatan!

As I watched this play, however, it seemed to me that we were not being shown any merely ordinary pair of traveling players, random individ-uals left over after the holocaust. "You know, it was me who launched those missiles," the male player, Gesaku, repeats on two occasions, by way of emphasis, as though he becomes in and of himself a manifestation of those who committed the insane folly of the war and so virtually struck down the human race.

Eventually, in the midst of a heavy snowfall, which quiets the folly of the continuing strife, these two comic travelers say to each other, "Well, why not give birth to some children?" In their own audacious way, they therefore become a new Adam and Eve. Here, it seems, the playwright has created a text that, while using words redolent of the vulgarities of this world, is actually a metaphysical drama.

Thus, it is that these two categories of voyagers, Christ and these all-too-human beings, continue to travel along together. In the last scene, however, there comes a parting of the ways. Christ goes to Jerusalem, and the two travelers prepare to make their way to that most ancient of sites, Harappa at Mohenjo-Dāro in Pakistan, to the "hill of the dead." As they move apart, the emotional impact is very heavy indeed. As the humans face toward "the hill of the dead," they begin again to drag along their cart.

It is said that Kitamura Sō is a great fan of the British writer G. K. Chesterton. So it is, then, that at the end of the play there is more than a hint of the work assigned to the artist as defined in Chesterton's *Orthodoxy*. Here, he, in his own terms as an artist, sketches the image of a God who has completed his composition. At the instant it leaves the hand of the artist who created it, the work of art begins its own separate existence. In the same way, after his or her creation, a human being begins to walk away from God. And no total return is possible.

Chesterton suggests that to create something is to part from it fully. Just as God created the world, this English author believes, so has he left it in freedom. If that is so, then the human beings as envisioned by the author and director, as God's "perfect play," are now free to wander onto the stage in what Chesterton would call the total confusion of the world. And indeed, this too is human, all too human, is it not?

42. A SHOCK FROM BELOW THE BELT

The Song of a Strange Family—the Case of the

On-Line Fraud of Itō Motoko

Written and directed by Yamazaki Tetsu

TRANSPOSITION 21

1982

We receive various emotional impressions in the theatre. There are those light ripples of excitement that run across the surface of your skin. There is the kind of hinted knowledge that can cause you to focus your attention, with a hushed clearheadedness. Or there might be a movement that can appeal to the heart directly, as though overflowing with a sweet fruit juice. Yet, for me, the most theatrical of all such impressions involves the force that goes right for the pit of the stomach, striking head and heart simultaneously. In this production by Transposition 21 of Yamazaki Tetsu's new play, it is precisely this force that assails the audience with such dark energy.

It must be said at the beginning that the exact nature of this force is never made clear. Quite the opposite. The strength of the play comes from the sense conveyed that nothing *needs* to or can be explained in words. They can do little to explain the appeals to these dark, lower forces in the body, which continue on without end. Such is the reality that these characters must bear unceasingly. Nothing can move outside them, and the force of the bold decisions made by the family involved emerges unconcernedly from them. This play makes no apologies. It does not chatter on. The quiet determination that it expresses is stretched taut, like a transparent thread, throughout.

So it is, by the same token, that, however dark the coloring of the drama itself, the feelings engendered bear no relation to any simple pessimism. However pitiful, indeed however comic, the situations presented may be, the characters in the play, theatrically speaking, bear up under them; indeed, they appear to face them undaunted. And so it is that we ourselves are urged to burrow deeper and deeper into that same gloom.

The present play is the newest in Yamazaki's series of dramas he has entitled *Field Notes for Crimes*, which began with his 1976 play *Dog Town—the Incident of a Murder of a Female College Student by a Police Officer*. Doubtless the most representative work in the series so far has been the 1980 *A Legend of Fish*, which I have described elsewhere and which, when I saw it produced, seemed to me a work that would be difficult to improve on.

Now that I have seen *The Song of a Strange Family*, however, I must gladly revise my former opinion. The present play does more than match *A Legend of Fish*; here and there it truly surpasses it. This is particularly true when one considers, as I have noted, that the earlier play owed something to *Thorns of Death* by the well-known novelist Shimao Toshio. *The Song of a Strange Family*, which is altogether Yamazaki's own work, shows to an even greater degree his capacity as a writer for the theatre. And the members of his company, whose unique performances reveal such a sense of rootedness, gain my sincere applause as well.

Opposing any commonsense approach, the author has chosen not to portray the actual events that took place on the day of the crime or during

The 1982 production by Transposition 21 of Yamazaki Tetsu's *The Song of a Strange Family. From left to right:* the Sister (Kuriyama Michi), the Father (Fujii Bin), and Minami (Kinouchi Yorihito).

the flight that followed. Nor does he chronicle the actual planning of the theft. Rather, he shows us the events of the evening before and the morning of the day on which the crime was to take place, concentrating on events that occurred in the garden of the house inhabited by this strange family. The play ends as Motoko (played by Tane Rakuko) leaves this house and goes off in the direction of the bank.

Yamazaki has no reason to shirk or evade the actual incident itself. Rather, he extends his imaginative powers in order to reveal the ordinary life of this family as it is lived in its deepest layers. In such a context, the actual incident itself seems no longer surprising. The drama rather becomes one chronicling the hideous lives that these people suffer through from day to day. They are more astonishing still than the crime itself. Their lives float up before us, an emotional vortex of peculiar and disturbing passions. In that sense, this is a play assembled from the daily routine of these lives. And when, in this dreary, repetitious desolation, Motoko can say, "Well, there is no doubt about it . . . this is a grave business," then it is clear indeed why she can repeat so often during the course of the play, "Our crime . . . is already finished."

In the play, the Mother (played by Ōkata Hisako) speaks of "the smell of the wind" in the evening, while Motoko's brother (played by Hama Kenji) uses the phrase "the color of evening." These lines seem consciously adapted from similar phrases used by Betsuyaku Minoru in his play *Bub-bling and Boiling*. And Yamazaki's attempt to emphasize the "everyday" character of the play interweaves with Betsuyaku's work as well.

Even though these two writers employ the same phrases, however, Yamazaki's work follows a very different trajectory from Betsuyaku's. Indeed, it goes in the opposite direction.

This situation is bluntly manifested by the way in which the playwright has emphasized the physiological urges of the very bodies of the characters themselves. Yamazaki's characters "violently belch" as they eat. One of them is always "grinding away" on an apple. They spread their saliva everywhere. Reality for them is their experience of misalliance with the actual world, which expresses itself in violent jerks and spasms. Indeed, they can find no other means, even for an instant, for release or solace.

When asked by her mother why she has chosen men simply because they are tall or own a car, Motoko's answer sums up the sense of reality conveyed by the whole play. A woman with no spiritual illusions, she insists that men are, in the end, not very reliable. "Is there any other way to make a choice?" she responds.

In the world of this play, any attempt at spiritual redemption is bound to fall short. The father of the family (Fujii Bin) is described as a former instructor of philosophy at some university. How ironic this seems. In the scene in which he sputters, "What a miserable field of study that was, don't you know," Fujii gives a performance that is nearly unparalleled in conveying a sense of comic despair.

Tane Rakuko's Motoko conveys most clearly this sense of cosmic desolation. Hers is a rich, fine performance. The role of Motoko's sister, played so well by Kuriyama Michi, full of distortions and eccentricities, and glittering with suppressed passion, is beautifully comic in its pain. The maid is played by a newcomer, Suwazono Mika, and her good work should also be noted. In sum, while maintaining their usual level of energy, author and company alike have succeeded in creating a performance even a shade more effective than what they have accomplished before.

43. TSUKA KŌHEI'S "STAIRCASE"

The Kamata Marching Song

Written and directed by Tsuka Kōhei

TSUKA STUDIO

1982

In a recent interview in the *Asahi Shimbun*, Tsuka Kōhei indicated that he was ready to "give up the theatre." He was quoted as saying, "It's all been a big bluff, frankly," and, "I'm really feeling all dried up." This January, his novel *The Kamata Marching Song* won the prestigious yearly Aoki book prize, and Tsuka has indicated that he may now turn his energies to the writing of fiction. When I met him the other day, in connection with some work I was doing for a Tokyo magazine story, he told me much the same thing. "Maybe I'll become a stock broker or something!" he joked.

If that is Tsuka's true intention, this is a sad day indeed. Since the 1970s, it has been Tsuka Kōhei who has staked out a new, indeed unique territory for the contemporary theatre. His productions employ a virtually naked stage, using no scenery and very few props. Even something as minimal as the telephone poles of Betsuyaku Minoru's plays are too much for Tsuka. Tsuka sets aside such appurtenances in order to focus directly on the depths of the human relationships he sets out to portray. It was he who rejected the theatrical artifice of his predecessors, using everyday conversation as a model and provoking a vivid emotional response thereby. And his dialogue continues to move audiences. Therefore, if his retirement from the theatre turns out to be in jest, I'll be happy to acknowledge that I've been fooled by his joke.

This present "last" production, which he has written and directed, is in fact a revival of his 1980 *The Kamata Marching Song*, and it is beautifully effective. In terms of text, direction, and acting, this presentation represents one of his peaks. In that sense, there is a connection between the skills revealed in this production and Tsuka's determination to "give up the theatre."

In watching the play I noticed a number of things. At the climax of the play, which uses newly edited film stock, the protagonist, a secondary actor in the Ikeya Film Studio named Yasu (played by Hirata Mitsuru), is murdered and thrown down the stairs by the star, Ginnosuke (played by Katō Ken'ichi and Kazama Morio; the part has been double-cast), tumbling and tripping all the way. This is a remarkable scene, in which the pressure of

Tsuka Kōhei's *The Kamata Marching Song,* produced in 1982 by the Tsuka Studio. *At the right:* Hirata Mitsuru, who plays a minor film actor, with his friend, played by Negishi Toshie. (Photo by Saitō Kazuo.)

Yasu's masochistic sense of tragedy is made clear. But it must be said that a similar device was also used at the climax of one of the finest plays of Tsuka's early period, *The Atami Murder Case,* produced in 1973. In that earlier work, a pitiful factory worker, Oyama, takes on the role of a "criminal" for supposedly killing a woman factory hand and happily decides to climb up the "thirteen steps." In this case, the stairs as such do not appear on the stage. Still, one might ask why Tsuka made use of the same device in his best plays from these two periods.

However one may wish to characterize Tsuka's theatrical vision, it is never a flat or level one. His world shows, even to excess, a strongly layered sensibility. In the present play, there exists between the star Ginnosuke, who is "sold," and the mediocre actor Yasu, who is "not," a sadomasochistic, master-slave relationship based on control and power.

Few of Tsuka's characters are among the elite; most are involved in an all-consuming attempt to rise above their demeaning lives. Like Yasu, or like Shige in *The Story of a Stripper,* they are all of a kind. They are trampled on and suffer hardship and humiliation; yet, because of this very state in which they find themselves, they experience a kind of exaltation.

So it is that Tsuka's dramas are always controlled in some way by an "unseen staircase." All the while that his characters make themselves glow with a theatrical passion, they are rushing earnestly up this invisible staircase. Or, as they fall headlong down those same steps, they may still be on the rise spiritually, hoping somehow to be saved by their holy agonies.

Thus, whether the play be *The Atami Murder Case* or *The Kamata Marching Song,* it is not surprising that, in the final scenes, we should begin to catch a clear glimpse of the outlines of the staircases. Given Tsuka's character, shot through as it is with masochistic tendencies, it is no wonder that his protagonists' fall, their tumble down those stairs, is inevitable.

Tsuka has gone to great lengths to polish his portrayal of the fall. The question now is how he will develop this theme further. What new direction will his vision take?

44. THE POWER OF IMAGINATION LAVISHED ON A HOUSE

Melancholy When the Flowers Bloom

Written and directed by Watanabe Eriko

THE THREE CIRCLE COMPANY

1983

When we approach a theatre piece by Watanabe Eriko, it is as though a storeroom of memories has unexpectedly been opened within us. The light shines into that hidden space that we had hitherto forgotten. Those things that had been sleeping, covered with dust, now begin to stir; they begin to speak. Things thrown away, things long dead, have breath suddenly blown into them again, and they start to sing.

Sensations long gone from memory are revived as well. The sense of wonder and fear engendered by the very homes in which we were raised, for example. The dark place above the ceiling, where there might be hidden a passageway to a frightening new dimension. Or the unsurpassed mystery of the space below the veranda, filled with spider webs. Deep at night, in the midst of our dreams, some interior closet might open, noiselessly. Such are the things that can profoundly strike us, again and again.

The plays of Watanabe Eriko are impressive magnets that can force the metal of the abandoned past to move again. They can drag anything back to the present, however long it has been discarded. Time therefore flows backward, and nothing disappears, nothing perishes. If something does appear to have been irretrievably lost, it is only because we ourselves have lost the key to its hiding place. This is what Watanabe tells us. As the curtain rises, the key is inserted, and the door is opened, and we are overcome by nostalgia and regret.

In *Melancholy When the Flowers Bloom,* her first work after winning the prestigious Kishida drama prize, Watanabe Eriko gives us yet another drama that dredges up the pain of the past. The mix of the past and the present in the play is even more complicated than before, at the same time revealing more of the seemingly endless secrets and hiding places of the house that is our lives and exerting an even stronger attraction on us.

As the bright sound of Pat Boone's nostalgic "April Love" is heard, we suddenly see the monkey cages in a zoo. The first remarkable event that occurs, thanks to the magical efforts of a middle-aged monkey named Ichi (played by Tōdō Takaya), is the transformation of a baby monkey named

Hachi (played by Mitsunaga Yoshie) into a teenage human being referred to as "Prince Ki." This young man, his remarkable female companion, Shiki (played by Sei Ayami), and his retainer (played by Shishido Kyūichirō), a middle-aged man with an obsessive fear of work, hit the road. Eventually, they arrive at a battered-looking grocery store.

In the old days, a wooden apartment had been constructed on top of the store, but that upper story has since been torn down, leaving only the original single-story building. Suddenly, however, as the girl who shows them around mounts the staircase that originally led to the second story, we hear the sound of music, the lights come on in this "second floor that should not exist," and the shadows of those who live there are reflected in the windows! Some young girls can be heard clattering their washing pans, chattering as they noisily descend the stairs!

This scene, in which the past is suddenly reborn, is of a virtually terrifying beauty and calls forth in us a powerful response. Indeed, the lights seem to come on in our own hearts, in our own second story, so long abandoned. From that point on, whatever surprising thing may occur, we can open the doors of our hearts without further resistance.

In this play, as in many of her others, Watanabe Eriko uses the notion of a "house" as a basic structuring device through which to create a sense of

The Three Circle Company's 1983 production of *Melancholy When the Flowers Bloom* by Watanabe Eriko. *In the center:* Watanabe Eriko herself as the Sleeping Princess.

wonder. This may be because for some reason we respond naturally to the correspondence between houses and human souls. Nevertheless, few writers have used this device so effectively. It seems that cherry blossoms are blown to us from that mysterious world that opens up beyond the ceiling and the staircase. Next, a sleeping princess (played by Watanabe Eriko), straight out of a fairy tale, bursts forth from that long covered passageway that must surely continue on the other side of the ceiling. Then a mummy appears right out of the wall. Such sensibilities are not those of one who simply passes absently through the space she has lived in. Rather, they represent the imaginative power of someone who has really come to inhabit her space, bringing to her sense of home all the fullness of love and hate now layered deep within her own heart.

At the center of this driving force, which gives rise to such a sense of wonder, lies an image of the soul of all our lost youth. The majority of the characters, clutching as they do at memories of regret and pain that they cannot yet shed, live in perpetual dusk. The shadows that surround Prince Ki are those of the drowned youth Kachi, the dead youth Akihiko, betrayed in a love suicide, and his paramour. And also there appears a middle-aged man who seeks with all his might to find again the spirit of youth that has wholly vanished from his heart.

And, for the men, there is always the image of the lost girl. It is the memory of that girl in the seat next to them who walked down that covered passageway leading from the school, never to return. Both the middle-aged man and his companion, an old, blind man, each acting out a childish drama in the chambers of his own mind, wait intently for her to reappear. Toward the final curtain, the old man (played by Azuma Ginnosuke) mutters to himself a phrase that strikes the audience as profoundly significant. "From one end of the passageway to the other, how is it different?"

The atmosphere that fills this play is both comic and painful. More important, it is warm and gentle. The author insists on nothing. No metaphysical lights shine down on us. Rather, we are shown those human beings who simply loiter, in the midst of a sense of regret and mourning. They reveal to us the very structures of their hearts in which those spirits of vanished youth live on. Nor is it a question of some vast "something" that is waiting to be buried. Rather, it is we as spectators who come to realize that we ourselves can seek out our own staircases, our own covered passageways, where those things we think we have forgotten can never truly pass away. Thus, we see things differently, as though for the first time.

The direction is as worthy of praise as the play itself. The actors give rich and individual performances that reveal that their skills have grown ever greater. This troupe has entered a period of new maturity of which we can expect even greater accomplishments.

45. MALCONTENT PASSIONS

Radical Party

Written and directed by Kawamura Takeshi

THE THIRD EROTICA

1983

This was the first presentation I have seen by this troupe, which I attended on opening night. There were lots of empty seats in the little Art Theatre Shinjuku, where the production was staged. I had been looking forward to the performance, but, as I took a seat in the front row, I began to wonder whether I would be disappointed.

Soon after the play began, there occurred the provocative scene in which the actors, ropes tied around their throats as though they were somehow bound together, passed from hand to hand a filthy piece of cloth that they squeezed out as they twitched and screamed their incomprehensible obscenities. Everything was suddenly caught up in this rough-hewn energy, just as if the whole stage had become alive with an electric current, which, in turn, surged outward, charging the audience as well. There were surely some among the spectators who wanted only to distance themselves from that force. Yet, opening myself up to this vision, I realized that this psychic electricity, which at first appeared merely crude and violent, flowed of necessity from the very energy that sustained Kawamura's whole conception.

The nature of this current was by no means a pleasing one. It rubbed the nerves raw, producing only a sense of pain. Yet by the same token it forced living breath into that sense of vile roughness that lies sleeping within all of us. And so it seemed that, in fact, we had all somehow become charged with that black energy as well.

Witnessing this production of the Third Erotica, I was reminded, first of all, of the early work of Kara Jūrō's Situation Theatre. Here was the same kind of energy that his troupe first showed in the 1960s, an force long subsided, a villainous energy, violent, oppositional. The kind of rough glitter that Kara first created has been reborn here. And for that, I was glad.

This troupe, which was founded in 1980, may find the comparison annoying. After all, Kawamura himself was born in 1959 and is now only in his early twenties. Most of the members of his troupe are twenty years younger than Kara. The two companies are of two different generations, as far apart as fathers and sons. Suggesting any such connection may thus seem untoward.

Be that as it may, however, the thick and gloomy energy that floods out of this play, and the technique supported by a physical sense of the power of violation that infuses the very structures of the production and that mixes serious purpose with extravagant nonsense, seem resolved to break open our restricted sense of reality and let in some fresh air. In its concentration on the centrality of physicality and the power of attack, and in the vision revealed in the play of a teeming urban underclass, this bold young troupe shows commonalities with its predecessor. That wild, villainous energy, so plentiful when the little theatre movement began but lost over time, now seems reborn here within the unclean atmosphere created by Kawamura. That energy seems also authentically of our time.

In a fancy Shinjuku apartment, a dour group of youths is engaged in an ominous business, providing not callgirls but callboys. Most of these youths already have criminal records and seem soiled to their very souls. The play presents this bizarre mode of life in a way that is surprisingly detached yet at the same time thrilling. One young man, named Kita Aohiko (played by Sasaki Hideki), who has a history of murder, screams out, as in the American film *Carrie*, that he "dreams of a pure terror." He brings about a veritable whirlwind as he demonstrates a virtually superhuman capacity for destruction, inviting a brutal catharsis in the scene in which he violently destroys their room in the apartment. Then too, there is a strange and dynamic power conveyed during the scene in which he ties together Torapisu (played by Arizono Yoshiki), Karuma (played by Ebihara Hiroyuki), and Tesu (played by Fukaura Kanako) to force them to see within themselves the extraordinary forces that lie within them.

Shortly before the final curtain, the group uses its power in order to hurry off to "that other world" that lies above and beyond ordinary reality. At that moment, the spectators gasp in surprise as the scenery at the back of the stage suddenly divides and the steel shutters behind slowly part in order to show the actual alleyway of the Shinkuju night. Now, in that larger space, the play continues, lit only by pine torches. This kind of play within a play, in which the drama must compete with reality, indeed, spurn that reality, represents a grandiose effort indeed.

Ropesu (played by Kawamura himself), who impersonates a member of a secret society, and his subordinate Samiira (played by Katori Satsuki) both give off a vital and glittering energy. And the fact that, in addition to writing and directing, Kawamura also plays a small part may well invite still another comparison with Kara Jūrō.

No matter how peaceful the times in which we see such a play, our human passions themselves are never completely at rest. "There is nothing to rebel against; indeed, there exists no rebellion itself"—such may be the sense we have of this time, yet underneath the surface squirm and wriggle these malcontent passions waiting to burst forth. This play gives them to us

Radical Party by Kawamura Takeshi, produced by the Third Erotica in 1983. *In the center:* Kawamura Takeshi himself playing the role of Ropesu.

at close range. The phrase "the shadow of the wind" occurs again and again in the course of the drama. We cannot see such a shadow with our ordinary eyes, used to the daylight as they are, but this play proposes to make clear to us the precise nature of that terrible darkness.

In one respect, then, this is not a "revolutionary play." It is worth noting that Kita remarks at one point, "We are the children of revolutionaries who do not believe in revolution." It is clear that this play is structured so as to get its message across indirectly, as do action and perhaps war films. The play is one of paradox; in it, "revolution" is meaningless, and this "party," itself so "radical," stands in opposition to nothing whatsoever. Yet, in all its sharpness, the play shows us a mercilessly clear outline of the author's malcontent vision.

46. A PAINFUL SENSE OF DISTANCE

Afternoon of a Man and Woman

Written by Yamazaki Tetsu

Staged by the directing unit of the Seventh Ward

Troupe

THE SEVENTH WARD TROUPE

1983

If you get off the subway at the Machiya station on the Chiyoda line, right in the middle of Tokyo, you can follow along a narrow path, go past the shops that are just putting on their lights for the evening, then turn right by the old lantern shop (which is pretty hard to spot), then finally bear left at the corner where the noodle shop is located. If you get that far, you will eventually come to an alley of row houses, with flowerpots lined up one after another in front of the doors. There you will find a tiny park, no bigger than a cat's paw, where the voices of children will be sounding out. Now you have located all the elements for a nostalgic evening collected here together in this old section of Tokyo.

The small theatre that serves as a headquarters for the Seventh Ward Troupe, run by Ishibashi Renji and Midori Mako, can be found here, on the first floor of one of these rows of two-story houses. Most of the small theatres in Tokyo are removed from the older parts of the city; they can be found in the Yamanote district, or in the suburbs on the main railroad line, or along some of the private lines that snake into the further reaches of the city. The obstacle presented by the troupe's location in the old section suggests in turn one aspect of the group's basic disposition. In those terms, it is not surprising, then, that their first production, in 1976, was staged in a rundown movie house, long empty, in a deserted factory area.

It had been three years since I made my way to this tiny theatre along the Ara River. On that occasion, the group presented Kara Jūrō's *Two Women*. Since then, no productions had been mounted. Would it be possible to re-create such a strong sense of theatrical power?

As it turned out, Yamazaki's new production, *Afternoon of a Man and Woman*, revealed a force that exceeded every expectation and left behind a powerful sense of shock. Of course, Yamazaki's text itself (originally titled *Pawnshop*) was outstanding. And, although I thought that to have such a gap between performances was not necessarily a good thing for the troupe, it turned out that this production was well worth waiting for.

At the beginning of the performance, we catch a glimpse of Midori Mako, dressed entirely in white, seemingly floating in the pale dawn before the pawnshop. She reads one phrase ᵐm *Gravestones of Spring*, a popular

Yamazaki Tetsu's *Afternoon of a Man and Woman*, produced by the Seventh Ward Troupe in 1983. The Wife (Midori Mako) and her Husband (Ishibashi Renji).

book of poetry published in 1965 by the left-wing student Oku Kōhei, who later committed suicide. "There are countless nights for human beings. But only one truly sweet night. . . ." In that instant, I found myself transported into the world of the play. True enough, this quotation possesses its own surprising sense of naïveté; yet, above and beyond that feeling, Midori Mako creates with her voice an unusual and acute power that can unlock the doors that hold us back within the world of everyday experience. It is a rare occasion indeed to find in the theatre the sound of a voice that can gather into itself all the dangerous sweetness of that portion of the human personality seeking to leave behind all that to which the flesh binds us, all the pitiful limitations of reality, in an attempt to soar upward, outward.

Then, instantly, we breathe the atmosphere, the raw and melancholy smell of the pawnshop, a veritable storehouse of frustration and disillusionment.

A drama about a couple whose marriage has been shipwrecked and washed up on the shoals of life is nothing special. And the device of a husband and wife who, as a way of getting through their crisis, share the illusion that they possess a child who has never been born is familiar to us from Edward Albee's *Who's Afraid of Virginia Woolf?* However, what is unique about the sharp sense of tension generated here is the fact that most of the characters who appear in the play have at one time dreamed of a "revolution." It is the gap between the former dream and present reality, or, more precisely, the pain of that reality, that serves to drive them on through their lives with great diligence, even though they are trapped in a pawnshop containing items whose value is tenuous at best. They too are unsure of their own human value, and so their own lives and dreams alike seem, in consonance with the items pawned, tenuous. In the end, the drama rushes to the moment when Midori Mako hangs herself in the storehouse.

All of these characters have been "comrades." This includes the Man (played by Ishibashi Renji), who, while running the pawnshop, is closely connected to the disasters that occur in the course of the drama, his Wife, the left-wing head of a now-closed-down factory (played by Asaka Tōru), and a young man (played by Masamura Kazuya) with a mental disorder who wears a dirty white helmet and devotes all his energy to trying to make his clumsily built tin-plated airplane fly. None of these characters can change the course of their lives. They must simply struggle through, even if they feel that they have somehow become pawned articles themselves. Yet they do not despair. They recognize the distance as distance, the pain as pain, as they continue to strive on, even in their roles as pawns.

At one point, the wife suddenly says to her husband, "You . . . who are you?" These words are peculiar, and they are truly frightening. Here, the ordinary, familiar connections that make up our daily lives are suddenly snapped off and the very basis of life itself questioned.

Is the wife really pregnant? Or, as a kind of compensation for her flowing "illusions," is this perhaps a device that the couple has created in order to push themselves through the crisis that they face?

So it is then that, after the woman has hung herself in the storehouse, the doors of the structure open wide again. That moment produces a moving spectacle indeed. Suddenly, for the first time, the sky is a blinding blue, and, to the strident sound of a Warsaw workers' song (!), the phantom girl who formed the object of her mother's dream (Midori Mako, now in a second role) actually materializes. She appears, smiling, in a bright red dress. There is no vestige of pain or heaviness; rather, we have manifested in an instant a sense of expansiveness, of brilliance.

The smile produced by Midori Mako is a strange and surprising one. It is bright, and there is no sense of conflict, yet it is aimed at nothing, it has no place of origin; it is a brightly hollow, dimly introverted smile. This smile now seems a manifestation of that "revolution" that still exists, even within the context of a painful sense of distance that has been created. Its appearance makes this final curtain unforgettable.

47. MANKIND, AND THOSE
THEATRICAL SLIPPAGES

Man of La Mancha

Book by Dale Wasserman, lyrics by Joe Darion,

music by Mitch Leigh

Directed by Nakamura Takao

A TŌHŌ PRODUCTION

1983

Those theatre works are rare indeed that you can return to see again and again without tiring of them and that not only show you something new each time but also reflect your own self as clearly as a mirror. So far as I am concerned, *Man of La Mancha* represents one of those remarkable accomplishments.

Since this musical was first presented in Japan in 1969, four years after its New York premiere, this is the seventh time this Tōhō production, directed by Nakamura Takao, with choreography by Edward Roll, has been presented (nine, if you count the Nagoya and Osaka productions); I have seen virtually all of them, and I remain struck by the high aims and accomplishments of the work.

The production remains as successful as before. Matsumoto Kōshirō, Kojika Ban, Tomotake Masanori, and Kijima Shinichi head up the superlative cast, which has remained more or less together since the first production. Since the fifth mounting, in 1977, Kōzuki Noboru has been added to the original cast in the role of the serving maid Aldonza. Their long work together in what has become virtually a commune-like atmosphere continues to reveal a fresh sense of intimacy. In fact, it is exceptional that, in the fourteen years since *Man of La Mancha* was first produced in Japan, most of the cast has remained together. I find it moving that they have been able to maintain the quality of their performances and the level of excitement generated after all this time. I have gone to see this present Tōhō production twice.

Fourteen years. Times have certainly changed. Our world has been much transformed since then. And I have changed too. When I think of the fact that *Man of La Mancha* has put on some years as well, the strong response that I feel is by no means an ordinary one. My own reactions to this work have altered depending on the times and my own situation. Yet my response remains just as strong. And, when the evening ends, I feel as grateful as ever. Why is this so?

One part of the secret of this work can be found in the ingenious three-tiered structure that Dale Wasserman has created, which resembles an exquisitely nested set of boxes.

The largest framework that envelops his conception is the dimension of "reality," which here takes the audience to a jail in sixteenth-century Spain, where a group of prisoners are confined as they wait to go on trial before the Inquisition. Cervantes (played by Matsumoto Kōshirō) and his servant (played by Kojika Ban) are among them.

Inside is a smaller box; here Cervantes and the prisoners act out a play within a play called *Don Quixote*. Yet this story as well is nested within still another box, that of the world of a poor country squire who lives in La Mancha named Alonzo Quijana. Quijana, caught up in his dreams,

Tōhō's 1983 production of the Wasserman/Leigh musical *Man of La Mancha. From the left*: Kojika Ban as Sancho Panza, Matsumoto Kōshirō as Don Quixote, and Kōzuki Noboru as the maid Aldonza. (Photo courtesy of Tōhō.)

becomes mad and sets out on his travels, transforming himself into the knight Don Quixote. In this dream world, the bedraggled maid at the inn, Aldonza (played by Kōzuki Noboru), becomes the woman his vision requires, the princess Dulcinea.

So it is, then, that reality, the first dimension (at least, this is "reality" from the point of view of the second dimension), allows us to witness the slippages between the other two, and so it is that Matsumoto Kōshirō, who plays Cervantes himself in the dimension of "reality," becomes both Quijana and Don Quixote. The same layers, in another sense, can be seen as one of the woman prisoners becomes first Aldonza and then Dulcinea.

Thus, what we see here is no simple dramatization of the novel *Don Quixote* but a multilayered tale chronicling that cruel gap between dream and reality that undoubtedly gave rise in Cervantes' mind to the concept for the novel, one that the great Spanish author himself never composed. We are given therefore one more startling turn in this complex drama.

I remember being very struck at the time of the first production by certain lines spoken by "Don Quixote" in the play within a play. For example, "Facts are the enemy of truth," or, "Too much sanity may be madness. And maddest of all, to see life as it is and not as it should be." Such lines still have a strong effect, and the audience continues to be moved.

However, I find that, on this occasion, I am moved not so much by the words of Don Quixote himself as by the fate of the characters in the play's two interior worlds. Even the most miserable of mankind must find the Don Quixote or a Dulcinea that lives within them, yet, should they try to look for their dreams in the real world, they can find them manifested only in a pitiful, ridiculous madman. Such a dramatic structure, which can highlight just these sorts of differences, reveals a closeness in feeling to the spirit of Cervantes, who, of course, never directly wrote such a message himself; I can only call out "bravo!" to Mr. Wasserman for this extraordinary conception, which can encompass so well the vision of this classic Spanish writer.

We as spectators are able to identify with any and all of these various levels; therefore, however we ourselves may change over the years, our point of contact can shift but never disappear altogether. Therefore, the excitement engendered by the original conception can never diminish for us. In other words, this structure, capable as it is of shifting between these three levels, can seize us all, wherever we may be in the trajectory of our own individual lives.

It should be said as well that the affirmation of the existence of just such refracted "slippages," in the case of the present work at least, does not lead to any sense of pessimism in the spectators. Indeed, in witnessing these terrible gaps, we are urged on ever more fiercely to go even deeper.

This is because, as the dialogue in the play indicates, even if the country squire Alonzo Quijana should die, the spirit of Don Quixote, which informs him, "will never die." This sense of hope and passion, this "slippage" from which mankind can never escape, is therefore transferred to the prisoners, like some vast movement of a pendulum, and so even we who merely witness this spectacle can now each begin to walk, one by one, with this "man of La Mancha" ourselves. It is not that "Don Quixote" merely equals the "man of La Mancha." We as human beings can allow that heaven-sent child, Don Quixote, to nest somewhere in that set of interlocking boxes we keep within each of our own hearts; we ourselves thus become the "man of La Mancha."

Matsumoto Kōshirō plays his role with admirable maturity and depth. At this moment (and in the future as well), it is hard to imagine a performer who could bring the strengths to this role that he does. Kojika Ban, as Sancho Panza, has perhaps lost a little something in the requisite fullness of his singing voice, but his performance in the role is altogether moving. Kōzuki Noboru brings to Aldonza exactly the right sort of vigor.

One last caution. This is not the first time the producers have engaged an orchestra inadequate to the needs of the score. During a period we can justly call the "age of musicals," and at a time when performers have learned to sing and dance, the low level of musicianship therein evinced is distracting.

48. A WORLD IN WHICH THAT'S ALL WE CAN DO

Memories of the Little Finger

Written and directed by Noda Hideki

THE DREAM WANDERERS

1983

The name of Noda's new play, *Memories of the Little Finger*, puts me in mind of a song made popular a few years back by the singer Itō Yukari; both suggest at first glance something both bashful and somehow nonchalant. But, in fact, despite its title, this play is exactly the opposite, for Noda has encompassed here a much more expansive world than usual, and, as a result, I found myself happily surprised. The theatrical images he has created here show a new vitality and maturity.

In *Memories of the Little Finger*, Noda goes beyond his usual theme of youth and coming of age, striking off in several new directions. Of course his old concerns make their appearance, but here youth is not glamorized or endowed with special characteristics as it is in his *Prisoner of Zenda*. Indeed, the central figure in this new play is a young man far removed from such a world, the perfect insomniac Akagi Keiichirō (played by Uesugi Shōzō) who is linked in turn to a witch-like mother, Kasuba Seiko (played by Noda, dressed as a woman, the kind of role he particularly enjoys), who will bring forth in the course of the play her own "deluded youths."

Having so often pictured the crystalline purity of youth, Noda now enters a new territory, one where women's blood flows and they become pregnant and give birth—the world of the true mother.

Noda's writing remains wholly personal and characteristic. For example, Seiko's image is overlaid with that of the mysterious youth Caspar Hauser (the abandoned child who became famous in nineteenth-century Germany because he learned to speak only as an adult; he was eventually murdered by an unknown assailant). Seiko carries within her body the ability to re-create her "youthful years" on any number of occasions. However confusing all this may be, it can at least safely be observed that she partakes of a larger sense of life than any of the "youths" to whom she gives birth during the course of the play.

Noda shows us that part of ourselves that idolizes youth as well as that other part that now feels estranged from youth in every way. Here, dream relates to illusion, which comes to equal delusion. All are battling reality. In his previous plays, Noda has concentrated on his conception of "youth" itself. Here, that idea now turns on itself again. In this newest play, humanity's enormous capacity to create illusions, "a whole family of delusions," now does battle with the enormity of actuality itself, "a whole family of reality."

Soon after the curtain goes up, there is an extremely touching and lovely scene that establishes impressionistically the sense of discord between reality and illusion. In the darkness, the sound of a telephone being dialed can be heard. On the left side of the stage, Akagi, unable to sleep, appears. He whispers to himself, "One . . . two . . . three," as he counts sheep, trying to fall asleep. Then, in the center of the stage, we see a group

From left to right: Enjōji Aya, Noda Hideki, and Takeshita Akiko in a fantasy scene from the 1983 production by the Dream Wanderers of Noda Hideki's *Memories of the Little Finger.*

of young people, clad in pajamas, who slowly rise up on their feet. They have on their backs small pillows and what appears to be some sort of bedding. As they begin to wriggle around and then turn their backs to us, it seems that they are all wearing Japanese kites!

In the midst of their gentle and pleasant sleep, these young people lightly and joyously rise higher and higher in the air, borne by the kites on their backs. This delightful image contrasts with that of the "real" young man, who is still counting sheep in a desperate attempt to fall asleep. Indeed, as any adult knows all too well, the kind of rupture portrayed here is altogether familiar.

Later, such ruptures reappear. For example, there is the scene in which the centaurs, half man, half beast, have the tops and bottoms of their bodies rent asunder.

When casting around in my mind for an example of another theatre piece in which the play between illusion and reality figures so importantly, I always think of Dale Wasserman's *Man of La Mancha.* In that musical, the gap between illusion and reality is the central feature of all the characters' lives; indeed, the point seems to be that we/they have no choice but to believe in illusion. No matter how often I see this musical, which dates originally from the early 1960s, I am still deeply moved.

These two works, in fact, often resonate directly with each other. In fact, in the latter half of *Memories of the Little Finger*, the theme song from *Man of La Mancha* sounds loud and clear through the theatre. It seems clear that, while retaining the idea of "youth" as his central conception, Noda is moving here into the very midst of life itself.

It goes without saying that in his play Noda takes the side of those "deluded youths." But his serious intent is mixed with his usual sense of fun, with puns and jokes abounding. Such a style has caused some to dismiss Noda's work as superficial. If we speak of the dichotomy between "truth" and "falsehood," many have found Noda a writer who chooses "falsehood" and never shores up any vision of the "truth." This current work, however, offers no opportunity for misunderstanding. With one sweep of his magic cane, constructed from all his word games, Noda can flip over a pun and so, by means of a joke, suddenly reveal the deep layers of truth that lie within his conception.

Noda himself wrote in 1983 that, "while the skin exists on the surface, it also constitutes the actual interior as well." In his vision, it is really that interior skin that in fact "wraps up the outside," and not vice versa.

At the risk of repeating myself, let me say that this fine play represents Noda's most mature work. The cast is vigorous, and the scale of the performance, so appropriate to the work, is much larger than what has been seen in his previous efforts.

49. THE BASIC PRINCIPLES OF A VISION ALREADY EXPERIENCED

Rules for Sleeping in the Universe

Written and directed by Kōkami Shōji

THE THIRD STAGE

1984

All those who express themselves artistically move, it seems, in the direction of one of two polarities.

One of these involves a talent for constructing a world of one's own making. By keeping strictly within the boundaries of this self-created universe, the talents of such a creative figure may at times not be in the closest touch with the problems of contemporary society. Digging into the deepest layers of the human condition, however, such a writer can give birth to a new world, sometimes with its own astonishing contours. This world can seem a new one for us, and at the same time it can represent an ancient one as well.

The other involves the journalistic talent of a genius who can accurately observe and thereby reflect on the world around him and also sensitively predict the future. Such a talent enjoys emphasizing the freshness of the break between the past and the present. Therefore, the originality of such a writer consists in finding a fresh way in which to treat a subject, rather than depending on the power of pivotal images.

Kōkami Shōji, who has been working as a playwright and director for the Third Stage, founded in 1981, was born in 1958 and so is, at this writing, still a relative youngster. Until now, his considerable talents seemed to lie in the journalistic end of the spectrum; that is, it seems to me, he has been a sharp observer of the actual state of contemporary society. In that context, this production of his newest play, *Rules for Sleeping in the Universe*, staged in a small theatre in the suburbs of Tokyo used by five small companies, is of particular note. For, in addition to finding reflected in his work, as I always have, a coloration suggestive of the mentality of the young these days, which is made to assume a decorative function in the drama, I find that, in this instance, those ideas have become part of the very structure of the work itself.

By the same token, I cannot say that I was particularly excited or moved by the production. Indeed, I was rather bored watching it and felt a certain disharmony with what I was witnessing. The endless gags that keep repeating themselves, amusing as they may be, did not generate heartfelt laughter. I had the feeling that quite a number of them were "variations" on things I had heard or seen before. I found no great originality in the dialogue; little of it was of the imaginative order to take wing and carry the audience along with it. Harking back to the same author's *Déjà Vu*, produced last year, most of the elements in the play seemed to me quite familiar already.

The real interest of the production, however, lies in the fact that the characters *themselves* are quite aware of the fact that they have already experienced these things. When Iwatani Shinji, who plays "the Male," begins to dance, he suddenly becomes aware of this situation, whispering to himself, "that's his dance step." He adjusts his thoughts and begins again; but soon he stops midway through, muttering, "I've already seen this."

This sense of déjà vu never goes away; indeed, it is the central notion

The ensemble playing games in Kōkami Shōji's *Rules for Sleeping in the Universe,* produced by the Third Stage in 1984. (Photo by Okada Hatsuhiko.)

around which the play is constructed. The boredom engendered by repetition reinforces the sense that somehow everything has already been experienced before, and through these feelings is manifested the author's vision of the world. In the end, the basic principles of the universe boil down to nothing more than that it's déjà vu all over again! The games represent the countless fragments that constitute our sense of the world, and, just like the interactions of the fragments, they are endless and interchangeable.

The play itself consists of a series or chain of imitations. A group of friends come and go, replacing each other as they perform a series of little tales and sketches that in and of themselves constitute certain kinds of games, particularly those that suggest those television game shows that seem to stretch on endlessly.

Other kinds of "games" have been seen in the theatre before now. Genet, Abe Kōbō, Shimizu Kunio, Tsuka Kōhei: all these writers have sharply distinguished between reality and the masks they create. Their plays set in high relief the vast gap, the sharp split, between those masks and the difficulties of real life. However, in the games played here by Kōkami, there is no difference articulated between the mask and reality itself. Any such boundary remains unexpressed; therefore one seemingly, endlessly, changes back and forth into the other. One "theatre game" resembles a popular Wednesday night television game show program, and the heroine's game of "Let's Play Gorky," based on the grim vision of society found in *The Lower Depths,* appears to be an imitation of a "theatre" related to the subject of nuclear warfare. And there appears to be no sense of verticality, no view expressed that one game is more important or significant than another. All are treated equally as a joke, held up for our amusement.

Seen from the outside, the play itself therefore seems to stand as a kind of game that creates patterns from all those sorts of things that we already know. Yet there is a strong sense expressed here as well that in and of itself this spectacle is consciously intended to manifest a sort of world vision, which has been created within a dramatic framework. This is no simple attempt to make the audience laugh. It seems clear that *Rules for Sleeping in the Universe* represents an attempt to dismantle the kind of theatrical structures so familiar until now.

The various actors involved in the production show great individuality. The attractive sparkle the dialogue possesses is largely due to their own creative power as performers.

50. A FIGHT AGAINST FIXED FORMS

Japan Wars

Written and directed by Kawamura Takeshi

THE THIRD EROTICA

1984

In recent years, one characteristic of the theatre created by the younger generation is a preoccupation with predicting the near future rather than finding meaning in the past. These plays do not comb the part for clues to understand the present. They seek to observe life as it will be lived in the future, positing, with a certain unease, the theatre as some kind of laboratory for observing the emerging human condition.

To put things in the most general terms, from the 1960s through the middle of the 1970s, much of the work of the little theatre movement involved searching for the significance of the past. The question was first posed by Kara Jūrō early on: "In the end, what kind of creature am I?" As if as in attempt to answer this, the majority of plays written in that period explore history, time, and memory in order to locate and establish the "I" or "we," whether in personal, group, or, occasionally, class terms. It seemed necessary for those dramatists to attempt to establish this relationship between the self and the past in order to create what they believed to be an authentic territory that the theatre itself could occupy.

In contrast, what we have been seeing recently has been an attempt to reflect in the theatre the nature of human existence within the science fiction–like projection of a mirror that locates itself sometime in the near future. Here, the break with the past, not the necessity of maintaining a connection with it, is emphasized. The power of the past has thereby been considerably weakened. Rather than stressing the characters' overwhelming passions, the demands of the flesh, or any special powers granted to them by virtue of their own individuality, the authors of these newer plays express with a certain lightness and a clearheaded comic sense a vision of some new human homogeneity. Such a development is doubtless the result of the increasing urbanization of our society as well as a general indifference to the problems of poverty during this time of relative affluence. I see these tendencies in such currently active theatre troupes as Kisaragi Koharu's group NOISE, the Third Stage, the Third Erotica, and Tsutsumi Yasuyuki's Neverland Musical Comedy.

Yet it should be said at the same time that, while the work of the Third Erotica does touch on these contemporary tendencies, at the same time the group pursues its own particular ends. This new work, which is part of a series of productions presented by a group of five new companies using a theatre in the Tokyo suburb of Shimokitazawa, certainly does gain my attention. *Japan Wars* is a powerfully attractive work.

The feeling that the play creates is akin to that of good science fiction, and the production certainly shows off Kawamura's skills as a storyteller. Indeed, one gets the feeling that, in *Japan Wars*, the story line itself takes undue precedence and that the emotive power of the actors has been curbed too much. This may, however, be necessary if the atmosphere necessary to effective science fiction is to be achieved. In fact, this production is the most polished that the troupe has so far presented, simple and straightforward rather than merely violent.

The goal of the play is to make clear the way in which the past is to be dealt with. At first appearance, *Japan Wars* seems to be a play composed in the style of those others that seek a means to search out the past and define the present through a solidarity with others; yet, in its concluding moments, such images vanish in the brilliance of a sudden reversal.

The protagonist of the play, a young man referred to simply as O (played by Sasaki Hideki), has obviously once belonged to a group of radical terrorists. He suddenly comes to his senses to find himself imprisoned on a gunboat along with of a group of young men and women he does not know. "Why . . . why should I be here?" he asks himself, thereby beginning a drama of self-discovery.

As it turns out, however, all the other young people who surround him are androids who have been cleverly programmed for use in war by the person known as the General (played by Kawamura Takeshi). What is more, it becomes clear by the end of the play that the sense of the past and of memory that these androids possess has been programmed in them; even their seemingly spontaneous rebellion against "the system" is itself a scrupulously prepared program intended to permit them to mature. "Programming called 'rebellion,' " or "the final lesson—'rebellion' "!

While the play uses androids as a central device, it is clear that the play deals with humanity and speaks to the present. There appear to be two major critical themes articulated here.

The first is a critique of the special privileges accorded our sense of individuality. This is, in turn, a critique of those plays based on the need for self-scrutiny.

A second is the question of whether many of the actions and senti-

Kawamura Takeshi's *Japan Wars*, produced by the Third Erotica in 1984. The androids attack.

ments so embedded in human beings, based as they are on ideas of "love" and "rebellion," are indeed merely examples of "programming" themselves.

It seems clear that the play is modeled on Philip K. Dick's novel *Do Androids Dream of Electric Sheep?* and is influenced as well by Ridley Scott's 1982 science fiction film *Blade Runner.* In that context, the touching beauty of the scene in which O's battle companion, I (played by Fukaura Kanako), speaks with such feeling of her memories, imprinted so long ago, of a high school dance party makes a very powerful impression.

The play is constructed so as to bring directly to our consciousness not only the structures that support us but all those devices that subtly control our words and our representations; indeed, the play asks how we might transcend those secret and repressive frameworks. In the last scene of the play, the androids, who by now have come to realize the uselessness of self-scrutiny, set out to face what they call "our war," so beginning a seemingly endless battle against these ideas so firmly implanted within them.

The work of the Third Erotica in *Japan Wars* suggests that the group is not at ease with the sanitized and innocuous "plentifulness" of the present; neither, however, do they dream of revolution in order to change the present system. Rather, they show us that both attitudes are the result of a kind of "programming" that must be dissected and investigated, with no hint that mischief or mayhem is among their motives. In this regard, I applaud the loftiness of their intent.

51. THE SYMPATHIES AND DISJUNCTURES OF NOSTALGIA

Tango at the End of Winter

Written by Shimizu Kunio

Directed by Ninagawa Yukio

A PARCO THEATRE PRODUCTION

1984

On the basis of past experience, I was certainly aware that "those first three moments after the curtain goes up" are often crucial to Ninagawa's methods as a director, but I must say that, even so, this time I was stunned by what I saw.

As soon as the curtain went up on this new play of Shimizu's, staged in Shibuya's comfortable Parco theatre, what should appear on stage but another audience, effectively a mirror image of the space that we were occupying. The real audience was stunned and silent, but the audience on stage was laughing feverishly, rustling around, swaying like a huge wave. It was clear that they were intently watching a film (something like *Easy Rider*), following the voice of the hero on the screen; then, with a loud noise, the "on-screen" protagonists fell, and we could hear sobs and groans from the watching "audience."

A direct, hot-blooded response from these lithe and clever young spectators. It suddenly seemed that they were meant as a portrait of ourselves as we had been ten years before, in the late 1960s and early 1970s.

Among the spectators were young men wearing helmets. Some were wrapped in bandages, and others had blood smeared on them. Separated from one another in the darkness, and caught up in the frenzy of their ideas and their sincerity, that on-stage audience seemed somehow connected with the "real," theatre audience. Of course, their theatre was old, dirty, and rundown, unlike our snug and attractive Parco. Clearly, Shimizu and Ninagawa wanted to take us back in time, and, as a starting point, they conjured up the atmosphere of their Shinjuku theatre when it first opened in 1977.

They certainly intended to create a feeling of longing in their audience, more precisely a nostalgia for the politically troubled 1970s. You could feel it.

A creepy sensation came over me; after all, I did feel a certain sympathy with the plays the two of them had produced during those years, now a thing of the past. For a moment, it almost seemed as if I were sitting in that theatre on the stage myself. I felt the wind of time on my face, and my yearning for the past brought me close to tears.

Yet, filled with nostalgia as I was, two disturbing thoughts disrupted my mood.

The first voice was critical. "Privileging my own past is a form of pride, the proof that I myself have grown old. What must these young actors, who know nothing of the reality of the 1970s, think of such an emotional response?"

The second voice was in turn critical of the first (to some extent at least). "Any human being, after all, puts down roots somewhere, sometime. What is cruel is that time changes everything, isn't that so? Even if it's a question of regression, Shimizu and Ninagawa can show us that they still believe in the truth of this period, as we all once did. Don't we have every right to appreciate what they are trying to do?"

And so discomfort and sympathy struggled within me as I watched this brilliantly polished production, which had been prepared with such evident skill by Ninagawa.

Shimizu Kunio's play, too, somehow looks toward the past. That is, rather than striking off in new directions, he has decided to allow his audience to glimpse once again those old techniques and motifs that he employed so well at the beginning of his career. Indeed, this new play seems basically a panorama of his old theatrical techniques. The moment the protagonist enters—a character fond of hills and stairs, which allows Ninagawa to indulge his well-known love for incorporating staircases in stage settings—the play begins to resemble a set of nested boxes.

Just as you would expect, an older brother and his younger brother enter, then a husband and wife, their relationship as usual frayed. Next a character appears who is losing his memory, a theme that figures prominently in Shimizu's earlier work. It is a powerful image, as though reflected deep in a mirror, providing the sense of an uneasy identity.

On this occasion, however, the atmosphere is ominous; the memory loss of this character, Kiyoura Sei (played by Hira Mikijirō), a middle-aged actor who was formerly a star, is far advanced. Now, whether on stage or in the midst of ordinary conversations, he continues to speak using the words of others; in order to escape from his sense of self-disgust and unease, he is purposefully destroying his memory. Nevertheless, what has the power to restore that memory is the glittering image of a "peacock" (an elegant sentence from Mishima Yukio's story "Peacock" is quoted), which triggers in him nostalgia for his youth; restorative also is his constant quotation of dialogue, "other people's words," which he should in principle abhor. No one, not even his great love (played by Natori Yūko) from the early days of his career, or a fellow performer (played by Shiojima Akihiko), or his wife (played by Matsumoto Noriko), all three of whom he has apparently forgotten, can elicit any response from him other than speeches from *Hamlet, Othello,* and Sartre's *Kean,* all plays in which he performed when a young trainee. Thus, all his actions become, in effect, mere theatrical quotations. Everything becomes a performance, a habit that spreads like poison through his whole body.

Shimizu Kunio has here captured a personality transformed through deprivation and displacement. As he shows us this unearthly portrait of a half-crazed person propelling himself into madness, Shimizu can indeed be

A photograph taken at the 1986 revival of Shimizu Kunio's 1984 *Tango at the End of Winter*, produced at the Parco Theatre. Hira Mikijirō is the former star actor, and Natori Yūko plays the actress with whom he once performed.

said to have achieved in *Tango* a vision of the final extremity. What we see is Sei's attempt to find freedom through performance; yet, poisoned as he is by performance, he finds himself trapped in a decaying movie theatre, literally the end of the road.

I could not help but shudder the moment this decaying figure resolutely chooses a phantom partner and, along with the ghosts of his past, begins to dance a tango. He alone can see his partner. And what he sees, what he holds in his arms, is the peacock, the ideal that he has pursued since his youth and that which ties him to "that part of his life that he can no longer see."

Anyone might find it easy to laugh at Sei's cold-bloodedness. Yet, by the same token, no one can deny the keenness of his vision of the peacock.

Just before the final tableau, the director repeatedly invites our applause through the scenes he places before us. Writer and the director alike clearly find it difficult to distance themselves from the atmosphere they have created. And so it is that, in the extremity of its vision, the final curtain perfectly suits the saturated sense of the nostalgic created by Ninagawa and Shimizu.

Asakura Setsu did the stage sets, Yoshii Sumio the lighting.

52. A TALE AFTER THE MYTHS HAVE CRUMBLED

Genocide

Written and directed by Kawamura Takeshi

THE THIRD EROTICA

1984

As I have noted before, the 1980s have seen a new tendency in the plays being written, the more widespread use of a futuristic, science fiction–like style. Such has been the case with the work of several troupes reviewed in this volume, including the Third Erotica.

This represents, I believe, a fundamental change. I have enjoyed science fiction ever since my high school days, yet I remember few if any examples of its use in the theatre of the 1960s and 1970s. Nor do I remember any great expression of enthusiasm for science fiction among theatre people active at that time. Most of the plays written then searched the past, using it to sketch an energetic new portrait of the present. Both the commercial theatre and the avant-garde theatre turned their backs on the rapid rise of a high-technology society, choosing rather to look into the complexities of the human condition.

Now another period has arrived, one in which that older goal is no longer sufficient. There is now the strongly held conviction among artists that contemporary reality cannot be expressed in terms of a human subject. They examine the present, not through an uneasy alliance with the past, but through a fabricated notion of the future.

The Third Erotica has already staged a superlative drama in science fiction style, *Japan Wars*, and now again they are presenting a production based on similar situations, Kawamura's *Genocide,* which also shows off the author's powerful and complex attraction to the medium of film.

At the time this production opened, Kawamura's first anthology of plays had just been published. In the afterword to that volume, Kawamura has written that those kind of soaring desires "to go far, far away" so typical of the exaltation felt in the 1960s, as well as the phantom of a "fixed sense of self" that accompanied it, have since vanished altogether.

"Now, the myths have crumbled. And to a happy degree. And now that this has happened, we can begin to spin our own tales, unprotected as they are by myth, and with no dependence on what may lie 'afar' or involve the illusion of the 'personality.' "

As a playwright with such an adventuresome vision, it might seem that Kawamura would establish some sense of distance essential to his conception. Yet, as he has rejected both the present, in which all illusions have disappeared, and the past, which created the empty present, his final recourse has been to face the future. Kawamura has not chosen the future because of any strong attachment to it. Rather, the collapse of the present has pushed him toward it.

Most science fiction novels and films, and many of these plays as well, convey an air of detachment; in them, all passions seem under control. The Third Erotica's production of this play is, however, so intensely physical and involved with life that it challenges many of our preconceptions about science fiction. In the afterword to the published version of the play, the author himself has spoken of "that 'self' that exists in a state of doubt, one that lies beyond the confines of the system." From this perspective, the world conjured up by Kawamura is a complex one, one that possesses a richly critical nature.

Genocide is boldly conceived, making groundbreaking use of film footage. In it a film is not simply projected on a screen; rather, the film incorporated in the play in turn contains the play itself, teasing the audience with a giddy sense of ambiguity. The creation of such an atmosphere is perfectly in keeping with that sense of a futuristic state of doubt that the play presents.

As a Young Man (played by Arizono Yoshiki) who dreams of making movies talks with a projectionist (played by Ishii Kōchirō), their "dreams of film" turn into a "film of dreams" as they begin to create a melodramatic tale for "a film they wish that they could see." In this film, the entire world has been at war; only a few human beings, arrogant because of their successful crimes, now remain in the collapsing, floating city of Ephemera; the stage therefore becomes the set where their film, *Ephemera Babylon,* is being filmed. A film within a play, then still a film within a film! A character named Miss Lennie (played by Katori Satsuki), who suggests in turn Leni Reifensthal, the famous filmmaker working under the Nazis, now appears on stage. It is she who emphasizes the concept of film as a tool in a power game.

Eventually, the Young Man chooses to become a character in the film himself and so becomes trapped inside the very movie he is helping to make. Humans thus create a framework of dreams, only to be manipulated by their own handiwork. Kawamura has created here an extremely tricky, multilayered structure in which it remains unclear whether the sense that terror and humor are obverse sides of the same coin exists within the play or within the film.

Kawamura Takeshi's *Genocide,* produced in 1984 by the Third Erotica. Arizono Yoshiki as the Young Man *(center).*

As I watched this play/film, I was reminded of Satoh Makoto's *The Comic World of Shōwa,* the series of plays produced by the Black Tent Company from 1968 to 1971 that included his *February and Cinema* of 1972 and other works of his as well. In terms of using a film within a play in order to "overprint" a historical event with events from our own time, thereby creating meaning in the juxtaposition of similar (or dissimilar) images, the work of Satoh Makoto has clearly preceded that of Kawamura in *Genocide.*

Yet there is a big difference between them. For example, the kind of judgment that Satoh brings down on the present through his sense of the common people and his revolutionary sympathies does not exist in Kawamura's work. *Genocide* begins just at that point where such myths can no longer be depended on. In the course of the play, the king of crime, himself named Ephemera, says, "The world has not changed. That's all there is to say." This speech sets the gloomy tone of the whole piece. This represents neither resignation nor nihilism. In the afterword to the play, Kawamura has described this stern and "brand new place" as the premise on which his play is constructed. This sharp, disordered energy and pointed critical spirit coexist within the structures of this striking production.

53. TWENTY-FIVE HUNDRED YEARS:
GAZING AT A SCRAP PILE

Earth Station

Written and directed by Ōta Shōgo

THE TRANSFORMATION THEATRE

1985

I heard from a friend, about a year or so ago as I recall, that Ōta Shōgo was looking around for a large, open theatrical space in which to perform. He apparently wanted to mount a production that needed more space than any of the small theatres in which he had worked before; ordinary stages or halls could not accommodate him. Needless to say, his search was a hard one.

Eventually, however, Ōta found just the kind of site he needed. And it turned out to be vast indeed. He chose the remains of an old quarry in the city of Utsunomiya, north of Tokyo. The space is now used as a kind of archive and museum, and art exhibits and occasional *nō* performances have been held there. It is a huge area, hollowed out of the rock, as big as a baseball field.

On the afternoon of the thirteenth of January, I boarded a tour bus in Tokyo, along with other spectators, and made the three-hour trip north. When we arrived, the sun was already setting quickly in a frigid sky. As we began to descend a staircase, I was completely bewildered to observe the enormous space that lay spread out before me. I was astonished to learn that there was an underground performing area of that size in Japan. This cavity was now brightly lit, and the scale was such that we felt reduced to the size of tiny insects. The stone walls and ceiling were cut into the rock in perfectly straight and geometrical lines. These lines seemed in turn to suggest some powerful strength, some holy quality deriving from the vastness of the space itself; it seemed as though we had entered some ancient and sacred chamber. As we descended further and further down the shaft, the temperature dropped several degrees. The troupe provided us with blankets and pocket warmers, and we finally arrived at the benches that had been set up as seats. They were filled to overflowing. Now, in the midst of this theatrical atmosphere, Ōta's *Earth Station* began.

As the staging area became visible, a huge black mountain appeared before our eyes, probably some five meters high and twenty meters wide. Then, on the zigzag road that ran over this peculiar terrain, a woman (played by Andō Tomoko) appeared. She looked poverty stricken, and she was carrying a heavy load. Moving from stage left, she began very slowly, and in a curious, almost supernatural fashion, to climb the hill. I was reminded of the opening scene of Ōta's *The Legend of Komachi*. The woman moved gently and seemed oblivious to her surroundings, the inward direction of her thoughts suggesting great self-denial, a centripetal force.

As I examined the mountain that filled the performing area closely, I realized that it was made up of discarded man-made objects. Televisions, radios, electric fans, automobiles, motorcycles, tires, inner tubes, umbrellas, wheels—all the debris of our daily lives jumbled together and painted black. The woman was surrounded by junk.

As the play continued, all kinds of people climbed the mountain road that ran through this trash, all of them proceeding just as slowly, and with the same inexpressive and inward-looking expression on their faces. As I watched this drama chronicling the efforts of these people, performed in such an apparently nonchalant fashion, I saw that eventually they too were led to the top of this mound, finally reaching the spot where a Y-shaped tree had been planted. There was no dialogue. In the second part of the play, only one phrase, and quite a poetic one, was spoken by the women on stage. That was all. Otherwise, there remained only the oppressive silence emanating from those stern stone spaces. As time went on, there could be heard only the sounds of Satie piano music, alternating with a Vivaldi piccolo concerto.

The present production obviously represents a variation on Ōta's 1981 *Water Station*. The scrap and tires piled around a water hydrant employed there have been enlarged on here. And, as in the earlier play, various people enter without speaking. Ōta's earlier, small-scale drama has here been magnified, but the two shows still have many points in common.

However, *Earth Station* hints at the existence of a world missing from *Water Station*. It goes without saying that we are surrounded by the debris of the manufactured goods that we use to get through our lives. Now, in this vast stone cavern whose layers of rock show evidence of such great age, we find ourselves confronted with nature itself.

Surely this vision of mankind bearing up under the burden of debris serves as some sort of cautionary tale. In the second part of the play, a woman dressed in black (played by Moriya Yuki), the very image of death as she takes back the body of a stillborn child, sits for a time at the foot of the tree planted on top of the mound. Surely she must stand as a living symbol of the fact that the top of the mountain represents the gates of death.

It seems, therefore, that the forces of nature are looking down on this drama of mankind and its man-made things. The characters on stage occasionally look up toward the sky, and the play continually emphasizes vertical elements. *Earth Station* thus represents one vision of the world, indeed, of

Ōta Shōgo's 1985 *Earth Station,* produced by the Transformation Theatre. The performers work on top of an enormous pile of discarded scrap. (Photo by Furudate Katsuaki.)

the universe; it is a larger-than-life-size drama conceived on a scale never attempted by Ōta before. And, because of the holy nature of the space in which it is here being performed, *Earth Station* seems to manifest almost a religious sensibility.

It is perhaps for this reason that Ōta here employs images used in earlier plays, a practice that is for him unusual.

One of these images involves the appearance on stage of a youth who wears a straw hat, a white shirt, and short pants; he has a flute in his hand and seems caught up in the refreshing odors of summer. (The character is played by the actress Itō Maki.) He pursues a girl (played by Ushiyama Kimie) who has appeared from an abandoned refrigerator car. He enters quietly from stage left, then moves in the opposite direction from many others on the stage, exiting stage right. The character seems to symbolize the element of time in retrospect, suggesting a primal image of some insouciant morning breeze.

Another is the image of two women who meet for a second time. The girl (played by Takeuchi Makiko), who seems to wait endlessly at stage right, manages to meet her friend (played by Tōi Akemi), who appears from stage left shortly before the end of the play. Suddenly, there is thunder and lightening, and a heavy rain falls (of course, it doesn't really come down!). A young man (played by Yoneda Ryō), standing to the side, crouches to protect himself from what must be a frigid rain, but the two women, in this bitingly cold atmosphere, do exactly the reverse: they take off their outer clothing and, wearing only their slips, thrust their arms out into the falling rain.

Yet it is not death that these men and women are facing, locked as they are in their own interior worlds. The image is rather that of a fresh meeting, a new encounter. Perhaps the recognition of the awesome power of nature as exemplified in these vast stone walls has drawn such a vision out of Ōta. For both Ōta and his company, this new turn of events holds great promise indeed.

54. A TIME BEFORE EVERYTHING DISSOLVES

Taking along a Sunset like the Morning

Written and directed by Kōkami Shōji

THE THIRD STAGE

1985

As I have written before, it seems to me that the presentations over which opinion remains sharply divided are often precisely the ones that stimulate audiences and involve crucial issues. Others merely invite a nod and the comment, "Yes, good, isn't it?" In my experience, only the former kinds of productions, those about which people hold strong opinions, opinions not easily relinquished, enter a theatrical territory that can be considered truly challenging.

To judge by audience reaction, the Third Stage's present production is just such a play, for opinions about it are sharply divided. Young people who love the theatre, as well as a number of my own friends and acquaintances, condemn it absolutely. Yet I have other friends whose faces light up with pleasure at the slightest mention of the subject. And there are those who have been critical of this troupe's work until now but who have gone out of their way to praise this production. There is no denying the wide range of responses.

As for myself, I found the production quite fascinating. While not greatly excited or moved, I nevertheless did admire the fresh intelligence and basic theatricality that it offered. It seems to me that Kōkami and this company have stretched themselves in order to represent the "now" of our lives faithfully, in order to show us, even if lightheartedly, the dissolution that has overtaken society and the kind of rebirth necessary if it is to be reintegrated. In this respect, that uneasiness that I have sometimes felt over the work of this company has been substantially laid to rest.

Taking along a Sunset like the Morning was originally staged in 1981 as the opening production offered by this troupe. It was revived in 1983 and here receives its third staging. I did not see the earlier productions, but apparently a number of changes have since been made. Although I cannot be absolutely sure about this, it would appear that, in this newest incarnation, a number of elaborate devices are employed in order effectively to realize the earnestness and ambition underlying the original production. These various contrivances, at once naively lyrical and intellectual, achieve a surprisingly organic flow in the midst of an flood of jokes and gags, the author's acknowledged specialty.

First of all, the performances themselves gave great pleasure. In both this production and last season's *Modern Horror*, Kōkami's strategy as a director seems to have been to privilege the skill of his young actors. Certainly he succeeded on both occasions.

The production uses a bare stage; there is no scenery, a trend quite different from that embarked on by such similar companies as Noda Hideki's or the Three Circle Company. The roles are large; the director employs only five male actors nevertheless manages to create a supple sensibility, a comic energy, and the kind of idiosyncratic individuality that sustains the interest of the audience throughout the production. If I had to make a comparison, it would be with the sort of techniques employed by a writer like Tsuka Kōhei in the early 1980s. Yet the kind of sentiment and physicality that he was capable of creating, so twisted and poisoned they were sometimes difficult to bear, is not part of this present equation. Such sensibilities are here replaced by a clearheaded vivacity.

A second aspect of the production that I found attractive was the structure of the play itself, complex and full of interwoven layers. The play begins with a comic depiction of the way of life of a group of workers in a toy factory, who rush madly about as they attempt to develop a new game. Yet, at the same time, two of them, who bear the names

The 1985 production by the Third Stage of Kōkami Shōji's *Taking along a Sunset Like the Morning*. Five actors share in the gags and jokes. *From left to right:* Nagoshi Toshiaki, Kosuda Yasuto, Ōtaka Hiroo, Ikeda Narushi, and Itō Masahiro. (Photo by Okada Hatsuhito.)

Urayama (Vladimir) and Esukawa (Estragon), shift into the world of Samuel Beckett's *Waiting for Godot*, where they pass the time inventing games or telling stories, full of gags in seemingly endless numbers. When these stories and games are interesting, the stage is lively; and, even when they are tiresome, one senses the empty souls of these characters, another skillful usage of the basic situation found in *Waiting for Godot*.

Toward the end of the play, there is a sudden and shocking reversal. The game of "real life" is played with too much energy; in a sudden reversal, the play now appears to have been written in order to provide a kind of self-therapy to the characters, in which the victims attempt to alleviate their troubled mental states. The making of games, the playing of games, becomes too complicated; all sense of reality is lost, and there remains only the world in which such games are played. The ultimate comedy of the situation now stands in high relief.

In the end, the play gives the impression of having been forearmed against all possible critical salvos. No attempt at conventional, sustained narrative has been made. Instead, a series of gags and sketches follow one on the other in rapid succession. And even these dissolve before the audience fully understands them and hence before boredom or a sense of the play's limitations can set in. The devices employed are always apparent, since the next joke depends on the previous one. When the audience becomes aware that the jokes are unresolved, that is to say, that the story will never end, their once spontaneous laughter is quieted. As they witness the playing out of this spectacle, like a long, long chain of events in a story that stubbornly remains unresolved, they find themselves placed in the ultimate Beckettian situation. And, once it is realized that all thought and action has been forestalled even before it can be initiated, all prior criticism is rendered meaningless. At that moment, we, like Vladimir and Estragon, can only continue to say, hopefully, "Well, shall we go?" or, "Well, yes, let's go." But we cannot move.

The title of the play, *Taking along a Sunset like the Morning*, captures in this fresh image a real sense of the kind of critical spirit that has become so much a part of our mentality in these final years of the century. The following words are taken from the published version of the text. "From the very beginning, there has never been any truth in the idea of utopia. Absolutely none."

The play skillfully conveys the difficulty of bearing up under the burden of the consciousness of loneliness. The author puts it as follows.

> Nothing can be depended on. There is nothing to wait for. As an individual, I have decided to try to envelop myself in my own sense of the cold.

55. THE JIGSAW PUZZLE OF SEX

Cloud 9

Written by Caryl Churchill

Directed by Kino Hana

THE BLUEBIRD TROUPE

1985

It has been said for quite some time that sex has become an important topic in our society these days; nevertheless, to a great extent, the plays we see that deal with the subject seem only fragmentary in nature. The kind of stage work that can put all the pieces together and come up with some sort of synthesis is apparently more rare that you might believe.

The British woman playwright Caryl Churchill's *Cloud 9* was first produced in England in 1979, then in New York in 1981. It constitutes one of those rare dramas that does in fact lay out an entire map for us. More remarkably still, the author has done this, not in a heavy, cumbersome manner, but, thankfully, in a light, comic, and totally original fashion, in which the spirit of laughter remains paramount.

In this first in a series of experimental productions, the Bluebird Troupe, which consists entirely of female performers, has cast most men's roles entirely from within their own company, and their highly unusual treatment of the original allows the play to shine brightly. In 1982, I was able to see the long-running Off-Broadway production, staged by Tommy Tune, and I saw the first Japanese production later that same year. So I thought that I knew pretty well what it was all about. As it turns out, there were still some surprises in store for me.

From her close and sympathetic reading of the script, Kino has derived a number of new interpretations realized by a string of clever devices. For example, in the first scene, just after the opening chorus, a British flag, which had been nailed to the wall at the back of the set, explodes, fragmenting into a million pieces. The suggestion here of course is that the future of the British Empire may be in danger. And these new discoveries continue as Kino's wit fires volley after volley, effectively stunning the audience. The production ultimately stands as a testament to Kino's unique talents as a director. And the members of the Bluebird Troupe are all very well physically suited to play the kind of comedy required. Matsuoka Kazuko's translation is smooth, the dialogue especially showing considerable charm.

The play is constructed in two acts. The first takes place at the end of the nineteenth century, and the events center on the lives of an English family charged with looking after a colony in Africa. The second takes place almost a hundred years later, in London. The characters, however, age only about twenty-five years between acts 1 and 2, a surprising device in and of itself. By juxtaposing the two periods and telescoping the time line, Churchill apparently means to highlight the changes that have occurred in society.

In the first act, the characters carry on with their lives as they are expected to. Clive, the head of the household, acts just as such a man should, boastful and stern; his wife, Betty, shows a unwavering feminine modesty; the son is always very masculine; and the black servant personifies all the expected stereotypes. Yet they cannot help but be troubled by the gap between the limitations imposed by their places in this oppressive society and their hopes and dreams as individuals. Their passions, fueled by the oppression they suffer, result in spurts of wild and foolish behavior, sending all about them into confusion.

The play is filled with devices that emphasize these gaps. In act 1, we are presented with the puzzle of sexual transformations, as the major roles of the men and women are reversed. Betty, the perennially chaste wife (played by Makigami Kōichi), was written to be performed by a male actor, so the character's chastity seems conspicuous in its peculiarity. The boyish actress (played by Izawa Maki) disguises herself as a young gay man, Edward; when she says nervously, "What father wants I'd dearly like to be. I find it rather hard as you can see," there is a kind of charm in the emptiness of the remark. The unnatural is piled on the unnatural as the plot calls forth one foolish and comic scene after another, climaxing in the absurdity of the gay explorer (played by Misawa Shingo) marrying the lesbian housekeeper (played by Kasai Saki) simply for the sake of his reputation.

In act 2, on the other hand, virtually no pressure to conform remains. The characters are free to divorce, live apart, or live together—even in a gay and lesbian ménage à trois. The old rules no longer apply, and everyone is now free to make up his or her own mind.

Be that as it may, even if they are now "liberated," ironically few of the characters enjoy their freedom, feeling instead desolate and confused. Their new world lacks elegance, and, the old mores having been abandoned, they are brought face to face with the dreariness of sex. The sexual arena is now a battlefield. This sense of desolation is magnified all the more when the actor (Adaya Toshiki) plays the role of the young girl Cathy in a scene filled with raucous confusion. The laughter generated by act 2 is subdued in comparison to that of act 1, and the lightheartedness of earlier passions disappears.

In act 1, fighting against the pressures of the system enables the characters to establish their own sexual identities. In act 2, when all restrictions have been lifted, their sense of sexual identity remains unfocused, insufficient. Edward (played by Kuze Ryūnosuke), who in act 2 has become a young gay man, lives with another gay youth named Gerry (played by Makigami Kōichi), yet this updating of the traditional monogamous relationship here seems purposefully grotesque and peculiar. It is worth nothing that, near the end of the play, Gerry and Betty (played by Tane Rakuko) achieve true friendship of a sort, each maintaining a lonely self-sufficiency. Evidently, having been released from their bonds, the inhabitants of this world can find solace only in solitude.

The cast of the Bluebird Troupe's 1985 production of Caryl Churchill's *Cloud 9.*

A sparkle of humor enlivens this desolate world when the characters from act 1 and their reincarnations in act 2 achieve a surprising fusion of past and present. This is beautifully brought out in the last scene, when the "present" Betty (played by Tane Rakuko) and the "past," younger Betty (played by Makigami Kōichi) walk up to each other, hug each other. The sense of joy conveyed at that moment is very much like that in the final scene of Shakespeare's *Twelfth Night,* when the two twins, long separated, finally meet again.

Here, the past is not simply exiled but allowed to live on. Despite the fact that it was created under the kind of restrictions we witnessed in act 1, the laughter and foolishness of the past can still exert their charms on the present. It is G. K. Chesterton who once said that tradition may well be the right to vote that we give our ancestors; that is, it represents the democracy of the dead. And how striking that the charm of such a very British tradition can still be felt even in a contemporary play, with its courageous overtones of women's liberation.

56. SURPRISING THINGS HAPPEN

Comet Messenger Siegfried

Written and directed by Noda Hideki

THE DREAM WANDERERS

1985

When I look back to my childhood, I remember that I always dreaded the last day of summer vacation. Like Aesop's grasshopper, who played all through the summer months with no thought of approaching autumn, I would cower before the mountain of holiday homework yet undone and frantically try to find some way to return to that blissful feeling I had only ten days before, that the summer would never, never end.

The science fiction writer Ray Bradbury commented in one of his novels that, for children, there are "good months" and "bad months." June is the obvious choice for the best month of all—school is almost over, and September seems many thousands of years away. I find the expression "many thousands of years away" a clever way of expressing an evident truth.

What so surprised me about this new production of Noda's is that those keen feelings of a childhood summer long past have been charmingly and naively reborn. And that is not all. The memories of those innocent days are interlaced with memories of the springtime of the human race. The two flow together, reaching all the way back to the beginning of time as we know it.

While the construction of this grand myth is clearly of enormous importance, it has not resulted here in a fixed and consolidated record of events; these myths float on the surface of a humorous and charming universe. A child discovers a rhyming game, and a young man digs up a small fragment of stone; both become connected to the cardinal principles of creation. In Noda's myth, the smallest of the personal and the grandest of the universal are thus made to reflect each other closely. *Comet Messenger Siegfried* is the second in a trilogy of plays, the first, *The Walküre of the White Nights,* having been produced by Noda earlier this year. It is a perfect example of his art at its best. I have always been a bit put off by the portentous nature of Wagner's Ring Cycle, his series of operas on mythical subjects, and so I cannot help but admire Noda's own version of our mythic origins, presented with such humor, comic movement, and charm.

First, there was light. . . . No, actually, in this case, first there was a pile of discarded children's rubbish. This is how the play begins. Tin soldiers, bits of glass, old guidebooks, corks for discarded bottles. . . . A group of children, surrounded by these treasures, is studying the heavens one night during summer vacation.

"You can see Halley's comet, so that means that the skies will be very different this year." So the children think. Through the power of their imagination, the night sky suddenly changes, and, to the happy accompaniment of music from Lehár's *Merry Widow,* a strange drama begins. This spectacle represents a chase among a set of most curious constellations. There are the constellations representing the living fossils of ancient birds and fish (played by Sadoi Kenta, Haba Yūichi, and others), which are pursued by the constellations representing teachers, beginning with Professor Ikigami (played by Uesugi Shōzō); these are pursued in turn by a constellation called the Vengeful One (played by Takeshita Akiko), who in turn is pursued by others. The audience is thus bombarded by one surprise attack after another, in that sort of a rapid turnover of ideas, so typical of Noda's work, that never allows the brain to rest as the scenario unfolds at an extraordinarily rapid pace.

At the center of this celestial sphere is Tob Sawyer (no Tom Sawyer he!), a role originally played by Noda but taken over by Enjōji Aya after Noda was injured during the run. Tob is accompanied by his companion Tokage [Lizard] (played by Danda Yasunori). In the play, the young man's dreams of traveling back in time over his forty-day summer vacation are realized. In the way first suggested by Bradbury, Tob is able to vault backward through "many thousands of years," indeed 300,000 years, on a trip of exploration to the most ancient of times.

What becomes clear is the fact that there exist unexpected truths about the beginning of the human race. When humans first evolved, moving from four legs to two, their forelegs, which had originally been wings, now (thanks to a series of clever puns in the Japanese language) are said to become useful for thinking.

Thus, from the very beginning, human beings have been flying; Noda's clever hypothesis that we look up at the sky because it represents our ancient home is thus in its own way deeply moving. And the fact that this beautiful and stimulating idea is, of course, born from a play on words is a fascinating facet of Noda's vision in and of itself. In Noda's dramaturgy, the most important matters are most often manifested precisely through this peculiarly effective comic means.

The dramaturgy that gives rise to depth through humor now continues to utilize this motif throughout the entire length of the play. Thus, in another set of puns, Tob's companion Lizard comes to represent the "shadows" of all those unborn children who have not experienced the fate to be born into the world. Finally, at the end of the play, all the constellations are

The 1985 production by the Dream Wanderers of Noda Hideki's *Comet Messenger Siegfried.* Noda himself as Tob Sawyer *(left)* and Danda Yasunori as his sidekick the "Lizard."

reborn as "children" in their old home in the sky, while the myriad stars both on the stage and above the heads of the audience in the theatre itself begin to twinkle. Just like these "children" who have been given life, those children as yet unborn also rise to the sky as constellations and begin to shine as well. This finale, so deeply moving, constitutes virtually a religious requiem for the repose of lost souls.

I saw the play after Noda's accident, so I cannot compare his performance to that of his replacement, but Enjōji's Tob was vigorously rendered and altogether successful. Perhaps he was not as skilled at conveying naïveté as Noda himself, but his performance made beautifully clear the basic structures of the play. Danda Yasunori, who played the Lizard, and Takeshita Akiko, who played Tamiko, also gave strong performances. It is clear that Noda's company shows great strengths, even without his presence on stage. This group of young performers now shows a welcome maturity.

57. THE DILEMMA OF A DRAMA WITH A CHORUS

Chorus Line

Written, directed, and choreographed by Michael Bennett

Music by Marvin Hamlisch

THE AMERICAN TOURING COMPANY IN

TOKYO

1986

The American touring company of *Chorus Line* is playing for a limited run in one of the large theatres in Tokyo, and I've been to see the production twice. The first time was on opening night, the second some two weeks later, halfway through the series of Tokyo performances. Even in such short succession, I never wearied of watching these performances, for the fine details of the construction and the direction became all the more impressive to me. I really enjoyed myself.

I first saw *Chorus Line* at the Schubert Theatre on Broadway in 1976, a year after it opened; yet, believe it or not, the present production is still more stimulating, although eleven years have gone by since this musical first appeared. Perhaps this is because the significance of the social situations that surrounded its creation have become increasingly clear to us.

On the evening of the second performance I saw in Tokyo, my friend Deguchi Norio came along with me. As the managing director of the Shakespeare Theatre and a member of my own generation, he is easy to get along with, and we can always talk quite freely with each other. On this evening, as on many others, we chatted about what pleased us in the production we had just seen. We went on talking and drinking late into the evening. Among the other things that my friend said, I found the following particularly suggestive.

"In this musical, the director to whom the dancers speak is lost in the shadows. He occupies the same position as a god in one of the Greek tragedies."

As soon as my friend made this remark, I realized that he was right and that any sermon on *Chorus Line* was spurred on an extra notch. His words provided me with a useful hint, and all sorts of thoughts began to wrestle around inside me.

Just as my friend had pointed out, in *Chorus Line*, the character Zach, the director who controls with one wave of his hand the fates of all those dancers who audition for him, does seem larger than life, a false god if you like. For the most part, the dancers have to look up to see him. This impression is only strengthened when Zach speaks. He himself seems conscious that he is above ordinary humanity. And he is difficult to see, lost in the shadows. Only the echoes of his voice can be heard, reinforcing the fear and awe that surround him.

In this context, the spectacle of the dancers confessing their most secret hopes and fears (including the psychic wounds exhibited by the young gay man who wore women's clothing on stage) seemed almost masochistic in its intensity. It was as though they were performing penance in church. In their first interviews, standing before the director, when most of the dancers confess their sins and shortcomings before the others, who are also seated there, the director silently sits in judgment like the false god that he is. And, at the feet of their god, the dancers dance frenziedly, petitioning for salvation. Considered from this "religious" point of view, the episode of the dancer Cassie (played by Donna McKechnie), who had left the director to go to Hollywood, failed to realize her dreams, and then returned to dance again for him seven years later, seems more than anything a variation on the biblical story of the prodigal son.

While I am highly entertained by *Chorus Line,* what really attracts me to this work is the fact that, at its core, the musical suggests that people can productively work together only in the service of some god or godlike figure. In this regard, I felt that Alec Teague, who plays Zach in this current production with a certain astringent reserve, rendered his role beautifully, while, in the 1985 film version (directed by Richard Attenborough, where the role was taken by Michael Douglas), I found the emphasis on the aspects of dark power in the role extremely unpleasant.

In any case, it is clear that the relationship between the director and the dancers is not that among equals but rather more closely resembles that between humans and their god, that power that controls their destinies, that they placate, and against which they occasionally rebel. The resemblance to ancient Greek tragedy is clear.

Yet there is one crucial difference that cannot be overlooked. In the variation on a theme that is *Chorus Line,* the hero, that most important element in Greek theatre, is missing. As the title of the musical suggests, only the chorus (like the Greek *choros*) is present. No single striking figure

The finale of Michael Bennett's *Chorus Line* as performed in Tokyo in 1986 by the American touring company. (Photo courtesy of *Asahi Shimbun.*)

appears; all the dancers resemble each other in what must be termed a most unusual musical.

The structure of nineteenth- and early twentieth-century European theatre, which also called for a hero, who during the course of the drama revealed his special character through his thoughts and actions, began to break down in the plays of writers like Chekhov. Now after the theatre of the absurd, we have come to a place where there are no longer heroes. To quote the scholar Nakamura Yūjirō, we have moved from the traditional, and orthodox, Western concept of "the dramatic hero" to a sense of a scattered, centerless drama inhabited only by the "chorus." Here, Chekhov provides the model for this "chorus drama," sometimes allied to a species of what has been termed "nonsense drama." This "nonsense drama" in turn, to quote a phrase from Nakamura's *The World of Chekhov*, is based on "the dissolution of values, the confusion of ethical standards, of ruptures, of insufficiency."

In this context, *Chorus Line* has profoundly changed the Broadway musical, which to this day perseveres in being structured around a hero. In that sense, it is an epoch-making "chorus" work. And it is well to remember that this musical was written in America at a time when that society was suffering a "dissolution of values, the confusion of ethical standards, of ruptures, of insufficiency."

Chorus Line therefore is closely tied to the soul of the United States in the 1970s, which was faltering in the face of Watergate and the escalating war in Vietnam. Michael Bennett himself said that he first began to conceive of the musical after watching the Watergate hearings on television: "When I realized the way in which the country was being governed at that time, I couldn't help but respond to these lies and lack of concern. . . . It made me feel like vomiting." He wrote in the program provided for the Japanese tour, "I wanted to try to show the appearance on stage of good and honest people."

Chorus Line therefore represents a symbol of the fact that the country had lost the kind of hero capable of leading it toward the American dream. It thus becomes a true "chorus musical." Having, however, relinquished the need for an inevitably soiled hero, the production now becomes dependent on a counterstructure of "honesty." This new vision also includes minorities of all kinds, both racial and sexual.

Yet, by the same token, when we consider *Chorus Line* as a drama that embraces the structures of loss, we cannot overlook the role of Zach, with his false, godlike station. Even though what we have here is a drama in which the hero has dissolved and the center has collapsed, the "heroic" role of the director in pulling together the chorus and completing the action of the drama does suggest that *Chorus Line* contains its own inconsistencies.

While the production suggests that new values can be found in the newly constituted "chorus," a yearning for a hero to save us from confusion and fragmentation can still be detected. The contradictions inherent in these two themes cast their shadows over the work. To quote Mr. Nakamura again, "The *choros* [in a Greek tragedy] represents the manifestation of a surpassingly group unconsciousness"; and, since this is the case, the dilemma of this "chorus musical," pulled as it is in two directions, must mirror the collective American unconscious that has wrought such turmoil recently.

This musical calls forth our sympathy precisely because it is trapped in this profound dilemma. And the fact that *Chorus Line* continues its long run in New York should give us much food for thought.

58. THE ADVENTURES OF NOSTALGIA

Children of Night

Written and directed by Ikuta Yorozu

THE SPONTANEOUS TIN TROUPE

1986

"The past is always new, and the future is surprisingly nostalgic."

Such are the unforgettable lines spoken by one of the characters in Ikuta's new play, *Children of Night*. Actually, Ikuta used the same lines in an earlier version of this play, *The Three Stigmata of Nancy Tomato*, first staged in 1984. Yet, when you think over the significance of these words in terms of the kind of vision that Ikuta has consistently presented in his work, in many ways they seem to me to express the true nature of his theatrical vision.

On the surface, this phrase would seem easy enough to understand, yet these words are not as ordinary as they seem. From a commonsense point of view, of course, the past equals that which is nostalgic, the future what is new. Yet, here, that commonsense view is dramatically reversed.

Why is this? In Ikuta's theatrical vision, the past does not merely occupy the place assigned to it but sometimes moves on ahead into the future, to serve as a strange and foreign object to mount a surprise attack on unsuspecting mortals. By the same token, the future can also reverse itself, disguising itself as nostalgia and tempting us with some masque-like drama. It is not simply a question of time or space. The author and the characters who inhabit his plays, including even those who take part in the play within the play, continue to exchange roles, so that the author is able to achieve a tumultuous drama of sudden reversals. As the curtain opens with a cry from one lone voice, all the physical laws of space and even time seem suspended; everything begins to float, to gently move.

The vision created here is therefore not merely one that suggests a simple, retrogressive nostalgia. As past and future reverse themselves, they can steal the present from these characters and so break down our settled notions of the world. This is an adventuresome sort of nostalgia, filled as it is with the dynamism of reversal and an unusually conceptualized sense of play.

Children of Night is truly a wonderfully wrought example of Ikuta's dramaturgy. The production is beautiful and moving. His structure is complex, packed with astonishing surprises like a children's box of puzzles. Yet how strange, how somehow bashful this vision is! Ikuta and his troupe face their audiences with great sincerity. Here, a small heart can reveal large thoughts, all clothed in the good humor worthy of a comedian, presented without force, without braggadocio.

Itō Keiji, the designer, has decorated every surface of the theatre—the stage and even the walls of the auditorium—with charming, child-like drawings of children's masks, the moon, the stars, cats, even robots. Then, as we watch this "band of night children" noisily carrying on with their drama—all wearing charming masks depicting trumpet-blowing twins, a comic-book-style robot, a golden-haired princess right out of a fairy tale, a black cape and silk hat, or some other disguise—we seem to be witnessing the kind of late night village carnival that in days long gone by we surely dreamed of ourselves, tucked into our own beds. What follows seems a bizarre festival traveling the road of sleep, lighthearted yet exuding a wistful charm. Doors to memories long forgotten are now opened, and, through this device, the real drama begins. The play thus represents a kind of dream that, even if never fully articulated, any one of us might have harbored, one that indeed *might* have happened, one that we think about again and again, one that we mull over in a corner of our minds.

To borrow words spoken by Kasumi (played by Yamashita Chikage) during the course of the play, *Children of Night* is a tale in which we experience "thoughts that have not been born. They are only things that stop at our thinking only how grand it would be if they did come to pass. Things that we didn't think of at the right time, things that have never been realized. . . ."

The 1986 production by the Spontaneous Tin Troupe of *Children of Night* by Ikuta Yorozu. Three of the children. *From the left:* Kasumi (Yamashita Chikage), Yasube (Gimpun Chō), and Hiruma (Katagiri Hairi).

In that context, the play is structured in an extremely arresting fashion. This tale of dreams that might well have happened parallels another story we are told about those who dream such dreams. And so this tale of dreams comes to wreak havoc on the dreamers, turning all relationships upside down, and therefore moving in a very different direction than the anticipated response that surely those who dream these dreams serve, in some simpleminded fashion, to represent the author's own point of view.

So it is, therefore, that Yasube (played by Gimpun Chō), who has trouble selling many of the cartoons she draws for girl's magazines and who must support her sick sister, Kasumi, creates a comic-book story—the dream —in which, in this play within a play, she has lost her own initiative because, long ago, she opposed her family in some fashion. Now, Yasube's other self, that is to say, the Yasube disguised as she was when she was a young girl (played by Mutaguchi Kazumi), suddenly jumps out of the cartoon, the play within a play, and the grown-up cartoonist, Yasube, moves into the story to take her place, causing no end of confusion within this new drama.

What finally emerges from the plot twists in this dizzying metadrama is the unhappy truth that both Kasumi and her brother, the diligent Hiruma (played by Katagiri Hairi), have never truly been born as living human beings. But the drama does not end here. In the final scene, both unexpected metadramas now suddenly twist themselves around still one more time. Yasube herself, who has helped move the drama forward, was expected to be born as a boy, but it is now clear that she is, in fact, a girl, still waiting to be born. Now all these unborn children like Yasube, expecting to be born in some long-distant future, send off paper airplanes loaded with ten-yen coins, which include messages for those of us who live our lives now, in the 1980s. And those messages call forth melancholy feelings —"Goodbye, then, twentieth century. . . ."

So then, does this drama tell a tale of a father, Kazumasa (played by Hara Kintarō), who never wished for a child, and his dreams of a child whom he had lost? Or is it a play about children of the future who have not yet been born? Do we ourselves weave the dreams of the past in what the author would define as the present? Or are the characters we see created in the course of the drama by some playwright of the future? This is a play quite capable of posing all these questions. It is not a drama that addresses significant issues. It speaks to small things, forgotten things, things that have never materialized, things that have never seen the light of day. It is a play that includes within its purview, however, large dreams and earnest thoughts, one that speaks of such things with droll humor as it bumbles and stumbles along.

The performers act and sing well, and the songs, by Kubota Sachie, are excellent. Finally, Ikuta's direction fully captures the atmosphere he is anxious to convey.

59. MEDIEVAL PREACHING IN AN OUTDOOR SPACE

Oguri Hangan and Princess Terute

Written and directed by Endō Takurō

Music by Yabuki Makoto

THE YOKOHAMA BOAT THEATRE

1986

One of the famous productions of the Yokohama Boat Theatre, *Oguri Hangan and Princess Terute,* was to be given a special run of three days in an outdoor performance space within the grounds of the Yūkōji temple, located in the town of Fujisawa, close to Kamakura, the old capital of Japan that lies an hour south of Tokyo by train. There are close connections between the historic events dramatized in the play and the site, so I decided to go see a performance. I was told that, because of rain, the first two presentations had to be moved to a spot within the temple itself; fortunately for me, the rain stopped, and the final performance was held outside, as planned.

Among the number of small theatre troupes now in operation, Endō's Yokohama Boat Theatre, founded in 1981, possesses two virtually unique features. The first, as the name of the company suggests, concerns the fact that performances are given on a small boat tied up to the wharf on a river that flows through the port of Yokohama. True enough, Kara Jūrō had given some performances in 1973 on a coal barge anchored in Tokyo harbor, but there are no other groups that regularly make use of such a creative setting for their productions. In the atmosphere created by the sound and feel of the wooden boat, the company's productions often seem to resemble in tonality the surroundings the company has chosen.

Second, as this particular play, first staged in 1982, indicates quite clearly, as does another of their productions, presented in 1985, one based on the *Mahabharata,* this troupe seems quite unconcerned with questions of nationality, presenting productions that, in their surprising mix of cultures, might well be classified as a kind of pan-Asian theatre. The masks created by Wayang Topeng of Indonesia, or those made by Endō himself, which closely resemble them, are routinely used in performance. Music composed by Yabuki Makoto and played on the gamelan or homemade

The Yokohama Boat Theatre's 1986 production of Endō Takurō's *Oguri Hangan and Princess Terute*. The ensemble.

instruments also lends an Asian flavor to the evening. Ogata Kikuko's costumes mix the 1960s hippie spirit with the traditions of Japan, India, Indonesia, and other Asian countries. And an emphasis on the physical nature of performance that is common to small theatre companies is here blended with the sensibilities associated with the modern, commercial theatre.

Although these productions draw on elements from many Asian cultures, the company clearly does not identify itself with any particular country. As the name *Boat Theatre* suggests, the troupe is not moored to the culture of any one nation but moves freely, just like a boat, from sea to sea, shore to shore. Such is doubtless their objective.

I saw the Boat Theatre's first production of *Oguri Hangan* in 1983, in a small theatre located in the Shinjuku area of Tokyo. For that reason, I thought that I knew pretty well what I was in for. Yet seeing this newer version, presented on an outdoor stage facing the front of the temple, surrounded by a grove of trees and illuminated by torches stuck into the earth on either side, my impressions were soon transformed into something quite different.

What had impressed me about the original production in Shinjuku was the sense of the world created by the medieval legend of Oguri Hangan, which was just one among a repertory of tales presented by roving performers during that period, a venerable form of entertainment called *sekkyō-bushi*, which means, literally, "explaining the (Buddhist) sutras." Now, through the use of masks and music, the tale was freed from our national traditions and therefore able to transcend its roots in Japanese culture and enter the larger context of Asian storytelling. In this production Japanese traditional culture has not been observed merely within the framework of our own national traditions but has been assigned a place within the terms of a larger Asian framework. The tale has been relativized; affinities with other Asian cultures were sought. Indeed, more than anything else, such connections were stressed. This was a fresh and arresting approach to take with the material, and I was greatly impressed.

Now, seeing the play restaged on this platform within the compound of a Japanese Buddhist temple, I was more struck by the importance of these surroundings than I thought I would be. After all, certain incidents in the legend were supposed to have taken place in this very temple. We as spectators thus felt a closer affinity to the events of the play as they were enacted before us.

More astonishing still was the energy that flowed from the stage, a power surely derived from the legend itself. For an instant, it seemed as though we were witnessing these *sekkyō-bushi* texts as they were performed in the medieval period, either on outside platforms or in the streets. The echoes set up by the rhythms of the text; the clever use to which the phrases were put, which seemed to carry our emotions heavenward; the excitement of the successive theatrical images: all these suggested the special characteristics of an outdoor performance. More than anything, there was created a sense of ingathering, of harvest.

I did, however, feel initially uneasy. Accustomed as they were to a smaller venue, the actors' gestures seemed too small and their energy level too low and their performances therefore unequal to such a large theatre space. Nevertheless, as the evening wore on, it became clear that their performances were based on the needs of the group. There was no effort to emphasize individual performances. And there were no "stars" in this performance. Such a communal quality seemed obviously more appropriate to the needs of the ordinary people who, in our imagination at least, originally performed and watched these medieval entertainments.

The original medieval version of *Oguri Hangan* was not the work of any one author. Just as Oguri's cart is pulled by one person after another, moving ever deeper into the mountains of Kumano, so did this tale grow by accretion as it was passed along from one nameless entertainer to another. And, as the story developed, at some point the protagonist ceased to be human, taking on gigantic proportions, the tale itself shaking free of the confines of ordinary life on earth and reaching out toward the limitless universe. (Oguri himself had been resurrected, brought back from hell, and reborn as a kind of evil priest.) Viewed in this light, Endō's actors achieved a truly satisfying fusion of images, one in which the nameless artists who created the story became one with the artists who simply but sincerely and powerfully recreated it.

In the final scene, fireworks shot up into the night sky behind the actors, who held cherry blossoms in their hands, making us all the more delighted with what we had seen. It was surely worth delaying my trip to Fujisawa so that I could take in this particular, remarkable performance.

60. THE RESULTS OF PRACTICAL ROMANCE

I Bit the Green Seed

Written and directed by Ichidō Rei

THE BLUEBIRD TROUPE

1986

Last spring, I found the all-female Bluebird Troupe's *Something I Saw One Summer* to be among the best productions staged during the season. Their opening production this fall, *I Bit the Green Seed,* rivals that earlier work. Or, to put it another way, last spring the troupe scouted out new territory, and this fall they have firmly staked their claim. And, as usual, the production has been created through the combined efforts of the entire troupe.

One factor that needs to be taken account of in assessing this new production is that Kino Hana, formerly so central to the troupe's work, has left the company. Yet, despite losing so key a player, the company has remained loyal to the principle of group effort, a principle on which their productions have been based since the troupe was founded in 1975. And once again they have shown us just how well the concept can work.

In the 1970s, the work of the French director Ariane Mnouchkine and her Théâtre du Soleil became well known, and her ideal of the "collective imagination" was much discussed. Actually, it seems to me, this principle has been best carried out here in Japan, and without undue exaggeration or self-promotion, by the Bluebird Troupe itself. The troupe functions in such a way that the work of no one person is allowed to stand out. Through discussions among the members of the troupe and improvisatory rehearsals, all details of the production, from subject matter to script, from costumes to staging, are put together by the troupe members themselves. This is a method that stands at considerable odds with most of the productions by small troupes here in Japan, where a director or playwright is usually in charge. As the Bluebird Troupe never engages in theoretical proclamations, their working methods may sometimes be overlooked, but that this troupe continues to function successfully should command our admiration.

The productions of the Bluebird Troupe do not require, therefore, any ostentatious display of genius or unbridled individuality on the part of the troupe's performers; there are no hints of mad genius or disorder. Rather, the troupe depends on the richness, and the depth, of what G. K. Chesterton has called the ordinary, common man. The attitude of the members of the troupe toward their work is indeed well described in the British author's phrase "practical romance," which he explains in his book *Orthodoxy*. Their plays fall well within the notion of a mix of the surprising and the certain; or, to employ another of Chesterton's insights, a mix of the miraculous and the emotionally attractive.

In its new production, *I Bit the Green Seed,* the troupe takes on for the

I Bit the Green Seed, an ensemble production created by the Bluebird Troupe in 1986. Izawa Maki plays an old woman of eighty dressed as a young girl *(seated in the center)*.

first time the theme of old age. The main character in the play is an old woman of eighty (played by Izawa Maki) who refuses to acknowledge the realities of her advancing years and determines to remain a child of ten. She is cared for by a group of four middle-aged women who are her "helpers" and who look after her as best they can. The old woman dresses, not as would be expected of someone her age, but in a way that expresses how she feels about herself, wearing a young girl's short skirts, and she sparkles with the energetic and childish charm of a ten-year-old.

This notion of the discrepancy between self-image and actual reality is clearly based on a well-known Japanese comic strip, and Izawa Maki's splendid performance fully encompasses the worlds of both the young girl and the old woman. She is particularly successful in a series of scenes in which the old woman thinks back to her childhood days, when she was waited on by a series of maids (played by the helpers). She plays a series of games with them, including a race with a string tied to an empty can, a game of hide and seek with curious creatures who come and go, and a boat game using a ship made, in origami fashion, of folded pieces of paper. The charm and naïveté of these gestures and attitudes soon send us in the audience nostalgically back to the world of our own childhoods. We become one with this vigorous old woman as we begin to rediscover within ourselves, and with real force, that sense of play and banter that we knew as children.

Yet, however beautiful or oppressive we find this nostalgic world of childhood, the central issue of this drama lies elsewhere. At the beginning, the old woman, with her helpers, plans a trip back to her old home, one that could verify the spot and locate her within her real past. At this early point in the play, however, she has absolutely refused to make the trip. The drama stresses the confrontation of the woman with her past so that, even while she manages to stay young at heart, at the same time she moves ever closer to an encounter with the realities of her old age. At the beginning of the play, when she refuses to board the ship, her age is indeterminate; by the last scene, she is wearing clothing traditional for old women in Japan, her hair is shot with gray, and she is every bit the old woman that reality demands. As she bids her helpers good-bye, she climbs up the gangplank of the ship, alone.

At this moment, the walls of the theatre behind the audience begin to light up with electric ornaments that blink on and off, adding an emotional freight to her nighttime sailing. The moment put me in mind of that splendid scene in the Fellini film *Amacord*, where the glittering ocean liner, blazing with lights in the night, sails past the child on shore. This use of the theatrical space by the troupe was particularly effective.

In the earlier sections of the play, the four helpers, dressed in raincoats, pursue the old woman, who has refused to board the ship and somehow escaped from them. They rush everywhere, even in the aisles of the theatre. Suddenly, they shed their raincoats, and we see that underneath they are dressed as the kind of traditional Japanese maids who took care of the old lady when she was young. Thus, in an instant, the stage picture moves seventy years back in time and space. It was a striking moment, and an affecting one.

As the troupe's name suggests, its work has often been connected to the conception of a "little girl," and their performances as well often show a genuineness of spirit and a winsomeness appropriate to just such girlish charm. Yet, if we continue to concentrate on this aspect of their work, our sense of their real accomplishments will remain far too limited. As *I Bit the Green Seed* suggests, their work far exceeds the restrictions of "practical romance." On this occasion, their vision encompasses nostalgia for the past and a sense of the comic nature of the present and even extends as far as old age. They have shown us a world in which youth and maturity can coexist fruitfully.

61. A CRIME EXPLAINED, A CRIME UNEXPLAINABLE

Memo from the Aliens

Written and directed by Yamazaki Tetsu

TRANSPOSITION 21

The Incident of the Salad Murder

Written by Betsuyaku Minoru

Directed by Fujiwara Shimpei

THE ATELIER OF THE LITERARY THEATRE

1986

It is often said that crime has changed. What this apparently means is that, not only have the ways of committing crimes changed, but the way in which crimes are explained to us has been altered as well. It used to be that, when journalists theorized about a crime, they used the work of detective story writers, criminologists, even psychologists. These days, however, it appears that such playwrights as Yamazaki and Betsuyaku have taken on the journalist's role. In explaining the criminal's actions, these writers are concerned not so much with recreating the crime as with ferreting out the motive where it lurks in the mysterious depths of the human soul. That is, while they are interested in the unique nature of the crime portrayed, their main focus is to use the crime as a means to sketch a portrait of the criminal. What is truly surprising is that the peculiarities of character they uncover turn out to be not so peculiar after all. We are shocked to see how commonplace the criminal mentality is.

Both these plays appeared at roughly the same time, and both are compelling works. Both treat crimes, or incidents, in which the family figures prominently, and both plays stand out even among the season's other successes.

Yamazaki's *Memo from the Aliens* concerns a frightening incident that took place in 1985 in the Nakano Ward of Tokyo. Owing to abuse ("in the form of a mock funeral ceremony") that he suffered at his school, a second-year middle school student committed suicide by hanging himself in the lavatory on the lower floor of a bus terminal in the city of Morioka. In constructing his play, Yamazaki used elements from the work of one of Japan's classic modern poets, Miyazawa Kenji, as well as from an early essay by the well-known literary critic Yoshimoto Takaaki entitled "Poetry and a Memo from the Aliens."

Before the play began, I must admit that I was rather, well, frightened to be faced again on the stage with my all too vivid memories of this horrible "abuse" about which I had already read so much. It all seemed too painful. Shortly after the curtain went up, a new performer, Kaji Tatsuya, who took the role of the student Hirofumi, slowly entered from stage left, wearing his school uniform. He stiffened his body like a wooden doll and let out a chilling, peculiar laugh; this gave me quite a start, and I felt an ominous premonition. "What does this peculiar laugh mean?" I asked myself. It seemed that the drama was considerably intensified by this puzzling laugh, which surely must have led to the "abuse" that the student was eventually forced to endure.

Again and again his irritated classmates told him, "You laugh in a crazy way." This was in fact what led him to be so abused by those around him. As it was sounded on stage, the laugh gave out a clear and petrified ethos all its own. It was a laugh that, while pathetic, sounded somehow distant, indirect;

The 1986 production of Yamazaki Tetsu's *Memo from the Aliens* by the Transposition 21 troupe. *To the left:* the student Hirofumi (Played by Kaji Tatsuya) with his
mother (Kiuchi Midori).

it seemed indeed to contain within it some unarticulated sense of the outcome that awaited this creature so much made sport of. This laugh is first
produced on stage when Hirofumi receives the unexpected "extra" abuse
applied so energetically by his classmates. Evidently, a masochistic personality is stimulated by severe treatment, which would explain why the young
man actively assumed the role of the abused. It would appear that, within

Hirofumi himself, the sensation of being alive had grown weaker and weaker and that, in order to cling to existence, he needed to experience increasing levels of abuse.

What is so peculiar and striking about the play, however, is the fact that this sense of dying slowly on the inside attacks not only the young man but his mother (played by Kiuchi Midori) and his teacher (played by Seshimo Kazuhisa) as well. Both these characters seem troubled by strange premonitions, and they repeat the same words over and over to themselves. "When? When was it? That I had something like this happen?" This sensation that they could only have gone through these experiences previously strips away any sense of the reality of their own feelings, indeed, of their own lives. They seem locked within two dimensions. They have a sense that their feelings and their lives are nothing more than quotations from outside that flattened frame. Thus, they become the "aliens" of the play's title, sad and cut off both from themselves and from the realities of their lives.

The drama thus distances itself as it poses questions. To whom do we assign responsibility as the assailant? And for whom must we feel pity as the victim? Without inflicting violence or damage, all these characters hold tight to their locked souls; they seem frozen, unable to move. It therefore seems that the crime was inevitable, that nothing anyone could have done could have changed things.

Kaji's performance as the young man is splendid, as are those of Kiuchi Midori and Seshimo Kazuhisa, who manifest their loss of sensibility quietly and without arrogance. They leave behind a strong impression. Considering the subject matter of the play, however, I have reservations about the music used, which is overly loud and assaults the ear.

As for Betsuyaku's *The Incident of the Salad Murder,* the experimental Atelier group at the Literary Theatre is quite accustomed to performing the author's work, and on this occasion all the necessary elements—script, direction, performance—are so polished that the results seem strikingly professional.

The central characters of the play are a poor, middle-aged couple (the woman is played by Yoshino Yukiko, the husband by Kadono Takuzō) who kill their daughter for the insurance money. Betsuyaku's peculiar and buoyant humor, the play of light and shadow brought to the stage by the performances of this couple, the droll performance given by Tamura Katsuhiko as the somewhat ambiguous man who is their "friend," all result in a highly polished production.

Watching Betsuyaku's play, I suddenly realized that, while both plays treat a crime, and while both do so by sketching the lives of family members, Betsuyaku and Yamazaki have chosen extremely different methods of presenting their material.

Betsuyaku Minoru's *The Incident of the Salad Murder*, produced by the Atelier of the Literary Theatre in 1986. *From the left:* the Husband (Kadono Takuzō), the Wife (Yoshino Yukiko), and the Friend (Tamura Katsuhiko).

In the case of Yamazaki, the major characters, driven into a corner, openly confess their problems. They display them for public consumption. We understand what motivated their crimes and in the process are brought to a realization of just how extraordinary human life can be.

In the case of Betsuyaku, however, things are different. Here, the results of the crime are merely hinted at. Indeed, every aspect of the "incident" is merely suggested. We have no idea what the killer's motives are or what the wife is thinking. All is hidden. Just as during the course of the play, a condolence gift changes from a teapot into a vase, nothing seems clearly defined, nothing is properly regulated. We watch in horror as this timid, comic woman, who, in her silence, knows nothing of her real nature, sits unconcernedly and embraces the uncanny.

We admire Yamazaki for the clear vision he gives of the crime portrayed and the people who perpetrated it. Betsuyaku, on the other hand, startles us with his understanding of the fact that, since explanations cannot be given, the world and those who inhabit it must remain mysterious as well.

62. A QUICK GLIMPSE OF THE MEANING OF THE WORLD

Wind Station

Written and directed by Ōta Shōgo

THE TRANSFORMATION THEATRE

1986

It seems that, these days, more and more playwrights have chosen to write plays meant to be watched as a series. Take, for example, the trilogy *Walkure* just completed by Noda Hideki or Kawamura Takeshi's *The Shinjuku Version of the Tale of Eight Dogs,* in five parts, written for the Third Erotica. Kōkami Shōji's *Nuclear War* is also a trilogy, as is Inoue Hisashi's *History of the Common People of the Shōwa Era.*

Since these playwrights attempt such large-scale works, they must imaginatively order, not a brief skirmish, but a long, drawn-out war. The troupes mounting such productions must make sure that they have the talent available to carry them off satisfactorily. Kawamura himself has written concerning his own *Shinjuku Dogs* series that, "to complete this project, I may need seven, even eight years." Such work demands patience. The real tale behind this new artistic development, perhaps, is that the powers of so many dramatists of this generation are at last reaching full flower.

Ōta's newest work, *Wind Station,* follows his *Water Station* of 1981 and his *Earth Station* of 1985. The whole "station" project, as I call it (this is not a phrase used by the author himself), has thus taken about six years. The three plays surely represent a period of sustained creative activity. And, in one important way, his series differs from all the others now being composed and presented.

This difference lies in the fact that, with the exception of a few lines of poetry spoken in the latter half of *Earth Station,* Ōta's trilogy is virtually dialogue free. He has thus laid claim to an area seldom explored by his contemporaries.

Most playwrights show off their talent through their clever dialogue or novel structural devices. Ōta's work, on the other hand, is far removed from any sort of chatter. He moves in the direction of a world sunk in an impenetrable stillness. And, unlike most playwrights of today, who choose to use ever faster tempos so as to move more quickly than the consciousness of their spectators, in these three works Ōta maintains an extremely slow pace, a virtual challenge to the patience of his spectators. In doing so, he

Wind Station by Ōta Shōgo, produced by the Transformation Theatre in 1986. Ōta's gifted performers in an enormous pile of sand. (Photo by Furudate Katsuaki.)

quietly forces his audiences to enter into a territory seldom glimpsed by eyes trained to respond quickly to the details of everyday life.

Ōta is not looking for new meaning in life or the world. Rather, the direction that his plays take obviate any search for meaning. Not that he sets out to dismantle the concept of meaning itself. His plays have shown us a complex and ambiguous vision of the world and of mankind, an ever-changing vision to which it is difficult to assign any precise meaning. And he provides no notes. Perhaps one might say that this trilogy forces us, if only momentarily, to acknowledge the gap that exists between "meaning" and the world itself.

Ōta's work does not, in any ordinary sense, leave any "new" impressions behind. He shows no quick wit; he does not startle us with some shocking devil's mask; rather, he creates in his audiences a reliable and a subdued feeling. In the work of other serial dramatists, there is usually to be found something that can be characterized as new and that leaves a strong impression behind of the creative power at work therein. In Ōta's three *Station* plays, however, even if there is nothing at all shown about what is "without," he nevertheless seeks to examine an area in the vicinity of the outer world, one unexplored by other playwrights. And, just as the performers move slowly but surely across the stage, Ōta just as slowly and surely—and taciturnly—moves us into uncharted territory. In this way, Ōta and his troupe suddenly do find themselves crossing boundaries.

This new play, faithful to such a dramaturgy, reveals a particularly powerful depth of meaning. A new element here appears, one that was not present in the first two plays and that may suggest a new point of departure for Ōta's art in the future.

The basic structure of *Wind Station* resembles that of the previous two plays: men and women, with a sluggishness of movement and gesture seen only in slow-motion film, make their way across the stage as travelers, bags and suitcases in their hands. As these figures move slowly on, the "station" where their paths cross is represented by the stage space itself. And, as in the other two plays, the world they observe with eyes seemingly robbed of all function and utility is meant to represent in itself some sort of fable.

In all three of these plays, material, inorganic objects constitute a central image. In the first of the three, *Water Station*, water runs ceaselessly from a hose attached to a pump. In the second, *Earth Station*, layers of stone were employed. In the present play, the stage is filled with a mountain of real sand that comes right to the audience's feet. Buried here and there in the sand are everyday, man-made objects that have been thrown away—a television set, an ice box, and so forth. The suggestion is that somehow the function, the meaning, of these objects has been stripped away. The image is that of objects that have been robbed of all utility and so become simply "matter"; at the same time, humanity has regressed to the point that existence is no more than movement, life a constant and meaningless crossing back and forth. However banal my observations, it really seemed to me that Ōta is showing us mankind returned to its original state.

But what startled me about the silence exhibited in *Wind Station* was the fact that this was not the kind of smug stillness we have seen before, a quiet trapped inside Ōta's characters. Now a laughing wind passes over, transforming that stillness into a sometimes light and carefree silence. Perhaps the wind is meant to suggest the emptiness of the sky as the wind blows through that space that exists between mankind and the world. Yet at the same time this image seems to entice us to move away from the desiccation and meaninglessness that fills the stage. I remember my delight at naming this image "the laughing wind." Ōta's silence, which until now has been associated with the darker and unreachable side of human nature, is taking on new meaning.

Yet at the same time it must be said that no precise meaning can be assigned to this laughter. For example, in one scene, four men and women hurl away shoes taken off by others. In another, they play a strange game, lining up their suitcases, on which they then sit. They embrace each other wildly, they tumble about on top of the heap of sand. . . . These comic scenes succeed each other in perfect silence, and, indeed, it is not clear what the meaning or the purpose of this humor might be.

This is laughter that slips through any net of understanding; it is a game. Here, the light of Ōta's laughter is doubtless meant to shine into that ambiguous space occupied by so many meanings, existing, as it does, in the space between sense and nonsense. This kind of comic touch, which he first revealed in his 1985 play *A Thousand Summers,* has returned, and with much greater force.

If meaning is to be denied, then the performances of Ōta's actors must be so calculated as to avoid any sense that they are "impersonations," a special characteristic of all three of these productions. In the present case, the faces of the performers are all by now well known to us. And their performances, carried out with virtually expressionless faces, emphasize their "being" rather than their "performing." They too are therefore walking in a new territory, far from ordinary conceptions of "acting." It would seem that, over the course of these three *Stations,* their performance skills as well have undertaken a long, long journey.

63. A NEST OF BOXES AT THE EDGE OF WAKING

The Tempest: A Rehearsal on a Nō Stage on Sado Island

Written by William Shakespeare

Directed by Ninagawa Yukio, translated by Odashima Yūshi

A NISSEI THEATRE PRODUCTION

1987

Among Shakespeare's thirty-seven plays, his late work *The Tempest* is regarded as one of the most cumbersome to stage. The magic world created there can easily seem a clumsily wrought juvenile drama, and the blending of these unrealistic elements with the deeper philosophical layers contained in the play causes further difficulties.

I have seen *The Tempest* several times before. On the occasion of the 1973 production staged by The Cloud Troupe, in a translation by the postwar playwright Fukuda Tsuneari, I remember being bored with the whole affair, except for the ravishing scenic effects created by Inoue Bukichi. When the famous Paul Scofield played Prospero in a 1975 production I saw in London's West End, only the somewhat portentous delivery of his speeches helped me pass the time. For me, *The Tempest* was little more than a burden—indeed, a burden within a burden—one that would remain difficult to bear unless some fresh approach to it could be developed.

Remarkably, however, Ninagawa Yukio's new production at the Nissei Theatre has found just that fresh approach, and his conceptual methods may well hold promise for future productions. By providing a new framework for the play, Ninagawa has turned Shakespeare's original into a complex, delicate, and intriguing set of boxes, and the whole play seems to glow in the light of this new interpretation. Now a drama in the true sense of the word, Shakespeare's play suddenly came alive to a contemporary audience. Ninagawa's direction will, I think, prove epoch making, and this production will represent a true milestone in the history of *The Tempest*.

When I entered the theatre, I thought that I had a good deal of time to spare before the play began, yet actors and stagehands were already busy on the stage, creating a noisy turmoil. Young men wearing devil masks were beating drums with great intensity, and actors were applying makeup and adjusting their costumes, putting traditional Japanese clothing on over their own modern street clothes, chatting together all the while. The effect was exactly as if the green room had been brought right up on the stage. In the middle of the stage itself had been constructed a dilapidated *nō* stage and walkway with its thatched roof, and around it was a thicket of trees. The idea was that we were now to witness a rehearsal of *The Tempest* on this rundown stage on Sado Island, for which all these actors and stagehands had been brought together.

When it came time for the play to begin, at a signal from the "director," who also plays Prospero (Hira Mikijirō), all the participants assembled in the center of the stage and formed a circle, then dispersed. Immediately, the stagehands arranged the device with which the shipwreck of the party of the king of Naples (played by Kanno Naoyuki) on the deserted island inhabited by Prospero and Miranda would be portrayed.

The framing device of a rehearsal propelled this production of *The Tempest*. Rather than being allowed to lose themselves in the beauty and fantasy of the drama itself, the spectators are forced to observe the action

Shakespeare's *The Tempest*, in a version by Ninagawa Yukio produced at the Nissei Theatre in 1987. Hira Mikijirō as Prospero *(at the rear)*, Hatakeyama Hisashi as Ferdinand, and Tanaka Yūko as Miranda.

of the play carefully since it is shown to them as a play within a play that the actors are in the process of presenting. For Ninagawa, this is an unusual way of staging Shakespeare. And he pushes these unusual methods to the extreme. When actors have finished playing a scene, they line up on either side of the stage to watch the progress of the drama, and the breezes that blow their robes come from the electric fans openly whirling on the stage. In the scene in which the banquet laid for the king of Naples and the usurper Antonio (played by Wakamatsu Takeshi) is snatched away before their eyes by Prospero's magic, Ninagawa resorts to no mysterious "tricks"; rather, the stagehands come in quickly and remove the trays that have been set before them, a device that in itself involves nothing out of the ordinary.

As a result, the production becomes a complex set of nesting boxes. The first of them, on the outside, is represented by the actors, who come from our contemporary world and are rehearsing the play. Inside that, serving as the second layer, is Shakespeare's text itself, with all of Prospero's magic here faithfully presented. Then, inside this second layer, is a third, for, in the middle of this *nō* stage, Prospero "directs" *his* production using gestures reminiscent of the traditional *nō* and *kyōgen* theatres. So, in one sense, we have a play within a play within a play. These three layers continually overlap, moving back and forth as though they were indeed a nest of cleverly constructed boxes that dovetail one into the other.

This kind of complex metatheatrical device gives superb results. Of course, the very fact that Prospero both plays in and "directs" this production provides a metatheatrical dimension in and of itself. And these repetitions of the dramatic structure also provide for the kind of dovetailing I mentioned above. As Jan Kott points out in his *Shakespeare Our Contemporary,* the stories of Prospero, Ariel, and Caliban are indeed variations on the same theme, that of "violence as a basic principle in the world." And the three interlocking boxes that Ninagawa has used in his staging reflect three variations in the structure of the performance.

Ninagawa has the more serious characters perform in a style suggestive of the *nō*, while the group of foolish characters—Stephano, the drunken butler (played by Daimon Gorō), the Jester (played by Ishii Ken'ichi), and Caliban (played by Matsushige Yutaka)—uses the devices of the comic *kyōgen*. The idea is a spectacular and highly successful one.

I believe that I was most impressed, however, with the final speech of Prospero, as beautifully delivered by Hira as his final good-bye. In abjuring his "magic powers" with the lines "But release me from my bands / With the help of your good hands," Prospero—and so Hira—presents a theatrical double image, one in which Ariel (played by Matsuda Yōji) is also "released," as are the actors themselves, who now may leave the stage.

The actors themselves are those who vow to play an assigned part and flesh out the life temporarily assigned them, and, just like the "spirits," they radiate their own glittering magic, which is not of this earth. But as this magic, like the play itself, comes to an end, the performers themselves return to the world of everyday life, "released," so that they too might well say with Prospero, "Now my charms are all o'erthrown / And what strength I have's mine own." Just at the point of emerging from the dream, their stage roles and their real lives fuse in momentary perfection. I can think of no other production of a Shakespeare play I have seen that, making use of the original text, has shown this sophistication in interlayering, in creating such intimate connections between fantasy and reality, acting skill and everyday life.

In this effort, Uzaki Ryūdō's musical score, Suzuki Toshiaki's stage devices, and Harada Tamotsu's lighting were extremely effective.

64. CLOSING IN ON THE SELF: ZEAMI AS "PERFORMER"

Zeami

Written by Yamazaki Masakazu

Directed by Sueki Hirofumi

A NEW THEATRE COOPERATIVE

PRODUCTION

1987

Just what is that "self" of the actor, which can exist only in the eyes of those who observe him? Such is the question that Yamazaki poses in his play *Zeami,* which had its first, and most famous, staging in 1963, twenty-four years before this present revival.

I did not see the original production, so, for many years, I have known the play only as it exists between the covers of a book. It seems surprising that this splendid drama, which has been performed in translation in Italy and the United States, has never been put on the stage again in Japan. Now that I have seen this production, mounted in honor of the thirtieth anniversary of the founding of the New Theatre Cooperative Troupe, with the famous *kabuki* actor Matsumoto Kōshirō playing the lead role, I became conscious again of the magnitude of this work and, at the same time, of the fact that, in the end, perhaps this revival was not delayed too long after all. For it may be that it is only now that we can fully grasp precisely why the work is so compelling.

It is certain that now, in our time, the ideas of "performance" and "performer" are no longer matters that pertain solely to the world of professional actors. Quite the contrary, those ideologies that would check or undercut the idea of "the self" have now lost their power. And, now that yet another set of standards, those of artistic merit, has become ambiguous, mankind, seeking to fill the emptiness that is life, has begun to enter into the realm of "performance" as a means of self-understanding. The idea, for example, that life and performance have become one is widespread, and the obstinate concept of "man as performer" remains strong in the thinking of a playwright such as Tsuka Kōhei. Similar ideas can be found in the work of other playwrights such as Kisaragi Koharu and Takahashi Isao. Indeed, in retrospect, many significant dramas of the 1970s and 1980s seem to have been filled with a real passion for "performing." The playwright and director Fukuda Tsuneari discussed this tendency in a prescient fashion in his 1957 study *The Theatrical Nature of Mankind,* and Yamazaki reveals in his *Zeami* a sharp distinction between "performance" and "person," taking the great medieval *nō* actor Zeami (1363–1443) as his referent. The play also gives us an exciting picture of what we have lost thanks to the current popular penchant for the concept of "performing."

The performance uses a raked stage, on which thick black pillars are ranged; indeed, black becomes the visual keynote of the production (in the design by Ishii Mitsuru). Ishii also designed the costumes, using a unique combination of Western and Japanese styles. In particular, the costumes worn by Lord Ōe (played by Inagaki Shōzō) and Lord Sanjō (played by Uchida Minoru) turn them into droll versions of European nobility. They appear to be quite fashionable, yet there is something strangely unsettled about their clothing; we in the audience know, therefore, that the play is not to be construed merely as a historical drama set in fifteenth-century Japan but can be seen as a universal drama that concerns the unease of all those who "perform." This device is most effective.

Yamazaki has made the most of the two contrasts that he constantly employs, light and shadow, and he exploits their significance in elegant rhetoric. Light becomes a symbol for those who possess substance and force; shadow, beginning with performance, is cut off from substance, re-

The 1987 revival of Yamazaki Masakazu's *Zeami*, first produced in 1963. Zeami (Matsumoto Kōshirō) addresses the villagers.

vealing the essence of emptiness itself. Zeami (played by Matsumoto Kōshirō) makes use of shadow as a reality and refuses to be influenced by the light that would use him for its own ends. Thus, he follows the path of shadow, of emptiness, to its end. What I found most moving was the vision presented of Zeami in the latter half of the play, where he is taken to task by both his sons, Motomasa (played by Kitamura Sōichirō) and Motoyoshi (played by Hayashi Tsuguki); estranged from both, his career seems to crumble. On one side are politics and power, on the other religious faith and a belief in the common people. Beset by both, as both claim the truth, Zeami finds only emptiness. Denying both sides, Zeami himself, who until shortly before the end had been able to bear his life as a performer, thus serves as a powerful symbol of contemporary man, whose attitudes concerning performance, as I mentioned above, are all too well known to us.

With his background in *kabuki*, Matsumoto Kōshirō plays the role of Zeami on a grand scale. It is a performance that reveals all the sides of this complex character—the depth of his unease, the chilling splendor of his glittering skill, his facility at manipulating others with his talent, the chagrin that he feels when being manipulated by others, and the bitter humor that remains hidden in the depths of his earnest and dark enthusiasms. Unfortunately, against this splendid realization, the other actors, trained in modern performance techniques, seem to give only small-scale performances. Still, at least one among them, Mita Kazuyo, who plays the role of Lady Kuzuno, has the skills to challenge Matsumoto. Nevertheless, when watching this "anniversary performance," sustained for the most part by an actor with a very different kind of training, there seems a certain irony in the fact that this production is meant to show off the level of skill possessed by modern theatre performers.

The director, Sueki Toshifumi, has chosen to employ a rapid tempo, so that the dialogue, written in a poetic style, never becomes pretentious, and he often allows the lines to be spoken in a humorous fashion, which is all to the good. The added dances, however, which are meant to show something of the lives of the common people of the period, are performed awkwardly and remind one of modern theatre productions back in the 1960s, and I must confess that I felt a bit embarrassed watching them.

65. THE DYNAMISM OF "THE CITY MULTITUDES"

Les Misérables

Written by Alain Boublil and Claude-Michel

Schonberg, based on the novel by Victor Hugo

Directed by Trevor Nunn and John Caird,

translated by Sakai Yōko, Tokyo production

supervised by Masumi Toshikiyo

A TŌHŌ PRODUCTION

1987

The Tōhō company has gathered all its forces together and begun a long run at Tokyo's Imperial Theatre of the Japanese-language production of the musical *Les Misérables*. Seeing the performance, I was fascinated by the fact that, contrary to my expectations, this is a musical that has been created without making any real use of its central characters. The flow of the story, of course, involves the celebrated pursuit of the protagonist, Jean Valjean (Takita Sakae and Kaga Takeshi in the alternating cast), by the notorious Inspector Javert (again Takita Sakae and Kaga Takeshi alternating). Intertwined with this drama of the chase are the stories of Valjean's foster daughter Cosette (played, depending on the performance, by three actresses, Saitō Yuki, Shibata Kano, and Suzuki Honoka) and her lover, the young revolutionary Marius (Noguchi Gorō and Azaki Motomu alternating); he, in turn, is loved by the forlorn Eponine (Shimada Kaho and Shiraki Mikiko alternating). These characters provide the backbone of the story.

Be that as it may, however, the chief interest in this adaption as conceived and staged by Trevor Nunn and John Caird lies elsewhere. The main "character" of *Les Misérables* is the crowd, those urban multitudes of whom the individual characters form a small part, and the space in which they live out their lives is the unruly urban setting of nineteenth-century Paris. Until now, it has been an unwritten law that a glamorous hero and heroine are necessary to the charm of any musical. But *Les Misérables* takes aim at a different target, for the individuality of its characters is subsumed within the chorus, the nameless, faceless downtrodden. It is the energy of these men and women that brings chaos to the city. Such is the vision chosen to guide this work.

However, in the early scenes of the musical, I did not realize this. Beginning with the moment in which the bishop attempts to reform Valjean through the gift of the candlesticks, I watched as the performance seemed to rush through the colorful incidents in Hugo's novel like some super express train. Simply observing, on one hand, the efforts of the people to find a political voice and, on the other, the severity of the police, faithful as always to their duties, seemed to me somehow an inadequate way of bringing the larger issues into focus since the individual personalities of the characters and their actions were never sufficiently developed. Even such characters as Fantine (played by Iwasaki Hiromi and Itō Hiromi), the mother of Cosette, who is forced into prostitution, and Cosette and Marius themselves seemed barely sketched out, with little of their true nature as human beings revealed to us. We seemed to be presented merely with stereotypes writ large, as though the piece was intended to serve as a quick digest of Hugo's long and complex novel.

Surprisingly, in the performance, the characters who escaped from this inevitable thinness were the scoundrel Thénardier (played by Saitō Haruhiko and Shintoku Akira) and his wife (Ōtori Ran and Achiwa Satomi). Both were portrayed in a truly droll fashion. Saitō revealed with great skill, and to exactly the right degree, his shady character in his song, and Ōtori

The 1987 Tokyo production of the musical *Les Misérables*. The scene at the barricades. (Photo courtesy of Tōhō.)

Ran's buoyant comic energy and outstanding dramatic and vocal skills became a central feature in the success of the production.

Toward the end of act 1, when the action of Les Misérables moves to Paris, however, we began to witness the misery of the lower classes and, with the appearance on stage of Enjolras (Uchida Naoya and Fukui Kiichi), the actions of the group of revolutionary youths. As this group of revolutionaries grows in size and energy before us, our point of view as an audience begins to change. Now it is clear that what we are witnessing is not with a theatrical narrative concerning the main characters, as might have been expected, but a drama about the urban masses of which they are merely incidental members. Thus, even though the central characters never really come to life on the stage, they nevertheless take their place in the larger, natural flow of events.

This kind of musical, dedicated to expressing the realities of urban life, is rare indeed. The scenery designed by John Napier is, in this context, astonishingly effective. And its importance to the total design of the musical is far greater than in any other work known to me.

On the wide stage of the Imperial Theatre, the dark and grimy walls of buildings rise up on all three sides, providing an overpowering re-creation of the oppression of the Paris slums. There is one particularly affecting moment when Eponine walks the night streets of Paris and sings her moving "On My Own." (And it must be said that Shimada performs the song spectacularly.) The darkness is broken only by the light of a few windows as she sings of her loneliness in the midst of this vast city. "The city goes to bed, and I can live inside my head. . . ." Suddenly, we are literally witness to what she is thinking. Most of these lighted windows have torn blinds, a detail so sensitive it takes your breath away.

I was also astonished at the two wing-like structures that slide in and out from the sides of the stage. They constitute an astonishing kind of movable space, sometimes small and recognizable (filled with those things found in the lives of the ordinary people of Paris—stairs, ledges, a place to store barrels), sometimes vast and unidentifiable.

When we come to the scene of the young people, these two structures tilt together to form a dynamic representation of the tall barricades where the revolutionaries will soon be fighting. This kind of scenic effect is moving despite its clear artifice, for the barricades seem to take shape before our eyes as if by magic.

One can see from the way in which the roles have been cast that this is a musical that centers on the crowd. For, although this production of Les Misérables uses a number of well-known performers, they are not utilized as they normally would be since they take small parts as well as large. In the program's production notes, it is mentioned that Noguchi Gorō, who plays

Marius in the latter scenes of the musical, also portrays a farmer and a jailer; indeed, he plays some eight roles in all. Some actors perform as many as twenty. The system of double and triple casting employed for this production thus mixes seasoned performers with newcomers. One might call it a sort of "ensemble system," since even the leads melt into the chorus.

The songs function in the same fashion. Schonberg's music is filled with dark emotions, and his tunes are memorable. The music is skillfully integrated into the fabric of *Les Misérables* in an opera-like fashion quite unlike the juxtaposition of song and dialogue in most musicals. Many numbers are striking: Fantine's particularly beautiful "I Dreamed a Dream," sung so beautifully by Iwasaki Hiromi; the tune sung by Cosette as a child, "There's a Castle on a Cloud"; the "song of the people" sung by Enjolras and the chorus; as well as the nostalgic melody sung by Grantaire (played by Tashiro Takahide) and the students on the barricades, "The Days Gone By." Then there is the number "Empty Chairs at Empty Tables" sung by Marius when he is left alone after the failure of the revolution to stare at the bodies of his slain comrades. (Noguchi does this number well.) These all make a powerful impression.

Yet, as the production continued, I found to my dismay that many of the melodies were recycled. For example, the tunes of the bishop's song, toward the beginning of act 1, and Marius's song are virtually identical, and the melody of "Lovely Ladies," sung by the prostitutes and their customers in act 1, turns up again in act 2, this time sung by the women on the barricades. Just as the words in their song has it, these melodies keep "turning, turning, turning through the years."

For me, the most astounding example of recycling was when the melody of "Who Am I?" sung by Jean Valjean in act 1 surfaces again in act 2, this time sung by Inspector Javert just before he kills himself. These two men are opposite in character; they are enemies. How startling that the same melody should be used in two quite different climactic scenes. Had this ever been done before? The program says on that "the fact that the same musical theme appears again and again is effective in strengthening our impressions."

It seems to me that such a technique brilliantly underscores the critique of the human condition that is *Les Misérables*. Valjean and Javert, the hunted and the hunter, the people who seek justice and the cold-blooded men who wield the power: at first glance they seem to be altogether different, but from our point of view in the audience we come to realize that both function like a reciprocal plus and minus within a larger system, so that their apparently fixed values can shift, depending on the circumstances. (Perhaps it is for this reason that Takita Sakae and Kaga Takeshi both sing the same melody and that they switch roles before the eyes of the audience.)

In this context, it is no longer the confrontation between Valjean and Javert that drives the drama. If indeed "melodies" are interchangeable, what is to stop the people from becoming fully as autocratic as their oppressors after they seize power? With that in mind, this musical, in which the red flag is freely waved and a saintly white light plays over the dead bodies of those failed revolutionaries, is no "left-wing" production, no piece of "revolutionary theatre."

It seems to me that there lurks within this musical more than a trace of the experiences of the 1960s and early 1970s, a time when so many young people worldwide embraced the revolution. Just like the young people of nineteenth-century Paris, these latter-day revolutionaries sought to "face the fortress before them" and dreamed of a new world order; but they soon learned about fear and defeat. As the women sing, "Nobody is coming to help you fight!" "Nothing changes. Nothing ever will." The champions of the people have met with yet another reversal, and the spectacle of the bureaucracy returning to power is for us all too commonplace.

I must confess that I had never imagined that I would see such a work as this on the Tokyo commercial stage. This is a production mounted by neither an avant-garde troupe nor a commercial theatre company. Paradoxically enough, the production was underwritten by the powerful Shiseidō cosmetics firm, yet another sign of the times in which we live. If this indicates that we have lost our way, we can nevertheless still be moved by what we see on stage.

Finally, I would like to say something concerning the performances of Takita Sakae and Kaga Takeshi. As both an actor and a singer Kaga performs his two roles admirably. His Javert is strikingly cold-blooded. Takita shows a nice sensitivity to his roles, but his conception of them is much too general. More sharpness is needed to convey the essence of Javert. Finally, more care should have been taken with the Japanese translation in order more effectively to render the emotional niceties of the text.

66. THAT FIRST KISS WITH THE TASTE
OF RADIOACTIVITY

Godzilla

Written and directed by Ōhashi Yasuhiko

THE FREEDOM BOAT COMPANY

1987

Among the monster movies that Tōhō made some years ago, I was particularly fond of *Mothra* (1961) and *Ghidrah, the Three-Headed Monster* (1964).

In the movie *Mothra,* the monster Mothra built a huge cocoon in the Tokyo Tower; after his metamorphosis, when he took wing, the director succeeded in creating a large-scale fantasy that seemed absolutely wonderful to me. This film's carefully prepared script must surely be quite unique.

Ghidrah included Godzilla, Radon, and Ghidrah, an ultimate all-star monster cast in a battle that was both ridiculous and joyous; I remember going to see that film twice. The popularity of Godzilla, the monster who was "friendly to humans," had apparently waned in recent years, but it is once again on the upswing. The wild and evil Ghidrah, the one who refused the food offered to him by human beings, played a totally scintillating role as a revolting force of evil.

Perhaps it was because I saw these films as a child that in later years I would dream about actually seeing these monsters on the streets. In my dreams, these monsters symbolized an absolute fear that bore down on me. I would be walking down the street when suddenly the dark monster Godzilla would appear in front of me; he seemed so tall that his figure rent the clouds themselves. His roars would make the earth echo, and, as he crushed buildings with his huge feet, he seemed to be coming right toward me. In my fear, I would duck my head, yet at the same time I recall a feeling of secret joy as I watched the buildings crumble one after another. In my dreams, Godzilla would strike fear into the heart of every citizen of Tokyo; yet, for some reason or other, at the same time I felt in some secret way the pressures within me happily begin to unravel.

Seeing this production by the Freedom Boat Company of Ōhashi Yasuhiko's *Godzilla,* I was most struck by the obvious fact that the author surely must have had a very different experience with Godzilla than I had. Here the monster is treated in a charming and original way, and his image is theatricalized most effectively.

The 1987 Freedom Boat Company's production of *Godzilla* by Ōhashi Yasuhiko. Matsudo Shunji as Godzilla *(at the rear)* and Kanno Miki as the love-stricken Yayoi. (Photo by Miyauchi Katsu, taken at a revival of the play in 1988.)

In this production, Godzilla wanders on stage quite nonchalantly. The original Godzilla engaged on occasion in violent battles with some of the human beings he came across. But in this case he behaves very differently than the Godzilla of the films. The young actor Matsudo Shunji, who plays the role, doesn't wear an animal costume or use special makeup; clad in a "Japan" T-shirt, he brings the role down to human scale. Still, imagination takes over, and he turns into Godzilla. It was very exciting. So it was that this production, drawing only on the audience's imagination, was able successfully to re-create the power of the original movie, even derived as it was from special effects.

The basic concept for Ōhashi's play is quite striking. In January of 1986, a volcano erupted on the island of Ōshima, near the Izu peninsula not far south of Tokyo. The playwright added to this the appearance of Godzilla himself, who emerges from the mouth of the spouting volcano, just as though he were some powerful force of nature. He descends the mountain to the town of Motomachi at the base of the volcano, coming right along with the flowing lava. The townspeople quickly begin to evacuate their homes, more afraid of the monster than of the lava.

Another clever idea has been added as well. Living in Motomachi is a beautiful young girl named Yayoi (played by Kanno Miki), who falls in love with the monster. Beauty and the beast, King Kong and Fay Wray—there have been endless variations on this theme for centuries. This play, however, shows a crucial difference: the young girl is not afraid of the monster at all. From the instant they meet, they fall madly in love. Godzilla, supposedly fifty meters tall, and the lovely girl replay the tale of Romeo and Juliet! Within the framework of this delightful nonsense, an exchange like the following becomes even more amusing.

> YAYOI: One day, that fellow [Godzilla] gently held out the palm of his hand and asked me to climb on top, and then he carried me to his lips. . . . Our first kiss . . . had the taste of radioactivity!

After Godzilla proposes to Yayoi, her family is thrown into turmoil. There ensues a marvelous series of conversations, first between Godzilla and the family, then with Yayoi's fiancé (played by Komori Hirotada), a policeman. This comic family, theatrically self-conscious to excess, seems to have emerged right out of some drama by a writer like Tsuka Kōhei. They posture for all they are worth—which is precious little—claiming, for example, that they are related to Kyoto's Sen family, famous for carrying on the rituals of the traditional Japanese tea ceremony. There follows a delightful "play within a play" scene that, in terms of wordplay, is clearly written in the manner of Tsuka Kōhei. In fact, the plays quotes Tsuka's plays with the same reverence that it quotes monster movies.

As the quotations pile up, one after another, the clever ideas combine to create a true "nonsense drama" before our eyes. These days, this kind of inspired silliness is rare indeed, and on few occasions have I laughed as heartily as I did watching this delightful play. There is no symbolism, no moral teaching behind this inspired nonsense, only a healthy desire for a good laugh.

Yet, as the laughter continues, the nonsense is tinged by a peculiar sadness. For eventually, this parody by quotation begins to lose its value. Godzilla's frightening monstrosity dissipates, and he seems to become just another ordinary mortal, one who might well be felled by a single bullet. Mothra (played by Takahashi Katsumi) says, "The movie has been given up long ago, and the cocoon has been sold off piece by piece. . . ."

Just at the point where their heartless quarrel makes the nonsense and the monsters themselves lose their value, a sudden switch is introduced right before the final curtain. The reversal involves a vision that comes to Yayoi just as she is ready to evacuate the town. What sustains her vision is the fact that, while she maintains her heartfelt desire to encompass within the ordinary scale of things (mankind, the world) something that exists on a far greater scale, in the real world such a thing can never be. It is a perplexing moment.

In the end, Yayoi is forced to realize that her dream has lost its value, but at the same time it becomes clear to her that such illusions are what make everyday life possible. Yayoi's existence now becomes altogether real and, in the final analysis, a *real* nonsense comedy for sure. Ōhashi finds the human situation comic, and he wants his audience to laugh along with him. I for one am certainly in sympathy with him.

This company, which uses the word *freedom* as part of its title, has been performing since 1983, but this is their first production I have seen. *Godzilla* opened in May 1985 as a revival, but it remains a powerful and wholly successful production. Kanno Miki plays Yayoi with the fresh beauty of the wind itself, and all those playing major roles bring to them interest and individual personality.

67. A REFRESHING WIND SURPASSES ITS DOMAIN

ALEJO—to Praise the Wind

Written and directed by Koike Hiroshi

PAPPA TARAHUMARA

1987

It would appear that the flourishing of so many small theatre companies in Japan has given rise to a variety of differing performance dimensions. In our generation, the quantity of theatres has grown considerably, and there now exist a substantial number of young companies capable of attracting substantial audiences, while various playwrights, directors, and performers vie to exhibit the individual character of their art.

Yet might it not be said that, despite the seemingly multifaceted nature of the theatre phenomenon and all this apparent activity, it is in fact quite standardized and that most theatre productions are more or less similarly structured? The production that has forced these ideas on me is the recent presentation of Koike Hiroshi's *ALEJO—to Praise the Wind*. It was one that made a strong impression on me. The least that can be said is that Koike's company seeks to develop a new kind of theatre, one entirely different from the work of the host of other groups that is structured along the usual, more ordinary lines. Koike has rejected conventional, received notions of both theatre and dance and taken his company into uncharted territory.

In stating this, it is by no means my intention to criticize the "regular theatre" as such. It continues to hold more than sufficient appeal. Yet, amid the current plenitude of theatrical activity, is there not a real virtue in such a bold experiment as this, which by abandoning tried and true theatrical formulas dares to seek out new means of expression? For example, when we think of the experiments conducted by Terayama Shūji and his company in the 1960s and 1970s, it is clear that they created a "new" kind of theatrical experience, one that was difficult to describe, at least in terms of previously accepted standards. And don't we lack just those kinds of experiments at this time? If I may exaggerate just a bit, this production of *ALEJO* brought to mind Terayama's achievements. And, since I hope that such experiments will continue in the future, perhaps I have discovered here a fresh approach to what has until now constituted the grammar of the theatre.

Koike Hiroshi (born in 1956), who, unusual among theatre practitioners, graduated from Tokyo's Hitotsubashi University, helped form this young company in 1983. I have seen one of their productions before, their 1986 *Monk*. This is the second time I have written about their efforts. Compared to that relatively cool and serene presentation, with its monochrome sensibilities based on the use of white and gray, *ALEJO* gives us the sense of an overwhelming rainbow of red, green, and yellow. This transformation into a technicolor world of the kind that would bring delight to the playful spirit of a child was quite startling to me. The title, *ALEJO*, is taken from the name of the novelist Alejo Carpentier, born in Cuba, whose novels of "magic realism" such as *The Kingdom of This World, The Lost Steps,* and others have been so well received in Japan. What has brought such a change to Koike's vision is surely his encounter with the author's vibrant and unexpected vision of the world. During the course of the play, glowing colors in South American style, evening clothes, and hats appear on the stage. And the music used during the performance as well seems imbued with the kind of "magic realism" somehow suggested to us when we hear South American music.

Yet there is actually no connection whatsoever between *ALEJO* and the kind of "narrative" so important in contemporary South American fiction. Quite the contrary, this production, which loosely links eighteen separate scenes, relates virtually no "story" at all; no major themes are verbalized, and the ordinary stage conventions do not even seem to apply. Nor do the performers adopt personalized roles. Just when each episode seems to be coalescing toward a narrative structure of some sort, the scene changes, and the illusion dissolves.

Burgeoning out on the stage comes a sort of children's frolicking sensibility. It seems as though the whole world had been set up to function as a giant playground, and, within it, eight actors move in an often dizzying, sometimes gently beguiling manner, sometimes with humor, sometimes in a loosely stylized fashion, as they repeat certain actions again and again. Their vocal production seems rather like that of Meredith Monk, reminiscent of the twittering of birds, and they speak in fragments of everyday speech, sometimes using bits of incoherent word games. Yet through these movements they have succeeded in cheerfully distancing themselves (even when they emphasize the body or the sentiments) from received ideas, for these "actions" by the cast resemble neither mime, which seeks to reproduce the gestures of everyday life, nor the rhythms associated with the dance. There is no attempt to attach meaning to them. Here, whatever the originally assigned "meaning"—if any—might have been, it seems as though a fresh wind now blows nimbly past it. Nor is there any sense of physical effort on the part of the actors; they seem liter-

The Pappa TARAHUMARA Company's 1987 production of Koike Hiroshi's *ALEJO—to Praise the Wind.* The company engages in beguiling fun and games.

ally not to perspire, this beguiling breeze having borne away all traces of exertion.

In this context, the elements of the production that lie outside the province of stage dialogue take on a much greater importance as they float to the surface. The artistry of the pure white box-like structures (designed by Matsuhima Makoto) that are used as scenery, the exquisitely detailed minimalist-style music (by Sugaya Masahiro), and the brilliant idea of using gadgets for props (also an inspiration of Matsushima) all contribute in important ways to the success of the overall conception. In particular, the use of these various gadgets is truly marvelous. There are strange objects that the actors enter and then propel by paddling their feet. There are huge deep-sea fish with transparent bodies that appear on stage equipped with tiny lamps, sedate and beautiful in the deep gloom. Such sights turn us into children again, and we feel so happy that we would shout with joy.

Objects suggesting the image of "wind" appear on the stage as well. For example, there is a gently turning windmill. There is also a kind of totem pole, designed like a bird. Linen cloth is spread around the floor near the windmill, which continues to turn as creatures wearing varicolored masks frolic about magically to the increasingly loud music. The beauty and charm of this scene left me deeply moved.

But this wind is not stable. It cannot be seen. It is always moving and so escapes any accretion of meaning. Here, the wind symbolizes a contrivance that can reduce to nothing any set frameworks that might lead to the verbalization of a subject or the creation of any structures suggestive of a narrative.

In Koike's work there is no sense of confrontation with the audience that has remained central to the work of the avant-garde theatre. In this production, we seem to witness a vital, happy whirlwind pass before us, and we are free to interpret or explain as we will. The various cheerful performers appear before us, dressed in loose white pantaloons reminiscent of cartoon clothing. The play, like their clothing, is loosely constructed, and, in the refulgent spaces that their performances create, we can assign story and meaning in whatever fashion may please us.

And, while it is true certain aspects of the performance seemed amateurish, for all I know this may be related to the genuine freshness of Koike's conception.

EPILOGUE

Theatre depends more than anything else on actual stage performances. Like that of a burst of fireworks, the fate of the theatre is to achieve a rapid birth, only to quickly vanish. Even if the text of the play itself remains behind, the production itself cannot return. And, even if the play is revived on stage, each presentation will by its very nature be different. We can record performances on videotape, but what is preserved can constitute only a memory locked within a fixed, selected line of vision. Inevitably, such a record is seldom consonant with our own lively memories that remain with us.

In this sense, is it not important, then, to pay a bit more heed to theatre criticism—to that theoretical record through which the memory of the theatre lives on? It is to that purpose that I have collected these various reviews together. In those private interior worlds inhabited by any given hundred spectators, there will perforce be a hundred separate critiques, a hundred differing, dazzling memories. Today, when the fact that the theatre is so prosperous is so often spoken of, various kinds of memoirs have appeared, and they are not limited to discussions of playwrights or dramatic texts. So it is that this modest collection of mine follows after and, I hope, connects in some way with the work of a number of fine writers interested in many of the same topics.

I have collected here for translation a number of articles and reviews from the past seventeen seasons, from 1972 to 1987. Some were originally written as reviews in the conventional sense, but others derive from other sources, beginning their lives as columns, editorial commentaries, and essays on particular playwrights. I hope that my readers will look on them as a commentary on the theatre, conceived of in the broadest sense.

During this period, I have written many more reviews for various periodicals than could possibly be included in a volume of this size. When it came time to choose among them, I gave preference to those that I had found particularly moving and those that I felt had the greatest significance for the development of the contemporary Japanese theatre. Unfortunately, because of the inevitable limitations of space, reviews have been omitted that by all rights should have been included.

I hope that readers will pick up this book with the idea that they can read in it at random. Japanese readers in particular should begin by reading about productions they found memorable, their favorite theatre troupes, playwrights, performers, and directors. And, with the appropriate indexes having been provided, I hope that the book can serve in its way as a kind of dictionary of contemporary Japanese theatre and so can be used as a useful source of material on the subject.

Then too, if there should be a reader sufficiently intrepid to read these brief essays in order, from beginning to end, he or she will be able to observe the way in which our theatre has developed during these years, what new branches it has sent forth, where the leaves have grown thickest. They may catch a glimmer as well of how the meaning and significance of this new period in which we are living has made its appearance on our stages, and this account may, for all I know, serve as some sort of panorama, a historical testimony to these times. At the same time, that same reader will discover some traces of the ways in which I myself, caught up in the movement and confusion of these times, have come to change the way in which I observe the performances I attend, as well as the way in which I came to think over their possible value. I regret that, as I read them over, many of these pieces strike me as inferior. Yet I cannot help but feel that this childishness is, after all, a part of this "history" as well.

Appendixes

PLAY TITLES

Since translations of titles are provided throughout for readers who do not know Japanese, the following list is intended as an aid in locating texts and reviews using the original Japanese titles of productions. Some of the translated titles are, inevitably, considerably changed from the Japanese originals. When possible, the titles of published English-language translations have been used, as have translations of titles already in use in Japan. Plays that are the subjects of individual reviews are listed first, followed by plays mentioned only briefly in the text (these latter listed by author).

Plays Reviewed

Japanese Plays

Afternoon of a Man and Woman
Otoko to onna no gogo
Yamazaki Tetsu

ALEJO—to Praise the Wind
Arehho—kaze o tataeru tame ni
Koike Hiroshi

Anthropology Museum
Jinruikan
Chinen Seishin

The Bacchae
Bakkosu no shinnyo
Suzuki Tadashi

Bubbling and Boiling
Aabukutatta, niitatta
Betsuyaku Minoru

Chairs and a Legend
Isu to densetsu
Betsuyaku Minoru

Children of Night
Yoru no kodomo
Ikuta Yorozu

Comet Messenger Siegfried
Suisei no shisha—Jiikufuriito
Noda Hideki

The Comic World of Shōwa
Kigeki Shōwa no sekai
Satoh Makoto

Diary of a Voyage to the West
Saiyūki
Tokyo Kid Brothers

Directions to Servants
Nuhi-kun
Terayama Shūji

Double Suicide, after Chikamatsu
Chikamatsu shinjū monogatari
Akimoto Matsuyo

The Dressing Room
Gakuya
Shimizu Kunio

Earth Station
Chi no eki
Ōta Shōgo

Genocide
Jenosaido
Kawamura Takeshi

Godzilla
Gozira
Ōhashi Yasuhiko

Great Doctor Yabuhara
Yabuhara kengyō
Inoue Hisashi

I Bit the Green Seed
Aoi mi o tabeta
Ishidō Rei

The Incident of the Salad Murder
Sarada satsujin jiken
Betsuyaku Minoru

Japan Wars
Nippon Woozu
Kawamura Takeshi

The Kamata Marching Song
Kamata Kōshinkyoku
Tsuka Kōhei

The Kara Version: Matasaburō of the Wind
Kara ban kaze no Matasaburō
Kara Jūrō

Knock
Nokku
Terayama Shūji

The Legend of a Flying Dragon: And Then a Crow
Hiryūden: soshite karasu
Tsuka Kōhei

A Legend of Fish: The Teacher Kills His Student at Rikkyō University
Uo densetsu—Rikkyō Dai jokyōju oshiego satsujin jiken
Yamazaki Tetsu

The Legend of Komachi
Komachi fūden
Ōta Shogo

Lemmings
Remingu
Terayama Shūji

Lemon
Remon
Takeuchi Jū'ichirō

Melancholy When the Flowers Bloom
Hana saku goro no yūutsu
Watanabe Eriko

Memo from the Aliens
Erian no shuki
Yamazaki Tetsu

Memories of the Little Finger
Koyubi no omoide
Noda Hideki

Night Shadows—a Gentle Ghost Story
Yoru no kage—yasashii kaidan
Watanabe Eriko

A Night's Feast
Utage no yoru
Suzuki Tadashi

1981—Jealousy
1981—Shitto
Shimizu Kunio

Oguri Hangan and Princess Terute
Oguri Hangan—Terute hime
Endō Takurō

Radical Party
Radikaru paatii
Kawamura Takeshi

The Rats of Hamelin
Hāmerun no nezumi
Kara Jūrō

Rules for Sleeping in the Universe
Uchū de nemuru tame no hōhō ni tsuite
Kōkami Shōji

Run, Merusu—a Girl's Lips Are Dynamite!
Hashire Merusu—shōjo no kuchibiru kara wa dainamaito!
Noda Hideki

Shanghai 'Vance King
Shanhai bansukingu
Saitō Ren

The Song of a Strange Family—the Case of the On-Line Fraud of Itō Motoko
Izoku no uta—Itō Motoko onrain sagi jiken
Yamazaki Tetsu

Song of Praise and Thanksgiving
Hogi-uta
Kitamura Sō

The Story of Mannen-town in Shitaya
Shitaya mannen-chō monogatari
Kara Jūrō

Taking along a Sunset like the Morning
Asahi no yō na yūhi o tsurete
Kōkami Shōji

A Tale of Smallpox
Hōsōdan
Hijikata Tatsumi

A Tale of the Original Japanese
Wajinden
Okabe Kōdai

A Tale of Two Cities
Nito monogatari
Kara Jūrō

Tango at the End of Winter
Tango—fuyu no owari ni
Shimizu Kunio

That Raven, Even
Ano ōgarasu sae mo
Takeuchi Jū'ichirō

The Theatre Train of Iihatōbo
Iihatōbo no geki-ressha
Inoue Hisashi

Thirty Days Hath September
Nishimuku samurai
Betsuyaku Minoru

Tosa Genji
Tosa Genji°
Sakamoto Nagatoshi

Travel of Twenty-seven Thousand Light Years
Ni-man nana-sen kōnen no tabi
Noda Hideki

The Trojan Women
Toroiya no onna
Suzuki Tadashi

Two Women
Futari no onna
Kara Jūrō

When We Go Down That Heartless River
Bokura ga hijō no taiga o kudaru toki
Shimizu Kunio

Wind Station
Kaze no eki
Ōta Shōgo

Zeami
Zeami†
Yamazaki Masakazu

°Personal name.
†Personal name.

European and American Plays

Chorus Line
Michael Bennett et al.

Cloud 9
Caryl Churchill

Lady of the Camellias (La dame aux camélias)
Alexandre Dumas fils

Macbeth (NINAGAWA Macbeth)
William Shakespeare

Man of La Mancha
Dale Wasserman et al.

A Midsummer Night's Dream
William Shakespeare

Les Misérables
Claude-Michel Schonberg et al.

The Seagull
Anton Chekhov

A Streetcar Named Desire
Tennessee Williams

Sweeney Todd
Stephen Sondheim

The Tempest
William Shakespeare

Japanese Plays Mentioned but Not Reviewed

Abe Kōbō

Involuntary Homicide
Mihitsu no koi

Akimoto Matsuyo

  Kaison the Priest of Hitachi
  Hitachibō Kaison

Betsuyaku Minoru

  A and B and a Girl
  A to B to onna

  Elephant
  Zō

  Kangaroo
  Kangarū

  The Little Match Girl
  Matchi-uri no shōjo

  Landscape with Red Bird
  Akai tori no iru fūkei

  The Move
  Idō

  The Revolt of the Soyosoyo Tribe
  Soyosoyozoku no hanran

Chikamatsu Monzaemon

  The Courier from Hell
  Meido no hikyaku

Fukuda Yoshiyuki

  Going Far, Far Away
  Tōku made yuku n da

Hijikata Tatsumi

  The Revolt of the Flesh
  Nikutai no hanran

Ichidō Rei‡

A Tale of Imposing Appearance
Monogatari ifūdōdō

Ikuta Yorozu

The Three Stigmata of Nancy Tomato
Nanshii Tomato no mittsu no seikon

Inoue Hisashi

History of the Common People of the Shōwa Era
Shōwa shomin den

Kobayashi Issa
Kobayashi Issa♦

A Strange Bible
Chin'yaku seisho

Izumi Kyōka

The Castle Tower
Tenshu monogatari

Kanasugi Tadao

An Uneasy Feeling after School Is Over
Munasawagi no hōkago

A Thief Who Lectures: The Story of Tama no I
Sekkyō gōtō: tama no i yodan

Kara Jūrō

A Beggar for Love
Ai no kojiki

The Bengal Tiger
Begaru no tora

---

‡The name of an ensemble project.
♦Personal name.

Fang of the Sea
Umi no kiba

Hoffmann of Shitamachi
Shitamachi Hofuman

Iron Mask
Tekkamen

John Silver
Jon Shirubā

More of John Silver
Zoku Jon Shirubā

Rival Courtiers in Love
Ai no saya-ate

The Sixth Room
Rokugōshitsu

The Vampire Princess
Kyūketsu-ki

The Virgin's Mask
Shōjo kamen

The Virgin's City
Shōjo toshi

Kawamura Takeshi

The Shinjuku Version of the Tale of Eight Dogs, Vol. 1, The Dog's Birth
Shinjuku hakkenden, dai-ichi maku: inu no tanjō

Kisaragi Koharu

Romeo and a Dining Table with Freesia
Romeo to Furiijia no aru shokutaku

Kitamura Sō

DUCK SOAP
DUCK SOAP

Kōkami Shōji

    Angels Who Close the Pupils of Their Eyes
    Tenshi-wa hitomi-o tojite

    Déjà Vu
    Deja vyu

    Modern Horror
    Modan horā

    Nuclear War
    Kaku-sensō

Noda Hideki

    Boy Hunt
    Shōnengari

    The Demi-God
    Hanshin

    The Prisoner of Zenda
    Zendajō no toriko

    Run Merusu: Do You Like the Burning Underwear?
    Hashire Merusu—moeru shitagi wa o-suki?

    Walküre of the White Nights
    Byakuya no warukyūri

Ōhashi Yasuhiko

    The Red Bird Has Fled
    Akai tori nigeta

Oka Kiyoshi

    The Heart of the Japanese
    Nihonjin no kokoro

Ōta Shōgo

    Nine Scenes about Buses
    Noriai jidōsha no ue no kokonotsu no jōkei

A Thousand Summers
Sennen no natsu

Water Station
Mizu no eki

Saitō Ren

Red Eyes
Akame

Trust D.E.
Torasuto D.E.

Satoh Makoto

Abe Sada's Dog
Abe Sada no inu

Shanghai in Spring: Killing Blanqui
Buranki goroshi Sanhai no haru

February and Cinema
Nigatsu to kinema

Cinema and Spies
Kinema to tantei

The Comedy of Abe Sada
Kigeki Abe Sada

My Beatles
Atashi no biitoruzu

Nezumi Kozō: The Rat
Nezumi Kozō Jirokichi

Suzuki Tadashi

On the Dramatic Passions II
Geki-teki naru mono-o megutte II

Takahashi Isao

   Goodbye to Walter Mitty
   Worutaa Miti ni sayonara

   The Never-ending Tomorrow of the Eternal Optimist
   Gokuraku tombo no owaranai ashita

Tamaki Michiko

   Cosmos Columbus
   Kosumo Korombusu

Tokyo Kid Brothers

   The Golden Bat Comes Home
   Kaette kita ōgon batto

   Tokyo Kids
   Tokyo kiddo

Tsuka Kōhei

   The Atami Murder Case
   Atami satsujin jiken

   Revolution for Beginners: Legend of the Flying Dragon
   Shokyū kakumei kōza hiryūden

   The Story of a Stripper
   Sutorippaa monogatari

Tsuruya Namboku

   The Scarlet Princess of Edo
   Sakura hime Azuma bunshō

Uno Nobuo

   The Phosphorescent Blind Doctor
   Shiranui kengyō

Yamazaki Tetsu

*Dog Town—the Incident of a Murder of a Female College Student by a Police
Officer*
Inu no machi—keisatsukan joshidaisei satsujin jiken

The Family Adrift—the Jesus Ark Incident
Hyōryū kazoku—Iesu no hakobune jiken

Field Notes for Crimes°
Hanzai fiirudonōto

Pawnshop
Shichiya

°This is the title of a series of plays.

NAMES OF THEATRE
COMPANIES MENTIONED
IN THE TEXT

So as to make the text as clear as possible for English readers, Mr. Senda and I have rendered the names of the various theatre companies mentioned in the course of the text into English. They are listed here in alphabetical order, along with their original Japanese names. Inevitably, some of these terms or expressions can be transformed into any English equivalents only in a rather awkward fashion, but it is our hope that these English renderings will at least give some sense of the way in which the names of these groups are perceived by Japanese theatregoers.

In particular, those familiar with the Japanese name of Terayama Shūji's troupe, *Tenjōsajiki*, often used in English-language sources as well, may be surprised to see it here translated as "The Peanut Gallery." Mr. Senda tells me that Terayama named his company in homage to the famous French film of 1945 *Les Enfants du Paradis*, directed by Marcel Carné. The title of that film refers to those who sit in the highest (and cheapest) seats in the theatre. Thus, although "The Peanut Gallery" may seem plebeian by comparison, Mr. Senda felt that English-language readers too might enjoy the reference.

Theatrical producers already well known in Europe and the United States, such as Tōhō, Shōchiku, and others, are not included in the list below.

The Actor's Theatre
Haiyūza

The Bluebird Troupe
Aoitori

The Cherry Company
Sakurasha

The Cloud Troupe
Kumo

293

The Creation Troupe
Sōzō

The Dream Wanderers
Yume no yūminsha

The Four Seasons Theatrical Company
Gekidan shiki

The Free Theatre
Jiyū gekijō

The Freedom Boat Company
Riburesen

The Group of Thirty
Sanjūninkai

The Hands Company
Te no kai

The Human Theatre
Ningenza

The Isolation Theatre
Tsunbosajiki

Katō Ken'ichi Studio
Katō Ken'ichi jimusho

The Literary Theatre
Bungakuza

The May Troupe
Gogatsusha

The Modern Peoples' Theatre
Gendaijin gekijō

The Mystical Zero Troupe
Hihō zero bankan

Pappa TARAHUMARA
Pappa TARAHUMARA

The Peanut Gallery
Tenjōsajiki

The Rekuramu Company
Rekuramusha

Seibu Theatre Production
Seibu gekijō seisaku

The Seventh Ward Troupe
Dai shichi byōtō

The Shakespeare Theatre
Sheikusupia Shiata

The Situation Theatre
Jōkyō gekijō

68/71
68/71

Space Performance
Kūkan engi

The Spontaneous Tin Troupe
Buriki no jihatsudan

The Theatre Troupe
Engekidan

The Third Erotica
Dai san erotica

The Third Stage
Dai san butai

The Three Circle Company
Gekidan sanjūmaru

The Tokyo Kid Brothers
Tōkyo kiddo burazaazu

Transformation
Henshin

The Transformation Theatre
Tenkei gekijō

Transposition 21
Ten'i 21

The Tree in Winter Troupe
Mokutōsha

The Troupe of the Slanting Light
Shakōsha

Tsuka Studio
Tsuka jimusho

The Waseda Little Theatre
Waseda shōgekijō

The Yokohama Boat Theatre
Yokohama bōto shiataa

The Youth Theatre Arts Troupe
Seigei

SELECTED BIBLIOGRAPHY

Translations of works by certain of the Japanese playwrights included in this volume are listed below. Bibliographic data concerning the anthologies in which certain of these works are located is provided in the section after the individual listings.

Akimoto Matsuyo
> *Kaison the Priest of Hitachi* (in Goodman, *Drama and Culture*)

Betsuyaku Minoru
> *The Cherry in Bloom* (in Rolf and Gillespie, *Alternative Drama*)
> *The Elephant* (in Goodman, *Apocalypse*)
> *The Legend of Noon* (in Rolf and Gillespie, *Alternative Drama*)
> *The Little Match Girl* (in Rolf and Gillespie, *Alternative Drama*)
> *The Move* (in Takaya, *Modern Japanese Drama*)

Fukuda Yoshiyuki
> *Find Hakamadare!* (in Goodman, *Drama and Culture*)

Inoue Hisashi
> *Make-up* (in *Encounter,* May 1989, 8–18)

Kara Jūrō
> *John Silver: The Beggar of Love* (in Goodman, *Drama and Culture*)
> *Two Women* (in Rolf and Gillespie, *Alternative Drama*)
> *The Virgin's Mask* (in Rolf and Gillespie, *Alternative Drama*)

Ōta Shōgo
> *Vacant Lot* (*Asian Theatre Journal* 10, no. 2 [Fall 1993]: 133–162)
> *Water Station* (*Asian Theatre Journal* 7, no. 2 [Fall 1990]: 150–183)

Saitō Ren (see also Satoh Makoto)
> *Red Eyes* (*Concerned Theatre Japan* 2, nos. 1–2 [1971]: 45–109)

Satoh Makoto
> *My Beatles* (in Goodman, *Drama and Culture*)
> *The Dance of Angels Who Burn Their Own Wings* (with Yamamoto Kiyokazu, Katō Tadashi, and Saitō Ren) (in Goodman, *Drama and Culture*)
> *Ismene* (in Rolf and Gillespie, *Alternative Drama*)
> *Nezumi Kozō: The Rat* (in Goodman, *Apocalypse*)

Shimizu Kunio
  The Dressing Room (in Rolf and Gillespie, *Alternative Drama*)
  The Legend of Noon (in Rolf and Gillespie, *Alternative Drama*)
  The Sand of Youth, How Quickly (in Rolf and Gillespie, *Alternative Drama*)
  Tango in Winter (adapted by Peter Barnes [London: Amber Lane Plays, 1991])
Suzuki Tadashi
  Clytemnestra (in Suzuki, *The Way of Acting*)
Terayama Shūji
  The Dog God (*Asian Theatre Journal* 11, no. 2 [Fall 1994]: 163–189)
  Knock (with Kishida Rio) (in Rolf and Gillespie, *Alternative Drama*)
Yamazaki Masakazu
  Sanetomo (in Rimer, *Mask and Sword*)
  Zeami (in Rimer, *Mask and Sword*)

Anthologies and Other Volumes Mentioned Above

Goodman, David. *After Apocalypse: Four Japanese Plays of Hiroshima and Naga-saki.* New York: Columbia University Press, 1986. Reprint. Cornell Series on East Asia Ithaca, N.Y.: Cornell University Press, 1994.

Goodman, David. *Japanese Drama and Culture in the 1960s: The Return of the Gods.* Armonk, N.Y.: M. E. Sharpe, 1988.

Rimer, J. Thomas. *Mask and Sword: Two Plays for the Contemporary Japanese Theatre.* New York: Columbia University Press, 1980.

Suzuki Tadashi. *The Way of Acting: The Theatre Writings of Tadashi Suzuki.* New York: Theatre Communications Group, 1986.

Takaya, Ted T. *Modern Japanese Drama: An Anthology.* New York: Columbia University Press, 1979.

Rolf, Robert, and John Gillespie, eds. *Alternative Japanese Drama: Ten Plays.* Honolulu: University of Hawai'i Press, 1992.

General Bibliography

Benito Ortolani's *The Japanese Theatre: From Shamanistic Ritual to Contemporary Pluralism* (Leiden: E. J. Brill, 1990; paperback ed., Princeton, N.J.: Princeton University Press, 1994) contains a full and wide-ranging bibliography on modern and contemporary Japanese theatre. The reader will find listed there a number of unusual and useful materials helpful for a greater understanding of both the playwrights and the theatrical background to Mr. Senda's book. For reasons of space, and because Professor Ortolani's study is easily available, these items are not listed here.

INDEX

About the Author

SENDA AKIHIKO, born in Tokyo in 1940, has written drama criticism for Tokyo's prestigious *Asahi Shimbun* (Asahi newspaper) since 1968, and his articles on Japanese theatre and performance have appeared in a wide variety of publications in Japan. He has composed a number of important full-length studies of postwar Japanese theatre, most recently his 1995 *Japanese Contemporary Theatre*.

About the Translator

J. THOMAS RIMER, professor of Japanese literature at the University of Pittsburgh, has written on various aspects of Japanese culture, art, and literature. In the field of theatre, he has translated postwar plays by Yamazaki Masakazu and Shimizu Kunio as well as treatises by the great *nō* master Zeami and the writings of the contemporary director Suzuki Tadashi.